BLOOD OF THE INNOCENT

P C PROSPERIE

RediscoveringSETX
Press

Blood of the Innocent

Copyright © P.C. Prosperie 2013

ISBN -13: 978-0-9888842-0-5 (paperback)

Library of Congress Control Number: 2013935585

www.rediscoveringsetx.com

Cover Art by Sorbis

Book cover by Steve Bagwell Enhanced Images Publication Design

DEDICATED IN LOVING MEMORY TO
FELIPA RAMIREZ URQUIZA
(1925-2011)

ACKNOWLEDGMENTS

There are several people without whom this first book would not have been possible. Their contributions have been priceless, and I wish to thank them here:

My editor, who continuously makes me strive to better my writing.

Linda Prosperie, who has been there since the beginning.

My lovely wife, Eugenia Prosperie, for her support and Spanish translations.

Susan Prosperie and Jessica Medina, for their multiple manuscript readings, and suggestions.

And last but not least, a special thank you to Author Kristen Taber, who has been my guide on this magical journey into the world of publishing.

CHAPTER 1

Katy ran swiftly through the brush near the river. Her heart was pounding with fear, and she heard the barking of the bloodhounds as they drew closer. She surely felt her world was coming to an end. Katy could probably outrun the two men on horseback but not the dogs. She might wade into the river, but her demise would perhaps then be evenly shared among the alligators and the snakes.

Katy ran faster and faster through the darkness until she finally reached a patch of cypress trees near a shallow inlet. She ran through the water, splashing her way to the other side. Just then, only seconds behind her, the dogs appeared through the brush. They were barking fanatically. All three dogs had her in their sights but stopped at the edge of the water. Katy, now on the other side, raced through the trees. There seemed to be a path on which she could make her way more easily.

The two men on horseback caught up with the dogs at the inlet. They had noticed the dogs barking at the edge of the water. One of the men trotted his horse up to the water to see why the dogs had not followed the girl. As he lowered his torch to shine on the water, a sudden splash and a hissing sound came from the bank. This spooked the horse and made it buck. The man fell backward off the horse and into the mud. Meanwhile the dogs, still barking wildly, began snapping at something in the water. The man hurriedly grabbed the torch from the ground to see what had spooked the horse.

"It's a 12-footer!" yelled the other man on the horse. "Hell, there's another one over there!"

The man on the ground jumped up and staggered nervously away from the water. The dogs seemed to be able to keep the 12-foot gator in the water, but he didn't want to push his luck.

"Shoot the damn thing, Ben!" the man said, still backing up.

"Ain't no point in it. It'll jest pick out the bullet and spit it back at ya," Ben grinned.

"Well do somethin' dang it." The man was now grabbing the reins of his horse.

Ben pulled out his revolver and fired two shots in the air while shouting for the dogs to get back. He figured it would be better to cross at another point than to lose three good hunting dogs.

"Mount up, Wes. We'll cross a-ways down from here. Dang girl must be in league with the devil to get through them. Don't matter though. She's headin' south. I reckon them Creol's gonna enjoy that little lassie if you know what I mean. Hell, if she makes it that far."

Wes mounted his horse. Raising his torch, he noticed the inlet was full of alligators. He counted seven sets of eyes peering at him from the water. Being from east Texas, he seldom saw alligators in the hollers and rivers, and he had never had to deal with these nasty creatures before. Maybe the odd bear or hog but not these foul monsters, surely spawned from the devil himself.

Katy, still running as fast as she could, noticed that the sound of the barking dogs was getting farther and farther away from her. Then she heard the two shots in the distance. For some reason, she had been given a chance to escape. She knew this was a gift, and she had better make good with it.

Her heart pounded, and fatigue began to set in. Katy stumbled and fell to the ground. Clambering to get up, her legs began to cramp, but she knew she couldn't stay there or they would eventually catch up with her. Finally rising to her feet, she began to limp toward a thicker patch of trees. Katy's eyes peered through the darkness in search of a place to hide from the dogs, but there was nowhere that she would be safe. Exhausted or not, she had to keep moving in order to stay alive.

At that moment, she heard a ruffling on the other side of the trees near another inlet. It sounded as if something was near. Told by the locals that there were possibly Indians in the area and knowing those men were chasing her, she crept silently to find out who—or what—was making the noise.

Katy, hidden by the trees and brush, could make out the silhouette of a person on a flat-bottomed boat. With the moon now peeking through the clouds, she could tell it was a woman although her face was mostly hidden behind a hood. Katy knew this was her last hope. She raced out of the brush and fell to the ground near the water's edge.

"My lady . . . Please," she gasped, falling to the ground before attempting to get up.

The woman turned her head toward Katy and thrust the guiding pole into the mud to halt the craft. She then guided the boat toward where Katy knelt in pain. The woman had heard the commotion minutes earlier, along with the gunshots. She sensed Katy's despair.

Katy now made it to her feet. She limped into the water and onto the boat.

"Thank you, my lady," Katy whispered graciously.

"Here, take this and push us off this bank. We need to leave." The woman handed the pole to Katy.

Katy took it and heaved the pole into the bank. The boat began to back up and move down the inlet. The woman guided the boat toward the river, knowing whoever fired those gunshots would soon be on their trail. It was time to get across the river. And fast.

The boat reached the river quickly, and both women could hear the barking dogs coming closer and closer. Wes and Ben had found a spot to cross a bit down the way and were now back on the trail. The dogs ran to the bank and stopped. They had lost the scent.

Wes rode up to the water's edge and used his torchlight to search, unsuccessfully, for signs of where Katy had gone. Since there were no alligators at this point, they crossed the shallow inlet and let the dogs search the other bank. Still no success—it was as if Katy had disappeared into the darkness.

Wes, worried about Indians and all the things that slithered and hissed in the night, felt it was time to head back to the plantation. Even if she was still in this godforsaken swamp, an immigrant girl of 15 would not survive.

"Let's go," he commanded Ben. "She's dead, eaten by the gators."

Ben looked at him with a smirk. "And you're gonna tell Lady Falsworth this?"

"Yes, it's obvious she didn't make it. And I'm not gonna stay out here all night. Let's go," he said, crossing to the other side of the inlet.

Ben didn't really care to be out in the swamps either, and he was not in charge. He knew going back empty-handed would not sit well with Lady Falsworth. But he wasn't paid to think, he was paid to follow orders.

Both Wes and Ben, along with the dogs, headed out of the swamp and back to the plantation. They knew that the night wasn't over by far, but at least they wouldn't be in this wretched swamp.

By this time, the woman and Katy were halfway across the river. Both now paddled because the Neches was too deep to use a guiding pole. Katy paddled vigorously. Although she did not know this woman, she felt her chances of survival were greater with her than by herself or with the ones on the other side of the river.

The nearly full moon now seemed to permanently clear away from behind the clouds, which brightened their way across the river. They finally reached the other side and proceeded into a small shallow inlet. The woman, now with the guiding pole, pushed her way toward the bank. Katy limped off the boat and began trying to drag it onto land. The woman also stepped out of the boat and began helping her.

The woman turned to Katy "My cabin is not too far from here. Can you walk?" she asked, noticing Katy's limp.

"Yes. I can," Katy said, with a noticeable hint of pain in her voice.

"Good. We're safe here. You don't have to worry." The woman tried to console Katy. She felt that this young girl had been through a lot, though what, she did not know. Only time and a little prying would tell.

The woman grabbed a sack from the boat along with a large knife and proceeded to walk down a trail leading into the woods. Katy, trying to hurry, followed the woman. Both walked until they came upon a cabin. In front, the remains of a fire glowed in the darkness. The woman picked up a stick from the smoldering fire and lit a lantern hanging near the front door. They went inside the cabin.

"It's not much but it's safe. Now let me have a look at that leg of yours," the woman said, placing the lantern, bag, and knife on a table.

Katy limped up toward the light and revealed her injury. "It's just cramping," she said rubbing the back of her calf.

Just then, both noticed the lower part of Katy's dress was covered in blood. "Oh," Katy said, a bit distressed. The woman quickly grabbed a bucket of water, a towel, and a bottle from inside a cupboard, then proceeded to clean Katy's wound. After she had cleaned all the blood off the leg, the woman took the bottle and began to pour the contents onto the open wound. Katy shrieked in pain.

"It's Tennessee whiskey," the woman offered. "It may burn but it will help."

"Thank you, my lady," Katy said, still grimacing in pain.

The woman wrapped Katy's injured leg with a cloth then handed the bottle to her. Katy took the bottle and drank a healthy swig from it. The woman chuckled.

"You are lucky. The gods are watching out for you, young lady," the woman said while pulling back the hood from her face. "You are not from around here, are you?"

Katy, finally feeling the burning subside, replied, "No, my lady. My name is Katy. I am English."

"Ah, England I know well", the woman replied. "I lived in Portsmouth a time, before coming here."

Katy took another swig of the bottle. She was beginning to feel a sense of calm now that she was away from the earlier horror. She was indebted to this woman whom she didn't know, and she felt more thankful with each passing minute.

"We left Portsmouth two months ago I believe. I do not remember much of the city. We left in a hurry, under cover of darkness," Katy mumbled. "I'm from Newcastle originally. Tell me my lady, what's your name? You've saved my life and I am indebted to you. I don't know if I can ever repay you."

The woman looked at Katy and smiled. "You owe me nothing. I do not know what happened earlier, but you seem like a girl out of place. My name is Angelique."

6

Katy looked at Angelique with a sense of comfort, her turbulent mind feeling more at ease. She hadn't experienced peace in a long time, but this cabin felt like a guarded castle for her tired body.

"Where are you from, my lady?" Katy asked noticing Angelique's slight accent. "You yourself do not seem to be from England or here."

Angelique lit two candles and placed them on the table for more light. Katy saw the woman's long pitch-black hair and dark eyes almost glowing in the candlelight. She looked maybe twice Katy's age but was as beautiful as any maiden or duchess she had ever met.

"France, I gather," Angelique replied with a snicker. "I was born in Hungary, but we moved to France a year later. I don't remember much about that time."

Angelique now took the bottle of whiskey and took a healthy swig of her own. She was a bit shaken from the events that had taken place earlier but felt peaceful, too. "I lived in France for eight years, traveling with my family from village to village. But the French do not take kindly to gypsies." Her tone changed thinking back to her childhood. "I will spare you most of this dark history, but when my mother died, I was put on a boat to Portsmouth to live with a distant aunt till I was fifteen."

"So you're a gypsy then?" Katy blurted out, almost excitedly.

A faint smile now glowed on Angelique's face because she saw that Katy was a bit tipsy from the few swigs of whiskey.

"I'm a poshrati," Angelique answered.

"A what?" Katy was puzzled.

"A poshrati. My father was a gypsy and my mother was not. A half breed I think you would call me."

Angelique now saw Katy had relaxed. The pain in her leg had subsided, and she looked more content.

7

"Well, enough about me," Angelique said, turning the conversation to Katy, "So why is an English girl running through the swamps of the Neches? Better yet, how did you get here?"

Katy's calmness began to wither at that question. It had brought her back to the reality of what have taken place only a few hours before. She knew her struggle was not over, and they would be searching for her soon.

"It's a bit of a long story. I am . . . was a servant for Lady Falsworth," Katy spoke nervously. "She is a baroness back in England. My parents died when I was eight years old. I had no more family so I was put in an orphanage till I was thirteen. I felt I could no longer live in that wretched place, so I ran away." Katy's eyes began to tear up thinking back to her life in the orphanage. With the tragic death of her parents years earlier, she had had no choice but to be housed there. For five long years, she was treated as if she were the property of strangers. Her dreams of escaping to a new life became reality one night, as she climbed out of a window and ran for freedom. "I remember that night well," Katy remembered. "I ran down the street toward the main square and hid in an empty factory in an off-street. I stayed there for about two days, but I had no food, no heat, nothing. I was coughing so much I thought I would die."

As Katy spoke, Angelique felt the sorrow in her voice, but also strength given that she had weathered these troubles as a child. Still there was more to this story that she would find out over time.

"I finally left the factory and walked down to the main square," Katy continued. "This is where I met Lady Falsworth. She was an old woman but well taken care of. I was hungry and tried to steal some bread from a small shop." Katy's eyes began tearing up. "Well, I was caught because I am not a thief. The shop owner grabbed me by the back of the neck and pushed me hard against a wall. I hit my head and lay unconscious for a few moments." The more Katy remembered, the more she began to weep. "I never meant to steal—honest! I am not a thief! I was just hungry."

Angelique, seeing Katy's despair, put her arm around her and tried to comfort her as best she could. "I believe you. You did well to survive," she said, thinking back to her own childhood. "And what of this lady?"

Katy, sniffling, continued, "I remember waking up to an old woman standing over me. She glared at me as if I was the devil. She yelled at me, poking me with her cane. 'Wake up! Thieves will not be tolerated here!'

"I managed to scramble off the ground but my head was still woozy from being pushed into the wall. I asked for her mercy. I was crying and I couldn't look her in the eyes. I explained that I had no money and that I hadn't eaten in two days. She looked at me without showing a hint of sympathy. She was such a cold woman. I remember so clearly what she said. 'Mercy? You want mercy? Why should I show mercy to a worthless common thief? You are hungry . . . no? Well then, you will work for your food.'

"I was so desperate that I accepted immediately. I did not hesitate for a second. I told her that she could ask me to do anything and I would do it. And I meant it. The old lady then nodded to the shop owner, who then handed me the bread. I ate it all immediately. I was told to follow her, which I did. There was a carriage waiting at the end of the street. The old lady and the people with her climbed in, so I did the same. We rode out to a huge mansion outside the city.

"It was there that I was given food, shelter, and work," Katy explained, wiping the remaining tears from her eyes. "The lady was mean and unkind, but at least I had food and a job."

Katy spoke more of her time in Newcastle. It was obvious that this had been a painful episode in her life, and she could not help but tear up as she spoke. Angelique listened on, feeling both sympathetic and surreal. For a lot of what Katy explained was in her past as well, bringing back many unhappy memories of her youth.

"So how did you get here?" Angelique asked.

"I remember one morning, Lady Falsworth was very angry with a new servant. The girl did not know her new job, and being French, her English was very bad. The lady was so mad that she slapped the poor girl till she bled. I was ordered out of the room, along with everyone else. I never saw her again, and the next morning Lady Falsworth was gone, too. A young lady took her place as our mistress. We were told she was Lady Falsworth's granddaughter. Her name was Annabelle. I remember a painting hanging over the fireplace at the manor. Miss Sterling told me that it was of Lady Falsworth in her youth, but it seemed as if the painter had painted Annabelle. Lady's Falsworth's granddaughter could have been her twin."

Katy paused. "I can remember that after about a fortnight, the police began to visit the house. They were looking for a missing person. We left for Portsmouth that night, then from there, we got on a ship to New Orleans. There were about thirteen of us in all. I still don't know all that took place. Annabelle is as vicious as her grandmother could ever be, if not more so. We ended up here at a plantation near the Texas–Louisiana border where I finally had enough." Katy began to tear up again, "She is evil! I would rather die than be with her!"

"And this is where you departed from her?" Angelique asked.

"Yes. I had had enough of her abuse tonight and forever. Now she will kill me as she did the French girl. I know it!" Katy began to cry.

Angelique gently cupped her hand under Katy's chin. "Look at me," she said softly. "Do not fear her. You are not alone now, and you shall overcome this."

Katy looked up and stared into Angelique's eyes. They seemed to calm her. She truly wanted to believe her, but in the back of her mind she knew Annabelle would eventually find her, and this is what she feared the most.

"Bless you, my lady." Katy put her arms around Angelique. "There aren't enough words that I could find to thank you for your kindness and bravery tonight. For your name truly matches your heart. An angel definitely came to my aid this evening."

Angelique began to smile. "Oh . . . Some would take issue with that. As I have said, you must be strong, and you will see this time through. You have been through so much and seen such horrific things, but you will overcome this one day. I promise you by the gods that you shall have peace."

Angelique saw the weariness in Katy's eyes and knew she needed sleep. She walked to the cupboard and took out a blanket and a spare gown.

"It's not Windsor Castle but it will do I believe," Angelique grinned. "Here is something dry and clean for you to change into while I check on something outside."

Katy took the gown and changed while Angelique went outside and grabbed a bucket. No sooner had she picked up the bucket than a ruffling of leaves could be heard in the distance. It was getting closer and closer. Suddenly a little black shape was seen running from the brush.

"Ah! There you are," Angelique laughed as her cat ran into the house.

Katy, now dressed, saw the cat and began to smile. The cat, on seeing Katy, stopped in its tracks and peered at her with its glowing yellowish eyes. It then promptly went up to greet her. Angelique walked back into the cabin and watched the cat run up to Katy and began to purr.

"That's odd," she chuckled. "He hates everyone. You must be special."

Katy knelt down cautiously because her leg was still hurting her, but all that didn't matter because she loved animals.

"Hello," she said, with her arms extended.

The cat looked at her and then jumped straight into her arms. Katy caught him and began to pet and hug him. Angelique just stood watching, in shock. Her cat had never reacted toward another human like this. "Well, it looks like you will have a warm pillow tonight," she smiled. "But first he must eat."

Angelique walked to the table with the bucket and began to open the sack that she had brought in from the boat earlier.

"Hmmm . . . What do I see here, my furry friend?" she said removing a fish from the sack.

The cat saw the fish and bailed out of Katy's arms just as fast as he had jumped into them. He belted a loud 'meow', almost begging. Katy, looking on, began to laugh. Another 'meow' was heard before Angelique dropped the fish onto the floor. No sooner had it hit the ground than the cat began to devour it.

"What's his name?" Katy asked.

"He doesn't have a name really, but sometimes I call him Pwyll. I believe he will answer to anything as long as you have food."

Katy began to laugh. The presence of the cat seemed to make her problems go away, and a stillness now rested in her heart. She watched Angelique remove some plants and herbs from the sack and put them in the bucket. There were so many questions still running through her head. But she was most curious to find out why Angelique was out in the swamp at night. It would seem that this extraordinary lady had many things to tell. In time, Katy would find out her story.

Katy looked on until her eyes grew heavy, and she fell asleep. She had been through so much in the past day, but she felt she was safe and protected for the moment.

Angelique divided the plants and herbs while thinking of the events of the evening. She wondered how this young girl, from so far away, could actually survive in the swamps and escape death. As with all things, the answer would slowly reveal itself.

CHAPTER 2

Wes and Ben maneuvered along the swampy edge of the river with the three dogs close at hand, inspecting every step of the path. They were still a good distance from the plantation, but that was fine with Wes. He still needed to come up with a satisfactory explanation for Lady Falsworth as to why the young girl had not been found. Ben's earlier question had haunted him. Lady Falsworth would not accept a standard excuse without proof. She was not someone to be reckoned with.

Wes had only known Lady Falsworth for a short time. He had previously been employed by a prominent cattleman in south Louisiana and had herded cattle to Missouri on a regular basis. One day he had received a message from a longtime friend, Douglas Anderson, who was working as a consort to a New Orleans port official, that a Baroness from England was to arrive in New Orleans in a few weeks' time and would be looking to employ men as security for her trip through southwest Louisiana and southeast Texas. The pay was to be five times more than he made herding, and the work would supposedly last at least a year. This was too good an opportunity to pass up, so Wes was dead keen to get the job.

Two weeks had elapsed and Wes had made his way to New Orleans. The ship arrived from Portsmouth, England, with the Baroness and her entourage, which included twelve other people, onboard. The Baroness stayed at a local hotel, and a constant stream of persons tried their luck in the hope of being hired by her.

Two people sat at a desk in the den of the newly constructed Ambassador Hotel, taking the names and information of interested jobseekers. Basil Thorton seemed to be the more senior of the two since he asked all the questions. Both he and Agatha Sterling were in charge of all things relevant to Lady Falsworth. There was nothing that Basil didn't know about the people surrounding the Baroness. He kept a close eye on her dealings, particularly her security. Agatha, on the other hand, handled the servants and all social gatherings and events. She kept things running smoothly for the Baroness.

Wes entered the hotel lobby with his wide-brim hat in hand. His eyes scanned the area looking for clues of where he needed to go. A small line had formed at the entrance to the den, and he could see some of his fellow herders vying for the same jobs. The line grew quickly shorter because Mr. Thorton was a fast and excellent judge of character. Wes soon was at the front.

"Your name, sir?" Mr. Thorton snapped. He had had a long day of interviews, and his patience and tolerance was wearing thin.

"Wesley, sir," Wes nodded. "Wesley Harris."

"And your qualifications?"

Wes proceeded to tell him all that he thought would qualify him for the job, from being head of security at a ranch in Nacogdoches to frequently transporting cattle and goods—without loss—to the employer. Mr. Thorton listened without expression until Wes was through. He then turned to Agatha with a blank stare before facing Wes again.

"Can you read? Write?" he asked, almost sarcastically.

"Yes sir! I was schooled six years in reading, writing, and arith . . . arithm . . . and I did math as well." He smiled innocently.

This made Mr. Thorton crack a smile—a departure from his usual conservative nature. He nodded at Agatha. "Thank you sir, please be here tomorrow morning at eight in front of this hotel for your orders."

Wes stood with his mouth open, thinking of what had just been said. Excitement raced through his veins. "So I'm hired then? I got the job?" he asked, almost in disbelief.

Mr. Thorton looked up and acknowledged Wes with a nod. "Yes, sir.

Now please be here at eight tomorrow."

Wes donned a huge smile, and a sense of happiness flooded his body. He found it hard to control his enthusiasm. "Thank you, sir. Thank you very much." He walked out of the den and out the front door. He almost glided; he was thrilled to have been hired. As he made his way down the street, he felt victorious. Finally he would have a good job, away from herding, and this would probably lead to other things. Only time would tell.

The next morning Wes was at the front of the hotel, bright and early, as requested. He saw nine others standing around as if waiting for something. No sooner had the clock hit eight than Mr. Thorton was outside, motioning to all to enter the hotel. The men piled into the hotel and entered the den.

"Good morning, sirs," he said. "I hope your morning is well. Now let's get to the business at hand shall we." Mr. Thorton explained details of the job. "You, sirs, shall first and foremost be responsible for protecting Lady Annabelle Falsworth and her companions. There will be three carriages along with five on horseback. Two horses will lead, one will follow behind the second carriage, and two will bring up the rear. All carriages shall have two persons at the helm. Mr. Branson and I shall be on the third carriage, which will transport Lady Falsworth, Miss Sterling, and three maids. This carriage is to be guarded and protected with your life if need be. Does everyone understand this?"

A scattered "yes" could be heard throughout the room.

He continued, "The first carriage will hold the rest of Lady Falsworth's companions, along with some supplies. The second will hold supplies and Lady Falsworth's property; this, too, is to be guarded and protected at all costs. If this is understood then we shall get underway."

All agreed and proceeded to the stables where the three carriages were loaded and waiting, together with the horses, which were saddled and ready. Wes took his place on the first horse, as he would be leading the caravan. The others mounted up and waited for their passengers.

Four ladies exited the hotel and walked toward the carriages. They were in modest dress and seemed very subdued, which was unusual given that they were beginning an exciting journey in a new country. A bit later, a further five ladies walked out of the hotel in the same fashion, followed soon thereafter by the last three: first, a young girl, who Wes would be chasing in a swamp five days later, and then Miss Sterling and Lady Annabelle Falsworth herself. The latter two were dressed exquisitely, as if royalty had come to Louisiana.

Such a young lady, Wes thought, looking at Annabelle. He wondered how such a young lady could almost have the stature of a queen. Well, it didn't matter. He would get her where she was going and hopefully prosper in doing so.

The caravan left New Orleans without a glitch, and there were no problems as they made their way toward the Texas border. Through swamps and rivers, and over bridges and ferries, they took two days to get close to the border. Most of the hired help, including Wes, felt no pressure and thought they would be over the Sabine River within a day or so.

There was also no sense of apprehension as the caravan moved into a dense forest. Most of the time only birds were heard along with the other animals, and this kept Wes at ease. They rode into a bend, and all of the wildlife seemed to go silent. The only sound heard was the horses and carriages. The silence went on for a few moments before the reason was made clear.

A man darted out in the front of the caravan with a shotgun and aimed it alternately at Wes and the other horseman. Meanwhile two more gunmen came out from the trees alongside the carriages. Wes stopped his horse, halting the entire caravan. The men all raised their hands in surrender to avoid being shot by the bandits. All except Basil Thorton, who pulled out a pistol and pointed it at one of the gunmen. The gunman shot Mr. Thorton in the chest, and he returned fire, hitting the gunman in the head and killing him instantaneously. That was to be his final act, as Mr. Thorton himself hunched over and died.

Another gunman ran from the trees and stopped in front of the caravan. He seemed to be the leader of the pack of bandits. "Drop your weapons!" he yelled, and seeing that they were surrounded, the men in Lady Falsworth's entourage dropped their guns to the ground.

One of the gunmen jumped onto the second carriage and gasped. "It's a good day, Luke!" he said as he began rummaging through the contents. The other gunman jumped onto the third carriage and proceeded to open the door.

"Well looky what we got here!" he said as he tried to climb inside.

Just as he began to put his first foot in, a shot was heard, and he fell backward off the carriage. The first gunman looked on in silence; he could see the bullet wound in his friend's head. As he looked up at the carriage, he saw a woman standing over him with a Colt revolver. She fired swiftly, hitting him in the chest. Only one gunman remained. He attempted to fire his weapon at the woman but was unsuccessful; it misfired. The lady looked on and gave a devilish grin.

Annabelle hopped off the wagon and walked to the front of the caravan. She stared at the one lone gunman with the same evil smile on her face. "And you, sir, are you trying to rob me?" she asked. "Go on, explain yourself." And with those words, she raised the Colt and fired, hitting the man in the knee. He fell to the ground in agony. "Well . . . I'm listening," she said again, raising the revolver and shooting him in the other knee. "Thieves will not be tolerated!"

The man was screaming, in tremendous pain, which had no effect on Annabelle. Some of the others cringed at the man's anguish. This went on for a few moments then, like a cat tired of torturing her mouse, Annabelle raised the revolver a third time.

"Mercy, lady!" the man pleaded.

"Mercy? Is mercy what you want?" she asked the dying man. "Well then, you shall have it."

A shot rang out. The man was hit in the head, putting an end to his pain. Annabelle looked down on the dead man with a smirk. "You're very welcome," she said. She turned to Wes. "Idiots!" she shouted. "Damn your incompetence! You are all bloody incompetent idiots!"

Wes knew that it was his fault for not paying more attention to the surroundings. "Sorry ma'am, I take full responsibility," he said, by way of apology for what had taken place.

"Sorry? As well you should be. Now clean this mess up!" she said angrily.

"Madam!" a voice called out. "It's Mr. Thorton. He's dead." Miss Sterling was in tears.

Annabelle looked at Basil's lifeless body, then back at Wes. "He was my number one. Now bury him!" She walked back to the carriage. Just at that moment, the last surviving bandit moved his arm in pain. Without missing a step, Annabelle walked alongside of him, pointed the revolver to his chest, and shot him a second time. "Clean this up! And bring me more ammunition! I'm out," she yelled, still walking.

Annabelle returned to the third carriage and changed into her riding clothes. She knew that if she was to get out of this wretched country alive with her property intact, then she would have to be in front and ready. While Annabelle changed, some of the men buried Mr. Thorton in a shallow grave and a few of the others went in search of the bandits' horses and supplies, and took them for the caravan's own.

A while later, Annabelle stepped out of the carriage and walked to the front of the caravan. She noticed all the maids and Miss Sterling standing around Mr. Thorton's grave. She knew Miss Sterling was very fond of him, and she could see the pain in her eyes. But in Annabelle's world, things happen in life, and Agatha would get over it. She took a horse from the second rider and climbed into the saddle. Another man handed her Colt to her, reloaded and ready for anything out of the ordinary. "Mount up!" she ordered, ready to leave. "We'll ride on till dusk then camp in an open field. I do not want what happened here to happen again. Do you hear me? Be on guard!" And with a slap to the horse's side, she led the way through the forest.

Wes rode next to her, now more alert, listening and looking for anything unusual. He felt totally at fault for what had happened but just rode alongside her in silence. She, on the other hand, could see his remorse, but that wouldn't bring back her number one.

They camped at dusk and traveled to the edge of the Sabine River the next day. They crossed at Burr's Ferry, then headed south to just east of a small town called Beaumont. Annabelle had plans to stay at a plantation house for a few days; the owner was away in San Antonio but had had business dealings with the Falsworth family in the past, so he had agreed to let the caravan stay there.

The next morning, after a night of sleep in a comfortable bed, most members of the entourage felt well rested and revitalized. All except one maid. She had suddenly taken ill that night and now lay almost lifeless. This wasn't the first time a maid had come down with a mysterious illness. They had left England with thirteen maids, and three had died on the ship en route to New Orleans. The maids felt cursed and uncertain as to the origin of the disease.

As the maid lay dying, Katy entered the room, along with Annabelle and Miss Sterling. She watched on as Miss Sterling, schooled in medicine and healing under Mr. Thorton, began bloodletting to try to take away whatever was causing the malady. Normally, Mr. Thorton would do this with both Annabelle and Miss Sterling, but since he was no longer there, Katy was included.

Katy stared at Annabelle intensely, taking in her hands. For young woman of no more than twenty-four who had never had to do the washing or any hard labor, she had very old hands. They almost mirrored her grandmother's, but Katy would never have brought this up for fear of the consequences it might bring.

After the bloodletting, the maid did not seem at all better; in fact she looked weaker and was subsequently not able to wake up. It was at this time that Annabelle ordered Katy out of the room. A few hours later, the maid was dead.

The house servants took the body out of the house and buried it in the servants' cemetery that same evening. Katy, noticeably distressed, sat alongside a big cypress tree, pondering her life and her future. A servant girl from the house, walking past, noticed her distress. "Missy, you alright?" she asked.

Katy looked up and tried to speak but couldn't, so she just nodded her head in the affirmative.

"That woman not right. She a devil," the young woman said, as if trying to warn her.

Katy found words to reply. "I do believe you're right. She is a bad person, but there is no escape for me here."

"You need leave this place before you end up like that other girl. That woman has no soul. She black as the night. She dangerous."

Katy listened to her words and could not help but think that she was absolutely right, but what could she do? She was in a foreign land with no means of help.

"That woman gonna kill you," the young woman said, looking around to make sure no one else was near.

"Possibly, but where do I go? I have nothing here," Katy replied miserably.

"Anything better than this. You need leave tonight. From here go south along the river. You can hide in the marsh till daylight. Across the river you find good folk. You work, they helps you." And with those words, she left. Swiftly. As if someone was watching her.

Katy began to think that this was probably her best option, but fear crept in. How could she survive alone out there?

A few hours later, Katy left the house, undetected, and traveled south, as the servant girl had suggested. Not long thereafter, word of her departure was brought to the attention of Lady Falsworth. She ordered Wes after her with the help of Ben Drayson, a hired hand of the plantation owner, and his hunting dogs. They set off into the dark to find the girl.

When Wes and Ben returned to the house, Lady Falsworth was on the porch waiting for them. She did not see either Katy or her body. Her eyes stared unflinchingly at Wes. Both men stopped in front of the porch and climbed off their horses.

"And? Is she not with you?" She directed her questions at Wes.

Wes' words stumbled. "Ma'am, there is no way she could have lived through all this . . ."

"Damn your opinions! I want facts, you incompetent fool!" she interrupted. "Is she alive?"

Ben, listening to this, decided to add to the discussion. "Ma'am, I am from here, and I know my dogs. If that girl was still running around the swamp, we'd a got her. There's only two ways out of that swamp. By boat or swim, and I don't care how good you swim, the current is too dang strong. She either drowned, which means we'll find her in a couple a days, or the gators got her."

Lady Falsworth felt Ben's answer was adequate, but she still wanted proof. "Alright then, but first thing in the morning I want you both, along with every man you can spare, out by that river. I want her found dead or alive. Do you understand me?"

"Yes ma'am," Ben agreed. "If she's out there, I'll find her."

"Good. I'm glad at least one of you is somewhat competent," she said, glaring at Wes.

Wes stood silent, knowing he could not live up to the expectations of Lady Falsworth.

"Enough. Leave me." She turned around and walked into the house, the cue for Ben and Wes to take their horses to the stables.

After the horses and dogs were settled, Ben headed to the ranch hands' quarters to get some well needed rest ahead of the next day. Wes, on the other hand, sat outside on the porch to do a little soul-searching on his own. He couldn't sleep, and the events of the last few days haunted his every thought. He knew he was working on borrowed time, and another mistake would bring sure dismissal. Only time would tell.

CHAPTER 3

Angelique sat at a table with a deck of cards in hand. Her gypsy roots had not waned, even after 15-plus years. Her early life had been one of pain and struggle, but like Katy, she had accepted it and did the best she could given her circumstances.

By nine and a half, Angelique had already learned the ways of the gypsies from her grandmother. Her ability to read the cards came to her as naturally as her judge of character. Her life in France though, was far from ideal. Most of her family earned little, if anything, and money and food were scarce. Although they tried hard to improve their situation, bad luck always seemed to prevail.

One day Angelique's mother took gravely ill. Her father had tried to find someone to help her but was unsuccessful. Since she was not of gypsy blood like her husband, the gypsy clan showed her no compassion. Likewise, any doctor who saw her family would deem her a gypsy and wouldn't see her without payment. Finally, the illness took its toll, and she died. Now motherless, Angelique was sent to England to live with her aunt whom she did not know.

Angelique walked off the ship in Portsmouth, frightened and alone. She saw a woman walking along the docks. She was staring at Angelique but had a glowing smile.

"Angelique?" she called out.

Angelique looked at the lady, afraid inside, but feeling a sense of comfort owing to the lady's smile. The lady stood in front of her and began stroking Angelique's hair out of her face. She tried talking with her in French, but unlike her sister, she was not able to speak the language well. Luckily Angelique had learned some English from her mother, which would be a tremendous help at the start of her relationship with this kindly stranger.

Angelique and her aunt became very close. Her aunt had never married and did not have children. However, she loved having her niece around and regarded her as her own daughter.

Angelique learned much from her aunt over the next five years, particularly about herbs and healing. Mixed with the teachings from her grandmother, it would seem that she would be well prepared for whatever life would present her with—or so she thought.

One day, when Angelique was 15, she was walking back to her aunt's cottage when she noticed her aunt slumped over in the garden. Angelique ran swiftly toward her to see what was wrong. She saw that her aunt was immobile and unresponsive. She immediately grabbed her arm in a vain attempt to help her up but without success. She simply could not lift her aunt's limp form. A man, who happened to be walking down the street at just that moment, saw Angelique struggling. "Hold on, lass!" he shouted as he ran to them. The man lifted the woman up into his arms as Angelique ran ahead to open the cottage door.

"Thank you, sir," she said as she grabbed a bucket of water and a towel.

The man placed her aunt on the bed. Both he and Angelique had already noticed that she was burning with fever. Angelique attempted to calm the fever with the damp towel. The coolness of the water seemed to give her aunt a measure of life, and although still delirious and weak, she lay on the bed, moaning.

"Lass, she needs a doctor," he said, watching the young girl wiping her aunt's brow. "There is a doctor not too far from here. I will try to bring him here at once, but because of the influenza epidemic, he may be a while."

"Bless you, sir," Angelique said, appreciative of his help.

The man left hurriedly down the street toward town while Angelique searched for something to help her aunt. Influenza was deadly to most, but there still had to be something she could do.

"Elderberries," her aunt groaned softly. "Dear, please make tea . . ."

With those words Angelique's aunt fell back to sleep. Her fever was still high and showed no sign of breaking.

Angelique went outside to the elderberry tree and began picking off the berries. This was what her aunt had been doing earlier before the sickness had become too much. Gathering a healthy amount of elderberries, along with some yarrow and mint, she returned to the cottage. The fire from the hearth was already lit, so she immediately began preparing the berries, yarrow, and mint to make tea.

A little time later, after the tea had boiled, Angelique took the hot brew to her aunt, together with some elderberries. She placed the cup to her lips and helped her drink. Still weak and delirious, her aunt drank the tea before falling back to sleep.

Angelique stayed at her side most of the night. Finally, in the wee hours of the morning, the fever broke, and her aunt began to wake.

"Dear . . ."

"Yes aunty, I'm here," Angelique said gently, feeling her aunt's forehead. "You must rest. You are still weak."

"Yes, I know," she whispered, trying to smile, "but I am in the hands of an angel."

"By the gods and your own knowledge, you are still here. I am merely following your instructions," Angelique soothed.

"And the yarrow . . . and the mint? You shall be great healer one day." Her aunt was speaking very slowly and quietly. "You are special, my dear . . . the gods look upon you as I do . . . with love and happiness."

Angelique looked on, wiping her aunt's brow, making sure that the fever had broken. Just then she heard a knock at the door. She stood up and walked to the door to see the man that had helped her earlier that day. He had brought the doctor. She let them in.

"I'm sorry, lass, that it took so long. How is your mother?" the man greeted as he entered the cottage with the weary-eyed doctor.

"I'm . . . fine." The lady was coughing.

The doctor stood over her, feeling her forehead, "You are weak and need rest, but it would seem that luck is with you tonight."

"By the grace of God, you have come back to the living," the man said, amazed to see her conscious.

Still very frail, the lady attempted conversation. "Yes . . . with a little help from my angel."

"And to this man—if it were not for him, you would still be in the garden," said Angelique, nodding in the direction of the stranger.

"Yes, permanently I am sure," the lady chuckled weakly.

"It is alright, madam," the man said. "I am glad to be of assistance. I lost my wife to this epidemic only a month ago. I saw the lass in peril and, in my heart, I felt that both you and she needed help."

"And I thank you sir for this good deed which you have done. Truly . . . from the bottom of my heart . . . you are a true Samaritan." And with those words, Angelique's aunt began to fall asleep.

The doctor looked at Angelique. "You have done well. Please look after her for the next night and day. I believe she will recover. She is very strong willed."

"Thank you, doctor, I will," she replied.

The doctor and the man left the cottage while Angelique looked over her aunt that night and the next day. She made a full recovery.

The memories of that time seem so far away now, Angelique thought, as she turned over another card and placed it on the table. "Times change yet they stay the same," she said softly to herself, as she glanced at Katy's sleeping body.

A while later, Katy awoke and moved slowly toward the table. Her leg was still swollen and sore after the previous night's trauma. Finally making it to a chair, she noticed the cards on the table. "Ah, you're a seer of the cards."

"And you know of these?" Angelique asked.

Katy looked at her excitedly, "Of course I do. My mother did this every October after the Hunter's Moon. She wanted to know the future of the year to come." Katy paused for a moment. "So what is to come?"

Angelique looked up at Katy and replied, "Do you need the cards to tell you? I believe not . . . I believe you already know what is to come, but it will be on your terms. Now it is time to go." Angelique stood up from the table and grabbed a sack from the cupboard. She placed it on the table and began opening it. Katy looked on, still trying to decipher her words but also curious about the contents of the sack.

"Biscuits!" she proclaimed with excitement.

"And . . . jam," Angelique said as she handed Katy a jar along with a biscuit.

"Bless you, my lady," Katy thanked her as she began to devour it.

"It has been a while since you have eaten no doubt." Angelique watched Katy eating.

"Yes, my lady. Two days, I think." She had taken another biscuit.

"Well then, worry not child . . . Finish them, you need the strength."

Angelique handed the rest of the biscuits and jam to her.

After Katy had finished eating, they set off together up the path. Angelique carried a huge sack filled with hides, some herbs, and her deck of cards. Katy limped alongside her with another sack, but she was having trouble with her injured leg. She kept stopping to alleviate the pain. "I don't know if I'll be able to go on—I'm sorry."

"It's alright, let's rest here," Angelique said, taking the sack from her.

Rubbing her leg, Katy looked around. There was a huge mound in front of them: it was twenty feet tall and seemed to be as long as three hundred feet. Given the otherwise flat albeit forested terrain, it looked out of place.

"What is this, my lady?" she asked her, sitting down on a log near the pathway.

"What? The mounds? It's a cemetery. The Indians built this."

"The cannibals?" Katy gasped, shocked that the area might be unsafe. Her visions of savages hiding behind every tree startled her. When Katy had arrived in the area, the locals had told her tales of large Indians, some as tall as seven feet, who walked the beaches and swamps of the area.

Angelique saw the concern on Katy's face and began to smile. "Yes, but worry not. These Indians have long since perished." She was amused but tried to reassure Katy. "There are Indians here but their numbers are few, and they favor the taste of alligator meat over a 15-year-old English girl."

"But why did the people at the plantation say this? They made a point of telling us not to travel south," Katy explained, trying to justify her fear.

"The locals usually tell Northerners to stay away for their own good. There is more in this swamp that will harm them than just the ghost of an Indian. To the south is also where bad people dwell. I also do not go there. Murderers and thieves, it is the land where Lafitte used to dwell."

Hearing Angelique's words, Katy began to relax, but still the pain of her leg still consumed her. Just then, a noise was heard close by, further along the path. It sounded as if horses were coming nearer.

Angelique stood up. A smile appeared on her face as she looked down the path. "Worry no more, lass," she said, "Help is on the way."

Both could now see a horse-driven wagon coming up the path toward them. Etienne Broussard, Angelique's neighbor to the south, was heading to Beaumont to purchase supplies. Etienne saw Angelique and halted the horses in front of her. He tipped his hat. "How are? Ladies." He spoke in broken sentences. Etienne's English was fair, but he also knew Angelique was fluent in French so it made it easier to talk with her. Angelique proceeded to explain to Etienne, in French, the problem with Katy's leg and asked if they could get a ride into town. He was only too happy to oblige. "Well now, I think I can," he spoke in English so Katy would understand. "There is plenty of room on this wagon for both of you, and me, too. We are headed to the same place so come on up."

"I always know I can count on you, Frenchy," Angelique smiled. "Thank you." Both women placed the sacks in the back of the wagon and then climbed up front.

Katy was happy that she didn't have to walk anymore and turned to Etienne, thanking him profusely. "Bless you, sir," she said over and over.

"It's my pleasure little lady," he said. "It's not often I get the company of two beautiful ladies on my trips."

The wagon made its way up the trail through the little settlement of Grigsby's Bluff, riding north till they came to the outskirts of the small lumber town of Beaumont. It wasn't much to look at, but it did have its finer points—especially to a weary traveler who was out of supplies and in need. Etienne parked the wagon near the supply store and began unloading a few huge sacks of furs and hides. Angelique did the same while Katy stayed in the wagon and watched the horse. "Tell me, Gitane, where you find this girl?" Etienne asked. "It seems she a long way from home."

"The river gives up many strange things and this be one of them," Angelique said with a faint laugh.

"If you found her in the river, she lucky to be breathin'. And I'm sure somebody gonna want her back."

"Possibly. Time will tell, my friend. Time will tell."

A short time passed as they both traded the contents of their sacks in exchange for much needed supplies. Winter was coming swiftly, and they needed to prepare for what could be a very cold season. They packed the back of the wagon with supplies of sugar, flour, tobacco, assorted spices, and other commodities, which were needed to make life in this desolate place a little easier.

When all of the supplies were loaded, Etienne climbed up and took the reins from Katy while Angelique went back to the store to do a few card readings. This was a common practice for her when in town. All knew of her gypsy background, and many wanted her insight into their future.

"Well now, little lady" Etienne said, trying to strike up a conversation. "What is your name?"

"Katy, sir," she said, "Katy Morgan."

"Nice to meet you, Katy Morgan. My name's Etienne, but no one round here can say Etienne so they call me Frenchy instead."

Katy laughed aloud. "Well, hello Mr. Frenchy. I'm glad to meet you."

The two carried on talking, learning each other's origins. Finally Angelique left the store and was walking toward them when a wagon pulled by two horses suddenly came racing down the path toward her. The wagon was going too fast, and although he saw Angelique, the driver did not slow down. Angelique stood peering into the eyes of the horses, not with fear, but with disgust. No sooner were the horses upon her than they stopped abruptly in their tracks. This sent the driver of the wagon into a rage. "What is this, gypsy? You bewitch my horses?" he snarled, dismounting the wagon. "Out of my way, you heathen harlot." The man walked up to her. He was in a rage. He raised his hand, as if to slap Angelique in the face. Angelique saw this and almost instantaneously revealed a long-handled knife she had hidden under the sleeve of her coat. She jabbed it near the man's lower torso. He stopped in his tracks. He could feel the sharp knife digging into his lower regions.

"Calm you will be or you will never sire children in this world!" she muttered, holding the knife steady and looking him in the eye without a trace of mercy. Sensing that Angelique was serious, the man calmed himself and drew away from her with his hands raised.

The man was Thomas Leopold, a rancher from a county to the north. He knew Angelique and did not like gypsies in any fashion or form. Angelique had had dealings with him before, but this time things had become extreme.

Angelique watched Thomas slowly make his way back to his wagon and silently climb back up and pick up the reins. She reached out to the horses, kissed and patted both on the head, then walked back to Etienne's wagon and climbed up. Thomas looked over at her as he rode past. "You will pay for this, Gypsy! By God Almighty, you will pay!" he shouted.

Angelique just stared at him and then winked at Etienne. Etienne did the same. "Gitane, you special," he said, laughingly as they rode away.

Angelique became quiet. She was deep in thought and remained silent for most of the trip until Etienne suggested having dinner at his house. She knew Sophie, Etienne's wife, was a good cook, and Katy would gather a lot more strength from a big dinner than if she ate at her cabin. Also it was the night of the Hunter's Moon, and Sophie always wanted a reading at the last full moon in October. Both women agreed and headed off with Etienne to the Broussard's household. Angelique thought it would be a good night in preparation for what was to come. Exactly what, she could not tell, but the feeling was there all the same.

CHAPTER 4

Wes, along with a few of the ranch hands, had been searching the swampy trails near the river since dawn. There was still no sign of the girl. Ben had patrolled the river and inlets in a flat-bottomed boat. Everyone knew that looking for her was a waste of time, but Lady Falsworth had demanded that they continue the search, and whatever Lady Falsworth wanted, rest assured, Lady Falsworth got. And quickly.

Ben pulled the boat alongside the bank where Wes sat on horseback staring at the water.

"This is a waste of dang time," he said. He was feeling a bit fed up about the whole incident. "She ain't out here. And even if she was, she'd been supper to some critter already."

"I know . . . I know," Wes replied. He was just as frustrated. "Let's head back. We already have a boat downriver, and we'll send two hands to search on the other side. I just hope that's good enough for her."

"You know it won't be," Ben muttered. "I don't see why this girl is so damn important. Then again, I don't understand the English anyways."

"I'm beginning to wonder as well." Wes waved his hand in the air as a sign for everyone to head back to the plantation.

Ben stepped off the boat and signaled one of the ranch hands to take his place. After giving the ranch hand orders to search the opposite bank of the river, Ben climbed on his horse and began to ride toward the plantation.

An hour and a half had passed before the search team returned home. As usual, Lady Falsworth was waiting for them on the porch. She stepped out into the pathway and met Wes and Ben. "Well I see you haven't any news," she growled irritably.

Both Wes and Ben nodded and kept silent. Lady Falsworth turned to Ben. "So . . . your thoughts?"

Ben was silent for a moment. "She is definitely not out there, ma'am. Like I said last night, if she drowned then we'll find her in a couple of days, but there is no trace of her. Them dogs would have picked up on her scent. If she's still alive, she would have had to make it across the river, and she would have had to have help. There is no way she could've swum."

Lady Falsworth looked at Ben. Although she did believe him, she felt that Katy was still alive and needed to be found. "Very well, I honor your opinion but feel that we need to look more across the river. She is still out there, and I want her found at all costs. Do you understand?"

Ben looked at her and nodded, "Yes'm, if she is out there then we will find her. But beggin' your pardon, ma'am. I believe she was eaten up and don't think we'll find even a bone from her."

"Fair enough . . . Just keep searching across the river."

"Yes, ma'am. We will do."

Lady Falsworth began walking in the direction of the house but stopped for a moment and turned back toward Ben. "We leave tomorrow for Beaumont to replenish supplies," she said. "We will then head south to Sabine. I would like it if you would accompany us on this journey. You would be paid well for your services."

Ben's reply was immediate, "Yes'm. I greatly accept your offer and think it would be an honor to accompany y'all."

Wes looked over at Ben. The tone coming out of Ben's mouth was very different to that which he had used earlier in the swamp. Ben glanced over at Wes with a devilish grin on his face. "Looks like we gonna be partners for yet another day." He slapped Wes on his back as he walked past. Wes just shook his head and headed to the stables.

Lady Falsworth walked back up the porch and sat near Agatha, who was rocking back and forth on the swing. Agatha's mind appeared distant as she stared out at the trees. The events of the previous few days, especially the loss of Basil, had changed her. The normally stern, punctual, emotionless woman had removed herself mentally from the day's concerns. Annabelle saw this and felt the need to give her time alone.

"Hana," she called to one of her maids, who were also sitting on the porch with two other servants.

"Yes, my lady?" Hana replied, rising from her chair.

"It's nearly three, and Miss Sterling and I shall have our tea here," said Annabelle.

"Yes, my lady. Immediately." Hana curtsied and scampered to the kitchen to put a kettle on. The other two maids followed.

"You know, he was only forty," Agatha said. "His last act was to protect us. Even after a fatal wound, how could one feel the desire to protect another? One's last thought was for another."

"Because he did his job well," Annabelle replied. "He knew the risks of his job, and he accepted them."

"But why him?"

"Because the others had no desire for confrontation, only self-preservation. He of course was an exception."

Annabelle stared at Agatha. She knew Agatha was in pain over a lost love, but she needed someone stable whom she could trust.

"And you? How are you, my dear friend?"

Agatha thought for a moment. "Me? I'm fine. No need to worry. I am here for you."

"That is very good to hear," Annabelle said as she looked into Agatha's eyes. "The time is upon us, and we cannot afford another mistake. Do you hear me, dear friend?"

Agatha returned Annabelle's cold stare. "As I have said, worry not on my account. I am ready."

Annabelle's face took on a nefarious appearance. She could indeed always count on Agatha, no matter what the problem or situation.

Annabelle and Agatha chatted for a while on the porch while having tea. Both looked on as some of the last of the ranch hands returned from their day of searching for the young girl. They had all finally made it back, except for the two who had gone across the river in the flat-bottomed boat.

* * *

Benjamin Reed and Ezra Jacobs paddled down the river. They had searched the riverbanks for signs of the young girl all afternoon but to no avail. Finally Benjamin thought it best to search inland. They moored the boat near the burial mounds of Grigsby's Bluff then set off on foot.

Benjamin made his way up the mounds with Ezra close behind. From the top he could see most of the flatlands. There was no trace of anyone.

"Well, I guess Ezra," Benjamin said looking toward the path, "we gonna just have to start walkin'."

Ezra looked at Benjamin with a hint of disgust. "That girl dead. Why the hell we out here?"

"I know, I know. But I guess we doin' what you call foreign relations."

"I don't give a damn what you call it," Ezra began to rant. "That damn evil woman making us waste time out here when we got cattle to tend to." Benjamin smiled and nodded his head in agreement. "You know, Sister Betty says that woman has no soul," Ezra continued. "Sister Betty is a third cousin to Marie Laveau, and I believe her. That woman may be

Queen of Europe or something but she the devil."

"I'm sure she is, Ezra," Benjamin replied, trying not to laugh. He knew Ezra's lady friend dabbled in voodoo, and he had heard the story of her relationship to the voodoo queen, but he himself always dismissed it as superstition.

They talked together for a while on the mound before wading back through the thick vegetation to the path. It was then that they both heard the sound of a horse and wagon heading toward them. The men quickly ducked behind the tall grass and brush where they crouched, hidden from sight. As the wagon passed, they saw a man, a woman, and a young girl traveling southbound. Ezra's jaw dropped and his eyes grew wide as he stared at the young girl.

"That her," he pointed, whispering to Benjamin. "That the girl. As God is my witness, she there."

Benjamin knew Ezra had been around the girl enough to know what she looked like, but he also knew Ezra's wild imagination. "Are you sure?"

"Yeah, that is her," Ezra hissed.

Both remained hidden as the wagon passed. Benjamin knew that there were only a few people living down this path, so it would be easy to find out where she was staying.

"If I didn't see it with my own eyes . . ." Ezra was shaking his head.

"I think we need to go," Benjamin whispered. "We need to tell Ben and let him handle this."

After the wagon had passed and was out of sight, Benjamin and Ezra hurried back to the boat and proceeded up the river, back to the horses, and to the plantation. They were exhilarated by what they had discovered and were eager to share their news.

* * *

Ezra had been right. The wagon that had passed the mounds had been carrying Etienne, Angelique, and Katy, who were on their way to Etienne's house. All three had been chatting, enjoying the afternoon sunshine. Etienne was especially talkative. He had been relaying information about the things of interest that Katy had noticed along the trip, such as the different types of birds they had seen near Elisha and Mary Brewers' tract of land halfway home from the supply store.

Katy had had many questions, especially when it came to the mounds. Ever since she had arrived in this area she had been obsessed with Indians. Her imagination had run amok with all the talk of savages and cannibals. Etienne explained the real stories of the seven-foot-tall giants that had lived on the land years before. "I was told that they roamed the land for over a thousand years," he said, turning his head to face her. "Some say you could smell 'em before you saw 'em . . . And ornery. They say they were as mean as the alligators they ate." Katy listened attentively to each word as he spoke. "They were feared all across the coast of Texas. Although there was one that did befriend them, and that man was Jean Lafitte. I guess he thought having savages at his back door, so to speak, meant nobody gonna sneak up on him."

Katy looked at Etienne a little oddly. "Did they drink the blood of their victims?"

Both Etienne and Angelique glanced at Katy, surprised of the question.

"I don't really know, child. I think they stuck them in a stew pot," he joked.

"What happened to them, the Indians?"

"Well, I believe they were too mean and kept killing the settlers, so the Texicans and the Mexicans killed them off."

"Dear." Katy was mortified.

39

"Yep. These times and places are dangerous and hard, but we gonna be alright. Right, Gitane?" He winked at Angelique.

"But of course, Frenchy." She smiled back. "But of course."

They rode for a few minutes more before coming to a fork in the road. Etienne turned the horses to the left. It was his land. He took the long winding road past some dense brush and trees until they came to a clearing near a garden where Sophie, Etienne's wife, was working. Etienne called out to her and waved as they rode up to the barn. While Etienne attended to the horse, Angelique and Katy unloaded his supplies from the wagon and carried them onto the porch of the house.

"My, this place is lovely" Katy said, admiring the two-story structure.

"Yes, he is an excellent carpenter. One of the best," Angelique explained.

Sophie had left her work and walked over to the porch. She greeted the women with a joyous smile and hug. She and Angelique rambled on in French for a few moments, and it seemed to Katy as if they were the best of friends. Katy didn't mind being left out of the conversation. She was too busy examining her surroundings—the nice house, the big vegetable garden, and especially the dog that had met them on the porch.

Etienne headed to the house after settling the horse. He walked up and noticed Katy with the dog. "I see you've met my Jacque," he said as he reached out to pet his dog.

"Why yes indeed," Katy replied. She was kneeling next to Jacque.

They all chattered for a brief moment before Sophie picked up the basket of herbs and vegetables that she had picked in the garden, along with a few rabbits that Etienne had hunted that morning. She then headed to the kitchen, which was alongside the house, to begin preparing dinner. Both Angelique and Katy followed her while Etienne and the dog walked down toward the river.

An hour passed as the sun began to set. They had all settled into the kitchen to prepare the night's meal. It was always special when visitors came, thought Sophie, and even more special when it was on the night of the Hunter's moon.

* * *

Across the river, the two men, who had now made it to the plantation, were not thinking of a holiday dinner. Their only thoughts were to report to Lady Falsworth that they had found the girl alive. Benjamin and Ezra quickly dismounted their horses and rushed up to the house. Ben, who was sitting on the porch, greeted them. "Well?" he asked.

"She there!" Ezra blurted out for most of the house to hear. Annabelle, sitting in the study, stood up and walked to the porch. "She there Miss Falsworth! She there!" Ezra repeated excitedly.

Annabelle glanced at Ben and nodded her approval. "Well now," she said looking back to Ezra and Benjamin. "It would seem that things are looking up."

"Yes'm, Miss Falsworth. It was her. It was definitely her."

"And where did you see her?"

"We were at the mounds by Grigsby's Bluff, and Ezra noticed a wagon heading south," Benjamin said. "She was on it with two others."

"Could you tell who they were?" Ben asked.

"No, not for sure, but it looked like Frenchy. There are not many houses down there, so she's not too far away. I can head that way with Ezra tomorrow at daybreak and find out."

"I think we all will go," Annabelle interrupted. "We leave before dawn." Annabelle turned to Agatha, who was now at the door. "Make sure they are ready." Agatha nodded and headed back in the house.

Ben, on the other hand, had questions. He knew of Frenchy but had never met him. He also knew from others that he was a good fine man but didn't take well to strangers on his land. "I believe the best thing to do is to have a few of us ride up and see." He was addressing Lady Falsworth. "I think it would be less trouble that way."

"As you wish," said Lady Falsworth as she noticed Wes approaching. "At least someone is thinking tonight." Annabelle turned on her heel and headed into the house. She did not even acknowledge Wes. He just bowed his head and listened to the others as they made their plans.

* * *

The night air was crisp and cool, and there were no clouds in the sky. It was at about the time that Annabelle went inside the house that the moon began to rise. It would seem to be a perfect night. Perfect and calm ahead of the oncoming storm that would change the lives of many here in this small sparsely developed area.

CHAPTER 5

Sophie walked over to the large pot that was hanging over the fireplace. The sweet smell of herbs and rabbit spread through the kitchen, to the enjoyment of all, especially Katy and Angelique, who had had nothing to eat aside from the biscuits and jam that morning.

Angelique always loved to visit her friend Sophie. Not because she was a great cook, although that was admittedly a plus, but because she saw in Sophie a strong woman who, like herself, had traveled away from hardships to start over in this new world.

Sophie, like Etienne, was born in France. Both of their families had traveled to Canada, but the wretched winters—and the English—had forced their families south to Louisiana. They had met in a small village just north of New Orleans, where they had married a few years later.

Etienne, a carpenter by trade, worked at a local mill. He was a true craftsman, and the quality of his work was well known. He had offers to build cabinets from all over Louisiana, but he usually stayed local in order to be near Sophie. One day a cattle baron from Southeast Texas, who also had a lumber mill, was in New Orleans and noticed some of Etienne's work. The next day Etienne was headed for Texas with an offer he and Sophie couldn't pass up.

Sophie and Etienne had arrived in their new land, south of Grigsby's Bluff, both excited and nervous. They were a long way from what they called home but seeing that this new life would enable them to make good money, they believed it was worth the move.

Etienne had acquired about fifty acres, built his house, along with a large vegetable garden, and prospered greatly. Although he and Sophie lived a simple life and did not dabble in what others called upper-class living, they lived off the land and worked hard for what they had achieved. They were a proud people.

The food was at last ready to eat. Sophie picked up the big pot with Angelique's help, while Katy carried the bread to the main house. While walking from the kitchen to the house, Angelique noticed the full moon rising over the river.

"Ah, the Hunter's Moon rises. Beautiful," she said, coming to a stop at the bottom of the steps.

"Indeed," replied Sophie. "Thank you, Mr. Rabbit."

Both Katy and Angelique began to laugh and also thanked "Mr. Rabbit" for his presence. Once up the steps and through the doorway, they set the pot on the table. Katy was close behind and placed the bread next to the pot. Sophie walked back out to the kitchen and returned with some tea that had been boiling. "Etienne!" she called. "Supper's ready."

Etienne, who had been outside on the porch, almost ran into the dining room. "Eeeew yah!" he shouted. "That smells good!"

They all gathered around the table as Sophie began serving the stew. Katy, determined to be of help, poured tea into each cup while Angelique sliced the bread. With the food and drink served, they bowed their heads as Etienne said grace. "Dear Lord. Bless this food that we have before us, and keep watch on all of us here, especially our new friend Katy. She's in a new land and needs special attention. We know that you will show her the way that she needs to go. Amen."

With the blessing said, they began eating the food that Sophie had prepared, or rather, devouring it, as there was very little left of the big pot of stew once they were finished. Katy especially, ate and ate, until she could not eat anymore.

"My . . . young'un?" Etienne said grinning profusely as he watched Katy gulp down her dinner.

Katy looked up and noticed everyone looking at her. She looked embarrassed. "Sorry, my manners are atrocious," she said, still with spoon in hand, ready for another mouthful.

"Oh no, no, no, you go right ahead, lass." Sophie handed her another piece of bread.

"Thank you, my lady. I haven't tasted a meal this good for a long time. You are all too generous."

It had indeed been a long time since Katy had had such a meal. She, along with the other maids, were usually fed after everyone else, and she mostly only had leftovers to look forward to.

Etienne, also enjoying the meal, nudged Katy. "Little lady . . . You are our guest. You can eat as much as you need to. Good Lord knows that if you don't, I will!" he said, patting his protruding belly.

"Thanks, Frenchy. I am ever so grateful to have met you three."

"And we too are glad that you are here," Etienne replied.

Katy was thankful because her life had been one of tragedy and bad decisions. She felt her luck had finally changed when she had met Angelique and Etienne. However, she also felt that her past was still there and could rear its ugly head at any time.

After supper, Katy and Angelique removed the dishes and put them aside while Sophie cleaned the dining table. Etienne opened the window that faced the river then sat down in his chair, like he always did after supper if the mosquitoes weren't too horrendous.

"Well, would you look at that," he said as he peered out the window in the direction of the moon.

"It is beautiful tonight." Angelique walked to the window to take a closer look.

The moon was bright over the river, lighting up the night sky almost as if the sun still were still shining. This was the Hunter's Moon, the moon after the fall equinox and a time at which most hunters took advantage of the light for gaming. Even in this small community, the sound of occasional gunshots could be heard as the night progressed. This made Katy a bit nervous because of the previous night's events.

"Sounds like ol' Peloat is having good luck in the woods," Etienne commented. He noticed Katy twitch at the sounds. "Don't worry, young'un," he said, trying to comfort her. "It's just my neighbor to the south trying to get him a critter or two."

Katy smiled politely but Angelique could tell she was physically shaken from the noise. Angelique made a quiet gesture in an attempt to comfort her, then gave a warm smile. "Tonight is special for a few reasons," she said, walking back to the table with her cards in hand.

"To me it always has been," Katy muttered. "I can vaguely remember my mother watching my grandmother read the cards each year and telling tales of my great-great-grandmother. She was a healer and helped the villagers with any illness or problems they had. Legend has it that they had burned her mother and two sisters for witchcraft. One man tried this with her, and he paid the ultimate price."

"I believe we all have our skeletons hidden away in the shadows," Angelique remarked, thinking of her own history.

"I remember as a child back in France, my cousin was a healer," added Sophie. "She was very good, too. Many people, even from other villages, would seek her out whenever someone was ill or needed help. But all that changed when two children became sick with something mysterious. She tried to cure them but couldn't. They died within a week. Normally this wouldn't be her fault but some said it was sorcery and being who she was, people pointed to her. It was never the same after that. You could have painted a big red devil on her face and the people would not have flinched."

"At least she lived," Katy stated, thinking of her great-great-grandmother.

"True, but it's like being a carpenter and having your hands cut off—you're ruined. She finally moved away to somewhere I forget. I never heard of her again."

"She probably ended up here, as we all have," Angelique joked.

"Could be," Sophie replied. "She would have fit right into Louisiana."

Angelique sat at the table shuffling the cards, then placed some of them on the table. Sophie sat close by, in keen anticipation of what the next year might bring. Angelique stared at the cards for a moment. It looked as if she was in a trance. Many thoughts and pictures came to her with each card she turned over. At length, she turned and faced Sophie.

"I believe you will have a good year, but there is something soon . . . a decision you will have to make. This decision is important for you, but more so for a traveler. Go with your heart, and the wheel will keep turning. Go with another's, and you will become stuck for a very long time. It is this decision that lies in your future."

Sophie began to ponder Angelique's words. Normally the reading was for a year, but it seemed as if her whole year hung on one decision. This frightened her a bit because she always had a plan to fall back on. She was not at all comfortable with doing anything at the spur of the moment.

"I don't know what to say." Sophie was still taking all of it in.

"Do not fret Sophie. Your life, as with your husband's, will be abundant and sound. It is this decision that will affect another, but you will know when the time comes what is right and just."

Sophie felt a little bit relieved that at the least her life with Etienne would be one of plenty for another year.

"Is that all you see?" Sophie asked, daring to learn of any other revelation that the year would bring.

"There is something I see. A visitor of great importance shall arrive in May. He . . . he will change your life forever . . ." Angelique was gathering her thoughts. She took her eyes off the cards and turned her attention to Sophie. She looked at her with a little confusion—and excitement.

"What? What is it you see?" Sophie blurted nervously, as she saw the change in Angelique's manner.

Angelique kept staring at her, now with a playful grin. Finally she spoke. "Sophie Broussard, are you with child?"

A loud clang came from the chair where Etienne was sitting. He had been rocking and semi-listening to them while whittling on a piece of wood. With the sound of the words "with child," Etienne dropped everything and turned his attention to Sophie. Sophie just sat still, dumbfounded, not knowing what to say. They had been trying to fall pregnant for years but without any luck.

"I . . . I don't really know . . ." Sophie was almost totally speechless.

Angelique couldn't help but smile at Sophie. She knew they had been waiting for this news for a very long time, and it would seem that it was coming true.

"What you say, Gitane?" Etienne said, now standing up from his chair, walking to the table.

"I believe you're going to be a father, Frenchy," Katy said excitedly.

"She is correct!" Angelique confirmed.

Etienne began to jump up and down with excitement. He grabbed Sophie and embraced her. "Oh momma! This is a good day!" Etienne was holding her tight.

Angelique watched the couple embrace, as tears of happiness fell from their eyes. The thought of having a child meant more to them than anything else in their world. For years they had wanted to hear the cry of a newborn, the laughter of a child at play, to see a little one reaching out for their mother or father.

Katy moved quietly over to the table where Angelique was sitting, her eyes still on the happy couple. She then looked at the cards, then at Angelique. "Well? What is to become of me?" she asked in a playful yet concerned tone.

Angelique looked at Katy then picked up the cards from the table. She began shuffling but then put the cards aside. Angelique looked at Katy once more, this time with a firm stare. "As I said this morning, you do not need the cards to tell you what you already know. This will be on your terms." And with those words, she took the cards and placed them in a pocket in her gown.

Sophie and Etienne were now ready to interact to their guests and sought them out to bring them into the celebration. Katy smiled politely at the couple but, again, felt confused by Angelique's words.

"I believe this calls for a toast," Etienne exclaimed as he walked to the cupboard and took out a bottle of French wine. "I have been waiting to drink this for a few years." He also took four wine glasses out of the cupboard. They seemed out of place in this house, but they did fit the joyous occasion. Sophie carefully opened the wine bottle and began to fill the glasses. Her demeanor was bubbly. She was filled with an immense happiness now that she knew that she would be a mother.

The four raised their glasses high as Angelique spoke, "A wish of peace and happiness to those who are expecting. May the gods look on and protect this family through this happy time and beyond." They drank to the toast then placed the glasses on the table. Sophie, pouring another glass for Etienne and herself, noticed Angelique had put the cards away and looked as if she was ready to leave.

"What? No reading for you, Angelique?" she enquired playfully.

"Me? No, I live for the present. Whatever will pass, will pass and the present says it's time to go feed the cat."

"Well I have something for him," said Sophie putting some scraps together.

"I thought you might." Angelique smiled.

Sophie placed some scraps in a sack and gave the rest to Jacque. She then handed the sack to Katy, who took them and headed for the door along with the rest of the dinner party. As they said their goodbyes, Sophie reached out and hugged Katy and thanked her for coming. She did the same to Angelique, thanking her especially for the good news she had brought them. Etienne also expressed his gratitude but was a bit worried about Katy's leg. "Young'un, you gonna be alright?" He was concerned that she would not make it back to Angelique's house.

"I believe so, Frenchy," she replied. "Whatever she put on my leg last night did wonders."

"I think she'll be alright," Angelique added. "She seems to heal fast this one. I believe she'll be chasing down deer in a few days."

"Hey, now that I wanna see," Etienne laughed with Angelique.

Katy grinned and gave Etienne a hug before leaving. Angelique followed, picking up the sack of supplies she had purchased earlier in the day. She waved to the Broussards then walked to the path that led to her home. The night was crisp and clear. The pathway was illuminated by the full moon, which hovered in the night sky. As they walked, Angelique and Katy spoke about the events of the day.

"You know you brought joy to their hearts, my lady. Well done," Katy said looking at Angelique with a smile.

"I am only the messenger," Angelique replied, "but I am glad to see them like this. They deserve all the happiness that falls upon them."

"Yes, they do, but what of you?" Katy asked.

Angelique looked at Katy in a strange and a confused manner.

"What do you mean?" Angelique asked.

"Are you happy?" Katy asked.

"I believe so. For my days are good and somewhat prosperous."

"But living alone in the wilderness?"

"One is really never alone. I am well."

As Angelique walked down the path, she looked up at the moon. Its brightness had faded a bit, and she quickly realized why. The moon was not full anymore. The bottom had gone away. Katy saw Angelique peering up at the moon. "Gorgeous," she said, noticing the eclipse.

"Yes, it is," Angelique agreed.

"And the meaning of this?"

Angelique thought for a moment before answering. "It would seem that the dark shadow of the earth has gobbled up part of the moon," she said grinning mischievously. "Actually who knows what lies waiting in the darkness? We can only live life as best as we're able, then hope for the wheel to turn our way."

"I truly hope it turns my way," Katy blurted.

"You have come to a crossroads, dear girl. Your time at hand is changing as swiftly as this season will change to winter. Behind you, you have seen the past. Before you, lies an uncharted future." Angelique stopped and turned to Katy. "You will need your strength and endurance going forward. It will not be easy, for there are many challenges that will be forced upon you to disrupt your path. Do not be disarrayed by the source of the power that you will encounter. You must meet this face to face."

Katy looked into Angelique's dark eyes as she spoke. It was as if another person was now walking beside her. Although it was a bit frightening to hear, Katy understood her words and took them to heart. She knew Annabelle would be looking for her, and the time would come that she would have to face her yet again.

"You asked me what is to come," Angelique continued. "This is what I have seen, for just as the darkened shadow covers the light of the Hunter's Moon, it will only last a short time. When the time is right, you will know—your true self will emerge. This will be on your terms." Angelique's tone became softer and a smile graced her lips as she moved forward down the path again. "Well enough of that. I believe something is waiting on us with great anticipation," she said.

Katy, walking beside her, let out a chuckle, "Oh, I'm sure with great anticipation, my lady."

The two walked down the path until they reached the cabin. As expected, Angelique's cat was waiting hungrily at the entrance. The day had been long for both of them. Long but fruitful, especially for Katy. Meeting a few allies would certainly be an asset, but all in good time.

Angelique and Katy began to settle down for the night. Weary eyes and sore bones made it fairly easy to fall asleep. Peace and quiet now reigned. A pleasant change from what had transpired the night before, but a far cry from what tomorrow would bring.

CHAPTER 6

The sun had not yet risen on the caravan, which had left the plantation at around four thirty or so that morning. The three wagons and five horses were making their way toward the ferry crossing to Beaumont. Annabelle, in light of what had happened the week before, rode on horseback along with Ben and Wes at the front rather than the comfort of the wagon. She didn't trust anyone's ability to lead, least of all Wes. It was no secret that the only reason she had kept him on was as an extra gun in case of trouble.

Annabelle did feel that employing Ben was a plus. She felt he knew the area, and he had a sense of competence that she felt slightly confident about. Wes, on the other hand, was not to be trusted. To her, he was incompetent and a fool.

The caravan made its way along the path until it finally reached the ferry. The sun was now peeking through the horizon. The ferry took over an hour to get all the wagons and horses across the river, but to Annabelle, they were making good time. The next stop would be the supply store, then to Grigsby's Bluff to track down her rogue maid.

After about another hour or so, the caravan halted in front of the store in Beaumont. While some of the riders tended to the horses under Wes' direction, Annabelle went into the store with Agatha and a few maids. Ben, after taking care of his horse, moved about the wagons checking on things when he noticed a couple of maids talking in front of the store.

"Would you look at that?" he said to Wes, who was walking up to him.

"What?" Wes asked, unaware of the maids.

"Looks like this trip is going to be a very profitable," Ben said, as one of the maids, Hana, glanced at him with a smile.

Wes, who still did not know what Ben was talking about, saw him return the smile. "Ahh…" Wes looked at the blushing maid. "I do believe she's takin' a liking to you, Ben."

"Yep, that's what I'm hopin'," he said as he walked away from Wes toward the maids. Wes shook his head and continued walking back to the wagons.

Ben walked up to where Hana was standing. "Mornin', lovely ladies," he said as he tipped his hat.

Both Hana and the other maid, Sara, both giggled playfully at the sight of Ben. "Good morning, dear sir," Hana replied shyly, a smile still gracing her lips.

"And how might y'all be this fine mornin'?" Ben enquired, his gaze firmly on Hana.

"They are doing just fine thank you," a voice from inside the store roared. It was Annabelle. She stormed out of the store to confront the three. Hana's innocent smile vanished instantaneously and was replaced instead by a look of fear. She bowed her head at Annabelle.

"And you? Aren't you needed somewhere?" Annabelle scowled at Ben.

Annabelle's swift actions caught Ben off guard. "I'm truly sorry, ma'am," he said, trying to back away. "I was only being cordial. I meant no disrespect."

"And no disrespect taken," she answered. "Hear me, be advised that these ladies are not harlots to your desired wishes. They do not mingle with outsiders and certainly do not need a companion. It would seem that if you need to sow your wild oats somewhere, let it not be here. This is your only warning. Now, do we understand each other?"

Ben, still bewildered by Annabelle's tongue-lashing, could only nod and agree.

"Well now, since that is settled let us get back to our chores. Hana, Sara, follow me."

Both maids entered the store with Annabelle and left Ben to contemplate what had just happened. He came back to his senses in a few seconds and headed out to the wagons with a disturbed look on his face. Wes, in the meantime, had seen what had taken place and grinned as Ben walked toward him. He tried to hide his amusement without success.

"Not as profitable as you thought, was it?" Wes joked, although he was hardly able to keep his composure.

"Shut up," Ben scowled as he walked by. A scatter of laughter was heard among the other ranch hands, who had also witnessed the events.

Back in the store, Annabelle and her entourage moved about the place while Agatha read items off a list to the merchant. Even this early in the day, the store seemed most popular given the steady stream of patrons entering and departing with their goods. Obviously the locals, as well as those passing through, were stocking up on supplies for the coming winter. Agatha finally finished giving the list to the merchant. The last of the supplies were collected and loaded onto the wagons by some of the men. The merchant, Jonathan Brown, had noticed the ladies' accents and had become curious. "I believe that is about all you needed," he said. "Will there be anything else, madam?"

Annabelle thought for a moment, glanced at Agatha, and replied, "No, I believe this will be sufficient." She motioned for the maids to leave the store and head back to the wagons.

At the same time, both Ben and Wes entered the store and walked up to Annabelle. "Ma'am, the horses have been watered and fed," Wes said, as he glanced around the store.

"Excellent. Then we shall be on our way," Annabelle replied.

"Begging your pardon, madam. You are English? Yes?" Jonathan asked.

"Yes we are. Why do you ask?" Annabelle said quizzically.

"No reason . . . Just we had another English girl here yesterday as well. Just wondering."

Both Wes and Ben looked at Annabelle inquiringly. Not too many of the English came this way, and it was possible that the English girl was the one they were looking for. Annabelle smiled at the merchant. "Oh? And this girl, would she have been about fifteen years old perhaps?" Annabelle was obviously interested.

"Yes, I would say so. Very young and stayed with the horses most of the time. I just heard the accent is all."

"Who was she with?" Ben interrupted.

"Oh, she was with Frenchy and the gypsy lady. Angelique, I believe her name is."

Ben knew of Frenchy but had only heard of this gypsy woman on a few occasions.

"Yes, they were here yesterday." The voice was from a man who had just entered the store. It was Thomas Leopold. He had overheard the conversation while he had been talking to someone else on the porch. "She was with that harlot witch."

Jonathan lowered his eyes and became quiet. Thomas was a good customer but so was Angelique. He had a soft spot for her because, eighteen months before, she had helped cure his three-year-old daughter of an illness.

"You mean that gypsy woman?" Ben asked.

"Yes, that heathen."

"And whereabouts would we be able to find this lady?" Ben asked Thomas, giving Annabelle a quick glance.

"'Lady' is a word you should use loosely, my good man, but she would be just south of Grigsby's Bluff and just north of Frenchy's tract."

Annabelle smiled at the man again and thanked him, "Excellent. I appreciate your information tremendously, dear sir. The young lass we speak of is in need of serious medical attention. Every hour of her absence places her life in further peril."

"You are very welcome, madam" Thomas replied, tipping his hat. "I hope this young girl will soon be with you and receive the help she needs."

"Oh, and I as well," Annabelle flirted, "I as well."

Annabelle and her entourage departed the store and gathered near the wagons to make plans for the journey south. Her ambitions, first and foremost, were to retrieve Katy at any cost. Now that she was aware of her whereabouts and the possible dangers, she felt that they must move swiftly before Katy disappeared from her grasp once again.

"Ma'am, I believe it best that we send a small detachment of no more than five," Ben suggested. "The wagons and the other horses can be left at the crossroads for a time. The area here is safe from bandits, and it would be better not to bring the wagons south only to have to return north again. It would tire the horses considerably."

Annabelle listened to Ben. "This would make sense, but I am counting on you for the protection of the wagons and my maids. Are you sure that it is safe?"

"Yes, ma'am. The danger is south of us. The wagons will be fine for a couple of hours. The crossroads are grasslands, and there is no brush."

"Excellent, then mount up," Annabelle replied. "I will be accompanying you and Wesley. Please pick two more riders, and then we're off."

Wes, upon hearing his name, mounted up, ready for the journey. Ben picked two more riders based on Wes' suggestions and then led the caravan south to the crossroads. The journey was a swift and quiet one. They made it there in no time. Since everyone had their orders, everything went like clockwork. Annabelle readied the search party to head south to Grigsby's Bluff.

"I take it we all know the plan, correct?" Annabelle asked, expecting no less than affirmation.

"Yes, ma'am," the hired hands murmured their assent.

"Okay, we're off then," she said as she jerked on her horse's reins. And with a few nudges of her boots, the horse was off down the trail, along with the other four riders, heading south toward Grigsby's Bluff.

It appeared that they were still ahead of schedule for the time being, although they wouldn't really know that for sure until they had located Katy. They knew her whereabouts but had a large area to cover.

* * *

About ten miles south of their location, Katy was helping out in Angelique's garden. After a restful night, both she and Angelique had woken up bright and early. Katy was feeling especially well because the pain in her leg was subsiding. She was now able to walk without a limp.

Angelique was hoeing the weeds between the rows of her fall vegetables while being entertained by the cat and Katy. It would seem that the cat felt a bit frisky in the cool morning air, and Katy was up for a game of chase around the plants.

"Careful now," Angelique warned, "Your leg."

"It feels fine," Katy replied in between giggles. "Your medicine works wonders."

Angelique watched both Katy and the cat chase each other around in the dirt. Hearing her ceaseless laughter brought a smile to her lips. She knew this young lady had been through much pain and many hardships.

To have the simple luxury of a pet or time to just be a child had obviously been absent from her life. It was again surreal. It had seemed as if Katy's life could've been taken out of her own past as well.

Katy, now winded and still giggling, looked at Angelique. There were questions running through her mind. "My lady," Katy said, catching her breath, "as good as you have made your life here, I am still puzzled as to how you settled in this harsh land."

Angelique, still with a smile, answered, "A boy."

Katy returned the smile and listened.

"Well, a young Welsh lad," Angelique went on. "I was fifteen, and he was twenty. We met by chance in Portsmouth one day. I was walking back from town and just happened to see a man running passed me. He looked as if he was in dire straits. Seconds later, I saw why he was running. A horse had broken free and was galloping down the high street dragging parts of his harness. I leaped out of the way just in time so as not to be trampled." Angelique's face now glowed with delight, thinking back, "Seconds behind the steed, another passed by with Gareth at the reins. He chased the horse till he came alongside. Then without showing any fear, he leapt onto its back and grabbed the reins to slow the horse down. Gareth managed to bring it to a halt but fell off and landed in the dirt, injuring his arm. I ran to him to see if I could be of assistance. He was in serious pain and needed care . . ."

Angelique smiled wistfully as she remembered her first encounter with Gareth.

"Are you alright? Let me help you," Angelique said as she tried to help Gareth out of the middle of the street and away from the horse.

"Yes, lass," he replied in obvious pain.

Angelique put her arm around him and helped him to his feet. She guided him toward the side of the street away from the horses until they reached a stone fence.

"Sit here," said Angelique as she maneuvered him to the fence.

Gareth sat on the old stone fence, his hand still grasping his other arm. As painful as it was, he couldn't help but wonder who this beautiful young girl was.

"Take your jacket off and let me look at your shoulder," instructed Angelique.

Upon hearing this, Gareth began to laugh. Even with the immense pain, he found this young lass' ability to take hold of the situation astonishing.

"Yes, lass, at once," he said, both laughing and grimacing at the same time. "My name's Gareth, fine lady. I can't thank you enough for your help."

Both Gareth and Angelique's eyes met as he continued to smile at her.

"And what may I ask is your name?" he asked while slowly taking his jacket off.

"Angelique . . . fine sir," she replied a bit more shyly and not with the same decree as before.

"Ah, yes you are. An angel sent by the gods no doubt to come to my aid," Gareth said. He took her hand in appreciation. "Thank you, lass. I am indebted to you."

Angelique began to blush and lowered her head to hide her shyness, but she couldn't help but keep looking up into his eyes. She had never felt these feelings before and it frightened her a bit. But she did not want Gareth to know how she felt, and she hid it well.

After inspecting the injured arm, Angelique noticed it had begun to swell. It seemed to her that it was severely sprained, but it didn't appear to be broken. "I believe my aunt should look at this. I believe she would best know what you need to do," Angelique said.

"Then we shall go see your aunt. For if you think that is best, then I will follow you," Gareth replied, grinning, "even if it's for eternity."

Angelique and Gareth became very close as time passed, and within six months, they were married. It would seem that they were a perfect couple. Both worked really hard and dreamed extravagantly. Gareth held two jobs, one as a rancher and the other working at the docks. He had dreams of sailing to the new world and riding amongst the buffalo and the wild horses on the plains. Meanwhile Angelique dreamed of getting more involved with medicine. For the first time in her life, she felt unconditional happiness, and she knew she would follow Gareth to the ends of the earth if need be.

Angelique peered out into the horizon, watching her life story unravel in front of her, while Katy listened intently.

"We left for the new world a year later. We were frightened but oh so happy. We sailed into Galveston two months later and saw our dreams turn into reality. It was hard—no food, no jobs, but we pushed on. Finally Gareth heard of a job east of Galveston. It was a ranching job, and we settled there. I did some work for the Hildebrandts and we paid off our deed, but in 1862, war was inevitable. Times became hard again and disease spread. That is when I lost him."

Katy noticed tears running down Angelique's cheeks as she spoke of the illness and subsequent death of her husband. She loved him dearly, but there was nothing she could do in the end. He had succumbed to yellow fever and that was one disease she knew nothing about and could not cure.

"He taught me the ways of old. How to hunt, how to live from what life has given me. I am forever in his debt."

Angelique wiped the tears from her eyes and continued with her hoeing. Katy had also begun to tear up as she listened. She knew Angelique's life had been similar to hers, with pain and hardships, but if this lady could overcome her anguish, then she should try too. "In all the sadness that came to pass, you still loved a great man as he did you," Katy replied. "At the very least, you were loved, and that is most important." Angelique noticed Katy's tears falling down her face as she continued, "Taken by death from your family to be put in a house of non-caring strangers, then to live thankfully in the house of a heretic. I guess I should be thankful. I did end up here, and for this I am grateful."

"By the gods, young Katy, you are welcome here as family. This is your home if you so desire. Whatever troubles you will soon pass. As I have told you, you are not alone."

Angelique knew Katy's sorrow ran deep, and it would take much time to heal her wounds, but through time, she felt she would make it.

"As I have said, your kindness and goodwill toward me has been tremendous. My only wish is that when the time comes that my new friends are protected from the evil that still lingers and haunts me."

"Do you remember the eclipse?" Angelique asked.

"Yes," Katy replied.

"Have you ever seen a full eclipse?"

"Yes my lady, once, long ago," Katy answered. She felt that Angelique's questions were a bit odd.

"The sign was there in the night sky. Not a sign of the moon splattered with blood but only wounded and able heal. The signs are there, Katy. Be strong, be vigilant, and above all, be true to yourself."

Angelique's eyes turned toward the trees as if she noticed something. She then began to smile. Katy slowly turned around out of curiosity, but her nervousness was still evident.

"Behold, young lass. For even in this foreign land, the gods still watch over you."

Katy observed movement in the trees. She saw some of the limbs moving but couldn't see what was there. She walked a little closer as an antler appeared from behind the trunk. Her eyes lit up with excitement that yet another animal in her presence. She kept looking until its face became visible. "Oh!" she gasped.

The stag walked out away from the brush, looking curiously at both Angelique and Katy. He was a big buck, and it was unusual for him to be this far south, but here he was all the same, and both stood amazed at the sight of this proud beast.

"Let this be a sign to you, Katy," Angelique said in a low voice.

"Oh, it is my lady. It is."

And just as soon as he appeared, the stag was gone from sight. Katy knew that trouble was near, but for the first time in her life, she felt a sense of calm and courage that would help her as the minutes ticked slowly away. For her life, from then on, would be far different from what it had been, as would life for the rest of them.

CHAPTER 7

Minutes passed as Katy lifted a basket of vegetables and slowly walked toward the cabin. Angelique stood in the garden wiping her brow—she had finished weeding. Just then a burst of cold wind blew in, bringing a shiver to her body. Something was wrong. She could feel it in the air.

"Katy," she called out, "please grab the sack from the table in the cabin, and go hide!"

On hearing her instruction, Katy became frightened, but she did as Angelique asked. She put the basket down, ran into the cabin, and took the sack from the table. She then dashed toward the trees beyond the perimeter of the garden to hide.

Seconds later, both Angelique and Katy heard the approach of galloping horses. Angelique walked to the edge of the garden near the path. She could see five horses barreling down toward her, but she held her ground. The five saw Angelique standing near the edge of the path and slowed to a trot, coming to a standstill in front of her. Ben tipped his hat and greeted her while the others remained silent. "Mornin' ma'am," Ben said as he tried to settle his horse. "We are looking for a girl."

"A young girl of 15," added Annabelle. "She wandered off near the river two nights ago and has disappeared. She is very disturbed and in dire need of her physician."

Katy, on hearing what was being said, felt anger rise above her fear. She knew Annabelle was a devious liar, just like Lady Falsworth the elder.

"I have seen no one such as this, and you are trespassing," Angelique replied coldly.

Annabelle attempted to convey a sense of caring about Katy's wellbeing, but to Angelique it sounded empty and false. She stared at the young baroness as a cat to a dog.

"Are you sure you haven't seen this girl?" Ben asked.

"No, now go away," Angelique snapped.

Tensions rose instantaneously, and even the horses could not remain still. A sense of apprehension fell upon them as Annabelle again attempted to determine Katy's whereabouts.

"Some have spoken and said you do know where she is," Annabelle declared, her tone changing. "They have said you were in Beaumont yesterday gathering supplies, is this true?"

"I have no business with you, young lass. I suggest you ride back into the darkness from which you came."

Annabelle was irritated with Angelique. "You are wasting my time," she said tersely.

"And you, mine." Angelique's reply was swift and cold.

"Hear me, gypsy witch! I am Lady Annabelle Falsworth. You will tell me where she is or else . . ." Annabelle pulled her colt revolver from her holster and pointed it at Angelique.

"Your status does not have meaning here, English tart. Remember you are a guest here," replied Angelique, her face taking on a wicked grin.

Katy, watching this unfold, became more frightened. Seeing the gun pointed at her friend was horrifying, and she didn't know what to do. Angelique had told her to stay hidden for her own safety, but she couldn't bear to see her friend killed.

"Wait a minute!" Wes said, looking at Annabelle's revolver. "Ma'am, put the gun away."

Annabelle, surprised by Wes' interference, turned to him. "What?" she scowled.

"Ma'am, this is not right," Wes responded, trying to defuse the situation.

"You are not paid to think! You are paid to follow orders."

The confrontation with Wes and Annabelle went on for a minute or two. The horses remained nervous and fidgety, as if they sensed something. Angelique gazed in the eyes of the horse that Annabelle was riding. The horse slowly calmed down.

"You will leave now!" Angelique shouted, wanting to be heard over Annabelle and Wes' dispute.

Annabelle turned back to Angelique and pointed the revolver at her again. Katy, seeing this, could not stand by and see her friend being shot. She ran out from the trees and yelled to them. "That for which you are searching is now visible! I am here! Now kill me, dear lady, if you wish, but leave her alone!"

Angelique, seeing Katy away from the safety of the trees, turned to face Annabelle's horse. Her eyes glanced up at Annabelle. She gave her an evil stare. Just then the horse began to squeal, spooking the rest of the horses. Annabelle pulled on the reins with her free hand, but it wasn't enough. The horse began to buck violently, which made the rest do the same. Annabelle and the men all fell off their horses to the ground. Angelique quickly grabbed the reins of Wes' horse and laid her hand on the side of its head. This immediately calmed the animal. She then kissed and patted it on the head. The horse stood motionless, while Angelique mounted it and gave a quick tug on the reins. The horse broke into a canter, running through the garden toward Katy. "Take my hand!" Angelique hollered as she got closer to her. Katy took her hand as Angelique pulled her onto the horse. As they rode away, Annabelle, now rising up off the ground, retrieved her revolver and fired two shots at them but missed.

"Bloody idiot!" Annabelle screamed as three of the four men rose from the ground. Wes had injured his arm in the fall and still lay in pain.

Annabelle, irate due to the escape of her maid and the gypsy, climbed back on her now-passive horse, wielding her revolver. "Mount up!" she yelled. Her eyes turned to the injured Wes. "You fool! You have troubled me for the last time." Annabelle lowered her revolver and pointed it at Wes. Without so much as a blink of an eye, she pulled the trigger. Wes became lifeless within a split second. But the nearly maniacal Annabelle was oblivious to this—her thoughts were now on pursuing Katy and Angelique. "Mount up! Do you hear me!" she yelled.

Ben and the other two riders stood in shock as they looked upon Wes' motionless body. "I will pay a thousand dollars to each of you three to kill that harlot witch. Hear me now!"

"Yes, ma'am," Ben replied. The promise of money seemed to break him free of his shock.

"Where does this path lead?" Annabelle asked.

"It eventually leads to the road to Sabine," Ben replied quickly.

"Good. One hundred dollars apiece to you both," Annabelle said as she looked at the two remaining riders. "All you have to do is ride back to the wagons and take them south. Can you do this?"

Both riders looked at each other and nodded. They felt happy to take the money and were even happier to be able to ride away from this insane woman. As they two set off for the wagons, Ben and Annabelle proceeded down the path following pursuit of Angelique and Katy. Ben now saw Annabelle as she was, just a wretched lunatic who could not be trusted. But a thousand dollars was a huge amount of money all the same.

* * *

Silence now swept over the pathway where Wes lay. His body remained quiet and motionless, but he could not hold it in any longer. The pain of the gunshot to his shoulder was so immense that he had found it almost impossible to lay silent even while Annabelle had been near. He remembered the thief in Louisiana who had suffered a fatal shot to the head after he had survived the first. Wes knew she was brutal and felt fortunate that he had survived.

As Wes rolled over in agony, trying to make it to his feet, he was met with another click of the gun chamber. The barrel of a shotgun was poking into his face. He looked up to see a heavyset man standing over him. It was Etienne; he had heard the gunshots earlier and felt that Angelique may have been in trouble.

"Slowly now," Etienne commanded as he watched Wes freeze at the sight of the shotgun. Etienne also saw that Wes was bleeding profusely and needed help, but the question in his mind was still, who was he? And why had he been shot?

"Okay now, what happened here?" he asked, "And where is Gitane?"

Wes sat up, wincing in pain. "The lady that lives here is in trouble. This lady that I worked for is looking for a young English girl, and she will stop at nothing to get her back."

"And how I know you don't work for her still?"

Wes looked up at Etienne. "Well dear sir, I think when she shot me in the shoulder, our business partnership ended."

Just then two other men walked up and peered down at Wes. "She not there. Her cabin is empty, and there's a basket full of food by the door," said Henri, Etienne's neighbor. "Look like she left in a hurry."

"Yes, but they're not safe," Wes added. "That woman is vicious, and she won't stop till she finds them."

Etienne was aware that Wes was in a lot of pain and bleeding. He knew Wes needed help desperately, but he still felt Wes couldn't be trusted until he found out what was going on.

"Okay young'un, what happened?" Etienne asked as he handed his shotgun to Henri and bent over to look at Wes' wounds.

Wes proceeded to tell them what had happened earlier, while Etienne tried to stop the bleeding in Wes' shoulder. Hearing his explanation of the events that took place and the tone of his voice, Etienne couldn't help but believe him.

"How many is after them?" he asked Wes, wrapping his arm with an old sack to absorb the blood.

"Right now, it's just Lady Falsworth and Ben, a hired hand from the ranch across the river," he replied, grimacing in pain.

"We need to get you to my house to tend to this arm and then we gonna go lookin' for this woman."

Wes thought of Lady Falsworth's penchant for violence and Ben's tracking skills. He did not know this woman Gitane, or Katy, but he just couldn't stand by and allow murder and abduction take place without making amends for his role in it.

"But don't you think they need help now?" Wes asked.

Etienne looked at Wes and smiled. "I know Gitane. She knows this land. She gonna be alright for a time till we get there. Now, let's git."

Etienne helped Wes up and guided him to a wagon, which was now heading toward them, driven by another friend and neighbor, Thomas. When the wagon stopped, Wes climbed into the back with the help of Etienne, and all four made their way toward Etienne's house.

Wes, although still in extreme pain, did feel a bit of calmer as a result of the help he was getting from this stranger. It was a welcome relief; far removed from the ridicule he had endured over the past week from his previous employer. Bitterness had never been a problem in his life, but it had seemed to be start creeping into his mind lately. His only remedy was to extract the two pursued women from Lady Falsworth's tentacles.

The wagon proceeded down the path, finally halting in front of Etienne's barn. Sophie, who was sitting on the porch, saw them approaching. She also saw the injured man in the back of the wagon. Etienne yelled to her, explaining the situation and what was needed. She quickly rushed into the house and gathered the things she would need to help.

Sophie ran out of the house clutching a few items. Normally she would have been in the garden at this time of day, but she had felt ill that morning, further proof of Angelique's assertion that she was with child.

Wes stepped off the wagon and staggered to a wood stump, which he used as a chair. He removed his shirt along with the makeshift bandage, which Etienne had put on. Sophie looked at the wound and poured whiskey from a bottle to sterilize it. The pain from the liquid made Wes scream in agony. She then proceeded to wrap the wound in a cloth. In the meantime, Etienne had brought a clean shirt for Wes so that he could get rid of the blood-stained garment.

"How you feel?" Etienne asked Wes.

"Like hell, but thanks to you for this," he replied sincerely. He knew that if Etienne hadn't found him, he would most likely be dead.

"Good, now we need to find Gitane and her little friend."

"I'm ready, just point me in the right direction," Wes muttered, staggering onto his feet.

"Whoa now, take it slow. You're weak from the loss of blood," Sophie said while trying to hold him steady.

"I do believe you are right. Sorry ma'am," Wes responded, now regaining his balance.

Etienne met up with Henri, as Thomas mounted his horse and headed toward the river. Some of the Peloat boys had been fishing around the banks that morning, and Thomas thought that, under the circumstances, it would be a good idea to take more firepower with for the ride. Both Etienne and Henri, now walking over to Wes, had started devising a plan to find Angelique and Katy.

"Okay, young'un. Tell me what that woman is up to." Etienne laid two rifles and a pistol on the back of the wagon.

"She's headed for Sabine," Wes said, rubbing his arm. "She and Ben went off down the trail while the two other men went back to the crossroads to fetch the wagons. There will be nine guns in total on the wagons; eleven when Lady Falsworth and Ben meet up with them."

Wes dropped his head for a second, as if he had had a passing thought, then continued, "Word of advice, gentlemen. Whatever you do, do not turn your back on that lady. She's mean, quick, deadly, and shows no mercy. I have already seen her kill three men so far. There would have been a fourth, but I believe she was more interested in going after the two ladies than finishing me off."

"Well now, Gitane does that to people sometimes," Etienne laughed. He mounted his horse while Henri and Wes prepared the wagon.

"Alright, let's go," instructed Etienne. He gave Sophie a farewell wave.

"Hey, don't forget your fourth gun. He don't like being left out if there's trouble," Sophie said as she blew him a kiss.

"Oh yeah. Jacque!" he yelled. "Oùest le Gitane? Go, go find her now!"

Suddenly Jacque dashed out from behind the trees and ran toward the path at full speed. The three followed close behind. As he reached the path, Jacque began to sniff around for her scent.

"Oùest le Gitane?" Etienne shouted once more.

Jacque finally turned to south and ran down the path toward the road leading to Sabine. Minutes later, Thomas and five young men, all on horseback, met up with them. All armed and ready for a fight if need be.

Wes looked around in astonishment at all the help Etienne had managed to muster in a matter of mere minutes. Etienne, noticing Wes' curiosity, rode up to the wagon.

"We a nice and friendly people here," Etienne told Wes, "but don't ever cross with one of us, especially with one of our women. We don't like that very much." And with those words, Etienne rode away, toward the path.

* * *

An hour earlier, Angelique and Katy had galloped down the same path trying to escape from Annabelle's wicked grasp. Luckily, their horse was fast and strong and did not tire in their time of need. They rode a few miles south before Angelique became nervous. She surveyed the area; she looked very troubled.

"This is not good," she said, "not good at all."

"What's wrong?" Katy asked, becoming concerned.

"This is all grasslands—there are no trees. We need to get off this horse and this trail." Angelique slowed the horse to a trot, still scanning the area. The tree line was at least two miles back, and there was no cover for them to hide, only the tall grass. But that would have to make do.

"Why are we stopping here?" asked Katy, her fear rising.

"There is no place to hide if we go on. At least here we have a chance," Angelique replied while stopping the horse and dismounting.

"Here? Please my lady, think of what you're doing. What if we head to Sabine? Will there not be someone there to help us?"

"Two women on a stolen horse? We'd be lucky to survive an hour. Trust me, lass, we'll do far better this way."

Angelique helped Katy off the horse and took the sack from her. She dug deep, finally pulling out a cloth with something wrapped in it. Angelique opened the cloth and removed two cubes of sugar, which she fed to the horse. After the horse ate, she kissed and patted him on the head. The horse then took off down the trail toward Sabine.

Katy scanned the area. She could see nothing but grass for miles. Katy trusted Angelique, but that trust was somehow not fully unconditional at the moment.

"Well, we are here, all alone in a field. What do we do now?" Katy rambled.

Angelique looked at Katy, amused at her words. "Don't worry, Katy. We are not alone. Now let's move to the river."

Katy again surveyed their surroundings. There was no one in close proximity.

"I do trust you, my lady, but I am frightened."

Minutes later, as they walked through the tall grass, the rumbling sounds of horses could be heard.

"Oh no!" Katy gasped.

Angelique turned to Katy with her finger over her lips in a shushing motion. As both kneeled silently in the tall grass, another sound was heard—it seemed to be in front of them. It was the sound of something ruffling through the grass. It was followed by snorting.

Katy's eyes grew big with fright. She felt surrounded but dared not make a sound. Angelique on the other hand gave her a wink and a confident grin to try to ease her nervousness. The rumbling drew closer.

* * *

Annabelle and Ben raced down the path following the hoof prints made by Wes' horse. Ben noticed there were more tracks on the ground, as if the horse had stopped. Both slowed their horses down and began to search the nearby grass for any sign of a trail.

"They stopped here, but the tracks continue," Ben commented as he walked his horse into the grass.

"Well if the tracks continue, then why have we stopped?" Annabelle scowled.

"Ma'am, they're light. As if someone got off."

Katy, close enough to listen, was nearly paralyzed with fear. Ben's horse kept edging closer and closer, as he searched. Suddenly, the ruffling began again, which caught Ben's attention. He moved toward the sound, even closer to Angelique and Katy. Then, from out of the grass, a hog appeared, rummaging, followed by another, then another . . . One of the hogs eyed Angelique. Her presence had piqued its curiosity.

Angelique returned its stare and shushed the hog to try to get it to move but to no avail. It remained in front of her. Finally, she drew back as if to hit the beast and eyed the hog in an almost threatening way. The hog jumped back and looked visibly uneasy. Then, with a frightened leap, it ran out of the grass, squealing along with ten others and scaring both Annabelle's and Ben's horses.

"Dang it!" Ben moaned.

"And why are we still here!" Annabelle shouted, visibly irritated.

Ben moved his horse back on the path and again proceeded to follow the horse's hoof prints. Whether the trail was light or not, he did not want Lady Falsworth to see him as a problem in the same way she had Wes. Annabelle followed close behind. She was anxious to find Katy but also to meet up with the wagons.

Angelique listened closely until she could no longer hear the sound of the horses. Her devilish grin became a huge smile as she winked at Katy. Katy, trying to calm her nerves, had felt huge relief at the sound of

Annabelle galloping away from her.

"Now, let's go," Angelique said as she stood up and made her way back to the path.

"And these creatures?" Katy pointed at the herd of hogs now rummaging on the path.

"Thank them, for they have been noble friends," Angelique replied, hoisting the sack over her shoulders.

Angelique knew that luck was with them this day, but she also knew that this ordeal was not over. Annabelle would be back. The time for closure was nearing. She could feel the winds of change blowing amongst memories of her life; some good, some bad, but to her, this was life, and nothing could slow its ever-turning wheel.

CHAPTER 8

Angelique and Katy walked back up the path toward the tree line and Angelique's cabin. The stiff southeastern breeze now brought a few clouds to dim the sunshine, which had been ever-so-present for the last couple of days. Angelique looked to the sky, as if she were studying the future. She knew there would be rain that night as was always the case when the wind blew in this way.

Katy, now feeling more at ease, took the large sack from Angelique and slung it over her own shoulder. The turmoil of the past few days had altered her normally sweet demeanor but, with Angelique around, she had managed to maintain her stamina.

"You don't think they will double back?" Katy asked, thinking of Annabelle's penchant for trickery.

"I doubt it. She was very frantic, and I believe the other one went down the path just to silence her," Angelique replied with a chuckle.

"So luck was with us then?"

"But of course. Luck seems to follow you." Angelique turned to face Katy. "Yes, your life has been one of hardship and pain, but luck always seems to wait in the shadows for you."

Katy thought back to her life in England. Yes, her life was one of pain, but it did appear that just when her life was at a standstill, another situation would arise. Even given the hardship of her employment with Lady Falsworth, she had had a place to live and food to eat. Looking back, there was nothing in England for her. She had more in this foreign land than anything that had ever been presented to her in her life.

Both descended toward the tree line when suddenly a loud rumbling was heard from the path. The sound grew louder and louder. Angelique stopped, grabbed Katy's arm and dashed into the tall grass. She knew the sound was coming from the north, the same direction as her cabin, but she did not know who might be approaching. Hiding was the best option.

Katy's fear returned instantaneously. With the sound of horses drawing closer and closer, there was another noise: a barking dog. Her body trembled violently at the notion of another chase through the swamps.

"No . . . please, no," she wept, shaking her head, "I can't."

Angelique saw the terror in Katy's eyes and reached out to her. "No, lass," she whispered, pulling her down, "put it out of your mind. You must feel with your heart, not think with your mind."

The rumbling of the horses fell upon them, as Angelique and Katy hid in the tall grass. The barking also sounded very close—they could both sense the dog moving near them through the grass, searching. Angelique sat in front of Katy to protect her as best she could. Just then, a black shadow could be seen frantically moving through the grass until it appeared in front of Angelique.

"Jacque!" Angelique shouted, a tremendous sense of relief falling on her.

Jacque, his tail wagging, ran up to Angelique and began licking her face. She reached out to him and hugged him tightly. Although tired from his run along the path, he was excited to see his friends, and he showed it, bouncing back and forth between Katy and Angelique, barking incessantly.

Etienne, hearing the commotion in the grass, brought the horses and wagon to a halt near them. Angelique and Katy finally stood up and walked to the path.

"Merci, good friend," Angelique said to Etienne, a huge smile on her face.

"What the hell have you done now, Gitane?" he laughed, as he dismounted his horse.

"Oh, I guess I can't keep my mouth shut!" she grinned.

Etienne looked at Katy. She did not look at all like the charming gracious young girl he had met the day before. She looked exhausted and agitated from yet another run to save her life.

"You alright young'un?" Etienne asked tenderly.

Katy wandered out of the grass toward the wagon as if in a daze. She was silent and unemotional. It was then that Wes stepped off the back of the wagon and walked to the front to face Katy. He tipped his hat to her as a show of respect and went to check on the horses. Katy stopped and turned toward Wes, a look of disgust on her face. "You . . . why are you here?" she said, staring coldly at Wes. "Why are you here?"

Angelique and Etienne, who had been talking to each other, turned to Katy, disturbed by the tone of her voice. Wes stopped what he was doing, not knowing what to say.

Katy, holding the sack, now thrust it at Wes, hitting his injured arm again and again. "You wish to kill me? I am here! Now!" she screamed, still hitting him.

Wes did not fight back. The pain from the blows was excruciating, but in Wes' mind, he felt he deserved it.

"Wait, Katy, no!" Angelique shouted.

"You want to kill me? Finish your job!" Katy shouted, now in tears, "Now that I stand before you, you do not have the stomach for it?"

Angelique grabbed Katy's arms in an attempt to stop her. "Hold on, young'un!" Etienne shouted. "Whatever happened before I don't know, but I do know that I found him shot and bleeding to death just a couple of hours ago. Shot by that same woman who wants you."

"He's right!" Angelique added as she tried to calm Katy down. "If it wasn't for him, I would be dead in the garden. You saw this! He stood up for me. For us."

Katy fell to her knees and began to weep uncontrollably. She didn't know what to think anymore. Finally, all the things in her life had exploded in her head, and she just couldn't take it. Angelique held her, trying to comfort her, but she could only let Katy weep until she had let it all out of her system.

Wes, now crumpled on the ground from the sheer pain of the beating on his injury, held his arm. He had begun to bleed again. Etienne bent down and helped him off the ground. He motioned for a couple of the young men to help him put Wes back on the wagon.

"I'm truly sorry, ma'am," Wes muttered as he passed Katy, "I should have known."

Katy could not respond, she only wept.

After the three had finally placed Wes on the wagon, Henri immediately turned it around and headed back to Etienne's house. The rest of the riders did the same, leaving one horse behind for Angelique and Katy. Etienne, still with the two, walked up to Katy and put his hand on her shoulder. "Young'un, I know it don't make no sense right now, but life tends to fix itself. Sometimes you gotta go through a lot of bad things to get there, but you will. Look at your friend. She's been through more hard times than anybody I know, but she still gonna fight, harder and stronger than the rest."

Katy, still silent, wiped the remaining tears from her eyes, then grabbed his hand to stand up. She hugged Etienne tightly before walking to the horse. Angelique mounted and then helped Katy up. "And a good fight it will be, my friend," Angelique said to Etienne before the horse took off down the path.

"You better believe it!" Etienne shouted in reply.

They all returned to Etienne's house. Both Etienne and Angelique rode in silence, their minds troubled. They both felt that this situation would become deadly in the near future, and neither knew how to bring it to a peaceful conclusion. At least they were all safe at the moment. They would regroup later and come up with a plan for the next encounter.

* * *

Down the pathway in a southerly direction, toward the Sabine Road, Annabelle was riding with Ben. They were planning to meet up with her entourage at the crossroads and hopefully find Katy. They rode swiftly down the path, but there was no sign of Katy—or anyone else for that matter. Just a grassy dirt path that bore no insight into what was to come. Ben noticed that the horse tracks were still light, even in the mud. He knew that Lady Falsworth would not be pleased to say the least when she determined the obvious.

"It should be just another mile," Ben said.

"And the others?" asked Annabelle, thinking of her entourage.

Ben thought for a moment, "Once we get to the crossroads, I believe it will take them about an hour at most to catch up with us."

Annabelle nodded and kept riding till they finally reached the crossroads. Both halted and looked around for signs of Katy and Angelique or the horse, but none were found. Ben checked the tracks, and it seemed as if the horse had headed north, back to Beaumont.

"The tracks head north, ma'am," Ben said. "I believe we need to stay here and wait for the wagons. If they're on this horse, then your hired hands will pick them up. If not, then they might be around here."

"And you're not sure?" Annabelle asked quizzically.

"No ma'am, I'm not." Ben sounded a bit irritated. "As I said before, the horse tracks are light, and I do not even know if they are on the horse. I cannot see any other tracks around."

Annabelle sensed his annoyance and also felt that she may have been a little too hasty earlier. She could also feel that Ben was doing the job as best he could, which was far better than what she was used to from Wes.

"So it is possible that they escaped earlier?" Annabelle asked calmly.

"Yes ma'am. But now that we know where they are, we should be able to find the girl again easily," Ben replied, both pleased and astonished that she was actually being civil.

"Point taken, although I do not believe it will be easy. I'm sure she has accrued more allies. This may be a problem."

"Possibly, but there may be ways around that."

Annabelle, upon hearing Ben's last comment began to grin, "I do like your thinking."

Ben stared at Annabelle inquiringly. Ever since the night in the swamps, he had been very curious about this young lady of 24 years who acted as if she were a queen most of the time. He figured she had been born of money, which in his mind always brought status. But there was something about her that he just couldn't pinpoint.

"So ma'am, forgive me for askin', but how did a young woman like yourself achieve such great stature?" Ben asked, letting his curiosity take over.

Annabelle turned to Ben, as a lioness to a gazelle. "Through force and determination. Everything that I have has been earned. My family has had cattle and sheep for centuries, but the isle that I am from is changing. It would appear that this land would suit me better. For I am the last of my kind, and what better way to start anew than here in this land."

Ben was always on the lookout for an opportunity to profit. With Annabelle's mention of a new life, this could possibly mean new work for him at better pay. He had to be sure to stay in her good graces though. He surely didn't want to end up like Wes.

"And this new venture, will it be in this area or further west?" Ben asked, attempting to show interest.

"I do not know as of yet, but if you are interested in new employment, I believe we can work something out. I am a man short as of now," said Annabelle with a devilish smile.

"Yes ma'am, I am definitely interested," Ben replied aspiringly.

"I'll keep that in mind. Now let us try and find that horse."

Forty-five minutes passed as Annabelle and Ben searched the area, but there was still no sign of the horse or Katy. Finally, Ben followed the tracks on the road northward for a short distance and noticed they had veered into tall grass. Though a little wary of heading off the trail, Ben wanted to show Annabelle that he was indeed competent, so he continued following the tracks.

Annabelle, also riding north, stared out into the grassy plains for any indication of her wagons moving south. But still, she saw nothing. Just then a shout was heard from Ben within the tall grass.

"Ma'am!" he yelled.

Annabelle raced off the trail and into the tall grass just in time to see Ben get off his horse and take the reins of Wes' horse.

"Here he is," Ben said as he walked the horse near his own. "It looks as if he just got tired of runnin' and stopped for bite to eat. Those ladies are not here."

Annabelle saw the horse. Her facial expression immediately soured, and a sigh escaped from her lips. Once again, this young lass was a thorn in her side, but sooner or later they would meet again.

"Well, that's that. Come, let us meet up with the wagons. I do not wish to lose them as well," Annabelle said as she turned her horse toward the trail.

Ben mounted his horse and followed Annabelle north toward Beaumont with Wes' horse in tow. They rode for a few minutes until he spotted riders in the distance, heading south. Annabelle also saw them and felt relieved that at least her wagons and possessions were still intact.

Minutes passed before Annabelle and Ben finally reach the wagons. Both of the riders, who had been with them earlier, led the way.

"I see you made it back to the wagons with no problems?" Annabelle asked them.

"No problems, ma'am," one rider replied, the other nodding in agreement.

"Excellent. Now let us head to our destination. If you, Ben, have everything under control, then I will travel in my wagon. I have many things to prepare," said Annabelle, dismounting and handing the reins to another rider.

"But of course, ma'am," said Ben cheerfully. "But one question. Whereabouts in Sabine do you wish to go?"

"The docks. We will be meeting up with a ship. There is already someone waiting for us in town. He will seek us out."

Annabelle climbed into the wagon in which Agatha and three maids were riding. Agatha knew from the two riders who had returned of the earlier problems; however, she was in the dark about what had transpired thereafter, including the absence of Wes.

"Well, I see that our dear friend has not been found yet," Agatha said, not really wanting to say much in front of the maids.

"In time . . . in time," Annabelle replied, removing her hat.

"And Wesley?"

"Dead. Unfortunately he fell off his horse and hit his head on a stone."

The three maids became uneasy. They were saddened to hear of Wes' death.

"Pity," Agatha replied, looking out the window at Wes' horse that was walking alongside the wagon.

Agatha also noticed that the horse did not carry Wes' body. Of course, her mind was whirling with thoughts and possibilities of what was going on, but she knew Annabelle would not speak aloud with the maids near.

"Que es lo que realmente paso?" Agatha spoke in Spanish to try and tempt Annabelle to explain. It was a method they had used many times before since none of the maids understood the language.

Annabelle replied in Spanish, "Tenemos un problema (We have a problem). It would seem that there are other obstacles in our way."

The three maids bowed their heads with the sound of the foreign words. They knew that this conversation was not intended for them, and it was best not to acknowledge either woman unless spoken to.

"Que paso?" Agatha asked speaking only Spanish. "What kind of obstacles?"

"She has befriended a woman. There is something dangerous about her that I can't explain," Annabelle replied. "This woman is a problem, a very big problem."

"And the man?" Agatha said, not mentioning Wes' name because of the maids.

Annabelle sneered, "He was expendable. He irritated me for the last time."

"I thought as much," Agatha grinned, knowing Annabelle's hatred for Wes. "So? What of the plans?"

"The plans stay as is. We sail to Galveston as planned. We will resolve this situation upon our return. She will be with us. I guarantee it. Now rest, dear friend."

Agatha sat back and gazed out the window, looking at the miles and miles of grassland and swamp. What a desolate place, she thought, a far cry from central England where she had grown up. A land such as this was years away from being tamed into something that she would call habitable.

She had heard over and over from friends who had visited this country their tales of the great west, open plains, Indians, and many other assorted adventures. Not that they had seen all this in person, she realized. Her friends had wild imaginations, and some of their stories were long-winded, yet she felt there was some truth in them. This only fueled the fire deep inside her to experience the west for herself. As she stared out of the window, she could feel that this was only the beginning of a great journey.

Annabelle placed her revolver next to Agatha as she started to change clothes with the help of her maids. She definitely wanted to look respectable when meeting with a possible future business partner. She changed out of her riding gear and opted for frilly feminine lace, although this was still business. Annabelle could be quite enticing when she wanted to be, especially to men. She managed to persuade them that they were in control for a time, but in reality, Annabelle was always in control.

After Annabelle finished changing, she and Agatha talked for a good while. Agatha repeated the tales that her friends had told her, to the delight of the three maids. They especially enjoyed the descriptions of the rolling hills and endless herds of cattle that dotted the landscape.

"My lady?" ventured Sara, one of the maids. "Do you think one day we will settle on lands such as these? It all sounds so wonderful."

"I do not know, Sara," Annabelle replied. "I believe that we will find out soon. Whatever place we settle will be adequate."

Sara smiled and looked across to Agatha. "Oh, I do wish Lady Falsworth was here to see this. I'm sure she would love this."

Agatha glanced at Annabelle and grinned. "Oh, I am certain she would, child. I am certain she would."

Sara was the only maid to have befriended Lady Falsworth. She had felt as if Lady Falsworth were her own grandmother. Even though the woman had treated her in the same wretched way as the others, she had felt a small degree of closeness to her.

Sara was 16 and had been with Lady Falsworth for almost two years. She, like Katy, was an orphan who had been without family for seven years. Both her parents had died an untimely death in a fire. At the age of nine, she was sent to live with a family friend until Lady Falsworth had found her and given her a job.

It would seem that this story would apply to all the maids somewhat. They were all orphaned and all between the ages of 14 and 18. To the elder Lady Falsworth, this was a very good age to mold them into competent workers.

As time passed, the wagons were driven south to Sabine, where steamboat captain Andrew Metzger was waiting for them at the docks. Upon arriving, the hired hands immediately began loading the contents of the wagons onto the boat. Annabelle, along with Agatha and the maids, also left the confines of the wagons and walked along the docks in anticipation of their trip to Galveston.

Annabelle walked along the docks, staring out across the river. She certainly looked out of place here in this little village, but she, along with her entourage, was secure. Ben, seeing Annabelle in a different setting and out of riding clothes, walked up to say a final farewell.

"So you're off then?" Ben asked as he took off his hat.

"Yes, but we shall return in three days," Annabelle replied with an unfamiliar smile gracing her lips. "I take it you will return with our horses and wagons?"

"Yes ma'am. I will be here," said Ben, returning the smile.

"Excellent. I do appreciate your help in all this. You will be handsomely rewarded."

Ben dropped his head, almost blushing. He was developing feelings for this woman. It was unusual for him, but he did feel a certain way toward her that he had not felt before for another.

"I appreciate the opportunity to serve you, ma'am, and hopefully one day we will be able to make this permanent."

"But of course," she replied, "this time will come soon."

Ben put his hat back on, tipped it to her and left to round up the wagons and horses to take them back to the plantation. Annabelle continued to stare out at the river. She also felt a cold wind blowing. No one else was aware of it. The cold wind of change, which she would have to deal with upon her return, seemed familiar; she had dealt with things like this before. Still, the uncertainty of a new problem had arisen with the introduction of the gypsy woman.

CHAPTER 9

Sophie stood in the garden. She felt a little better than she had felt earlier in the day, as her morning sickness had subsided. She needed to harvest the last of the vegetables. While picking, she heard the sound of Etienne's wagon barreling down the path with a cavalry of horses close behind. As she glanced at the wagon, she noticed Wes lying in the back in distress. She dropped her basket and hurried to the porch to get her bag of supplies. She knew he had been bleeding badly earlier, but she could only imagine what had taken place since.

The wagon stopped in the front of the Broussard's house, and Sophie climbed onto it with bag in hand. She saw that Wes was in a lot of pain and was still bleeding. "How are you?" she asked, as she began inspecting his shoulder.

Wes, clinging to his arm, nodded to indicate that he was fine, but Sophie could tell he was in tremendous pain, and he had started bleeding heavily. She took a bottle of whiskey from the bag, opened it and put it to Wes' lips.

"Here . . . Drink," she said encouragingly, trying to comfort him as much as possible.

Wes took a swig from the bottle and tried to get up. Sophie immediately pushed him back down.

"No, you stay down there," Sophie commanded as she removed his shirt and bandage. "Listen to me. Keep drinking the bottle. You gonna need it."

Wes did as Sophie told. He took another swig, then another. The pain was almost unbearable, but he thought he could handle it. Sophie, still trying to stop the bleeding, felt almost as if it were a losing battle. Somehow, someway, she needed to stop the bleeding, or he would die.

"Henri, amene-moi de la poudre à fusil!" She asked desperately for gunpowder in French so that Wes would not understand.

Henri had a pouch of gunpowder for an older gun that hadn't required any bullets. He quickly handed it to Sophie while she called on two of the young men to help her with Wes.

"How you doing?" she asked Wes again.

"Fine ma'am," he replied, still drinking the whiskey as Sophie had instructed.

"Good. Now listen to me carefully," Sophie said while taking the gunpowder and sprinkling it on the wound. "We need to stop the bleeding, or you gonna die. Understand?"

Wes nodded his agreement, as the powder in the wound began to inflict more pain with every passing second.

"This is gonna burn really bad, but we gotta do this," said Sophie, holding his hand.

Sophie looked to another one of the young men, who had dismounted and was standing around. She shouted in French to him to bring a stick from a burning pile of trash that was in the field. The young man brought the fiery stick to her, keeping it out of Wes' view. He was still drinking the whiskey as Sophie had instructed.

"Tiens-le bien!" she muttered to the young men to hold him down. Each man grabbed one of Wes' arms and pinned him down.

"What's going on?" Wes asked, now fully alert to the fact that something else was happening, something he hadn't anticipated.

Sophie took the burning stick and pressed it into the wound. Wes screamed in agony as the gunpowder ignited. The young men struggled to hold him still as the flames burnt through the wound. Finally, as all the gunpowder was spent, the flames diminished. Wes, in a state of shock, passed out from the excruciating pain.

Sophie peered at the wound. It would seem that her last resort had worked. The bleeding had finally stopped. She ordered the men to go down to the river and bring her a few cattails, roots and all. Now that the bleeding had ceased, she needed to heal the burn.

It was at about this time that the sound of horses was heard. Etienne, Angelique, and Katy galloped down the path until they came to a standstill in front of the wagon. All eyes were on Wes and his shoulder. Katy was especially concerned. She could tell that something had gone horribly wrong. She jumped off her horse and ran to the wagon, her eyes tearing up yet again. "No!" she cried.

"Hold on, young'un. I believe he's gonna be alright," Sophie said, putting her bloodied hand on Katy's shoulder.

"But it is my fault . . . This is all entirely my fault!" Katy began to cry again.

Angelique and Etienne, having dismounted, walked up to the wagon and took a closer look at Wes. Both saw the burns on his shoulder and were amazed by Sophie's ingenuity.

"Mama, you done good," Etienne commented as he helped her off the wagon.

"He lost a lot of blood," Sophie sighed. "I think he'll make it, but it not gonna be easy."

Angelique looked over at Katy's tearful eyes. "You hear that? He's going to live, but he needs care and looking after."

"I'll help. Anything you ask of me, I'll do," Katy blurted out.

"Are you up for it?" Sophie asked, wiping the blood from her hands.

Katy nodded and climbed onto the wagon. She wiped the last of the tears from her eyes and sat next to Wes. The smell of burnt flesh was almost unbearable, but she believed that if it weren't for her emotional outburst, he wouldn't have been in this situation in the first place.

"We need to get him off this wagon," Sophie said, looking for a way to carefully remove him.

"I'll heat the water," Angelique said, still staring at the wound and anticipating Sophie's next chore. Sophie thought for a moment and then dashed up to the porch, through the door to the house, and returned a minute later with a blanket. She handed it to Etienne, instructing him to spread it out next to Wes. Together with the three remaining men, they carefully lifted Wes onto the blanket.

"Bring me a few more blankets from the house and spread them on the bench on the porch," Sophie ordered Katy. Katy jumped off the wagon, ran into the house and quickly found the blankets. She then rushed out the door and spread them out on the bench, as Sophie had instructed. Etienne and the three young men slowly moved Wes onto the porch and carefully laid him on the bench. Katy ran to the side of the porch and retrieved a bucket of clean water and placed it next to Wes, along with a chair.

Angelique also retrieved a bucket of clean water and poured it into the cauldron, which hung over a newly ignited fire. She wanted to bring the water to a boil in anticipation of the return of the young men with the cattails.

Time passed before the two young men finally got back to the house. The older of the two, David, handed the cattails to Angelique. She noticed they were already rinsed and cleaned. She took the cattails from him and gave him a big smile. "Merci, David," she said. "Merci for cleaning them so well."

David looked at her with a grin. "I have done this for my grandmother before and found out the hard way never to bring her a dirty root."

Angelique laughed then cut the roots off the plants and dropped them into the boiling cauldron. Within minutes, the roots softened. Angelique placed them in a bowl with a little milk and water before mashing them. She pounded and stirred the roots into a paste, adding crushed mustard seeds. She then handed the bowl to Katy and instructed her to apply the mixture to Wes' burn. Katy took the bowl and gently applied the paste, trying not to harm or wake Wes, as sleep had given him some level of relief from the pain. Angelique and Sophie watched as she did the best she could.

"Very good, lass!" Sophie exclaimed. "I believe you will do well at this."

"Yes, she seems to have healing in her blood," Angelique commented as she watched.

Katy listened quietly to the women as she worked, but in her mind, she was the reason Wes was in so much pain. It was her sense that it was not his fault that she had been chased through the swamps and the grasslands. He had been doing his job, and it had nearly cost him his life. She prayed that he would recover so that she could make amends.

As Katy applied the paste, she could hear Wes moaning quietly. Even though he was asleep, he was still in obvious pain.

"My ladies, is there anything we can give him for the pain?" Katy asked after she had finished applying the paste. "He is asleep, but I fear he is in torturous agony."

"I believe the whiskey will wear off soon," Sophie answered. "We have another bottle. I'll bring it to you. The poor soul has been through a lot, but he will be fine, lass."

"I will be here. If there is anything I must do, please tell me and I shall," Katy replied.

"You're doing fine," Angelique said, handing her a towel to clean her hands. Angelique saw in Katy a tortured soul but one with the determination to help another. It would seem that this was the best medicine for her. Most of Katy's life had been deplorable, but she had a natural propensity for helping others. Angelique could also see something else. Katy's help and care of Wes had brought back memories; memories of caring for her husband, Gareth. It had been thirteen years since his passing, but it still tormented her, as if it had happened yesterday.

Angelique had assumed responsibility for her husband's death. Despite all the years of helping and curing others, even those in the direst need, she could not get over the fact that she was unable to cure him. This thought haunted her every day and prolonged her grief to the point where many times she felt like disregarding life itself. She knew this was wrong, but she could not change the way she felt, nor could she shed the pain.

Sophie walked into the house and retrieved two bottles of whiskey from the cupboard. She promptly walked out the front door to the porch and handed one to Katy. The other she handed to Angelique.

"Merci." Angelique accepted the gift with a smile.

"Not a problem, Gitane. I feel you could use a drink." Sophie headed off the porch toward David and three of his brothers, who were cleaning fish.

Angelique opened the bottle, took a swig, then closed it and left it near Katy. She followed Sophie. It was time for supper, and the Peloat boys had had a good day of fishing before all the excitement had occurred. Instead of taking the fish home, the brothers had decided to have a cook out at Etienne's house, just in case of trouble. No one expected any problems, but there was always more tranquility and safety in numbers.

Sophie and Angelique prepared the evening's supper for thirteen with the help of the Peloat boys' mother, Aimee, who had brought fresh eggs and corn meal with her. With the boys having cleaned all the fish, it took hardly any time for Sophie and Angelique to fry them with some fresh eggs.

They all enjoyed the outdoor feast even as the weather started to turn. The wind still blew, but in the evening sky, the threat of rain was imminent as lightning streaked across the horizon. The Peloat boys, along with Aimee, Thomas, and Henri, headed south to their house before the bad weather arrived.

Etienne, now with a full stomach, walked up to the porch to check on Katy and Wes. Angelique followed, bringing their supper. Katy was sitting silently beside Wes, keeping guard over him. She thanked Angelique for the food but wouldn't eat until Wes woke up.

"How is he, young'un?" asked Etienne, taking note of her vigilance.

"He has much pain," Katy replied, wiping Wes' forehead with a damp cloth. At the sound of her voice, Wes began to show signs of life. He tried moving his arm but showed signs of pain with each attempt.

"Hold on, please be still, or you'll hurt yourself," Katy whispered, taking his hand into hers to comfort him.

Wes finally opened his eyes, surprised to see that it was Katy who was nursing him back to health. Even with the enormous pain he was enduring, he could not help but smile at her.

"Thank you, ma'am," Wes grimaced, as he held onto her hand tightly, a smile still hidden in his pain.

Katy's eyes began to tear up, as she gently stroked his forehead with the cloth. "I am so sorry, sir," she wept. "If it were not for me, you would not be in this pain."

"If it were not for you, I would be dead." He smiled as he looked into her eyes, holding her hand tighter. "Thank you, beautiful lady, for your care." Wes lifted his other hand to her watery eyes and began slowly wiping the tears from her face. "You don't have to cry. None of this is your fault. I think I just made too many bad decisions for my own good."

"True lad, but in the end, I believe it shall be worth it," said Angelique, grinning and holding the bottle of whiskey near Katy.

"I believe sh . . . um . . . it will be worth it, ma'am," Wes smiled, still looking into Katy's eyes.

Katy looked at Wes intently, as if hypnotized, and didn't notice anything else until the bottle lightly touched her arm. "Hmm . . .? Oh yes. You must be in tremendous pain. Let me get this for you," she said, fumbling with everything she touched, including the damp cloth. "Sorry. I don't know what's wrong with me."

"It's alright. Take your time, dear," Angelique said, handing her the bottle.

"Thank you, my lady," Katy replied, her voice betraying her feelings of confusion. She opened the bottle and held it to Wes' lips for him to drink. Wes took a few swigs, then tried to sit up on the bench. Katy slowly helped him rise till he was able to sit on the side of the bench. By now, the storm was moving swiftly from the north toward them. They all felt it was time to move into the house. Etienne checked the sky. Lightning had begun striking very near to the house, so he, Sophie, and Angelique hurriedly gathered all their belongings, including Wes and Katy's supper, and took them into the house. Katy put Wes' arm around her and gently lifted him to his feet. They moved slowly through the door and to the dining table where she helped him sit.

"Jacque!" Etienne yelled from the door. Etienne heard a faint whimper coming from behind him. It was Jacque. He had been lying underneath the table since first hearing the thunder. Jacque didn't like loud noises or bad weather, so he had hidden himself.

Angelique, the last to enter the house, grabbed both bottles of whiskey and rushed through the door. The wind, howling violently, nearly slammed the front door shut, as the rain started to fall. "Ah, that was close," she said as she put one of the bottles next to Wes. She walked to the chair near the back window and sat down.

Etienne was in his chair with Jacque now as close as he could get without being in Etienne's lap. Katy sat next to Wes, helping him to eat his food, as Sophie placed candles in various places around the room to provide light. Wes looked to be a lot better than earlier.

"L'amour est toujours le meilleur remède," Sophie said to Angelique, as she placed a candle next to her before walking to the sofa and picking up her knitting. Love is still the greatest healer.

"Oui, mon ami," Angelique chuckled as she took a swig of whiskey.

Angelique stared out of the window into the night, watching the rain fall. Unlike most people, she loved the sound of thunder and falling rain. It gave a sense of calmness to her sometimes tormented mind. She took another swig of whiskey, then another, sometimes glancing at Katy and Wes. She saw in both their eyes the beginning of an innocent and true love much like her own fifteen years ago with her husband. Angelique felt happiness for Katy and Wes but seeing their growing love conjured up memories, which all ended the same way—with Gareth's death.

As Angelique took another swig of whiskey, she slowly stood up and walked to the table. She patted Wes lightly on the uninjured shoulder, kissed the top of Katy's head and then walked into the other room. Noticing this, Sophie put her knitting down, picked up a candle and followed her.

"Mon ami?" Sophie called out as she entered the room. She raised the candle to see where Angelique had disappeared to. She saw her now, sitting on a couch in the dark with one hand over her face and the other holding the bottle of whiskey. Sophie walked up to her and placed the candle on the table in front of the sofa. She put her arm around Angelique, seeing now why she had left the room. Angelique was weeping openly.

"I miss him so much," Angelique said, crying uncontrollably.

Sophie could only nod and hug her tighter. She had been there from the beginning and knew this was something that was ever-present in Angelique's mind. Sophie knew that Gareth's death wasn't Angelique's fault, but she saw the torture that Angelique put herself through.

"Gitane, he was a good man, and I know you miss him dearly," Sophie said trying to comfort her. "I see the torture you put yourself through, and it is not right. You could not save him—no one could."

"With everyone I have helped, by the gods, why couldn't I save my own true love? It hurts. It hurts so much," Angelique sobbed.

"I can't answer that. But I do know there is someone else who is depending on you. Without you, I fear she would not have come this far. She would have disappeared into the swamps forever." Sophie sat next to Angelique on the couch and held her hand tightly as she continued, "I've watched you for all these years. There is something special about you, dear friend. Something that you were put on this earth to do. Even though life has thrown nothing but pain and hardship in your path, you still go on. I don't have all the answers, but I do know you will overcome this. When the right time comes, you and Gareth shall meet again. Of this, I am certain."

Angelique wiped the tears from her eyes, took another swig of whiskey and handed the bottle to Sophie. Sophie took it and laid it alongside the couch. "No more tears," Angelique sniffled, tightly clenching Sophie's hand.

"And no more whiskey for you," Sophie grinned. The two women hugged and laughed out loud before rising from their seats. Angelique loved Sophie as her own sister. Their friendship was a special one. She knew that she could always count on her if there was a problem, and vice versa. It was a blessing that they had found each other in this desolate land.

The rain continued to fall for the next couple of hours as they all relaxed in the comfort of the Broussard home. Even Wes, though still in considerable pain, seemed to hurt less under Katy's continuous care.

Angelique walked up to the table and inspected Wes' shoulder. "You've done well," she said to Katy. "I bet you will make a fine doctor one day."

Katy grinned and began to apply a bandage around the burn, "I believe there are not enough days left in my lifetime to learn what you and Miss Sophie know."

"With time, you will learn, and the Good Lord knows that Gitane and I have had plenty of time to learn," Sophie added with a smirk.

"You speak for yourself!" Angelique snapped back playfully.

"So, do you think this will be alright?" Wes asked. He was still anxious about his arm and shoulder. He had started to think about infection and didn't want to go through any type of amputation.

"I believe you will be alright," Sophie reassured him. "Just try to keep it from becoming infected, and you will be well in no time."

Sophie's words brought a welcome relief to Wes' mind. As much as he had been through in the past few days, he didn't want to go through life crippled and unable to work. Especially since he had a desire to settle down. And take a wife very soon, he thought.

As the rain subsided and the night wore on, they all headed off to sleep. This night, in complete opposition to the day, was one of peace and tranquility—and not a moment too soon for Katy. She lay down on the floor across from Wes, with Jacque snuggled up to keep her company. Many thoughts raced through her weary mind, as she pondered what life would bring. With all that had taken place and the new friendships she had made, this was the first time in her young life that Katy felt that she was not alone. But still, the fear of uncertainty stayed close. She yearned for the day when she would no longer have to look over her shoulder in fear.

CHAPTER 10

The three men stepped off the ship onto the New Orleans dock. The long journey from Portsmouth, England, had not sat well with Evan Giles, who was the first to put his feet on dry land. Evan had always hated sailing and coastal life in general. Having grown up in Central England, he was much more at home in the forest.

William Bannister, his partner, was quite the opposite. He had grown up in London near the Thames River, where he had spent most of his youth working in and around boats. Despite his joy at experiencing his first trip on the open sea, he had kept his excitement hidden in order to appear focused on the reason for their trip.

Evan and William were detectives, who had been hired by Monsieur Chevalier to determine the whereabouts of the elder Lady Falsworth and Lady Annabelle. Monsieur Chevalier's daughter had gone missing in the weeks prior to Lady Falsworth's disappearance, and she had been reported to the police as a runaway. Two weeks had passed, and no word about the girl had been forthcoming.

Finally, the police had received a lead from someone around the streets of Newcastle that the 15-year-old girl had taken a job with Lady Falsworth. The police had checked the lead but were not able to find any trace of the girl. Mere days later, another lead had appeared. A maid, no longer employed by Lady Falsworth, had gone to the police with a story of working with the girl they were looking for. The maid told the police that the girl, of French origin, spoke very little English and had obviously never been a maid before. Her basic cleaning skills were horrific, and she had seemed out of place in her role as a pauper.

The former maid went on to tell the police of a confrontation the girl had had with Lady Falsworth. Irritated that the girl did not have any useful skills, Lady Falsworth had slapped her. When the girl had protested, Lady Falsworth had hit her in the face with a walking cane, making her bleed profusely. Lady Falsworth had then ordered everyone out of the room. This had been the last time that the maid had seen either the girl or Lady Falsworth.

The following day, both Lady Falsworth and the girl were gone, and Lady Annabelle had arrived. The maid had never seen this woman before, but she bore a striking resemblance to the Falsworth family, especially the portrait of Lady Falsworth that hung over the fireplace. The similarities between the two ladies were so strong that they could easily have been mistaken for the same person.

Days went by and the police again searched the grounds of Falsworth Manor. By this time, Lady Annabelle had also disappeared with an entourage of maids and assorted servants. A day later, the police had finally found what they had been searching for. A body was discovered in the forest near a brook with its wrists and throat cut. It had been drained of blood.

The police had searched for Lady Falsworth as a possible link to the murder but were unsuccessful. As for Lady Annabelle, they didn't have evidence that she had done anything wrong, but she was nevertheless a person of interest. The police could do nothing since both suspects had disappeared. Distraught and irritated, Monsieur Chevalier had lost all faith in the police. It was then that he had hired Evan and William to find his daughter's murderer.

Monsieur David Chevalier was a prosperous French businessman who imported and exported goods to and from France and England. His wife, Marie, had died two years prior from an illness. He had spent a lot of money sending his daughter to the best schools in France, but with the death of her mother, the child had begun to rebel. Finally, while visiting her father in Newcastle, his daughter had run away, leaving no word of her whereabouts.

"New Orleans!" William exclaimed excitedly. "I've heard so much about this place."

"Yes, in history books I'm sure," Evan snarled. "Not a good ending for us there certainly."

"Come on, Evan, it's not that bad. We've only been here a few minutes. You never know, you might actually find the area appealing."

"Maybe once we leave this dreaded sea air then possibly I'll find this bug-infested place more attractive," Evan said as he swatted a few mosquitoes.

Monsieur Chevalier stepped off the ship and walked up to Evan and William. As always, he was most dapper, dressed in the best suit money could buy. Evan looked at him as he approached. His first instinct, given where they were, was that Monsieur Chevalier's apparel may be a problem.

"Good morning, sir," William greeted him, still giddy with excitement at being in a new land.

"And good morning to you both," Monsieur Chevalier replied pleasantly.

The three headed away from the dock toward a wagon, which was waiting to take them to the Ambassador Hotel where they would meet Thomas Benoit, a past business associate of Monsieur Chevalier. Thomas had received a telegram earlier that month about what had transpired. He had been summoned to keep a watch out for Lady Annabelle and her entourage.

The men boarded the wagon with luggage in hand. Evan, still thinking about Monsieur Chevalier's attire, felt obligated to say something out of concern for their safety. "Sir, you know we are in a desolate land filled with thieves and hooligans," he ventured. "Your attire is most excellent; however, I believe it may be a problem. You are showing your status, and this may give some of these ruffians a bit of an appetite."

"An appetite?" Monsieur Chevalier replied with a grin.

"Yes. I believe that making your wealth so visible may give a man too much insight into our status."

"I see. If you feel it is warranted, then I shall follow your advice."

The wagon made its way down the high street toward the hotel, passing a few lively shops filled with patrons. This intrigued Monsieur Chevalier somewhat. Even given the quest at hand, he still couldn't turn away thoughts of new business ventures. Sadly of course, this may have been the cause of the problem with his daughter following his wife's death. He had buried his thoughts and feelings into his work and had found that it made him a little more capable of moving on with life. Obviously his daughter had not shared these sentiments.

The wagon finally came to a halt in front of the hotel. Thomas immediately walked out of the front door, as he had been waiting for them to arrive. "Afternoon, gentlemen," he greeted.

"Good afternoon, sir," Evan and William both replied simultaneously, while Evan scanned the area out of habit.

Monsieur Chevalier also greeted Thomas as all three men stepped off the wagon. "And how are you, my good friend?"

"Life has been good since moving here," Thomas replied gleefully. "There are tremendous amounts of money to be made, but business will have to wait. Come, let us sign you in. I'm sure you are famished. I know a place where we can eat."

"Excellent. I am ready for something fresh after the long journey," Monsieur Chevalier replied.

Thomas led them into the hotel where he had made reservations earlier in the day. Evan and William scurried up the stairs to drop off their luggage and freshen up while Monsieur Chevalier stayed behind and conversed with his old friend for a moment before making his way up to his room to change as Evan had requested.

Monsieur Chevalier trusted few people in life, especially in business, but he did trust Thomas. They had met in France 10 years previously. Thomas had been working for a shipping company in Le Havre and was responsible for shipping most of Chevalier's goods to England and Spain. Thomas had been married only a few months at that time and had decided to take a chance. He had moved to New Orleans where he had taken a job as the leading importer to the city. He had profited greatly.

Evan and William walked down the stairs also anticipating something fresh and delicious to eat. The ship's stores had been stale after the long journey but at least that would change today. They stood at the bottom of the stairs with Thomas, who was waiting for Monsieur Chevalier to come down. They didn't have to wait long. After a few minutes, Monsieur Chevalier hurriedly made his way down the stairs wearing more conservative and simple attire that was better suited to his new surroundings.

"Much better, sir," Evan commented as they all walked out the front door. "This is still a strange country, and I have no idea of what to expect."

"But I'm sure you will have figured it out by this evening, no doubt," William joked, as Evan looked at him sourly.

One thing William knew and respected about Evan was his ability to stay ahead of trouble. His ever-cynical mind always seemed to be three steps ahead of any possible scenario. This made William feel secure about Evan's trustworthiness. The four men strolled down the street and stopped at a residence at the end of the business district. A woman stood in the doorway. She looked to be of French origin and greeted each with a smile. "Welcome," she curtsied.

They all acknowledged the woman, anticipating a tasty meal. She led them into the dining room where they sat and talked for a while until another woman began serving the food. The dishes were hidden beneath silver trays but that did not stop a delectable smell emanating from them.

"Ah, this smells wonderful," William commented with a wide smile.

"It most certainly does. Chicken I believe?" Monsieur Chevalier added. "Fresh chicken is always delicious."

"You are correct, Monsieur," the woman replied. "We have chicken and a rice dish that I am sure you will all enjoy."

The woman finished placing the food on the table, and with another quick curtsy, she left the room. With all of the food now on the table, the four began to devour the meal.

"These rolls are most exquisite," William commented as he tasted the hot bread, which almost melted in his mouth.

"Yes, Marie is an excellent baker and cook as well," replied Thomas, also tucking in but trying not to answer with a mouth full of food.

As the men enjoyed the meal, the talk around the table began to turn toward the business at hand. Thomas told them what he knew of Annabelle's journey into Texas, but he was unaware just how far she was going or what her reason was for traveling there.

"So, what of her contact here?" Evan asked. "She must have had someone planning her journey?"

"Yes, she did," Thomas sighed, "but he's been missing for about a week, and I heard today that he was discovered near an inlet, south of town. He had a bullet in his head. Apparently it was a suicide."

"How quaint," Evan said, disgusted. He knew it would be hard to find her in this country. He knew it would be even harder if those who potentially had the answers to his questions suddenly committed suicide.

"Do we even know where her first stop was?" Evan continued.

"Yes, it was a plantation near the border of Texas and Louisiana," Thomas replied. "I do not know if she is still there or how long she stayed." He thought for a moment, then continued. "There is a store in Beaumont. I am almost certain that, with as many people as she has in her entourage, she would need to purchase supplies. For your safety, before you think of going to the plantation, I believe you should to go to the supply store. I am positive they will know of at least some of her plans. I have discerned that the plantation owner is a very good friend of the family, and you might be getting into something you can't handle if you go there."

Evan sat back in his chair and thought briefly of the days ahead. He knew this wasn't going to be easy, but at the least he had hoped for some sort of insight into Annabelle's mind. Looking at the information in front of him, he would have to wait for something else to appear down the road that would add more value. He abhorred waiting.

"Well, that's that," William said. "We leave tomorrow and will hopefully catch a break along the way. As big as this country is, I believe she is out of place and will stand out, especially with her entourage so close behind her."

"So true," Thomas replied, "but be aware of the dangers here also. There is a lot of forest from here to Beaumont and beyond. There are a lot of people who would just as soon slit your throat than give you the time of day."

"Be well armed and watchful, I say," Evan added, eyeing Monsieur Chevalier. Thomas' observation had just confirmed his earlier belief about the Monsieur's apparel.

"Well armed and eyes on your back," Thomas replied.

The four sat and talked more over dinner for an hour or so, then retreated to the hotel to get some rest for the upcoming journey. Thomas had planned all the details, including their horses and a guide to take them to Beaumont. This made Evan feel a little bit at ease now that he had greater confidence in Thomas.

Nightfall brought heavy thunderstorms to the area. Fortunately, as violent as they were, they retreated just as swiftly as they came. The rain ended at around six, and a burst of cooler weather overtook the warm and humid early morning. It was just as well for Evan, as he enjoyed the cooler climate and had little care for tropical life.

Evan and William made their way to the stables, anxious to get moving. Monsieur Chevalier followed minutes later with a few sacks of personal items that would be put on a lone horse for the journey. After arriving at the stables, they met up with Samuel Cobb, a regular to this area and an expert guide. He had spent many years driving cattle through this region to both Missouri and Texas. He knew the land and the people plus, since he was a good friend of Thomas, they believed he could be trusted.

It took 30 minutes for all five horses to be loaded with the supplies and essentials for the two-day journey to Beaumont. With the extra horse for supplies instead of a wagon, Samuel thought this would save much-needed time. Once everything had been loaded and was ready, the men mounted up and headed off down the road to Texas, the same road that Annabelle and her entourage had taken a week earlier.

The four left New Orleans and rode through the wilderness toward the Texas border. With the air cool and dry after the storms, travel was very easy, especially on the horses. They passed through rivers and streams with ease and actually managed to bypass a few ferries since there was no wagon. They made good time, finally reaching a dense forest. Evan felt at home here. Whether in Central England or South Louisiana, he was comfortable in such an atmosphere. While most people would be on edge entering the forest, he was at his best.

As they made their way through the forest, the sound of chirping birds and the presence of forest life were welcome, especially to Evan. He felt it was a good sign that they were, at least for the moment, safe from an ambush.

"Hmmm . . . This place reminds me of Sherwood. Dense and damp," William said peering into the trees.

"Somewhat," Evan replied. "But at least in Sherwood I would be more confident that we wouldn't get accosted at any second."

"Come on, you worry too much," William laughed.

"Dear friend, it is because I worry that we are alive," Evan replied with a grin.

"I guess you're right," William acknowledged.

The group travelled through the forest without incident until they reached a narrow stretch of road. Samuel noticed multiple wagon tracks pressed deep into the soil, as if hauling a heavy load.   He had known of a caravan the week before but had been unable to reach New Orleans in time to apply for the job. After talking to Thomas though, he felt it may have been a blessing in disguise.

"The ones you're looking for definitely travelled this way," Samuel stated. "Looks like three wagons passed through here within a week, and it seems they were carrying a good amount of people and things."

"Good," Monsieur Chevalier replied coldly. "I look forward to the day when I meet up with this person. We have a lot to discuss."

Minutes later, a smell arose. Before long, a rotten stench filled the cool, damp air. It was the sour smell of death, and they all became aware of its presence. They rode down the road a short distance before finally locating the source. Lying alongside the road were four decaying bodies. It looked as if they had been there for at least a week.

"More proof, I would guess," Samuel said, covering his mouth and nose with a handkerchief.

Evan stared at the bodies, observing them as he would a crime scene in order to determine what had taken place. He noticed a freshly dug grave amidst the trees. He immediately stopped his horse, dismounted, and walked to the grave. William, who had come to a halt in the middle of the road, looked on while swatting at the flies buzzing around his face.

"Well, any ideas?" William asked.

Evan looked at the bodies and the grave again. "It's just a thought, but robbers don't usually leave guns and rifles around dead victims," he said, pointing to the firearms spread near the bodies. "They also don't bury their fallen brethren at the crime site either."

"So you're saying these are bandits?" Monsieur Chevalier asked, also examining the bodies.

"I would concur. He is right," Samuel added. "Judging by their clothes, these men are French. From what I have heard, only herders were hired by the Baroness. And none of them was French. These were no herders."

"And the grave?" William asked.

"They may have been ambushed, but they only lost one person so they definitely have fire power," Evan replied, now mounting his horse. "I believe we need to move on, but since the bandit's guns are still here, I do not believe we are in imminent danger."

The four moved on down the road finally making camp in a field before dark. Evan thought that it was the best place so no one could sneak up on them, but he knew that one could never fully trust this area or its people.

Evan sat in front of the campfire in deep thought about what the next day would bring. By all accounts, they should arrive in Beaumont tomorrow unless unforeseen problems ensued, which was not out of the question in this desolate place. His biggest concern though was what awaited their arrival. He knew Lady Annabelle was well armed and protected, and she was not going to go back to England willingly. The situation he felt would not be a pleasant one. Evan did feel that the element of surprise was on their side, and this could be the factor that would decide their triumph or failure. And failure would surely mean death.

CHAPTER 11

Night fell on the plantation as Ezra Jacobs walked toward the stables to check on the horses, as he usually did before retiring. The night was cool and damp after the previous night's storms, and even the wretched mosquitoes were absent, which allowed for a pleasant night to sit outside and enjoy the breeze. Ezra passed the three wagons left behind by Lady Annabelle and slipped into the stables. All was quiet except for the horse, which was closest to the door where Ezra entered. The horse seemed fidgety and nervous.

"All right, you. Ain't nothing here gonna hurt you," Ezra said, as he reached out and gently stroked the horse's head. The horse calmed slightly but kept looking at the door. Ezra paid no attention to her. The horse tended to spook for no apparent reason, and he figured that she would settle down when he closed the door. While walking through the stables, Ezra noticed that the door at the other end was open. He found this odd because no one ever used that door for anything other than to let the breeze in.

Ezra walked over to the door and shut and locked it, as it was supposed to be. He then made his way to the other side of the stables. Just then, he caught a glimpse of a shadow passing just outside the first door. His first thought was that it was Ben out checking on things, as he also did at about this time each evening.

"Ben? You there?" Ezra called, but he received no answer. Ezra knew Ben Drayson well, and he knew that Ben was a trickster, so he didn't pay much mind to it.

"Yeah, mister Ben. Why you creepin' around here?" Ezra spoke out loud, trying to get him to say something. But again, there was only silence. Ezra walked out of the door and looked around. No one seemed to be near the stables, and this fact began to make him feel uneasy. He hastily closed and locked the stable doors then turned toward the ranch hand quarters. As he passed the wagons again, he heard a faint voice call his name.

Chills ran down Ezra's spine, as he heard his name called yet again.

"Ben, quit playing with me now. It ain't funny," he said nervously.

Ezra looked around but still could not see anyone. He could hear the horses in the stables acting up, so he was sure his imagination wasn't getting the better of him.

"Ezra . . . Help me," the voice said a third time.

Ezra looked toward the wagons. The voice seemed to be coming from inside the wagon closest to him. He slowly walked closer and peered through the window, but he could see nothing. A cold chill came over him, and even his breath seemed to freeze in the air. Ezra trembled with fear as he placed his shaking hand on the door of the wagon.

"Who's in there?" Ezra shouted, nearly overcome with fright.

Ezra opened the door, and there, sitting quietly in the middle of the seat, he saw the figure of a young girl. He recognized her as the young girl whom he had helped bury in the servant cemetery. He began to shake uncontrollably.

"Why has my Lady abandoned me?" the ghostly figure asked, then looked directly at Ezra. "And why have you sentenced me to the ground?"

Ezra, paralyzed with fear, began screaming, which got the attention of Ben, who was near the ranch hands' quarters. Ben ran to the stables and saw Ezra slam the door to the wagon and stumble away.

"What's wrong?" Ben shouted, as he pointed his revolver in the direction of the wagon.

Ezra began mumbling something before he jumped up and tried to run away from the wagon. Ben grabbed Ezra by the back collar and shook him violently.

"What the hell is wrong, dang it?" Ben asked again, seeing the fear in Ezra's eyes.

"She . . . she there," Ezra stuttered and pointed to the wagon.

"Who's there?" asked Ben.

"That . . . that girl. The one that we had to bury. She knows my name!"

Ben let go, and Ezra's trembling body quickly fell to the ground. He ran to the wagon and opened the door but saw nothing. He quickly moved to the other side of the wagon and looked around. Still, he could see no one. Ben walked to the front of the wagon in disgust. Seeing Ezra on the ground and shaking with fear, Ben again asked him what had happened, "Ezra, get a hold of yourself and tell me what the hell happened?"

Ben could see the total fear in Ezra's eyes. Whatever he had seen had undoubtedly affected him to the point of a mental breakdown. Ben knelt down next to Ezra's shivering body, trying desperately to find out what had indeed happened. "Okay. Settle down and tell me what happened?" he asked calmly.

"That woman . . . she bringin' all this stuff here," Ezra replied, as if speaking out of his head.

By now, others from the ranch hand and servants' quarters had heard the ruckus and had rushed outside to see what was happening. Betty was the first out and ran to Ezra's side. "You alright, Ezra?" she said, placing her hand on his shoulder.

"Betty, it's true! It's true I say," Ezra began to rant. "She bringin' all this down on us! What we gonna do? What we gonna do?"

Just then the loud sound of a gunshot was heard, frightening all who had gathered. Ben had grown tired of all the yelling and noise and had thought it was time to put an end to it all. He took control of the situation. "Alright! Everyone go back to your quarters immediately. Looks like Ezra had a little too much rheumatism medicine tonight. Me and Miss Betty gonna take him to bed. The show is over."

A snickering was heard from within the crowd, as they walked back to their quarters. Miss Betty, on the other hand, wasn't laughing. She saw that something had scared Ezra to the point of breakdown, and she was determined to find out what it was.

"Okay," Ben said, as he helped Ezra to stand up and, with Betty's aid, led him to a bench under a nearby tree. "What the hell is going on with you tonight, Ezra?"

Ezra, now a little calmer by virtue of Miss Betty's presence, repeatedly shook his head in disbelief, "I don't know, Mister Ben. I saw the girl. She know my name!"

"Okay, okay, just keep it down. We don't want an epidemic of this seein' the dead girl stuff," Ben said in jest. But he was irritated about the earlier scene.

Betty looked at Ben in disgust, but she knew to be careful of what she said. She knew Ben and didn't want to face the consequences of losing her employment, among other things. "Mister Ben, there's something going on. I sense it," she volunteered cautiously. "There's something evil here."

"Enough! The only thing going on is Ezra's wild imagination and lack of sleep," Ben answered coldly. "Now, I don't want to hear any more of this voodoo stuff from either one of you. We don't talk about guests that way, especially important guests. One more peep out of either one of you, and you'll both be finding new employment. Am I making myself clear?"

"Yes sir," Betty answered at the same time as Ezra. She had hidden her silent rage. She knew she couldn't say more, or she would be sent away.

And around here, that would most certainly mean resorting back to living like an animal in the swamps.

Ben walked back to his quarters, as Ezra and Betty sat under the tree, whispering so as not to be heard. "But I did see that girl," Ezra mumbled, still wanting to be believed.

"I know you did, Ezra," Betty replied, trying to comfort him. "There's nothing wrong with you. You saw what I been feelin' lately."

"But she called me by my name . . ." Ezra said, once again becoming a little upset.

"Shhh . . . They hear you," said Betty, covering his mouth with her hand. "But it's alright. That girl don't want you, she wants the lady."

"But why come to me?"

"Maybe she reachin' out to you 'cause she don't have anybody else. All I know is that there is something going on round here, and we need to be careful. That woman's up to something. I can feel it."

Minutes passed as they continued talking. The talk seemed to loosen Ezra up because he began feeling a little more at ease with the situation. Although he was still frightened that there was a ghost walking around the plantation, he felt calmer with Betty around, explaining things to him. Finally, Ezra and Betty retired to their separate quarters to get some well-needed rest.

* * *

An hour had passed since the episode near the stables, and all was quiet as Ben sat on the porch, a bottle of whiskey in hand. He had tried to sleep but had been unsuccessful. His mind was filled with thoughts of the past days and visions of what would lie ahead in his life. If what Lady Annabelle had said was true, then would he leave here and start a new job with her? He would need to make several decisions in the coming days, and they would surely change his life forever.

He stared out at the trees, taking the odd swig of whiskey. The cool breeze, a few crickets, and a lonely owl were the only sounds disturbing this otherwise silent night. Everyone else had gone to bed, and his time was also drawing near. Fatigue, along with the whiskey, slowly made him nod in and out of sleep.

With his eyes closed, Ben felt moments of peace until a sound interrupted his meditative state—the faint sound of giggling. Ben opened his eyes and got up from the chair, leaving the whiskey bottle on the ground. Half-awake, he struggled to bring his eyes back into focus and was unable to sense where the sound had come from.

Seconds passed before Ben heard the giggling once again, but this time he saw a shadow out the corner of his eye. He immediately turned his head but saw nothing. He grabbed a lit torch and proceeded to the tree line where he thought he had seen something, oddly enough near the stables. As he peered out into the darkness with the torch, he still saw nothing.

By now Ben had raised his revolver in front of him as a precaution. He didn't know what to expect, if anything, but if something did happen, he wanted to be ready. Slowly moving down the pathway, he again heard the giggling. And the crunching of leaves as if someone was in front of him, also walking along the pathway. He strode faster, trying to catch up with whomever or whatever was out there. "Who's out there?" Ben shouted, his eyes still focused on the pathway.

With every step Ben took, the sounds grew louder. Faster and faster, he hurried through the trees but never seemed to catch up enough to see anything. Finally, he came to a small clearing. The sounds also stopped. Out of breath from running, Ben lowered both his revolver and the torch. The light illuminated a few headstones. He had run into the servant cemetery, nearly stepping into the recently dug grave of the newly departed maid.

"Hello!" Ben called out, but heard no reply nor saw any sign of someone or something else there. He put away his revolver and raised the torch to have a better look around. He still saw nothing. He was now irritated that he had wasted his time. When he turned to head back to the plantation however, he came face to face with the ghostly figure of a young girl in white. This startled Ben, and he fell backwards.

Ben awoke from his chair on the porch of the house. His hands shook, and cold sweat ran down his forehead. He had been dreaming. All this talk of ghosts seemed to have affected even him. As he scanned the area, all seemed quiet and only the usual night-time sounds were heard in the darkness.

Now on his feet, Ben walked swiftly to his quarters. Ghosts or not, he needed to sleep. As he opened the door to his quarters, he yawned and lit a nearby lantern, which was hanging near the door. He sat on the edge of his cot. He was half asleep and still a little tipsy from the earlier whiskey. As he began to pull his boots from his aching feet, he noticed that the boots were full of fresh mud. Puzzled of as to why this could be, he mentally retraced his steps of that evening but was still unaware of having walked to any place where he could have picked up the mud.

Then a thought entered his mind. He thought back to the dream he had had on the porch. But he could only dismiss it as ridiculous. There was no way he could have been trouncing around the woods earlier, he thought. Ben extinguished the lantern and lay down on his cot. As he lay there in deep thought, he clutched his revolver tightly.

* * *

With the cool breeze of the night, Ben hadn't been the only one awake in the wee hours. Annabelle sat on the second floor balcony of a newly constructed house near the beach in Galveston. She had spent most of the day discussing land deals with a few land brokers from Central Texas. At first, it had not gone well, as most looked upon her youth disparagingly, but they quickly learned of her ruthlessness in business.

What Annabelle wants, Annabelle gets. Her philosophy held steadfast when trying to obtain prime land at a decent price, and of course, showing gold as payment certainly helped to change some minds.

Annabelle sat looking into the darkness of the morning, with a glass of French wine, which had somehow made it to Texas. Agatha, who also couldn't sleep, joined her.

"Ah, dear friend," Annabelle greeted Agatha with an intoxicated grin, "what a wonderful night. Do be a dear and join me."

Agatha saw that Annabelle had been there a while and had indulged in almost two-thirds of a bottle of wine. She could tell Annabelle was a bit tipsy at the very least.

"And how are you this morning?" Agatha asked, pouring herself a glass of wine.

"Adequate. I cannot complain," Annabelle replied, looking out over the water.

"And are we ever so closer to our new home?"

Annabelle turned to Agatha, her wine glass extended for a refill. Agatha refreshed her glass then sat in the chair next to her. As Annabelle spoke, her distaste for Texas land brokers became increasingly evident.

"Yes," she said, taking a sip of wine, "yes, we will soon have our own abode. Though it will be with no thanks to these ruffians in whom I am so greatly disappointed."

Agatha let out a sudden chuckle. She knew that when Annabelle did not get her way, there would be hell to pay for all who crossed her. "I believe they would be called snake oil salesmen in these parts," she said, still with a grin on her face.

"Thievery, would best describe it," Annabelle replied, a small smile curling the corners of her mouth. "But I have an audience with the final two brokers in the morning. I feel that something will be of use from this meeting."

Agatha took another sip of wine and nodded her head in agreement. "Hopefully, for this adventure is becoming enormously expensive. Couldn't we just travel to Central Texas and pick and choose for ourselves? I'm sure with the right price anyone there can be bought out."

Annabelle glanced at Agatha, then turned her thoughts to the ever-present sound of the sea rushing on the shore. "Perhaps, but I believe our interests quite possibly will be best suited to the east. Vast prairies and open terrain do not satisfy my needs."

"And those needs are . . .?" Agatha asked.

"Privacy of course," Annabelle replied with an inebriated chuckle.

Just then a soft knock on the door to the upper living area was heard. Agatha stood up from the chair, left the balcony and walked across the room. As she slowly opened the door, she could hear a faint sniffling behind it. Agatha saw Sara standing in the doorway with tears in her eyes.

"So sorry, my lady" she said, upset with her head bowed. "I've had dreams of Alice. I know they're just dreams, but they are so horrendous and disturbing that I cannot put them out of my mind."

"Dear child," Agatha comforted in a woeful tone. She knew Sara missed Alice considerably, since Sara's befriending of Lady Falsworth had made her somewhat unpopular with most of the other maids. Hana, Brigit, and the recently departed Alice, were the only maids to be civil toward her. All the rest seem to mock and despise her.

Agatha led Sara into the room, then closed and locked the door. By this time, Annabelle had called to her from the balcony. "And who knocks at my door in the middle of the night?" said Annabelle in a rare, playful mood.

Agatha and Sara stepped onto the balcony, now in clear view of

Annabelle. Sara's eyes were bloodshot, and her head was still bowed as if ashamed for having disturbed her overseer.

"Now what seems to be the matter, sweet, sweet Sara?" Annabelle asked, looking at her with a kindly, atypical smile.

"My lady," she replied curtsying, "I am so sorry to bother you. I have been dreaming of Alice. Terrible, wicked dreams."

Annabelle saw Sara tearing up but was able to keep most of her own emotions hidden. "And what of these dreams, child?" she asked. "What disturbs you?"

"I see her asking me for help. I could not help her when she was living, so how am I to help her now?" Sara replied, confused.

"Dear child," Agatha added, "you were having a nightmare. I understand you and Alice were friends but to think that she is contacting you is preposterous." Agatha put her arm around Sara to comfort her. "Alice was very ill and in pain. She no longer feels this pain or illness because she is in a much better place now."

"And Lady Falsworth? Is she in a better place as well?"

Annabelle smiled at Sara and took her hand, stroking it lightly. "You really miss her, don't you?"

Sara nodded in agreement, "Yes, she was the mother I never had. The other girls thought she was always too cross with us, but I felt she was this way because she loved us. I miss her."

"Dear, dear sweet Sara," Annabelle clutched Sara's hand tightly. "Your lady loves you the most of them all, and I promise you, you will see her once again."

"It is my ultimate wish, my lady," Sara replied, tears filling her eyes.

"And I promise you, your wish will come true. Now go and sleep well.

You'll be accompanying me in the morning."

"Thank you, my lady." Sara wiped the tears from her face and smiled at Annabelle, as she started to back into the room. "I am so thankful that you are here, watching over us."

"Oh, it is definitely my pleasure, dear Sara," Annabelle returned the smile. "Definitely a pleasure."

Sara left the room and walked down the hallway back to her room, as Agatha watched from inside the door. Annabelle sat back in her chair and returned to listening to the waves rushing over the beach. The combination of the unceasing sound of the water and the effects of the wine made her relax to the point of sleep.

"Poor dear," Agatha said, walking back onto the balcony.

"A distressed and befuddled child," Annabelle replied, taking a sip of wine. "The orphaned, the abandoned, the unwanted, all thrown aside at one's leisure to fend for themselves. The darkness is where these children hide because they have no light to shine their way. It is solely in their dark, confused little minds that their essence incubates, along with the uncertainty of where their next meal will be coming from." Annabelle stood up from the chair and placed her hands on the railings of the balcony as she continued, "These daughters who emanate from the darkness have been given a chance to serve. They shall truly be rewarded in the end."

"To which I believe the only reward dear Sara wants is to have Lady Falsworth back amongst us," Agatha added.

"Oh, she will see her again, dear friend," Annabelle said. "That is a promise that I assure you will come to pass."

CHAPTER 12

The morning came swiftly as the sun rose over the steady rush of Gulf waves. Annabelle awoke, fatigued after a late night of French wine appreciation. Her mood reflected her thoughts, which were definitely focused on the agenda at hand. She understood the dire importance of finding suitable land for her new venture.

Agatha, also awake, rounded up the maids for the day's chores, which included packing for their return to Sabine that night. Agatha entered the room where Sara, Hana, and Brigit were already gathering items for the night's journey.

"Morning, ladies," Agatha said, as she inspected the room.

"Good morning, my lady," they all replied in unison.

"I take it all is well here. And how are you feeling, Sara?" Agatha asked, noticing that Sara's demeanor had improved since the previous night.

"I am feeling much better. Thank you, my lady," Sara replied with a glowing smile.

"Very good. You three will accompany Lady Falsworth and I into town after breakfast, so make haste, ladies."

A chatter of excitement arose among the girls. The three would certainly have an entertaining morning tagging along with Agatha and Lady Falsworth, seeing new places and meeting new and interesting people. As an added bonus, such outings would also get them out of having to do the breakfast dishes.

After breakfast, Annabelle, Agatha, and the three maids climbed on board an open horse-drawn wagon and set off for Menard House to meet with two more land brokers. The morning breeze and sunshine set a joyous tone for the maids, as they conversed openly about all the interesting houses and sites along the way. Jack Diboll, the wagon's driver and a twenty-year resident of Galveston, added a few tidbits of history and facts to make the maids even more giddy and animated about the short trip.

As the wagon pulled up in front of Menard House, three gentlemen came forward to greet them. The maids, still talking amongst themselves, exclaimed their love of the Greek-style pillared home, as well as their wishes to settle in a house such as this.

"Good morning, ladies," John Stiles, who was employed by the Menard family, greeted. The other two men followed suit.

"Good morning gentlemen," Agatha replied.

Annabelle and the maids remained silent as they stepped off the wagon behind Agatha. Annabelle scanned the area as if searching for one specific thing but never acknowledged what she was looking for. She finally turned her attention to the three gentlemen waiting at the steps to the house. Her demeanor changed instantaneously, and Annabelle greeted the three with the utmost affection.

"Good morning. I am so very glad to make your acquaintance," Annabelle said, as she shook Mr. Stiles' hand before doing the same to the other two.

"It is an honor and a privilege, madam," Mr. Stiles replied. "And might I say, you all are looking most wonderful this morning."

"Indeed you may," Annabelle chuckled, letting her charm flow.

Mr. Stiles led the ladies and two gentlemen in through the front door and down the hallway to an office. Originally, the office had been used by the house's founder, Michel Menard, to meet with those seeking to buy land in Galveston, until his death in 1856.

Mr. Stiles, a friend of the Menard family, was just beginning his journey into the world of land brokering and was grateful to have full use of the magnificent house. He felt the environment provided him with the credibility to do business. It was a jewel compared to his modest "two-roomed shack," as he called it.

"So, Lady Falsworth, Miss Sterling, I do hope you are enjoying our young up-and-coming city by the sea," Mr. Stiles said in attempt to draw attention to the island's attributes.

"Yes, it is a quaint little place, but I don't know if I would be comfortable living by the sea," Annabelle responded.

"What do you mean? Living near the water is the best part!" Mr. Stiles feigned astonishment. "There is always a breeze, and a dip into the ocean is most gratifying on a hot summer's day."

Annabelle looked at him in a bemused manner. "True, it is definitely wonderful, but I do feel that this area is plagued with storms, is it not?"

"Hmmm . . . We have our fair share of storms of a tropical nature but nothing to worry about. Those that do the most damage tend not to come this far west."

Annabelle looked at him in disbelief. "Oh? Well, that is good to know. Unfortunately your brethren in Indianola cannot say the same, can they?"

"Pardon? Oh yes." Mr. Stiles remembered almost a month to the day that a strong hurricane had blown into Matagorda Bay, Texas, destroying almost the entire port town of Indianola. "Yes, what a terrible and tragic situation," Mr. Stiles recalled, "but here in Galveston things like that just don't happen. I believe God shines down on our glorious little city and protects it."

Annabelle's smile grew wider on hearing his words. She looked into his eyes mischievously, "Well, if I may give you some advice regarding the future of your glorious little city. Heed this warning and remember those who perished in Indianola, because it may be you who finds yourself in the eye of destruction with no warning or means of escape." Annabelle paused for a moment and, noticing Mr. Stiles' blank stare, continued, "Well, enough of that. I believe we shall continue with other business at hand." She smiled graciously.

"But of course, Lady Falsworth," Mr. Stiles acceded, gladly acknowledging the change of subject.

Waiting quietly across from Annabelle with an amused grin on his face, was Johan Strauss, a spokesman for one of the Hillebrandt family members. He had been listening as Mr. Stiles had tried to unscrupulously sell the idea of Galveston Island to Annabelle.

"I applaud you, madam, for your knowledge of this area," Johan commented, partly to ridicule Mr. Stiles.

"Oh, your applause is well received," replied Annabelle. "I never go into an investment blindly. I am very thorough in my conclusions—both past, present, and future. I believe in leaving no stone unturned."

"As do I," Johan agreed. "Pardon me, madam, but if I am right, you are looking for a place to settle? Protected from the cyclones? Well, my client has land just east of here, which is well protected, even by Indianola standards. I believe you have traveled through part of it?"

Annabelle listened intently. Aside from the certain problems that had arisen, Annabelle did like the area and believed this was where she could begin a new dominance that, to her, would last for years. "Yes, I did, and I believe that this land would give me what I am searching for," Annabelle answered cryptically.

"Then I believe we can work out a deal," Johan replied cheerfully. "The family I represent wants to sell some of its tracts. Their problems are to do with internal friction and not the land itself. I would graciously encourage you to visit our humble place and look over it at your leisure."

Annabelle sat back and digested Johan's words for a brief minute. When she next spoke, it was with an upbeat tone: "I will do that. As I said, I do like the area and look forward to seeing more of it."

"You are staying east of the Neches, are you not?" Johan asked, displaying his interest in her activities.

"Why, yes," Annabelle replied coquettishly, turning the charm up a notch.

"Good. I can send a few wagons for you in a few days' time so that you can tour the site."

"Excellent, though we do have adequate wagons. I believe a guide would be sufficient."

"But of course. I will personally show you the area."

"Again, this is excellent. I look forward to the meeting."

After talking with Johan a few minutes more, Annabelle turned to the third gentlemen, Michael Eddingston. He was from east Texas, and Annabelle thought he also made a good presentation, but she would need to visit his property as well before making a decision.

An hour passed as the five made conversation. Later, Jack brought the wagon around to the front of the house while the three maids, Miss Sterling, and Annabelle gathered near the driveway. The three gentlemen had accompanied them out of the house.

"Well, I am sure I speak for all of us here when I say it was very enjoyable meeting you all, and I hope that we will meet again soon." Mr. Stiles was gracious toward Annabelle.

"Yes, it has been an enjoyable morning," Annabelle replied. "I am most certain I will visit this city again soon."

"Well, do please let me know if I can be of further service to you, madam. I am always here and ready to assist."

"Indeed I shall," Annabelle smiled warmly and boarded the wagon behind Miss Sterling.

With all five now on board, they began their journey back to the house near the beach. After completing their duties earlier in the day, the other maids had been treated to a morning of walking along the beach and collecting shells. Most of them had never set foot on a beach, and this was expressed through their joy and excitement. Watching the water rush in and out while finding small crabs and shellfish had put a long-absent smile on their otherwise somber faces.

The wagon arrived at the house just a little after noon. Agatha quickly stepped off the wagon and gathered some of the maids to prepare lunch. Annabelle sat back for a few moments in the wagon looking around the area. Sara and Hana also stayed behind, still asking Jack questions about the city.

"Okay, I am sure Mr. Diboll has told you everything there is to know about this place," Annabelle said, looking at Sara and Hana. "Now go help Miss Sterling prepare lunch. Hurry now. We will be leaving shortly."

Hana and Sara did as Annabelle instructed. They stepped off the wagon and headed into the house. Annabelle watched them leave, then turned to Jack. "Mr. Diboll, would you be a dear and take me a few blocks north, then make a turn left?" she asked, still scanning the area.

"Yes, ma'am," Jack replied, as he urged the horses to move again.

Jack did as Annabelle requested by going a few blocks north before turning left. Annabelle looked on as the horses made their way down the dirt street. As they passed a small modest two-roomed house at the end of the block, she stood up. "Stop here!" she instructed, preparing to dismount the wagon.

Jack stopped in front of the house, and Annabelle stepped hurriedly off the wagon and walked to the door. Before knocking, she shouted to Jack to leave and return in ten minutes. As Jack rode away from the house, he looked back just in time to see Annabelle entering the small house. He caught a glimpse of an older woman holding the door open.

Jack had lived in the area for twenty-odd years or so but never knew who lived in that residence, or in fact, never really noticed the house being there. Either way, his business was not to know the minutiae of Lady Falsworth's daily routine, and he was getting paid good money to chauffeur her around.

Ten minutes had passed by the time Jack halted the wagon in front of the small house once again. Annabelle walked out of the house and closed the door behind her. The other woman was not seen. Annabelle stepped onto the wagon and sat quietly while Jack guided the wagon back to Annabelle's house. Once there, Annabelle swiftly disembarked without saying a word and walked through the front door, leaving Jack at a loss for words.

Inside, Agatha had rounded up the maids, given them their orders for preparing lunch, and then informed them that at six o'clock they would all depart for Sabine. Annabelle walked silently passed them up the stairs to her room, where she closed and locked the door.

Within half an hour, lunch had been prepared. Sara sauntered up the stairs and gently knocked on Annabelle's door. Annabelle opened the door and smiled at her favorite maid, then walked down the stairs without saying a word. Sara followed. They entered the dining area and sat down in anticipation of a fine meal.

The planned trip to Galveston had been a positive one for Annabelle, and her plans were nearly in place. The last installment would be dealing with Katy. Or so she thought.

* * *

Evan, William, and Monsieur Chevalier rode into Beaumont around noon. They had made good time across the Louisiana border and through Burr's ferry. To be able to wade across the Neches into Beaumont was an unexpected plus. Samuel Cobb, seeing that the three had arrived safely under his supervision, now turned north for Nacogdoches to meet up with another client.

"I am famished," William said as they stopped in front of the supply store.

Evan dismounted his horse and headed inside. "Okay, William, I get the hint. You eat and I'll do the investigating."

William turned his head in Evan's direction as he chewed on a piece of jerky. "I believe I am entitled to food intake at least once a day?"

Evan shook his head and laughed. "Well, you've been nibbling since we left camp. I believe you are not in danger of starvation."

"True!" William agreed. "But this stuff is so damn good . . ." He took another bite of jerky.

Evan and Monsieur Chevalier walked into the store, leaving William to watch the horses. As they were looking around for what they needed, the owner, Jonathan Brown, greeted them. "Good day, gentlemen. May I be of assistance?" he asked.

"As a matter of fact, you can," Evan replied as he looked around the store. "We will need a few things for our journey through this area, but first, I was wondering if you could help us to locate someone?"

As Mr. Brown listened to Evan, he noticed his English accent. "Ah! English. You're the third visitor this week with an English accent. I'm beginning to wonder if there is an invasion taking place," he commented jovially.

Evan laughed along with him but couldn't help but wonder who the other travelers were. "So you've had others here, did you?"

"Sure. We've had a few."

"Well, we are actually looking for a young lady who goes by the name of Lady Annabelle Falsworth. She might have come through here with a caravan."

"Pretty young blonde? Highfalutin? Some kind of royalty?"

"Yes! I do believe you've met dear Lady Annabelle."

"Sure, she was in here two days ago with a band of hired guns and some pretty young girls. I believe she was headed for Sabine, but they were sure interested in another young girl who was here the day before. I believe they went to Grigsby's Bluff to find her."

Evan listened intently. He felt that this was working out to be even easier than he had hoped. "So who was this girl, and where specifically is Grigsby's Bluff?" Evan asked.

"Well, I really don't know who this girl is, but I believe she is staying with some French friends. I will warn you though, one in particular doesn't take to strangers too well," Mr. Brown cautioned, thinking of Angelique.

"That is fine. We will be on our best behavior," Evan grinned. "We have no quarrel with these people. We only want to find Lady Annabelle."

Mr. Brown explained the way to Grigsby's Bluff and also to Etienne's tract. He thought if anyone knew something, it would be Etienne.

"Well, sir, I appreciate your information and your help," Evan said as he shook his hand. "And now it is time for business."

Evan pulled out a list of things needed for the days ahead and handed it to Mr. Brown, who then headed to the back to get a few of the items. Monsieur Chevalier, who had been quiet and attentive all this time, approached Evan. "I think we will find what we are looking for in this Grigsby's Bluff," he said.

"I believe so, too," Evan replied. "I'm just glad you're here. We may run into a bit of trouble with the French. I don't think they would be English friendly here."

"It will be fine. I am anxious to see what has taken place here. I am hoping that they will be on our side."

"With your story, I believe they will."

Mr. Brown finally returned from the back and had a few hands bring out the supplies. William, now on the porch, directed the hands to the horses. With fresh supplies and the horses fed, the three were ready to head out toward Grigsby's Bluff. After a last minute explanation on how to get there from Mr. Brown, the group began their journey south.

"So, what we are riding into?" William asked.

"I believe—and hope—our allies," Evan replied.

"Great, so you don't actually know, do you?" William asked, a little uneasily.

"In one word? No. But I have a feeling it will work out to our benefit," Evan said optimistically.

"Don't worry, friend," Monsieur Chevalier added. "The French are good. I will deal with the French."

"I hope you're right," Evan added.

"Yes, I am right. It is true that some of these people fled Canada because of English persecution, no? But not all. I believe they wouldn't have befriended an English girl if this was the case."

"True, but stranger things have happened," Evan said out loud, as he thought more and more about the situation. "Allies make strange bed partners sometimes. Out of necessity they form a bond."

"Yes, Lady Falsworth seems to bring common ground to warring nations," William said jokingly.

"Maybe. We will see." Evan was non-committal.

With the three headed for uncertainty and no knowledge of where Annabelle was or what she was up to, they were, at least in their minds, at an advantage. One, Annabelle was unaware of their presence in the area, and two, if these people were indeed allies, this would be of great benefit to them.

Still, in Evan's mind, he tried to look at the broader picture of what could come their way. What was Lady Falsworth actually up to halfway around the world, so far from the comfort of home? And the bigger question, where was the elder Lady Falsworth? Was she also dead, and if so, where was her body?

* * *

As the three rode toward Grigsby's Bluff, someone else was also preparing to travel. Annabelle looked out over the water from the balcony of the house she had stayed in for the last couple of days. She was drawn to the hypnotic sound of the waves rushing onto the shore. Although she herself had never lived on the coast, Annabelle felt a passion for this area.

Agatha walked swiftly up the stairs and entered the room, calling out to Annabelle. "It is time. We must leave," she said turning around toward the door.

The wagons were packed, and the maids were aboard for the short journey to the ship. Annabelle stood up and gave a last look out at the sea, then walked through the room, across the landing and downstairs toward the front door. Agatha stepped onto the first wagon with Annabelle close behind. Now ready to go, the wagons left the house and headed for the port.

The wagons rolled down the street with the first driven by Jack Diboll. As they made their way toward the port, the caravan travelled along the street that Annabelle had, just hours before, made Jack take her down. As they moved closer to the house that Annabelle had visited, an old woman slowly crept onto the side of the street near the oncoming wagons. Her eyes focused steadily on Annabelle, as she silently watched her pass.

Jack noticed the woman and looked back at Annabelle to see her reaction, but her face was devoid of emotion. Jack became somewhat troubled. He knew almost everyone on the island, but this was the first time he had seen this old woman. As he looked behind the wagon to see her again, she disappeared. He slowed the wagon slightly so that he could get a better look at the side of the street, but she was gone.

Annabelle noticed him reducing the speed of the wagon. "Is there a problem here?"

Jack, still looking back, replied, "Oh no, ma'am. I thought I saw someone familiar. My apologies."

"Your apologies accepted. Now we must get to the port swiftly. The ship will not wait on us."

Jack jostled the reins, and the horses picked up their pace. Still in deep thought, Jack couldn't get the woman's face out of his mind, but he dared not stop again, or Lady Annabelle would have his head. He would just have to do a little searching once this job was finished.

As the wagons turned onto the street in front of the docks, a constant stream of chatter was heard from the maids, who were excited to be going on yet another boat ride. All except Brigit. She appeared to have taken ill. Sara, sitting next to her, noticed that Brigit looked dazed and in some sort of trance.

"Brigit? Are you alright?" Sara asked in a concerned voice.

Brigit did not answer. Instead, she closed her eyes and tried to sleep.

"My lady, it's Brigit. I believe she is ill," Sara said to Annabelle.

Annabelle and Agatha looked over at Brigit, who had passed out in the seat next to Sara. "Do not worry, Sara. We will tend to her on the ship. I'm sure she will be alright," Annabelle said, making Sara feel a bit more at ease.

The wagons pulled up to the docks. A few men were waiting there to help load all of the group's possessions onto the steamboat. The maids began filing out of the wagons one at a time and boarding the ship with Agatha guiding them. Sara and Hana were the last of the maids to step off the wagon, along with the barely responsive Brigit. Both helped her off the wagon and slowly up the plank of the steamboat.

Annabelle, the only one left on the wagon aside from the driver, stood up and walked to the edge. But before she stepped down, she turned to Jack and said, "I bid you a fond farewell, but with some important advice. Forget what your mind has conjured up. For one that sees nothing lives another day. One that walks in another's shadow shall feel the cold wind of death upon their soul. Now, she awaits your choice. For it is only you who can choose."

With that, Annabelle turned and stepped off the wagon. She walked up the plank onto the steamboat without looking back.

Her words had caught Jack off guard, and he had become unnerved. He took up the reins, and the horses and wagon were off, back to the house. Minutes later, as the wagon made its way down the street, the old woman again stood in front of the house, but this time, she stared at him. His eyes caught hers, and her face took on a wicked grin. Jack immediately turned his eyes to the street as he passed, never looking back. In his mind, he figured it wasn't any of his business anyhow. All he felt was that he definitely needed a stiff drink.

CHAPTER 13

It was a vibrant afternoon: a crisp cool wind swirled away the sultry heat that had earlier settled over the land. Angelique walked back from the river with a large sack over her shoulder and a knife in hand. She had been on her boat, gathering more plants from the river banks and catching a few fish. Katy was at the Broussard house, continuing to take care of Wes. Despite thinking that this beautiful day was a blessing, Angelique still had an odd feeling deep inside her, a feeling of emptiness, as if something was missing.

As she walked up to her cabin, she heard the faint sound of horses galloping in the distance. She dropped her sack near the door and moved quickly into the garden to get a closer look. She picked up a hoe, which was lying on the ground, and hurried toward the path. She was able to see three men riding on horseback in her direction. As they drew nearer, Angelique moved to the middle of the path where she was more visible.

Evan was the first to see Angelique standing in the pathway. He wondered whether or not she was alone and if he should draw his weapon to preempt a possible ambush. Monsieur Chevalier, noticing Evan's uncertainty, rode ahead of him and William, motioning them to stop so as not to threaten anyone who might be hiding in wait.

Monsieur Chevalier slowed his horse to a trot, moving closer to the woman, who now glaring at him as if ready to attack. "Pardon, madame," he said as he came to a halt in front of her, attempting to make her feel at ease. By her body language and facial expression however, it was clear that she was nowhere near comfortable with his presence.

"Who are you?" Angelique asked in English; her words were short and sharp. She looked behind Monsieur Chevalier at Evan and William. The two men sat silently on horseback, trying to appear as non-threatening as possible despite still anticipating an ambush. This in turn made them look very nervous—particularly Evan, as he kept looking at the outer edges of the path.

"I am Monsieur David Chevalier." He tipped his hat to Angelique. Angelique's eyes darted back and forth between the men, not trusting any of them.

"What do you want?" she asked, clutching the hoe tighter.

"Madame, we wish you no harm. We are looking for an English woman who goes by the name of Lady Annabelle Falsworth. She and her caravan may have moved through here three days ago."

"Friend of yours?" Angelique interrupted.

"No, madame. I believe she murdered my daughter back in England, and I am looking for answers."

Angelique recalled what Katy had said about a French maid disappearing. She began to feel that this man may be speaking the truth. "And what of the other two?" she asked, nodding in Evan and William's direction.

"They are detectives from Newcastle. They are the reason I have tracked her down this far. Please madame, if you have the slightest information that would help me in my search for this wretched woman . . . I beg of you."

"Get off your horse and follow me," Angelique said, lowering the hoe. "We can continue this conversation in my cabin."

"Bless you, madame," Monsieur Chevalier said as he dismounted and gestured for Evan and William to do the same.

Angelique felt that Monsieur Chevalier was speaking the truth; however, she wanted to be absolutely certain before she took them near Katy.

"You are French, no?" Angelique asked. "What are you doing in

Newcastle?"

Monsieur Chevalier explained some of his business affairs to Angelique as they walked, and he provided her with a brief history of his daughter's disappearance. She listened intently, trying to integrate his story with what she knew of Katy's. When they got to the cabin, Angelique laid down the hoe and opened the door. Monsieur Chevalier and Evan walked in while William stayed outside to look after the horses.

Before Angelique entered the cabin, she looked at William. "Please make yourself comfortable, but remember that those in the woods are watching. Be advised that you are a guest and should act accordingly."

William looked around nervously. He wasn't sure if her words were meant to frighten him or if there actually was someone—or something—watching. He nonetheless remained vigilant, aware of every sound.

"Please sit." Angelique motioned for the two to sit at the table while she went to the cupboard and removed a bottle of whiskey. "I apologize that this is all I have, but I believe we could all use this at the moment."

"It is fine, madame," Monsieur Chevalier replied. "I thank you for your hospitality."

"I concur, madam," Evan agreed. "Although please leave a drink for my friend outside. He is a bit nervous at the moment, and I'm sure it will do him good."

Angelique smiled openly. "This I shall do," she said, as she set three glasses on the table.

As the tension in the cabin subsided, Monsieur Chevalier felt more confident with this woman. He had his own questions for her. "So madame, you are also French, no?" he asked, picking up the glass of whiskey and taking a sip.

Angelique looked across the table at him. "Yes, I believe I am." She grinned cordially. "My name is Angelique, monsieur."

"I am very happy to meet you but am sorry that it is not under better circumstances," Monsieur Chevalier replied, referring to the business at hand.

"I am very sad to hear about your daughter. If it is of any consolation to you, I believe you will find the one you seek very soon."

"I hope you are right. Lady Falsworth is violent and cruel, and I believe she will kill again."

"So, madam, what do you know of this woman?" Evan asked, yearning for more information.

"We've met only briefly," Angelique replied, "but at the time, she revealed her true spirit. For some unknown reason, she is obsessed with an ex-maid, who escaped her grasp. I long to find out the true answer to who Lady Falsworth is."

"Well, madam, this is what we know of what happened in Newcastle," Evan said, and he began telling the story of what had taken place after Annabelle had left and how they had found the body of the French girl.

Angelique sat motionless, as she listened to every gruesome detail. "A very sad and tragic end to a young life," Angelique remarked somberly, noticing Monsieur Chevalier's eyes starting to gather tears. Although he portrayed himself as strong, she could sense the pain in his heart, and the dark anger that lay beneath his amiable demeanor.

"Tell me, monsieur, do you have a photograph of your daughter?" Angelique asked, as she reached out across the table and softly touched his hand.

"But of course." Monsieur Chevalier reached into his coat pocket, displaying a faint smile. He took the photograph out and laid it on the table in front of Angelique.

Angelique stared at the photograph and ran her hand gently over it. "A very beautiful girl," she commented quietly.

With her hand over the photograph, Angelique began to see visions of the young girl. The first, an image, showed her dressed in black, standing in the courtyard of a beautiful mansion of French design. Angelique guessed it was the girl's home. As Angelique looked closer, she noticed her bloodshot eyes and fatigue. It would seem that something had upset her greatly. In the second vision, Angelique saw the reason.

A casket lay in the courtyard, surrounded by flowers and mourners. The girl sat silently in the front row with her father, who was also visibly upset. As the priest began the mass, Angelique felt the pure anguish in the girl's heart.

In the next vision, the girl tiptoed quietly down an illuminated hallway. It was night time, and she was trying not to wake any of the visitors who were staying in the mansion. She walked to the end of the hall and down a large staircase, which led to the study. As the girl walked, she could hear giggling coming from behind the study doors. Finding this to be unusual given the circumstances, she crept closer. The giggling from inside the study continued, but this time she identified it as the sound of a woman.

Having been through the ordeal of her mother's funeral earlier that day, the girl was restless and unhappy. She needed to find out who was in such a jovial mood. As she turned to face the door to the study, she suddenly heard another voice. A male. His voice sounded very familiar. The girl flung open the door to the study to see who had been causing all the noise.

"Father?" the girl gasped, her eyes quickly filling with tears.

"Catherine? No . . . Wait!" Monsieur Chevalier exclaimed, as his daughter ran back up the staircase in tears. He hurried after her. Catherine was kneeling on the floor of the hallway, weeping.

"Catherine? It is not what it seems," he said, laying his hand on her shoulder to comfort her.

"Seems? It would seem to me that it is obvious! You cannot let the dust settle on my mother's grave, and you're already looking for harlots!" Catherine yelled, weeping uncontrollably.

"Please, Catherine, lower your voice," Monsieur Chevalier said, afraid that the guests would hear.

"Why? So that no one will hear just what kind of man you are?" she screamed. "One who lies with harlots while his wife is fresh in the ground!"

Monsieur Chevalier raised his hand to hit her. It only made Catherine yell even louder, "Go ahead! Marie thought little of you. She cried each night while you were in someone else's bed!"

"What you say is a lie!"

"Is it? Look upon her grave and tell her!"

Monsieur Chevalier was enraged by Catherine's accusations, and even more so as some of the guests began opening their doors to see what was going on. Finally, he could not take any more of her words, and he hit her across the face.

Catherine looked at him with contempt. "You are dead to me!" she shouted.

"And you to I," he replied, as he calmly walked away.

Catherine knelt on the floor, still weeping, as the guests retreated quietly back into their rooms.

Angelique's vision swiftly changed. She saw Monsieur Chevalier once again in a heated argument with his daughter, but the scenery had changed. The décor in the house was English. It would seem that they were both in England. Newcastle perhaps.

"But the letter explains it all!" Monsieur Chevalier shouted, "I spend enormous amounts of money on your education and for what? So you can waste your life away?"

Monsieur Chevalier had sent his daughter to elite boarding schools after her mother had passed on, but she never seemed to take advantage of these opportunities. Catherine's studies were always neglected, and she seemed unable to get along with her fellow students. She had been expelled from school after school for two consecutive years and was now in Newcastle under her father's supervision.

"I don't care!" Catherine shouted. "You can keep your money. I don't need you or anyone else!" With that, she turned on her heel and stormed out of the house into the night. Initially, Monsieur Chevalier ran after her, but he stopped at the door. He felt that he couldn't do anything else for her, and he believed she would be back.

Hours had passed as Catherine walked the streets of Newcastle, not knowing where her tantrum would lead her. As she wandered restlessly, fatigue set in. Strange men had begun approaching her. She did not know the time, but she figured it to be the early hours of the morning.

"Well lass, you're out late. Fancy a bit of company?" a tall thin man in a grubby brown coat asked her, his yellow teeth shining in the lamplight.

Catherine became frightened. Her English was terrible, but she could understand very well what the stranger wanted.

"No, no!" Catherine replied, as she rushed away.

An hour later, she was still walking the streets. She was exhausted, cold, and hungry. She yearned for some sleep. She realized that she had no choice but to go back to her father's house. No sooner had the thought crossed her mind than she heard a carriage slowly making its way toward her. As it approached, Catherine moved away from the street, closer to the buildings. She could only guess that this was another man craving her companionship for the night.

The carriage stopped in front of her, and the door slowly opened. As Catherine watched, a frail hand appeared, clutching a cane.

"Dear? Please come forward," a voice instructed from inside the carriage.

Catherine was frightened and miserable but noticed that the voice was that of an old woman. In her heart, she hoped that this may be a chance for her to befriend someone who would help her escape from her father.

"Madame?" she asked quizzically, moving closer to the carriage.

"Yes, come here, my dear," the old woman replied, as she beckoned to the young girl.

Catherine looked into the carriage and saw that the old woman was alone. She smiled at her politely and tried to communicate as best she could, but her English was limited. The old woman returned the smile and motioned for Catherine to edge nearer to her.

"Are you hungry?" the old woman asked.

Catherine nodded her head, as she moved closer to the carriage. "Please, madame, do you have work?" She struggled to find the right words.

"Ah, why yes, dear," the old woman replied graciously. "Please come with me, and I will give you work, shelter, and food."

Catherine was exhausted and felt she had no choice but to trust the old woman. She gave an appreciative curtsy and stepped up into the carriage. As she shut the door behind her, the wagon rode away into the night.

Angelique's vision turned black. She closed her eyes. Suddenly she heard the sounds of yet another argument ringing through her head. Angelique could see the old woman in front of Catherine, shaking her cane near her face. The old woman seemed very irritated with Catherine. Another woman stood alongside the old woman, sneering at Catherine.

"She doesn't understand!" the other woman scoffed, looking down at Catherine as if she were rubbish.

"I tend to agree, Miss Sterling, but she will learn or else," the old woman stared at Catherine in disgust.

Catherine became angry. She could not express herself as she wanted because of the language barrier, but she would not stand around and be treated like a dog.

"I will not take this from you two. I am human . . . No? Not a dog!" Catherine shouted, again struggling with the language.

The old woman took the handle of her cane and pointed it at Catherine's face. This enraged Catherine, and she slapped the cane away, mildly injuring the old woman's hand in the process.

"Show respect, you French tart!" Miss Sterling screeched, pointing her finger in Catherine's face. Catherine slapped it out of the way, which enraged Miss Sterling further. Meanwhile, the old woman had raised her cane again, and without warning, she hit Catherine across her right temple, cutting into her skin. The wound started to bleed profusely.

"Leave us!" the old woman bellowed, motioning for the other girls in the room to leave.

Catherine, weary but alert, looked at the old woman's arm where her blood had splattered. With her frail hand, the old woman took a finger from her other hand and rubbed the blood into her skin. She gave Catherine an evil smile. Suddenly, the old woman made a fist with her blood-splattered hand and hit Catherine in the same place that she had with the cane. Catherine passed out.

Angelique's vision again turned black. She saw nothing but felt the immense pain from Catherine's head injuries. A vision appeared to her again. This time Angelique knew who it was.

She saw Annabelle clearly. She was standing in front of Catherine. Catherine's weary eyes looked down at her own hands. Her wrists had been cut, and she had lost an enormous amount of blood. She felt weak. She looked up and saw Annabelle smiling down at her. One of her hands was soaked in Catherine's blood. Annabelle took the forefinger and gently stroked her lips. She then licked her finger, savoring the taste.

Still beaming, Annabelle said, "Dear, dear Catherine, so pretty you were. It's a shame really, but then again, the pain shall only last but mere seconds."

Annabelle's smile slowly turned into a sneer of unrivaled hatred. She raised her other hand and showed Catherine a large knife. Angelique could feel the fear in Catherine's heart, as Annabelle's cold stare turned to the knife. She held it to Catherine's neck and cut her throat.

"Avenge me!" Catherine's distant, ghostly voice could be heard at the exact time of the deathly vision.

Angelique's eyes bulged, and she felt an agonizing pain in her throat. She let out a terrified heave, as if she couldn't breathe. This stunned Evan and Monsieur Chevalier.

"Madame, are you alright?" Monsieur Chevalier asked, standing up from the table.

Angelique's head was spinning, but she finally stabilized herself against the table and tried to make sense of what had just happened. "Yes, yes, I'm fine," she said, putting her left hand over her eyes. "I believe the whiskey went down the wrong way."

Although the visions had seemed to last an hour or so, Angelique realized that in real time, it had only taken a few seconds to see what had happened to Catherine. It had shed new light on what Angelique was dealing with.

Evan looked at Angelique and the full shot glass of whiskey still sitting untouched in front of her. She was definitely in distress, and her hands trembled as if she were afraid. Evan silently slid the bottle over to her. Angelique picked the bottle up and first took a deep breath, followed by a swig of whiskey. She placed the bottle back on the table and took another deep breath.

"Okay then," she said staring blankly ahead, as if looking into nothingness.

"Are you sure you're alright, madam?" Evan asked, peering into her dark, glazed eyes.

"Yes, yes, I am. Thank you," Angelique replied, now recovering a little.

Monsieur Chevalier tenderly picked up the photograph, a smile appearing on his face as he looked at it. "You know, she looked very much like her mother. I did love her so," he said, stroking the photograph.

"Yes, she was," Angelique said, clearing her throat. "Were you two close? I'm sure it was hard spending all that time away from each other."

Oh yes, we were very close," Monsieur Chevalier replied, still gazing at the photograph. "Sure we had our differences, but in all, we were very close."

Evan listened to their conversation and watched Angelique's demeanor. There was something about her that was both mysterious and intriguing. Looking around her cabin, he noticed certain things that seemed out of place for a woman of French origin. There were symbols and trinkets that he hadn't seen since his early childhood. Symbols that could only be of Welsh origin. And of course, the Tarot cards sitting in plain sight near the cupboard.

"Madam, for how long did you live in England?" Evan asked, looking at a wood-carved charm hanging on the wall.

Angelique glanced at Evan, noticing his interest in her décor. "I lived there a few years. I have many good memories. My aunt still lives there."

"Wales?" he asked.

"No, she lives in Portsmouth," Angelique replied. "I had only been to Wales a few times before I moved here. My husband was from Cardiff."

"Ah . . . Your husband. So you live here alone with him?"

Angelique looked down at the table. "No, he has passed on."

"Oh, so sorry," Evan said, his voice taking on a sympathetic tone.

"You needn't be. It's been awhile," said Angelique, picking up the glass of whiskey in front of her and downing it.

"Well now, would it be possible to talk with the young girl?" Monsieur Chevalier asked, changing the flow of the conversation.

Angelique looked over at him and nodded, "I believe so. But be warned, henceforth you will find out things that could cause tremendous pain— and possibly death."

"I have travelled halfway around the world for answers and justice," he said, putting the photograph away in his pocket, "and I hope to get both at any cost."

"As you will, monsieur. As you will."

Angelique stood up from the table, quickly grabbed her cards and put them in her pocket. She also picked up the whiskey bottle, which had a small amount remaining, and took it outside for William. William, still among the horses, saw Angelique leave her cabin with Evan and

Monsieur Chevalier close behind. More importantly, he saw Angelique holding a bottle of whiskey. As she walked up to him, she handed him the bottle and said, "Here, may the gods reward you for being such an honorable gentleman. And may the French spare you, even though you are English."

With those words, she climbed onto Evan's horse and trotted toward the others. Evan mounted the spare horse and waited behind her while both Monsieur Chevalier and William got onto their horses. The four set off for Etienne's house.

Angelique knew that the horrific events that had taken place in England had not stopped there. They were ongoing. But what did the future hold for these people? She could not help but feel a fearful presence surrounding all who were involved in this story. The two ghostly words spoken in the vision haunted her. Was Catherine calling out to her? And what of her father? Unfortunately, these answers would soon be known.

CHAPTER 14

The four made their way down the path toward the Broussard house. Angelique and Evan's horse led the way just in case someone saw the strangers entering Etienne's tract. Evan, still intrigued by this woman, asked more questions as they rode.

"You seem to be a good judge of character," Evan observed. "Tell me, what are we getting ourselves into?"

"Why ask a question that you already know the answer to?" Angelique replied.

"Fair enough," he laughed, "but I am puzzled about this lady. The more we delve into this sick nightmare, the more questions I have."

"You seem more alert than the others," Angelique said with a faint grin. "That is a good trait. It will keep you alive."

"Oh, I do hope so," Evan responded amiably, "but my reasons for being here are to obtain justice and to keep my client alive in the process."

"Justice," Angelique paused, "or silence?"

Evan leaned sideways to get a look at Angelique's expression. He was confused. He did not have a clue what she meant. "Pardon?"

"If you remember anything from today," Angelique lowered her voice so that the others couldn't hear, "remember this: in the next few days you will learn many things, both good and bad. Trust only that which comes from within, for this shroud of darkness covers more than you know, more than any of us can see or comprehend. Trust no one."

Evan kept turning Angelique's words over in his mind. He knew that she was aware of more than she was telling him, but in time, he would hopefully make sense of them.

As the horses trotted down the path, they came to a huge garden where Sophie was standing. She normally would have had a hoe in hand, but since hearing the horses, she had picked up a shotgun and was pointing it squarely at the new arrivals. Angelique waved at her to let her know that all was well. Seeing Angelique, Sophie lowered the shotgun and put it in the basket near her feet. She then picked up the basket and began walking toward the house.

Sophie wasn't the only one watching their arrival. Katy had just brought a basket from the garden and was on the porch with Wes when they noticed the horses. Wes immediately picked up his revolver and waited in readiness. Katy also grabbed a shotgun from the porch and ran to the bottom of the steps. When they saw Angelique waving, calm and in control, they lowered their guns and met the arriving group in front of the house.

"All is fine," Angelique said. "I believe these men are here to help. They are also looking for the English devil."

Angelique and the three men had dismounted and gathered in front of the porch. Katy's eyes were glued to Monsieur Chevalier. She felt that she had seen him before but did not know where. Angelique introduced the men to Sophie, Wes, and Katy.

"Afternoon, sirs," Sophie greeted, as she stuck her hand out to the closest one.

"Afternoon, madam," Evan replied, tipping his hat and shaking her hand.

Once greetings had been exchanged, Sophie guided everyone onto the porch and invited them to sit down. In her mind, being seated was far more comfortable than standing in the pathway or at least that was what her back was telling her.

Aside from greeting the newcomers, Wes mainly stayed silent. He did notice the accents though, especially the English ones. Despite his normally passive, likable demeanor, the sound of an English accent— other than Katy's—made him think back to his past employer, and this made his stomach churn.

"So, monsieur," Sophie said, "what brings you here, half way across the world?"

Monsieur Chevalier looked around the group, his eyes finally settling on Katy. "Justice, madame," he replied, still watching Katy, "justice for the murder of my daughter."

Katy noticed Monsieur Chevalier looking at her. She still had a strong feeling that she had seen him before. A bit unnerved by being stared at, she walked over to Wes and sat beside him, placing her hand on his.

"So, this must be Katy," Monsieur Chevalier asked, looking straight at her. "You knew my daughter, no?" A smile warmed his face.

Angelique looked momentarily confused, an expression noticed only by Evan, who kept quiet.

Katy, not expecting the question, was caught off guard. "Yes . . . yes, sir, I believe I did. Her name was Catherine? Yes?" she stuttered.

"Yes," Monsieur Chevalier acknowledged, his face becoming solemn.

"I did for a short time. A very beautiful girl," Katy said awkwardly.

Just then, they heard the sound of horses trotting down the path toward them. Etienne and Thomas were returning from a day of hunting. Their return broke the discomfort that Katy was feeling, and she began to smile and point toward them. "Look, Frenchy is back from the hunt. I'll prepare the pots." She quickly scurried to the kitchen.

Angelique, watching Katy, was bemused by the scene, but she dared not say anything to offend Monsieur Chevalier. To her, this all seemed wrong. Nothing was making any sense, but rather, becoming more confusing. Hopefully she would find out the link between Catherine and Katy.

Etienne and Thomas, seeing the horses and the three men, rode up to the porch and dismounted. Sophie stood up from her chair and met them at the base of the porch. As she walked up to Etienne, she winked at him playfully, just to put him at ease about the unscheduled visitors.

"What you got for me, love?" Sophie smiled, as she took a sack from him.

"Looks like we eatin' duck tonight," Etienne replied, returning her smile but still curious about the visitors.

"Ah, that's good since we have visitors," she said, as they both walked up the porch.

Monsieur Chevalier, Evan, and William stood up and greeted Etienne and Thomas. The mood was cordial, and both William and Evan were on their best behavior. Evan was still feeling uncomfortable around these strangers and definitely did not want to make waves. William followed his lead, as he always did.

With the introductions out of the way, everyone sat down and chatted. All except Katy, who had appeared again when the men were greeting each other. She took the ducks from Sophie and immediately headed to the kitchen. Angelique sensed her nervousness, so she also slipped away to see what was the matter. Sophie, who would normally be preparing the ducks for dinner, was ecstatic to have Katy helping out. Noticing her uneasiness around Monsieur Chevalier though, she knew Katy was not just being her usual helpful self.

Katy took the ducks and began to clean them outside the kitchen. She prepared them swiftly, as if she had done this countless times before, but to her credit, her job had never been to prepare the meals. Angelique walked up to her and watched as she worked vigorously .

"You know, you're going to make someone a very good wife one day," Angelique told her, admiring her efforts.

Katy lowered her head and blushed at Angelique's comment. "Maybe. One day," she said with an innocent glow on her face.

"I'm sure you will," Angelique smiled at her. "You've taken very good care of Wesley, and I've seen the way he looks at you. You make a good match. He will be a fine husband for you."

Katy smiled, still blushing at Angelique's words. In her heart she felt, hoped and dreamed that those words would come to pass, and she and Wes would be able to start a new life without all the problems currently plaguing them.

"I would one day hope to fine peace with him, away from this nightmare," Katy replied.

"Isn't fate cruel? For without the nightmare, you would never have met. Love has arisen from the depths of tragedy. Your life will, for the first time, become normal, and all the bad will be washed away. I promise you this."

"I pray for normalcy," Katy said hopefully. "Away from all this. I understand the pain life brings, but I wish to have comfort in knowing that I am not alone."

Angelique smiled at Katy, walked up to her and gave her a hug. "By the gods, you shall never be alone, dear Katy. They are looking after you. You shall have the life that you wish for."

"I hope so. I really, really hope so," Katy replied tearing up slightly but still concentrating on the chore at hand.

Angelique stood beside her and helped clean the ducks. She knew it would not be long before the others would ask for Katy to see what she knew about Annabelle. Angelique had heard the story before from Katy, but she felt that there could be more to it than she was telling.

"So, you know they will be coming for you shortly?" Angelique said, knowing full well that Katy dreaded it.

"I know, but I don't know what I can add," Katy replied.

"How well did you know Catherine?" Angelique asked.

"Not well really," Katy said, thinking back, "I befriended her since the other girls didn't really get along with her. She was a bit cross with everyone, but I never had problems with her."

As Katy thought back, she kept seeing Catherine's father. "It is odd, but I feel that I have seen Monsieur Chevalier before. I do not know where, but his face is so familiar."

Angelique had felt something in Katy's reaction to Monsieur Chevalier when he was speaking to her. At the time, she had interpreted Katy's reaction as a return to the bad memories from her past, but this seemed not to be the case.

"What is your sense of him?" she asked Katy, already knowing the answer.

Katy stopped cleaning and looked into Angelique's eyes, confused. "I feel nothing; almost the same as Lady Annabelle. Yes, Catherine had her problems, but I believe they were more than I could fathom. She was just a troubled lass."

"Yes, not deserving the punishment of her fate but trouble all the same," Angelique nodded her head in agreement.

Katy stood speechless and perplexed, thinking back to the time she had spent with Catherine. Despite trying as hard as she could, she remembered little of their conversations or any other connection between them. Catherine was always alone, and when spoken to, she was distant and unfriendly. Seeing the way she was treated by the other girls, and especially Miss Sterling, Katy had thought Catherine had the right to act the way she did.

Sophie trotted out the back door to check on the progress of, as she put it, "her two helpers," but mostly Katy, since the visitors had been asking about her. Sophie had seen Katy's nervousness earlier, and she felt it best to let her get her composure back before she was put on a witness stand.

"Well?" Sophie grinned, as she saw Angelique and Katy's hands covered in blood and feathers.

"It's coming, dear friend." Angelique raised her eyebrows at Sophie in mock surprise. "Perfection takes time."

"Yes, and I believe this girl's got it down pat," said Sophie, looking at Katy's work.

"My, are you sure you haven't done this before?" Angelique praised her.

"No, my lady. I have never," Katy replied.

"Well then, this is gonna be good for our visitors and us," Sophie said, "but I think I got it from here. Gitane, they askin' for you and her. I tried to stall them, but they're persistent."

Angelique nodded to Sophie and picked up a bucket of fresh water and some soap to clean her and Katy's hands. "Okay, we will be there. Tell them we are coming."

"Okay I will, but I'm first gonna make sure my friend knows she is protected and safe here," Sophie said, as she hugged Katy. "You are now part of our family, little one. Do not be afraid of anything anymore. We are here for you, you understand?"

Katy tried to hug her back as best she could, but her hands were still covered in blood, guts, and feathers. She had begun to tear up upon hearing Sophie's kind and positive words. In her heart, she had never felt as loved as she did with Sophie and Angelique.

"There are no words to express just how much special you make me feel," Katy mumbled, her voice began to break up slightly.

Angelique chuckled, "And you are special; special to us, without a doubt. Now come on and let us find out what these men have to say. It's time we find out just what we are in the midst of."

After Katy had washed the blood from her hands, she walked in through the backdoor of the house with Angelique by her side. Although she was nervous, Katy felt thankful not to be alone in this turmoil. Angelique had been a great blessing in her life, which made her more confident to take on what seemed to be endless challenges, such as the one facing her now.

As Angelique and Katy entered the living room, they could both feel the calm anticipation of the three visitors seated on the couch. Katy again greeted the three and curtsied, extending her hand to Monsieur Chevalier. The Monsieur reached out and touched Katy's hand.

With the touch of hands, Katy suddenly became dizzy and aware of a vision, just as Angelique had done earlier with the photo: a vision of the elder Lady Falsworth ranting uncontrollably inside her study with someone who was not known to Katy. Katy had been doing the washing earlier that morning and had not seen the visitor arrive.

"What do you mean, you incestuous, marauding beast. I pay you good money for your goods and services, and this is how you treat your kind!" Katy heard Lady Falsworth yelling at the top of her lungs.

"Madame, I beg of you," another voice was heard in the heated discussion, although it seemed a bit calmer. "I apologize greatly, but as I said before, we can no longer deliver what you ask. The police are asking questions, and I will not be a part of it."

"Really?" Lady Falsworth replied in a lower tone but with all the spite of a venomous snake. "Well, you are already a part of it. I suggest you think again if you want to continue your services here in the north. I will not tolerate this. You know as well as I that the police have no hold over me.

I own them, as well as your competition."

"These are all grand words coming from you, but the fact is they're still watching me. I'll need more money to do your bidding."

"Ah, so, we find the basis of the problem. You greedy bastard. Do not cross me."

The man began to laugh at her attempt to intimidate him. "You do not frighten me with your little threats, madame. I have dealt with others more dangerous than you—with great success, I might add. The price is now double if you want your shipments to continue."

Lady Falsworth, hearing the self-assurance in his voice, calmed herself and stared blankly into his eyes. "Double is it?" she asked softly, with a slight confidence of her own.

"Yes, madame. I will take no less," the man replied smugly.

Lady Falsworth lay back in her chair and cupped her hands as if in thought. She was silent for a moment, then asked quietly, "So how is your daughter? Making any headway?"

The man became confused at her questions. "Pardon?"

"I'm sure it is very hard to raise a child alone with no mother to care for her," Lady Falsworth said, her face taking on a slightly wicked expression.

"What do you mean? What are you saying?" The man sounded confused.

"Oh nothing, I am just thinking how quickly life changes. One moment you're on top of the world, the next, you're cannon fodder." Lady Falsworth looked directly into the man's eyes. "Take your prices and your goods and leave me, but heed my warning: your life and that of those around you are a house of cards. You cross me, and I promise you, you will pay."

Lady Falsworth slammed her cane on her desk, making a terrible noise. The man, now infuriated, stood up from his chair and walked to the door. He opened the door forcefully but looked back at Lady Falsworth in anger.

"I bid you a good day, madame," he said, as he walked hurriedly out the door, almost stumbling over Katy. She was outside the door, eavesdropping on them.

"Oh, I'll have my day. I guarantee it, monsieur." Lady Falsworth was heard laughing.

The man stormed out of the house, pushing Katy out of the way.

With the touch of their hands, Katy now knew where she had seen Monsieur Chevalier. He had been the man in Lady Falsworth's study a month before Catherine had shown up. The vision frightened Katy tremendously, but she dared not show her fear to anyone. Katy had grown weary of these episodes in her life, but it was inevitable that this needed to be finished. And finish it would.

Katy removed her hand from the smiling Frenchman. Her head was still dizzy from the vision, but she managed to retrieve a weak smile for the man. Monsieur Chevalier noticed her hand had been clammy and shook slightly.

"Are you alright, madame?" he asked with concern in his voice.

"Oh yes, sir. I am very well and pleased to make your acquaintance," she replied, producing a bigger smile.

"And to you, dear, I have a lot of questions if you don't mind?"

"No, I do not mind at all, sir."

"Excellent. Then let us sit."

156

Katy sat next to Wes, again placing her hand on his, as if drawing the strength to help make it through this session. Wes noticed her hidden tension and gently took her hand and held it in his. He knew Katy was strong-willed and had endured much over the past few weeks. He knew the pressure was taking its toll on her, and he understood why. All he had to do was look back to his first meeting with Katy, which had nearly had a deadly outcome for him. A young girl of nearly 16 should not have to endure this.

"So Katy, I am trying to find out where Lady Falsworth may be," Monsieur Chevalier said, "as I believe she holds the key to my daughter's murder. Any information you can give me would be a blessing."

Again, Katy looked confused. She knew nothing of the whereabouts of Lady Falsworth. "I regret that I don't know anything, sir. The last time I saw Lady Falsworth was the same night your daughter disappeared."

"Can you tell me about it?" Monsieur Chevalier asked.

Katy was a bit hesitant to bring up old wounds but thought back to that night and told the men what she remembered of her final moments with Catherine.

"I remember being in the room with Lady Falsworth, Miss Sterling, and six other maids. Miss Sterling was giving us our list of chores for the next day. Catherine was next to me, a bit cross at being chastised by Miss Sterling. To the point that her temper regrettably took over . . ."

"Tell me if you can, French tart? What is wrong with you? They do not teach you to clean in France?" Miss Sterling scowled.

Catherine peered at the old woman as if ready to strike her. Even though her English was bad, she could still work out that insults were being slung her way. She just looked at the old woman silently but with a look of disgust on her face.

"She doesn't understand!" the other woman scoffed, looking down at Catherine as if she were rubbish.

"I tend to agree, Miss Sterling, but she will learn or else," the old woman stared at Catherine in disgust.

Catherine became angry. She could not express herself as she wanted because of the language barrier, but she would not stand around and be treated like a dog.

"I will not take this from you two. I am human . . . No? Not a dog!" Catherine shouted, again struggling with the language.

"Lady Falsworth took her cane and thrust it in Catherine's face," Katy explained. "Catherine knocked the cane away from her face, and I believe, injured Lady Falsworth's hand."

"Show respect, you French tart!" Miss Sterling screeched, pointing her finger in Catherine's face. Catherine slapped it out of the way, which enraged Miss Sterling further. Meanwhile, the old woman had raised her cane again, and without warning, she hit Catherine across her right temple, cutting into her skin. The wound started to bleed profusely.

"Lady Falsworth then told us to leave the room. I never saw them again," Katy said matter-of-factly.

"You said there were six others in the room as well. Who were they?" Evan asked.

"There were six maids," Katy replied.

"Are they still with her?" Evan delved deeper.

"I believe there are a few left." Katy lowered her head.

"What happened to them? Do you know?"

"Three passed on during the journey here. They were struck with illness and never recovered. Alice passed on the night I fled the plantation. I believe Sara and Brigit are still well."

Katy's eyes watered as she thought back to the night she ran from the plantation. Evan, seeing this, halted his questions and gave her a courteous smile. Wes, still holding her hand, put his arm around her. He knew that was a night that had unnerved both of them.

"I regret, monsieur, that this is all I know," Katy said, hoping that the information would suffice.

"Thank you, dear Katy," Monsieur Chevalier replied. "I know this is hard for you, but I am in need of any knowledge about the people who took my daughter from me."

"I understand, but this is all I have. I hope it helps you," Katy said.

"One last question. Do you know where Lady Annabelle is going? Why she is here?" Evan prodded one last time.

"I do know she wanted to start over. Raise cattle or something. I do remember hearing Miss Sterling and Lady Annabelle talking about buying land in Texas, but I do not know where."

As the night drew on, the conversation became more relaxed, with the subject matter turning light and cordial. After everyone had enjoyed a delicious dinner of duck and side dishes, the three visitors stood up and headed to the porch to leave. Etienne, Sophie, and Angelique followed them onto the porch to say their goodbyes.

"Are you sure you don't want to camp out here for the night," Etienne asked, as it was dark.

"Oh no, but thank you all the same," Monsieur Chevalier replied, mounting his horse. "I believe we need to camp closer to Beaumont. We have a long day ahead of us."

"He's right," Evan added, also getting on his horse. "But thank you very much for the food and the information."

Minutes later, the three rode off into the night, heading north toward Beaumont. Evan's plan was to camp out just north of Grigsby's Bluff and head into Beaumont early the next morning. As they rode, Evan thought back to all that had been said that evening. With all the information they had received from Katy, his mind still returned to Angelique's words. Does she know something I don't, he thought. Was she trying to warn me, or was it just a scare tactic?

To Evan, she seemed trustworthy, something which he rarely felt of anyone. He would heed her warnings and keep them close, along with his revolver.

CHAPTER 15

As the steamboat sailed eastward toward Sabine, Annabelle walked along the upper deck, gazing out at the waves. Agatha was below deck tending to Brigit, along with Hana, Sara, and the rest of the maids. Annabelle welcomed the strong, steady southeast wind that had taken over from the colder northerly winds of the previous few days. She detested the English weather with its cold and rainy conditions and definitely preferred the Texas climate.

Sara walked onto the deck in search of Annabelle. Brigit wasn't doing well, and Miss Sterling had sent her to inform Annabelle. As Sara turned the corner, she saw Annabelle leaning against the rail, silent, as if deep in thought.

"My Lady," Sara said softly, "It's Brigit. She is not faring well."

Annabelle turned to Sara and smiled. "Tell me, Sara, do you remember what I told you when we left Galveston?"

"Yes, my Lady. You said she would be alright."

"Go back to Brigit and see that she is awake. Tell Miss Sterling that I have requested her company."

Sara's sadness immediately turned brighter, and her face filled with happiness. "Thank you, my Lady. Thank you," she said, as she hurried back to Brigit.

Annabelle looked on with amusement. Sara was Annabelle's prized possession, never faltering nor swaying in her obedience to her mistress. Annabelle knew Sara cared deeply for Brigit and had lost many friends over the last few months. However, even with the losses, Sara had stayed true and loyal to her.

Sara ran down the steps to where Brigit lay, her heart pounding in anticipation of her friend's recovery. As she entered the room, she saw Brigit awake and coughing. She was weak but alert all the same. In Sara's mind, her recovery could only be thanks to Lady Annabelle. She was clueless as to how she could have made Brigit better, but to Sara that was unimportant.

Sara stood near Brigit's cot with a glowing smile and a sense of euphoria that eventually spread to the other maids. The last few months of illness and death had taken its toll on their young hearts. Some had all but given up hope of surviving these mysterious illnesses, but for now at least, there was a glimmer of hope.

"My lady," Sara directed her address to Miss Sterling, "Lady Annabelle wishes to see you on the deck."

Agatha, looking a bit irritable, replied, "Oh goody. Okay, ladies, I shall return in a bit. Please take care of Brigit."

"We shall, my lady, we shall," replied Sara, still giddy with happiness.

Agatha walked out of the room and to the stairs that took her up to the deck. The cool wind was a blessing to her, far better than the uncomfortable heat down below. As she walked up to Annabelle, she noticed her staring out into the Gulf, lost in what appeared to be profound thought.

"So how is our dear sweet Brigit?" Annabelle asked, her eyes still glued to the waves.

"Far better I suspect," Agatha replied.

"And so she should be," Annabelle added.

"Well you definitely have an ally in Sara. She worships the ground you walk on."

Annabelle stood silent for a moment, then with her own usual mischievous grin, she replied, "And so she should."

Agatha stared at Annabelle with a look of agitation, "You did call, your worship?" she asked, almost mockingly.

"But of course." Annabelle looked back at her. "Something is wrong. Something is dreadfully wrong. I can feel it."

Agatha's mood turned to one of concern. "What do you mean? Wrong?"

"My senses tell me something is imminent. I do believe we will have a visitor soon," Annabelle stated, her face motionless.

"The gypsy?" Agatha replied, her mind turning over the possible candidates that Annabelle may be referring to.

"Oh no. The harlot knows not to meet me at my strength. She is smarter than that."

"Well then, who?"

"I can't tell yet, but I do have a plan."

Annabelle looked around the deck for signs of prying ears but saw no one. The chance of anyone hearing their conversation from afar was slim since the noise of the steam engine filled the deck. All the same, she moved closer to Agatha and began to explain her plans for the following day.

"We will arrive in Sabine a little before daybreak. Mr. Drayson will meet us there with the carriages. After loading my things onto the carriages, we will set off toward Beaumont. It is there that I will take a separate carriage along with three hands."

"So you will take one of the carriages loaded with . . .?" Agatha asked, confused about the reason she would split the caravan.

". . . Our precious cargo, of course. It is our lifeline, and we must protect it at all costs," Annabelle replied confidently. "I'll take this along with a few other things and bury them in what I deem to be a safe place."

"But . . ." Agatha began to speak but was silenced by Annabelle.

"Fear not. I have never steered you wrong, have I?"

"No, but I feel your confidence could be your downfall," Agatha muttered.

Annabelle laughed as she turned to face the Gulf and the waves again. "In as many years as you've known me, has it ever?"

Agatha remained silent and retreated back below the deck to check on Brigit and the maids. She had confidence in Annabelle, but her way of doing things hampered Agatha's unconditional faith. She was not like Sara.

Annabelle continued to stare out into the enchantment of the waves. For the first time, there was concern in her mind, concern about an oncoming storm over which she had little to no control. Again, time would tell.

Hours passed, and the steamer finally docked in Sabine. As requested, Ben, the three carriages, and a crew of 11 were waiting for them. Instead of making a dangerous midnight trip, Ben had seen fit to make the journey earlier the previous evening—during the daylight hours—to reduce the possibility of unnecessary risks.

After the steamer was secured, Annabelle walked onto the docks where Ben was waiting for her. She was dressed in her riding clothes, a far cry from the gowns and perfume she had worn over the past few days. As she walked up to Ben, he could tell, even in the torch-lit darkness, that she was different. From the shadows, he could see that her face was fatigued and weary, as if she had the world on her shoulders.

"Good mornin', ma'am," Ben said, as he tipped his hat to her.

"Ah, well I see you made it, Mr. Drayson. Impressive. It's not often in this part of the world that someone actually does what they're supposed to do."

Ben gave a weak smile, but he did notice the obvious lack of warmth in her voice. He quickly changed his demeanor. "Yes, ma'am," he replied. "I figured you'd want to head out first thing, so we traveled yesterday evening."

"Excellent, Mr. Drayson. Now let's tend to the loading of my things."

With 11 men plus Ben in the caravan, loading the wagons took very little time to complete—especially with Annabelle standing out front barking orders in the same way that a drill sergeant would to his new recruits. Finally, as the last of the luggage and crates were loaded, Agatha disembarked with the maids.

Annabelle glanced at the maids walking down from the docks toward the wagons. They all looked tired from being up most of the night either looking after or worrying about Brigit. Brigit, on the other hand, was up and walking, though with help from Sara and Hana, but walking all the same. As they made their way, one by one, into the carriages under the steady gaze of Miss Sterling, they would have agreed unanimously that finding a new residence would be absolutely wonderful, just for the fact that the traveling would end.

Annabelle looked over the maids and the caravan as a queen over her subjects and then mounted her horse. The sun had begun to peek over the water and provided a beautiful panorama to the weary travelers. With everything now in place, the caravan headed north to Beaumont.

Hours passed as early morning turned to late morning. The caravan made good time and reached Beaumont before noon. As they stopped for a moment at the crossroads to turn east to the plantation, Annabelle decided it would be a good time to give them her new orders.

"Gentleman," Annabelle said loudly so all could hear, "listen closely.

We have a change in plans."

Ben found the change of plans a bit odd and dangerous, but it was her decision and her money.

"The caravan shall head back east as scheduled, under the guidance of Mr. Drayson, but with one less wagon. I, along with three hands and a horse, will travel north."

Ben did not like what he was hearing and, with due consideration to both her welfare and his paycheck, decided to speak out. "Ma'am? Pardon me, but it is not safe."

Annabelle looked at Ben as if she were almost looking through his soul. This made him uneasy, and silenced him. "As I was saying, Mr. Handle, Mr. Bedford, and Mr. Feldman will accompany me on my journey. I will return in a few days. The rest of you, please protect my dear girls from harm. Miss Sterling shall act as the mistress in my absence."

Ben's head became cluttered with a thousand different scenarios of what could go wrong, but he knew Lady Annabelle would not listen to him—or anyone else for that matter. He would have to just hope everything would go well or that at least Miss Sterling had the resources to pay him.

Annabelle dismounted and stepped into the wagon, and Mr. Feldman got on her horse. Both Mr. Handle and Mr. Bedford stayed on top of the wagon that they had been riding since Sabine. After feeding the horses and taking a brief respite, the four headed north while the rest of the caravan headed east.

As the afternoon progressed, the caravan finally arrived at the ferry along the Neches River. After waiting an hour or so, the carriages and the horses ferried across the river then headed straight to the plantation.

Ben, with Ezra on the horse next to him, rode in the front of the caravan. Ezra, still nervous of what had happened a few nights earlier, didn't relish taking this job. He felt everything about Lady Falsworth was evil, and he didn't want any part of it. But, alas, jobs were scarce, and he needed the money.

"Mister Ben," Ezra said, as he rode steadily alongside Ben, "I know it's not proper to talk about friends and business partners of the boss, but I still don't know about this."

Ben immediately became irritated. "Shut up, Ezra. I don't care what your lady friend says. If you don't like workin' here then there are always the sugarcane fields back in Louisiana."

Just the mention of the sugarcane fields brought Ezra's to a standstill. In his heart, he was a rancher, not a farmer of any kind, and he had hated the early years of his life, which were spent in south Louisiana harvesting sugarcane. He felt the best thing that ever happened to him was finding this job. Although normally he would be out tending cows, since Lady Falsworth had shown up, he had been obliged to do her bidding along with the rest of the staff at the plantation.

"I hear ya, mister Ben. I hear ya," Ezra said, as he dropped back to riding along the side of the carriage.

The caravan finally reached the plantation that afternoon to the sheer euphoria of the maids and Miss Sterling. Finally, there would be soft beds for them to sleep on—tonight and in the future. Or so they thought. Brigit, though still weak, seemed to have recovered swiftly. She even attempted to help with the luggage, but unfortunately, it proved to be too much for her.

* * *

While the caravan was safe and sound back at the plantation, Annabelle and the three others rode north into the wooded area. Tall pine trees now replaced the grasslands that they had come to know. The flat terrain gave way to hilly areas in between the burrows, thickets, and hollers, which splattered the landscape. Annabelle looked out of her wagon window, and the transition made her feel that she was back in Central England. The forest became thicker and thicker until the brush was so dense that it had drowned the light from the overhead sun.

As Annabelle sat silently looking out at the continuous blockade of vegetation alongside the carriage, she began listening to the sporadic conversations between Mr. Handle and Mr. Bedford. Both knew this area quite well and had herded cattle through Southeast Texas many times before.

"With all the birds around here, I don't hear any of them," Mr. Handle pointed out.

"Well, guess they afraid to wake up the ghosts," Mr. Bedford chuckled. "Damn, the growth here is thick. I wonder if we're gonna have to stay here tonight?"

"I hope not. I believe these woods don't take kindly to strangers," Mr. Handle responded. "I would sleep with one eye open, if at all."

Annabelle listened for a few more minutes until the thick brush finally gave way to a clearing. She immediately shouted for the wagon to halt. Mr. Handle swiftly pulled up the reins to stop the horses, then watched as Annabelle stepped out of the wagon and walked to the front. Not knowing her next move, all three men kept their eyes steadily on Annabelle.

"It is here," Annabelle said, pointing to the clearing. "Mr. Feldman and Mr. Bedford, do dismount and take a shovel from the carriage."

Both did as she requested, then walked beside her. Still surveying the landscape, Annabelle pointed directly to where she wanted a hole dug. With haste and precision, both men began to dig.

All three of the men knew about these woods and did not want to spend the night in this dark and dreary place. Mr. Bedford and Mr. Feldman dug vigorously into the earth. Four-by-four-by-six were the dimensions Annabelle barked out, as she supervised their progress.

"The same depth as a grave," she remarked, with her devilish grin. "Hurry, night is close at hand, and we need to leave."

An hour passed before the hole was complete. The men were exhausted from the constant digging but felt new energy with the knowledge that they would soon be leaving this ungodly place. As Mr. Feldman and Mr. Handle removed a chest from the wagon and carried it to the edge of the hole, Annabelle gave orders to put it into the hole. After lowering the chest, they removed another from the carriage and repeated their actions. With both chests at the bottom of the hole, Annabelle ordered the men to refill the hole with soil. With all three men burying the chests, it did not take long to finish the task.

The sun had now all but set on the four travelers. Annabelle had brought out a few lanterns from inside the wagon to help light the area while the men worked. With the chests safely buried under six feet of earth, the men loaded the shovels onto the wagon and prepared to leave.

Mr. Handle and Mr. Bedford climbed aboard the wagon but smelled the strong stench of kerosene. Annabelle, seeing their concern, remarked that when filling the lanterns, she had spilled some inside the carriage. The men paid no mind and prepared to leave. Mr. Feldman walked to his horse but was met by Annabelle.

"I'm dreadfully sorry, but would you be a dear and ride in the wagon for me?" she asked in the most charming voice. "I have spilled a bit of this awful oil, and I don't think I could handle the smell."

Mr. Feldman looked at her blankly, trying to keep from shaking his head in despair. In his thoughts, she was just a woman, plain and simple. But if it would help her nose for him to ride in luxury, then so be it.

"Sure, ma'am," he said with a faint smile, "I'd be glad to."

Mr. Feldman walked over to the wagon and grasped the door. He smelled the strong odor of kerosene but stepped up and entered the wagon anyway. Once inside the wagon, he noticed that the spill didn't just cover a small area. Someone had deliberately poured a can of kerosene throughout the inside of the wagon. Mr. Feldman became nervous and unsure about what was going on. As he turned around to exit the wagon, a shot rang out, and a bullet entered his chest. As he looked out, he saw Annabelle pointing a revolver at the top of the wagon. Then he saw her pull the trigger two more times.

Annabelle, now on the horse, a revolver in one hand and a lantern in the other, trotted next to the open door of the wagon. Mr. Feldman lay bleeding inside the wagon and could not get up. The others, Mr. Handle and Mr. Bedford, lay on top of the wagon. They were dead, each with a bullet in the head. As Annabelle looked at the dying man inside the wagon, her devilish grin appeared yet again. Now, like a cat tired of playing with a dying mouse, Annabelle threw the lantern into the wagon, shattering the glass and igniting the kerosene. This spooked the horses, and they began to run, galloping through the darkened forest toward the north.

Annabelle sat on her horse and watched the burning wagon disappear into the night. As elated as she felt, she couldn't help but feel a presence waiting for her. Even with her concern, she knew that the partial contents of her fortune and a few other relics were safe, buried with no witnesses. Now alone in the darkness, Annabelle headed south, down the path and back to Beaumont.

CHAPTER 16

Annabelle sat near a stream holding the reins of the horse. She had ridden all night and arrived at the road leading to Grigsby's Bluff just as the sun began to rise. While riding, her thoughts had turned to Katy and how she would get her back. At the very least, Annabelle would try to find out in advance just what and who she would be dealing with when the time came.

After the colt had finished drinking from the stream, Annabelle got on the horse and rode south toward Grigsby's Bluff. And Katy.

* * *

Just yards from where Annabelle had stopped to let the horse drink, three men slept soundly. The day before had been without incident for Evan, William, and Monsieur Chevalier, and they had not yet ascertained the whereabouts of Lady Annabelle Falsworth. Most of the day had been spent talking to people living near Beaumont, but they had not gathered any new information. Evan had therefore thought it best to return to Grigsby's Bluff in the morning to talk with Angelique again. They were blissfully unaware that Annabelle had quietly ridden past.

* * *

Annabelle wasn't the only person up at dawn. Angelique was walking in Sophie's garden, gathering what was left of the fall vegetables, while Sophie and Katy did some washing near the house. Perhaps it was the changing weather or just the excitement of the past week, but something had Angelique feeling down. Such feelings were normal for her, but they seemed to have been coming more frequently in recent years.

Katy, scrubbing clothes, looked over at Angelique. She had noticed that Angelique was distancing herself from the rest of the group, and Katy was worried.

"Is it me, or is something wrong with Angelique?" Katy asked Sophie with great concern.

Sophie glanced at Angelique then back at Katy. "She's alright. It's just her anniversary coming up, and it gets her down." Sophie paused for a moment then continued, "There's a lot of hurt there. I do what I can to help, but it's best to let it take its course. She'll be alright."

"I do hope so," Katy replied as she continued scrubbing.

As the morning wore on, Angelique finished in the garden and headed to the porch while Sophie and Katy finished the washing. The fresh morning air seemed to have done Angelique some good. Her silent walk through the garden had left her mind clearer and more at ease. Though totally not over her depression, Angelique did feel better and even managed to give the others a quick smile.

"Well, we've accomplished much today," Angelique said, walking onto the porch.

Sophie smiled at Angelique with glee, "Oh dear neighbor, what would I ever do without you?"

"Probably be out doing all this yourself," Angelique replied lightheartedly, regaining a bit of her playfulness. "But maybe not a good idea in your condition?"

Despite the fact that Sophie's pregnancy was still in its early stages, Angelique couldn't help but make joking references to it. But that was only when the newly present symptoms of morning sickness weren't visible. Sophie was elated to finally be with child. It was a dream that was finally coming true.

"Hey, I'm not helpless or contagious. I will be fine out in the fields."

Angelique paused for moment. "Oh! I am glad you are not contagious, dear friend."

Katy began to laugh aloud, which now made Angelique join in. Sophie, thinking back to what she had said, began to shake her head and laugh until she was nearly in tears.

The three women continued chatting on the porch for a portion of the morning until Sophie noticed the time. Etienne had gone hunting before daybreak and would be home soon. She needed to hang the laundry before his arrival so that it would not interfere with her cooking.

"Don't worry. I'll help you, again . . . dear friend," Angelique said, walking toward the house.

"As I will as well," Katy added. "I believe Wesley is still asleep and resting, so I can help as needed."

With all three hanging the laundry, the task was complete within minutes. It was only then that Angelique remembered that the full basket of vegetables had been left close to the front of the garden near the entrance to the Broussard's land.

"Oh!" Angelique exclaimed, "I forgot the basket."

Katy was eager to offer her help. "Don't worry. I'll go get it."

"Are you sure?" Angelique asked.

"Sure, I'll be right back."

Katy took off down the path to the edge of the garden until she came upon the basket near the entryway. Tired from the morning's chores, she knelt near the basket to collect herself before returning. As Katy gave a sigh of relief, she heard a noise coming from the nearby trees, which startled her. It sounded like a horse whinnying, but she had not heard anyone ride up. With curiosity getting the better of her, Katy stood up and walked slowly to the entryway to get a better look. She stared into the tree grove but saw nothing. Once again, Katy heard the horse, but this time she could hear it walking amongst the grove. Katy began to feel nervous.

"Hello?" Katy called out. "Frenchy? Is that you?" There was no answer. Katy's knees began to shake in fear. "Hello? Is there anyone out there?"

Katy felt an urgency to start back to the house. She turned around slowly, still looking into the grove, but a sound from the other direction caught her attention. It sounded as if someone was walking on dried leaves. Katy quickly turned her head in time to see the shape of a person standing behind some trees.

"Who are you?" Katy shouted in fear, but there was no answer.

As Katy turned around to run back to the house, she stepped in a hole in the middle of the path. She immediately fell to the ground in pain, feeling her ankle twist. Overcoming the sheer agony, Katy struggled to get up and head back to the house, but she could not. She turned her head back in the direction of the trees. She trembled as she saw a shape of a human, hooded, walk out from behind the trees toward her.

"Who are you?" Katy yelled.

As Katy lay on the ground in fear and pain, she could hear the sound of a snicker from the hooded person.

"Hello, dear Katy," the voice from the hooded person said, "dear, sweet Katy."

"No!" Katy shrieked as she saw who was heading toward her.

As Annabelle removed the hood from her head, Katy saw a big smile on her face. "Oh dear, dear, sweet Katy. Who will stop me now?"

Katy attempted yet again to stand up and run toward the house, but her ankle was causing her too much pain, and she fell back to the ground. Annabelle walked over to where Katy was lying on the ground. She stood over her and grabbed her hair tightly.

"No!" Katy screamed in horror. "I will not go with you! I will never go with you!"

"Oh, you will indeed," Annabelle replied as she swung her hand out and hit Katy hard on her temple, stunning her.

Annabelle grasped her hair tighter, kneeling next to Katy so that she could get a better look at her. "Just as Catherine brought me new life, you, dear Katy, shall bring etern . . ."

"Katy!" a distant voice yelled.

Annabelle looked up and saw both Angelique and Sophie running toward the garden. They had heard the yelling and rushed over to find out what was going on. Annabelle immediately dragged Katy into the grove where her horse waited. Katy still struggled with her, but after another blow from Annabelle's hand, she finally succumbed to the force. With Katy motionless, Annabelle lifted her onto the horse then climbed onto its back. Pulling a revolver from her holster, Annabelle watched the two women stop at the entryway.

Angelique had seen Annabelle's revolver and quickly grabbed Sophie's shoulder to bring her to a standstill. She knew without a doubt that Annabelle would shoot. Annabelle, sensing Angelique's hesitance, became cocky and confident. Annabelle trotted her horse in Angelique's direction.

Seeing this, Angelique looked at Sophie. "Run into the trees, make your way back to the house and get Wes. Hurry now," she whispered, trying desperately to get Sophie out of harm's way.

Sophie did as Angelique had instructed and ran into the trees and then toward the house for help. Annabelle saw her run away but did not attempt to stop her. Her attention was solely on Angelique. Now alone except for Katy, who had passed out and was lying across the horse's withers, Annabelle and Angelique stared at one another. Angelique knew Annabelle had the upper hand with the revolver pointed at her and tried desperately to think of a way out. If she didn't, she knew she would end up dead.

Annabelle halted the horse about fifteen feet away from Angelique. She knew Angelique was a capable of anything, and she didn't want a repeat of their first encounter.

"So, we meet again, Poshrati." Annabelle grinned, as she continued aiming the revolver at Angelique.

"You will not get away with this," Angelique said, sneering at Annabelle.

"Oh? And who will stop me?" Annabelle asked jovially.

"I will hunt you down, you English tart. You will never get away," Angelique replied, her eyes still fixed on Annabelle.

Annabelle began to laugh. "Even with your wonderful witchcraft, there is no way out of this situation for you. You made a crucial mistake befriending this child, and now you will pay for it with your life." An elated grin graced her face, as her fingers grasped the trigger of the revolver tighter.

"Any last words, gypsy whore?" Annabelle asked, looking into Angelique's eyes.

Angelique snickered at Annabelle's question and replied in the tongue of her Hungarian father, "Lo'fasz a seggedbe!"

Annabelle's grin was now wiped away and hatred quickly filled her eyes. Grasping the trigger tighter, she shouted, "Viszontlátásra! (Goodbye!)" then pulled the trigger.

Angelique held her ground, not flinching at the clicking sound of the trigger. There was no blast. Annabelle looked at the revolver puzzled as to why it had not gone off. She raised the revolver and fired a second time but with the same result. Annabelle then recalled that she hadn't reloaded the six shooter since being on the trail in Louisiana. One shot at Wes, three shots the night before, and two shots at Angelique.

Annabelle, in disarray and irritated, looked up to see Angelique grinning wickedly at her, almost laughing at her. Angelique knew that the revolver was useless and moved forward toward the horse. Seeing this, Annabelle quickly pulled the reins and turned the horse toward the pathway. In seconds, she was galloping away with Katy.

"Viszontlátásra! Poshrati!" Annabelle shouted.

Angelique's bones ached and her hands fluttered from the tension and stress of the revolver being pointed at her. She had feared that she would perish, but yet again, it would seem that the gods had other plans for her. It was then that she heard shouting coming from behind her. Angelique turned to see Wes and Sophie running toward her.

"Gitane!" Sophie yelled with a pistol in her hand with Wes close behind. His injury, although better, was still causing him pain, and it slowed him down.

They finally reached Angelique, but seeing that Katy was nowhere in sight, the realization that she was gone tore into their hearts like a jagged knife. Sophie, in tears, looked at Angelique. "Gitane, what should we do?" Sophie asked, confused about what had just happened.

"We will go after them," Wes interrupted, a look of anger in his eyes.

"But your injury . . ." Angelique started.

Wes looked into Angelique's eyes. "Don't worry about me, ma'am. There is nothing that is going to stop me from getting her back," he said with fiery confidence in his voice.

"Okay then," Angelique said, "we will need a horse."

"She's by the barn. I can have her ready in about five minutes," Sophie replied as she turned and ran toward the barn. "Five minutes!" she shouted.

Angelique turned her attention to Wes. As they walked hurriedly to the barn, she felt the strong passion in his words for Katy. She knew he wasn't ready physically for this journey, but she knew he would not stay behind as long as Katy was in danger.

Sophie opened the door to the barn, and although she was winded, she knew there was no time to waste. She grabbed the saddle near the door and headed out to the pen behind the barn where the mare stood eating grass. By this time, both Wes and Angelique had caught up with her. Wes tried to grab the saddle out of her hand but was scolded by Angelique. "No, I will do it," she admonished. "I need you healthy for later."

Angelique grabbed the saddle out of Sophie's hands and waited for the mare to trot toward them. Wes knew he wasn't in the best of shape for this, but somehow, someway, they would make it through this.

The mare trotted up to them, and Angelique and Sophie started to put the saddle on and ready it for the ride. Wes headed inside the house and brought out another pistol along with two rifles and extra bullets. He knew that the plantation would be heavily armed, that is, if Lady Annabelle and Katy made it that far, and that Annabelle's people would be waiting for them.

Sophie gathered a few things that the two would need for the short journey and loaded the items into the saddle bags. Wes, feeling the need to hurry, loaded the arms and ammunition. With everything intact and ready, Angelique walked up to Sophie. They quickly embraced and said a few words, then Angelique mounted the mare behind Wes.

"When Frenchy gets here, tell him what happened. Hopefully we'll return soon," Angelique said, ready to leave.

"You know he gonna go after her as well," Sophie said, holding back the tears that were edging toward the surface.

"I know, but gather an army of sorts. He may need everybody if it's at all possible," Angelique said. "To be safe, that is."

Now that they were both comfortably on the mare, Angelique and Wes rushed down the path to rescue Katy. Left on her own, Sophie wept openly. She felt helpless and weak seeing Wes and Angelique ride off. The only thing she could contribute was a prayer for an end to this nightmare. And she did, with another for Etienne's safe return.

As the horse cantered near her cabin, Angelique had a strong sense that she had forgotten something. "Wait! Turn to my cabin," she said authoritatively. "I need something."

Wes turned the horse toward the cabin, finally stopping the mare at the front of the door. Angelique swiftly dismounted and hurried into the cabin. She knew time was of the utmost importance so she went as fast as she could, dashing from one cupboard to another. Finally, after much searching, she pulled out a small box with a pouch lying beside it. She smiled as she opened the box and removed two necklaces. Angelique held onto them both, along with the pouch, then ran toward the door.

As Angelique stepped out of the cabin, she heard a lone caw behind her, and she froze. Wes, still sitting on the mare, watched as her face changed from a look of hope and hidden emotion to one of dread and fear. Again, there was another caw, followed by another, Angelique hesitantly turned around to see three crows perched above the door. Their caws grew louder with each passing second.

"Ma'am, what is it?" Wes asked, sensing her nervousness.

Angelique stood silently, watching the crows, as if in a trance.

"Ma'am? We need to go," Wes said, feeling slightly agitated.

"Hmmm . . . Oh yes," Angelique replied, as if awakened. She turned around to climb onto the horse. Wes grabbed her hand to help her up. He noticed something was definitely wrong with her. Angelique's hands were shaking and cold. He could sense that she was frightened, but of what, he could not tell. This made him very confused.

"A woman who stares down another with a revolver without flinching surely wouldn't be afraid of three birds?" he thought.

"You alright, ma'am?" Wes asked, as they trotted back to the path.

"Yes," Angelique said impassively. "Onward." Angelique patted Wes on the back as if to thank him, then became silent and kept to herself. Wes left her alone. He felt she needed to deal with this now, her way, before the trouble started. But his heart became heavy seeing her like this because he knew that he would need all her energy and support in order to rescue his true love.

* * *

A few miles down the path, Annabelle slowed her horse and stopped to load her revolver and tie Katy's wrists and feet. Katy was still unconscious, but Annabelle didn't want trouble if she awoke. With the gun loaded and Katy secure, she headed back along the path—until she heard a sound up ahead: riders were approaching. Annabelle quickly dashed into the trees for cover. The sound drew closer and closer until she could see three men on horseback heading south.

Securely hidden but still able to see the riders, Annabelle watched as they passed. Horrified, she recognized at least one of them: Monsieur Chevalier! The premonition she'd had on the ship had been correct, but to her, this was just another obstacle that would have to be dealt with later.

As the riders passed and the sound of their horses faded down the pathway, Annabelle headed north at a gallop. She knew she had to make it back to the plantation immediately as she was clearly outnumbered.

* * *

Evan, William, and Monsieur Chevalier rode hastily down the path toward Grigsby's Bluff and Angelique. Their time spent interviewing people along the Sabine Road and to the north had been a waste of time—at least in Evan's mind. He would have far rather listened to clues from the gypsy woman whom he felt he had at least befriended.

"Another day and all rubbish," William said, out of frustration.

"Yes, but I believe this day will be different," Evan replied.

"And how's that?" William asked.

"Well, for one, we are headed towards that woman who was a great cook. I guess or hope lightning strikes twice? Hmmm . . . ?" Evan joked.

"Fair enough," William replied, now feeling a little hungry. "I could go for a duck or two. How about you, monsieur?"

"Me? I would be delighted for a meal such as that again," Monsieur Chevalier acknowledged with a smile.

Many things crossed Evan's mind as the three rode southward. Over and over, he thought back to the first days in Newcastle when Monsieur Chevalier had explained the severity of the case. The next two weeks had been spent searching for clues about the whereabouts of Lady Falsworth. And who in fact was Lady Annabelle? And how did she get there?

There seemed to be more questions than answers. This frustrated Evan to no end. Records showed that Lady Annuska Báthory-Falsworth had lived in Newcastle for years, but he could never find her birth date or any other information about her. Her family had lived there for centuries. In fact, early records showed a Hungarian immigrant with the same name, Annuska Báthory, had shown up around 1612 and married William Falsworth, a prominent rancher of both sheep and cattle. William grew his business well and prospered greatly until his death in 1649. There was no record of Annuska's death, just the transfer of wealth to their child, Anna, in 1651. Surprisingly, no records existed for even the current heiress, granddaughter Lady Annabelle Falsworth. With all the questions surrounding this case, Evan still felt that the truth was close, and he would soon find the answers.

Time passed as the trio continued south. Suddenly, they heard a horse galloping down the path. Evan noticed Angelique and the young man, Wes, heading toward them. As Angelique and Wes reached the three men, they came to a standstill. They acknowledged the other party and sat eye-to-eye across from each other in the middle of the path.

"Good day, gentlemen," Wes said as he tipped his hat. "Did a lady happen to pass you by a short while ago?"

"It was your Lady Annabelle, and she has Katy," Angelique blurted out.

The three looked at each other, confused, since they hadn't seen anyone on this path. "No, no one has passed us," Evan replied. "Could she have gone another way?"

"No, I do not believe so. She would have had to have gone down this path," Angelique answered, feeling perplexed. "She must have seen you coming and hid in the trees."

"Possibly," Evan answered. "She is cunning."

"Yes sir. That she is," Wes added.

"You don't think she would have doubled back, do you?" William asked.

"No, she is outnumbered and needs her entourage," replied Angelique. "She will be heading back to where she came from."

"Across the river?" Evan asked. "So she would be heading to the ferry then?"

Angelique nodded her head in answer to Evan's questions, then turned to Wes, "I believe we should follow the path and cross near the ferry. I sense that she was alone, and this is where she is going."

On hearing Angelique's words, they all agreed, especially Evan and Wes. Evan sensed Angelique was wise and trustworthy. Actually, his sense was all he really had in this land, and he trusted it implicitly.

"So we turn back towards the river?" Monsieur Chevalier asked.

"Yes, but I believe someone needs to ride south and tell Sophie of our plans," Angelique said. "We may need more arms later."

Evan, who had been listening to the exchange, added his thoughts, "This sounds good. William can ride south and wait for the others."

"Yes, I believe so," William agreed.

"Well, that's that then," Evan said urgently. "Off with you."

William clicked his heels, and his horse galloped southward, down the path. "Godspeed all," he shouted as he rode away.

"And to you as well, my friend!" Evan yelled back.

Now with at least a small plan in place, the remaining four rode north towards Beaumont. Monsieur Chevalier was still thinking of how and where Annabelle had escaped their grasp. He also thought that, with two people on one horse, they would be considerably slower than with one rider.

"So she and Katy are on one horse, no?" Monsieur Chevalier asked.

"Yes, that is correct," Wes answered.

"What if I rode ahead and tried to catch up with them before she traveled to the river?" Monsieur Chevalier suggested. "This might save the girl and our lives."

Although she did not trust Monsieur Chevalier completely, Angelique agreed that it was a good idea to try to cut Annabelle off before she reached the other side of the river.

"I wouldn't advise it, sir," Evan said, thinking of his safety.

"It's up to you, but it could help the lass greatly," Angelique countered.

Monsieur Chevalier nodded to Angelique then rode swiftly down the path to try to catch up with Annabelle. Seeing the look on Evan's face, he shouted, "Don't worry I have dealt with worse foes in my life. All will be fine. I wish to see you later with the girl." He then disappeared down the path.

Angelique was happy that only the three of them remained. She trusted Wes and Evan and that trust would become a huge necessity in the future.

CHAPTER 17

An hour passed as Annabelle rapidly made her way to the river with Katy. She knew that the weight of two people on one horse had considerably slowed her speed and felt that Katy's friends would soon catch up with them. She also knew that the horse was tired from walking all night and half the morning. Tired or not, Annabelle had no choice but to push him to his limits if she wanted to escape the grasp of Katy's newfound friends.

Annabelle eventually made it to the edge of the river near the ferry. She rode the horse into the water without hesitation. This woke Katy up, as she was now half submerged in the river. Annabelle, seeing Katy struggle, took hold of her hair and lifted her head out of the ever-deepening river. When they were halfway across, Annabelle heard the sound of a galloping horse on the riverbank behind her. She turned to see Monsieur Chevalier stop at the edge of the water. He raised his hand, brandishing a revolver and pointed it straight at her.

"Madame!" Monsieur Chevalier shouted. "Stop, or I will have no choice but to shoot."

Still with one hand holding Katy's head up and the other clutching her own revolver, Annabelle turned to face him. Desperately pondering her limited options, she realized that she may indeed have to surrender to Monsieur Chevalier's demand.

"Madame! Again, I command you to halt. This is your final warning," Monsieur Chevalier yelled, determined to stop her from escaping.

"And what of the girl?" Annabelle asked, raising Katy's head higher above the water. "Do you not fear for her safety?"

Monsieur Chevalier looked at the women without showing any emotion. "She does not have value to me. Now turn around."

Annabelle stopped the horse, knowing Monsieur Chevalier would shoot through Katy if need be. As she slowly turned the horse around, Annabelle turned Katy's head to face her. She looked into Katy's eyes and whispered, "You will do exactly as I say or else you will stay in this river permanently, understood?"

Katy, half groggy and filled with fear, had no choice but to follow Annabelle's lead.

"Okay?" Annabelle confirmed, as the horse started heading back to the riverbank.

"Ride forward," Monsieur Chevalier said, his finger on the trigger.

Annabelle shook her head, as she began pulling the back of Katy's gown. A wicked grin now appeared on her lips as she stared at Monsieur Chevalier.

"What you seek is not here. I have hidden it, and no one but I knows where it is," Annabelle sneered.

"You're lying; now move forward," Monsieur Chevalier commanded.

"Oh really?" Annabelle replied, her voice laden with irony. "Well, you'll never know, will you?"

Monsieur Chevalier grew tired of Annabelle's games. He waved the gun barrel at her, motioning for her to move forward.

Annabelle seeing him grow increasingly irritable, quickly flung Katy into the water on one side of the horse while simultaneously raising her revolver at Monsieur Chevalier and firing. Seconds later, she fell into the water on the opposite side. Seeing Annabelle's attempt to escape, Monsieur Chevalier fired the revolver at her but missed. Unfortunately for him, Annabelle didn't. Her bullet hit him in the left shoulder. The force from the shot made him fall backward off the horse and to the ground.

Katy, now submerged in the river, fought fiercely to keep her head above water. With her hands and feet bound by rope, it was almost impossible to stay afloat. Katy kicked her feet downward, which gave her a slight jolt upward. She kicked again and again, inching her way to the surface. Finally, Katy's head popped out of the water for a few seconds, giving her just enough time to get some air. She gasped loudly, then as fast as she had risen, she sunk back into the water.

Annabelle, on the other side of the horse, grabbed the reins and turned the animal toward the opposite bank from where Monsieur Chevalier lay in pain. She slapped the colt on the side trying to get it to swim toward land. With the horse on the move, Annabelle swam to Katy. Seeing Katy rapidly exhausting her strength, she reached out, grabbed her hands, and pulled her head above water. Another loud gasp for air came from the girl, this time choking on inhaled water.

"Hold my hand and don't resist!" shouted Annabelle. "We need to get across the river."

Katy did as Annabelle instructed but couldn't keep her head above water. Annabelle hooked a hand under Katy's arm and dragged her toward the shore. Katy, weak and no longer able to pull herself up, lay limp in the water. Minutes, which had seemed like hours, passed as Annabelle swam to the bank, dragging Katy behind her.

Having reached shallow water, Annabelle hauled Katy out of the water and onto the sandy soil. Katy, fragile and exhausted, constantly coughed and choked up water. Although Annabelle was also fatigued, she knew they could not stay there for long. She stood up and looked across the river at Monsieur Chevalier. Although wounded, he had managed to stand up and get back to his horse. Luckily for him, the bullet had not hit a major artery, but for now, this battle was over. Monsieur Chevalier retreated south for help and reinforcements.

Annabelle stared at him, knowing he was too injured to cross the river, but she also knew he'd be back with the others.

"Why?" a weakened voice was heard from the bank. Katy, still coughing, tried to speak. "Why? Why are you doing this?"

Annabelle looked down at Katy, seeing her in tears.

"What have I done to you that I deserve this fate?" Katy said, starting to sob.

Annabelle stayed silent, knelt down in front of Katy and pulled a large knife from her pouch. Katy rolled back away in fear. Still with no words or emotion, Annabelle moved the knife to Katy's feet and cut the ropes, enabling her to move her legs.

"If you so much as twitch, your throat will end up like this rope. Do you understand me?" Annabelle threatened, waving the knife in her face.

Katy was petrified and didn't move.

"Now get up. We need to go," Annabelle instructed as she put the knife away. She grabbed Katy's bound hands, trying to stand her up. Katy struggled to her feet, slipping as a result of Annabelle's constant jerking and pulling on her wrists.

"On the horse . . . Now!" Annabelle scowled.

Katy stumbled up to the horse and slowly mounted it with Annabelle's help. It took all of what little energy she had left to mount the colt. Annabelle quickly got on behind her and, with a slap to its side, the horse was once again back on the path. Katy was too weak to fight against Annabelle. Her only hope was the thought of her friends coming to her aid.

* * *

Katy was the only thing on Sophie's mind as she packed a lunch for Etienne and the rest of what would soon be a posse. Etienne had arrived home shortly after Angelique and Wes had ridden off. The news of Katy's kidnapping angered Etienne. Not much ever swayed his fun-loving demeanor, but Annabelle's actions were wrong and he wouldn't stand for it. So he, along with Henri, gathered ammunition, a gun, and a few of the other things they would need. Thomas headed back home to find some of the boys to help.

It was at this time that Etienne heard the sound of a horse galloping down the path. He knew it was too soon for Thomas to return, so he grabbed his rifle and stood near the garden. Through a cloud of dust, he could make out a man riding furiously toward him. With his rifle poised, Etienne watched as the man slowed to a trot as soon as he neared the entryway. As soon as he was close enough, Etienne recognized the man as William from two days before.

William, seeing Etienne with the rifle, dropped the reins and held his hands up to show he meant no harm. Etienne lowered the rifle and motioned for William to ride up. Relieved that Etienne recognized him, William rode closer and greeted both him and Sophie, who had brought the lunch out to Etienne.

"A somber day indeed," William said, tipping his hat. "I was told by the gypsy woman to tell you that she, Evan, and the rest will be making their way toward the river in search of Lady Falsworth. If they cannot apprehend her before she crosses the river, they will follow her."

Etienne's face soured at hearing the news that Angelique and the rest would probably be pursuing Annabelle across the river. He knew they would be outnumbered—and especially outgunned.

"I don't like it," Etienne muttered, "I don't like it one bit. There are too many things that can go wrong there."

"I understand fully," William replied, "but I believe they fear for the young girl's life."

"I understand, but they can't save her if they themselves are dead."

"Gitane knows what she's doin'," Sophie chipped in. "She'll keep them safe till we get there."

"Mama, I hope you're right," Etienne replied with a sigh.

As time passed and the horses were stocked with the bare necessities, Etienne, Henri, and William prepared to leave. Luke, one of the Peloat boys, arrived on horseback, ready for the trip and with a message from Thomas. He explained that Thomas and the other four boys would be heading out in boats to the other side of the river. They would not be taking any horses with them. Thomas thought the strategy might be better just in case things went awry.

With everyone now ready to leave, Sophie hurried to join them. Etienne saw her holding a pistol and a sack of supplies. Etienne shook his head. The last thing he wanted was for her to go with them. He knew the danger, and he couldn't handle the thought of her being injured or killed.

"Oh no, mama," Etienne said as she walked up to him.

"What you mean?" Sophie asked. "I'm going. Katy's my friend, too, and dammit, I am not gonna sit around here and wonder."

Etienne gently clasped her hand. "Look, I don't know what's gonna happen, and you don't need to be out there, especially in your condition."

Sophie's eyes welled up with tears. "This baby also needs a father. Don't give me that; we're partners. We need each other, and if we don't stick together, then we can both give up the ghost. I'm goin', and that's it."

Etienne looked at her and knew she wasn't going to back down. Sophie was mild mannered, but when a friend was in trouble, there was no better friend than her. She cared deeply for Angelique, and Katy, too. There was no way she was going to be left behind.

"Okay," Etienne said. "Just promise me you'll stay out of the way. If something happens to you, I don't know if I'd ever recover."

"Promise," Sophie replied as she boarded the wagon and embraced Etienne.

Etienne knew she was a strong woman and had the heart of a thousand angels, but still in his mind, he would not be able to cope with her loss. She was everything to him. All the same, he knew they needed to get going, and every second was precious. So with Sophie straddling the horse behind him, the small group headed northward toward Beaumont. In his thoughts, Etienne knew Angelique would hold out as long as she possibly could, but deep in his heart, he felt they were doomed to fail across the river.

* * *

Angelique, Wes, and Evan hurried down the path toward the river. The trio made good time even though there were only two horses for the three of them. Evan, being in a talkative mood, asked Wes a plethora of questions about his time with Lady Falsworth. To his delight, Wes had plenty to say about her but no knowledge of her future plans.

"So she never gave you as much as a hint of where you were going?" Evan asked, trying to piece together some sort of next move.

"Nope, not really," Wes replied. "She always kept everyone in the dark about her plans. I'm sure Mr. Thorton knew, and of course Miss Sterling, but us? She didn't trust us."

"I believe she trusts no one," Evan said thoughtfully.

"I tend to agree. There was always a lot of stuff going on behind the scenes," Wes replied.

"Yes, I had this problem even back in England. It's as if she doesn't exist. There's no trail to follow."

Angelique, who had been silent for most of the trip, now added a few of her own questions. "So what you are saying is she just appeared on the night of the murder?"

"Yes, that is correct." Evan replied, "I've done extensive research and found no trace of this woman."

"But what about the family? The older lady must have had children or siblings?" Wes asked.

Evan shook his head. "I can't find anyone. Actually, the last person on record was back in the 1600s. Mind you, Newcastle doesn't have the greatest of people working in the department that keeps records, but this just couldn't be an oversight."

"With money comes power, and I believe she has both," Angelique stated matter-of-factly.

Evan shrugged. "I believe more than we can imagine."

"I'm sure she would say the same, but the time has come for her to find out that things in this place don't always go as planned," Angelique said.

Evan laughed. "Oh, I believe she has found this out. Hopefully we can give her more of the same this evening."

Angelique agreed, then fell silent once again, back to her deep thoughts. Both Evan and Wes continued talking, as the horses steadily moved forward toward the river. Wes, alert for anything out of the ordinary, could hear the faint gallop of another horse. As he looked down the path, he could just make out the horse and rider heading toward them. It was Monsieur Chevalier. He was slumped over but still riding at a staggering pace.

Monsieur Chevalier finally reached the three, who had stopped in the middle of the path to wait for him. Angelique noticed immediately why he was bent over: blood covered his one arm, and he was steeped in pain. Angelique quickly leaped off the mare and ran toward Monsieur Chevalier to help.

"What in God's name happened? Are you alright?" Evan blurted out.

"Yes, I believe so," Monsieur Chevalier replied as he slowly dismounted.

Angelique removed his jacket and saw that his shirt sleeve was covered in blood. The wound had bled quite extensively but, fortunately for him, had seemed to clot up and halt the bleeding.

"It seems as if you are a lucky man," Angelique said, looking at the wound closely.

"That I believe to be true, madame," Monsieur Chevalier replied, grimacing with pain as Angelique poked and prodded.

"What happened?" Wes asked, knowing very well just who was behind the Monsieur's injury.

"I found her crossing the river," said Monsieur Chevalier. "I raised my pistol and told her to halt, but she used the girl as a shield, and I couldn't take the chance of injuring her. Seconds later, I hear a shot, and the blow made me fall from my horse."

"So you didn't get a shot at her?" Evan asked curiously.

"And Katy? Is she alright?" Wes asked anxiously.

"I didn't have time to get a shot at her. She was too fast," Monsieur Chevalier answered as he turned his eyes to Wes. "I believe so. When I made it to my feet, I saw them ride off."

Angelique finished cleaning the wound as the others planned their next move. She knew time was a luxury they did not have, so she hurried to dress the wound with a clean cloth and a sprig of whiskey to prevent infection setting in. Monsieur Chevalier showed his discomfort, but he knew the efforts were for his own benefit.

"There. I believe you'll be fine," Angelique said, handing the small flask of whiskey to him.

"Merci, madame," he replied taking a gulp before handing it back to Angelique.

"Okay, time to go," Evan said as he mounted his horse once again.

"Yes, let's ride," Wes added. They could all see his desire to get back on the path and find Katy.

His anxiety was felt by Angelique as well. She believed Annabelle would not harm Katy for now but was unaware of what the future held—or Annabelle's plans for her. Nonetheless, she would do all she could to free the girl from her torture.

With the four now on horseback, they headed back toward the river and Annabelle's trail. The ride took a short time, and the horses seemed fresh from the earlier stop. This was a plus, especially with the uncertainty of what waited for them across the river.

As they trotted near the bank, Evan decided to be the first to ride in. They all agreed, especially Monsieur Chevalier, that they should go across one at a time just in case there was trouble. Wes, also wary of danger, stood guard on the bank with his gun at the ready, just in case. Moments later, Evan reached the opposite bank without incident. Next, Wes waded across, followed by Angelique and, finally, Monsieur Chevalier.

Now successfully across the river, the four found themselves in unfamiliar territory. Although Wes knew that most of the ranch hands were passive by nature, he couldn't rule out Annabelle's ruthless influence in making a good man do her dirty work; even if it meant killing one of his own. No one could tell for sure what each turn would bring, but Wes felt that they were ready as they could be.

Angelique stayed silent. She knew what lay down the path: nothing but trouble. While Wes held the reins to the horse, Angelique slipped her hand into her gown pocket and took out both of the necklaces she had taken from her cabin. She smiled as she placed one around Wes' neck. Wes was undaunted as he felt her do this.

"What's this?" he asked curiously.

"It was my husband's," Angelique replied. "He believed it gave him good luck."

Wes took the necklace off and looked at it. It seemed to be some sort of cross. Not being religious, he smiled and gazed down the path. "What is it?"

"It's a Celtic cross. He believed as long as he had it with him, nothing would harm him. Unfortunately, in his last few years, he lost it. After his death, I found it tucked away. I am certain this will help you."

Angelique put the other one around her neck. Unlike the cross, hers was round and obscure.

Wes became intrigued when he saw her necklace. "What is that?" he asked, almost in a joking tone.

"It was my aunt's. She gave it to me when I left England. It also brings good luck. She said Cerridwen herself put her love into this. She will protect us as best she can. We are far away, but the gods will still look after us."

"I honestly wish I had your faith, dear lady," Evan said sincerely. "I believe little of this earth. I have seen both sides of the good and bad of religion, and it sickens me so."

Angelique glanced at Evan, seeing in his heart that he was a fair and just man. "It is not religion you should seek, for it has been tarred and feathered by so many, nor should you be made into a learner of Latin. It is the feeling in your heart that you cannot sway. A feeling of peace when storms approach; a feeling of happiness when all around you turns to muck. This is where the gods thrive. Not in a structure, not in a book. They are in all things, watching you, as a parent to a child."

And with her words, Angelique withdrew into silence once again. Evan, like Wes, was not religious, but her words made him think back to his early years—and his grandmother. Her faith in the old ways nearly always conflicted with the rest of the family, but being as strong-willed as she was, it didn't matter. She held her beliefs openly for all to see.

Evan wasn't the type to delve into a religious conversation of any sort. He let life's cards fall as they may. He knew in his heart and soul what lay ahead meant misery and death to some of those riding beside him, possibly even he himself. After months of searching and investigating, judgment day had finally come. But at what cost?

CHAPTER 18

The horse trotted slowly through the entryway of the plantation. Fatigued from the long journey, both the riders and the colt displayed complete exhaustion. Annabelle looked at the raucous crowd that was growing in front of the house. Numerous ranch hands and maids had begun yelling when they saw her. The commotion aroused the attention of Miss Sterling and Annabelle's maids.

Sara, hearing countless shouts from outside, quickly ran to one of the upstairs windows to find out what was happening. As she looked out at the lone horse trotting along the path toward the house, her heart filled with happiness.

"My Lady! My Lady! She has returned!" she shouted, pointing excitedly at the window.

Miss Sterling was not at all happy with her outburst. "Sara! Settle down. This is not how a lady acts. Now get a hold of yourself."

"Yes, my Lady," Sara acquiesced, her head bowed. She fell silent.

Miss Sterling walked to the window and glared down at Annabelle with a disapproving expression then ordered the maids to meet her outside in front of the house. Sara and Hana were the first to scamper down the stairs and out the door to meet Lady Annabelle.

By now, Ben Drayson had caught wind of Annabelle's return. He didn't hear a wagon ride up, which made him curious. As he stepped outside the stables, he saw the gathering in front of the house. He walked hastily up to join it, making sure Annabelle could see him. Ben looked ahead and saw instantaneously why everyone was so interested in Lady Annabelle's return.

The sound of whispers filled the air, particularly from the maids who were watching Katy closely. Annabelle rode up to the front of the house and dismounted. As usual, there a sneer on her face as she surveyed the welcoming party. Katy, groggy and tired, had to be helped down off the horse by Benjamin and Ezra.

"Do take special care of her," Annabelle ordered.

"Ah, you do know how to make an entrance, don't you?" Miss Sterling smirked as she walked up to her.

"Yes, although I shouldn't have needed to," Annabelle replied. "This should have been taken care of days ago."

Ben took her comment as a smear upon himself, and he thought it was indeed deserved. "I do apologize greatly, ma'am," he said, his head bowed and his hat in his hands.

Annabelle turned to Ben. "Yes, as you can see, I get things done and will not tolerate failure."

"Yes, ma'am. I'm beginning to see this," Ben replied. "It won't happen again. We will have at least two guards outside the house at all times."

"Good. See that this is done," Annabelle instructed smugly. "Also, do place guards at the entrance. I expect visitors, and I do not want them near her."

"It's as good as done, ma'am."

"Excellent!" Annabelle turned to Miss Sterling.

Ben was not finished with his questions. He was wondering what had happened to the wagon and the three men. "Pardon, ma'am, but what happened to the wagon and your escorts?" he asked.

Annabelle turned back around to face Ben and gave him a look of bitter discontent, which transformed into a weak smile a few seconds later. "We had a bit of trouble, but we worked through it. I believe the three had no stomach for this kind of work, and they departed. So it would appear that I have three vacancies."

Ben listened intently but could not grasp her story. He felt she was lying but didn't want to make waves with his future employer, so he nodded and grinned like a good hand should. Annabelle quickly turned toward Katy, the maids, and Miss Sterling.

Katy, now off the horse and in the hands of Sara and Hana, staggered up onto the porch. Weak from her ordeal, she could not stand by herself much less walk on her own. Sara and Hana slowly helped Katy inside the house and to the washroom where she would get a much-needed change of clothes. Annabelle and Agatha remained on the porch talking over the events of the last few days, as Ben made plans to secure the plantation.

Ben smiled at both Ezra and Benjamin as he walked up to them. Both could sense his need and began preparing for guard duty at the front entrance.

"Well, I see you can read my mind," Ben stated, as Benjamin turned to head to his quarters to retrieve his guns while Ezra walked the horse to the stable.

"Yep, I kinda get that way," Benjamin replied, "We'll be there just as soon as Ezra gets through with the horse. Anything else, your majesty?"

"Yeah, tell David and Isaac to guard the house—one on each side. I don't want anybody going in or out unless Lady Falsworth or I know about it."

"Gotcha," Benjamin replied, striding toward his quarters.

Now with Annabelle's security needs taken care of, Ben walked to the back of the house and sat on the back porch checking the bullets in his revolver while he waited for the others to arrive to guard the house. In the front of the house, Annabelle, still soaked from her ordeal in the river, sat on the front porch with Agatha and spoke quietly.

"And all is well?" Agatha asked, handing Annabelle a towel.

"If you are referring to our precious cargo, then yes, it is safe," Annabelle confirmed.

"That is good to hear, but why you are sitting drenched in front of me is a mystery only you can unravel."

Annabelle glanced over at her with a look of concern. "We have a visitor," she said.

"A visitor?"

"Yes, it would seem Monsieur Chevalier has followed us here."

Agatha gasped in disbelief, "Monsieur Chevalier? Are you certain?"

"Oh yes, I am certain. I shot him as I went swimming in the river," Annabelle said.

"And? Did you fix the problem?"

"Unfortunately not. I expect visitors later today. We must be prepared. I am also certain that he has joined up with Katy's new friends."

Agatha began to feel uneasy. It was times like these that she missed Basil the most. He always took care of things, but now it was in their hands. Annabelle sensed her uneasiness and tried to put her thoughts to rest.

"We are fine, dear friend," Annabelle smiled. "I have everything under control."

"Do you? And what of the gypsy? Will she not want your dear sustenance back?"

"She will not be a problem. You are forgetting that I, only I, took dear Katy back from them; alone. I have lived many years, with many obstacles, and this is just another."

Agatha looked at Annabelle with distrust. "Obstacle she may be, but I feel your anxiety. Do not blind yourself with your own arrogance. It will be the death of us both."

Annabelle became irritated. "There is nothing that can stop me. We are here to start anew, and I bloody well will not let some poshrat or French thug dictate what my future holds."

"I understand, but all the same, we are here, and their arrival is imminent. We need to leave and leave now. We can head north where it will be safe."

"We will leave tomorrow," Annabelle said. "This is the safest place for now. We have extra hands here to protect us."

"I do hope you're right." Agatha sighed.

"Trust me, dear friend," Annabelle said confidently. "I have looked after you for all these years. Why would anything change?"

"It changed with Catherine," Agatha scowled.

Annabelle sat silent looking at Agatha. She was noticeably unhappy but did not want to continue this conversation further. Annabelle stood up from the seat, patted her face and hair with the towel and then walked into the house to get a change of clothing.

In the washroom, toward the back of the house, Sara and Hana removed the soaked clothing from Katy's body and gently dried her. Hana took a towel from a nearby closet and began drying Katy's hair while another maid, Fiona, brought in a fresh gown for Katy to wear. Sara noticed that Katy's swollen ankle was looking worse than before. She knew Katy could not walk and felt the need to tell Lady Annabelle.

"Look at your ankle," Sara pointed as Katy put on the clean gown. "It will have to be tended to. I must inform Lady Annabelle. She will know what to do."

Katy sneered at Sara, almost viciously. Still very weak, she reached out and grabbed Sara's arm, squeezing until Sara shrieked. "Ouch! What did you do that for?" Sara asked, pulling her arm away. "I am only trying to help. You're mad, you are."

Katy glared at Sara in disgust. "Go away," she hissed.

Sara, tired and shocked by Katy's behavior, returned the look. "Well, be that way then. Your antics this past week have brought nothing but misery and pain to us all. Lady Annabelle has been worried sick about your whereabouts."

"Go away," Katy ordered again, this time with a much higher tone of voice.

"You know, you should be a little bit kinder to us," Sara said smugly. "After all, that ankle of yours will need to be tended to. Lady Annabelle will probably heal it herself. You should consider yourself fortunate."

"Heal?" Katy retorted scornfully. "She is a beast that devours everyone and everything in her way. She's evil."

"You lie!" Sara shouted. "Our Lady is merciful and caring. She cured dear Brigit with just a thought. Her glory will enrich us all."

"And? What of Alice?" Katy replied, leaning toward Sara. "If Lady Annabelle is so powerful, then didn't Alice deserve to live? What of the other three on the ship? Were they not standing in the light of her glory? The reason they are dead is because of her and her alone, and I for one will not sit back and wait for my turn."

"Liar!" Sara shouted. "I hope to see you die for your insults and lies."

Katy grabbed Sara's arm again and pulled her sharply toward her, making Sara fall on top of her. Although her ankle was severely injured, her hands were not. Katy reached out and grabbed Sara's neck and began choking her. Hana shrieked in horror, as she tried to grab Katy's hands away from her neck.

"Help! My Lady, help!" Hana shouted, trying to attract attention.

Miss Sterling, walking down the hall, heard Hana's cries for help. She stormed into the washroom. Seeing what was happening, she quickly ran over to Katy and grabbed her long curly hair from the back and pulled forcefully. Katy, still furiously trying to hold onto Sara, could not endure the pain and let go of her. As she did this, Miss Sterling released her grasp. Then without warning, she stepped in front of Katy and hit her on the side of her brow. "Enough of this!" Miss Sterling shouted. "Behave yourself, or I will see to it that you make your new home at the bottom of the river."

Katy, holding the side of her head, looked at the elder Miss Sterling and spat in her face. "Damn you, old hag! Damn you to hell!"

Miss Sterling calmly wiped her face and then picked up a wooden dipper lying on the table beside them. Katy, seeing this, lunged at the old woman as best she could but fell short of her because of the pain in her ankle. Miss Sterling turned toward Katy raising the dipper to strike her.

"Enough!" a voice shouted from the door. It was Annabelle. She had heard the commotion from her upstairs room and had rushed down to see what was going on. Halfway undressed and holding her revolver, she entered the room. Miss Sterling, seeing Annabelle, lowered the dipper and placed it back on the table.

"Now please, tell me what is going on?" Annabelle demanded.

"It would seem that your beloved has attacked your favorite," Miss Sterling said, shaking with anger. "I fail to see the reason this one is here. She is obviously mad and cannot be controlled."

Annabelle ordered the three maids out of the washroom. Sara, Hana, and Fiona quickly left, leaving only Annabelle, Katy, and Miss Sterling. Annabelle finished dressing while Katy lifted herself off the floor and sat on a chair. Miss Sterling stood silent until Annabelle had finished, then walked over to her.

"Well?" Miss Sterling snapped.

Annabelle calmly retrieved a vial containing a finely chopped and dried substance from her pocket and handed it to Miss Sterling.

"Ten dale este a ella. (Here, give this to her.)" she said in Spanish so Katy would not understand.

"Que es esto?" Miss Sterling asked what was in the vial.

"Mandragora. (Mandrake.)" Annabelle continued in Spanish. "Put this in a tea for her. She will sleep."

"Where on earth did you get this?" Miss Sterling asked. "From my knowledge, it doesn't grow here."

Annabelle paused for a moment to straighten her dress. "I acquired it in Galveston," she replied. "It would seem we have an ally there."

"Who?" Miss Sterling asked. She was very curious.

"Before we left England, I received word from a business acquaintance that they too were on their way to Texas. His wife is an herbalist," Annabelle smiled.

"How useful," Miss Sterling remarked sarcastically.

"Very," Annabelle acknowledged.

Miss Sterling took the vial, left the washroom, and headed for the kitchen. She didn't know what Annabelle was up to, but she had no choice other than to trust her. If it was up to Miss Sterling, Katy would have been taken care of a long time ago.

Annabelle sat across from Katy with a grand smile on her face. Katy, still holding her head, looked up at Annabelle with anger. Knowing she could not escape, her rage boiled to the point of tears. She felt she needed to do something but was unable. Katy could only hope that Wes and Angelique would find a way to free her.

"Tears?" Annabelle sneered. "You resort to tears? Well, do not worry, dear child. Your time will end soon, and then there will be no more tears."

Just then, a thought entered Katy's mind; a dark emotion. It felt almost as if it were a vision, but the source was unknown to her. Katy's tears faded as she turned her head to face Annabelle. Her lips revealed a hint of a grin as she looked Annabelle straight in the eye. "Those whom you have murdered and those whom you have left for dead," Katy spoke with a devilish mien that was now becoming increasingly visible, "are returning. Your world is quickly coming to an end."

Annabelle watched Katy's transformation unfold but dismissed it as insanity. To her, the pressure had finally taken hold of Katy and driven her completely mad.

"Oh, I don't think so." Annabelle laughed. "They have had their uses, and I have moved on."

Annabelle stood up and made her way to the door, but before leaving, she turned around and gave Katy another look. But this time, she wasn't laughing. "And so shall you have your use as well, dear Katy. Right down to the last drop of your sweet . . . precious . . . blood."

Katy stared at Annabelle, emotionless. "And did Catherine know this? Before you bought her from the Monsieur?"

Annabelle gave Katy a menacing look. "What did you say?"

"You heard me." Katy smirked. "I was there that night, remember? Remember your words?"

In a flurry of sudden anger, Annabelle rushed over to Katy with her hand raised, ready to strike. "Silence or I'll . . ."

Before Annabelle could finish speaking, Katy grabbed her arm pulling it toward her. Annabelle recoiled, but Katy's grasp was tight. "Remember," Katy growled.

Annabelle became still as a vision of Katy listening intently behind a door appeared before her. Two familiar voices could be heard on the other side.

"Ah, Monsieur, what a pleasant surprise!" the elder Lady Falsworth had greeted.

"Madame, I believe you have my daughter?" Monsieur Chevalier replied, a bit agitated.

"Why, whatever do you mean?" Lady Falsworth grinned to the Monsieur's annoyance.

"Madame, you know what I mean. You are holding my daughter hostage."

"I hold no one hostage, Monsieur. People enter here of their own free will. They can leave at any time," Lady Falsworth said, almost mockingly.

Monsieur Chevalier was irritated by Lady Falsworth's antics. "Let me see her."

"She no longer wants to see you," Lady Falsworth replied.

"I don't care what she wants!" Monsieur Chevalier raised his voice in anger. "Let me see her!"

Lady Falsworth sat back in her chair, cupping her hands together as if she was in deep thought. Seconds passed, and she answered, "I'll pay what you ask."

"Pardon?" Monsieur Chevalier replied, confused by her comment.

"You wanted to raise your prices, and I will okay this. On one tiny condition."

Monsieur Chevalier now knew what she was talking about but did not trust her. "And what is the condition?" he asked skeptically.

"Let Catherine stay with me. It's obvious that she needs a woman in her life. Not as many as you have provided, but I believe it would be beneficial to you as well. Do you not agree?"

Monsieur Chevalier thought for a moment then agreed. He knew that Catherine's hatred for him wasn't just a passing childhood episode. At least with Lady Falsworth, Catherine might just become something other than a problem to him. "Okay, I believe you are right," he replied, "and I look forward to doing business with you again."

"Words spoken out of need," Katy said, releasing Annabelle's arm.

Annabelle instantaneously struck Katy on the side of her brow, but Katy stared at her unfazed.

"That was the elder, not me," Annabelle responded smugly.

"Ah, but one and the same," Katy said.

"As you shall find out, dear child," Annabelle countered and then turned and left the room.

As Annabelle walked down the hall to the kitchen, Agatha met her with a question. "The tea will soon be ready. Do you want to give it to her?" Agatha was calmer than before.

"No, I believe Fiona should take it to her," Annabelle replied, "I think she will be less threatening."

Agatha nodded in agreement then walked back to the stove where Fiona was sweeping the floor. Not long after, Agatha took the brew off the fire and poured it into a large cup. "Fiona!" she called. "Dear, would you please take this to Katy? This will help her heal and get some much needed sleep."

"Yes, my lady," Fiona replied. Fiona took the cup gently and carefully, a towel protecting her hands from the heat. She walked slowly down the hall to the washroom. Katy, unable to walk, sat quietly in a chair, deep in thought.

Fiona tapped on the washroom door, "Katy?" she asked in a somber voice. "It's me, Fiona. I've brought you some tea."

"If Miss Sterling has anything to do with it, it must be poison," Katy scowled.

Fiona pushed the door open slowly and walked in, holding the cup in front of her. "No poison, just something to help you," she smiled.

Fiona always seemed to get on well with Katy. Although a bit of a loner, she enjoyed Katy's company. Katy likewise enjoyed being around her and trusted her more than the others.

"I don't know." Katy looked at her.

"It's alright. Here, let me show you." Fiona smiled as she took a sip of the hot liquid.

"See? It is very tasty," Fiona said, trying to entice Katy to drink.

Katy watched as Fiona took another sip, then another. With her ankle throbbing badly, Katy finally gave in and began to drink the tea. It didn't take her long before she had finished it. Fiona, who had taken quite a few sips of her own, felt at ease and also a bit tipsy. Similarly, for Katy, the pain had begun to subside, but only as long as she had stayed off the ankle.

A short while later, Miss Sterling entered the room to check on Katy. She immediately noticed both girls inebriated and hunched over a table.

"Fiona?" Miss Sterling whispered, "Are you alright?"

Fiona only responded with a grunt, then nodded off to sleep. Miss Sterling shook her head and left the room only to return a few minutes later with three of her maids and Sister Betty. She instructed both Sara and Hana to help Fiona to the bedroom on the first floor while Sister Betty and the other maid, Elisabeth, helped Katy to a bedroom upstairs.

Elisabeth and Sister Betty laid Katy gently on the bed. Katy seemed delirious and was mumbling continuously.

"What's wrong with this child?" Betty asked.

"Lady Falsworth has given her some tea to help with her ankle, I believe," Elisabeth replied, laying a blanket over Katy.

"Tea, huh?" Betty grumbled as she looked into Katy's eyes.

As Elisabeth left the room, Betty quietly clasped Katy's hand and whispered, "Awaken your thoughts, awaken your mind, awaken your guardian through darkness, and peace you will find." She then made an x with her finger on the palm of Katy's hand and walked out the door.

Since the first night she had met Katy, Sister Betty had had a strong feeling about her. She felt a certain power in her aura that she had never felt in another. But time was running out for Katy, and Sister Betty knew it. Still, through all the tribulations, Katy continued to survive.

CHAPTER 19

Betty walked swiftly down the stairs, through the front parlor and onto the porch. A small pouch was hidden in her hand, which was tucked into the front pocket of her gown. Moving quickly and quietly down the wooden steps of the porch onto the dusty ground, Betty made her way to the front gate where Ezra and Benjamin were standing guard.

"Well, here she comes," Benjamin joked playfully to Ezra, knowing Betty was always checking up on him.

Ezra was not his usual self. He would normally take Benjamin's jokes in his stride, but ever since the episode at the stables, Ezra had felt confused and isolated from everyone around him, except Betty. He had enjoyed his two years working here, but since the arrival of Lady Falsworth, he had felt it was time to move back to Louisiana.

Betty walked up to the men, repeatedly glancing over her shoulder as if someone was watching her. Benjamin noticed Betty's guarded mannerisms right away but dismissed them, as he had grown accustomed to seeing her act this way.

"Afternoon, Miss Betty," Benjamin said cheerfully.

"Afternoon, Mr. Benjamin." Betty returned the greeting with much less enthusiasm.

"What brings you out here, Miss Betty? Is everything alright at the house?" Benjamin asked.

Betty's eyes rolled. "No . . . There's a lot of bad stuff goin' on there. Evil things."

"Yes sir. Something ain't right here," Ezra added. "I can feel it."

"I just came from upstairs. They have done somethin' to that poor girl," Betty rambled. "I fear she's not long for this world."

"What do you mean, Miss Betty?" asked Benjamin, starting to sense her trepidation.

Betty looked at Benjamin with tangible fear in her eyes. "Something's comin'. You need to take care. Let me see your hand."

Benjamin extended his hand to her, curious about what Betty might do next but skeptical at the same time. Betty removed the pouch from her gown. She opened it and placed two fingers inside. When she removed her fingers, they were both covered in a black powdery substance. Betty opened Benjamin's palm and drew an x in the center. "Darkness be free, free from me. Protect from evil's hand these two that stand in front of me. So shall it be."

As Betty finished reciting her words, she placed an x on Ezra's hand as well. She then handed the pouch to Ezra.

"Put that in your pocket," she said. "It'll protect you wherever you may go."

Ezra placed the pouch inside his pocket and thanked her. Benjamin could sense Ezra's anxiety, but he seemed to be better when Betty was around. Her charm and words calmed him considerably.

"I think we gonna be alright," Benjamin said to Ezra, as he tipped his hat to Betty.

"I sure hope so, Mr. Benjamin," Ezra replied.

"You'll be alright," Betty added, "Just remember that the power that surrounds you is now a part of you, like a fire that nothing can penetrate. All you got to do is keep it lit." Betty grinned.

Benjamin smiled back, but more out of politeness. He didn't really believe any of this, but if it kept the others in check, then so be it.

* * *

While the three continued to chat about lighter subjects and the possibility of new jobs in East Texas, three horses made their way east along the swampy edge of the Neches River. The sun was shining brightly but was filtered out by the large cedars and willows blanketing the path. There was still plenty of daylight left, but Angelique realized that time was running short. She knew Katy was in imminent danger and that they were her only hope of being rescued.

They were silent as they drew closer and closer to the plantation. The four had thoughts of what lay ahead, and most were not pleasant. Wes was particularly pensive, especially when he contemplated Katy's safety. In the past few days, he had grown to care for her deeply—what had started out as empathy had changed as Katy had taken care of him on her own and nursed him back to health. Wes knew deep inside his heart that the feelings were mutual and that Katy would be his wife someday.

As they made their way around a bend in the path, Wes recalled from previous travels that they were near the plantation. He stopped his horse and called out for the others to do the same. "Okay," he said, dropping his horse's reins, "the plantation is not far from here. I'm sure it's guarded well and that they are waiting for us." He paused for a moment while dismounting from the horse and then continued, "I've got an idea. Now I don't know if it will do any good or not, but we can try anyways."

"Any idea is a plus, my good man," Evan said, trying to hold his horse steady.

"What is it?" Angelique asked.

Wes stared silent down the path for a moment then extended his hand to Angelique. "Ma'am," he said quietly, "I believe I need to go on alone first. You can ride with Mr. Evan here."

Angelique took his hand and dismounted. She did not know what he was up to, but she was very curious.

"Okay, so what's your plan?" Angelique asked, standing in front of him.

Wes looked at the three, not somber as expected but in an almost mischievous mood, "Well, you know I'm dead right?" Wes grinned. "And if I could, I would like to borrow your shirt, Mr. Monsieur."

Angelique began to laugh, but Monsieur Chevalier was unaware of Wes' reason for needing his shirt. Evan, on the other hand, began to put the pieces of the puzzle together.

"But of course," Monsieur Chevalier replied, "but may I ask why?"

Wes nodded. "Yes, you may. It's simple really. Everyone over there thinks I'm dead. Wouldn't it be a sight to see me ride up to the front gate alone? I know some of these people are really superstitious. It's worth a try to see what happens. Meanwhile, you three can sneak around the side. Just in case anything happens, you will remain hidden."

"If that is your wish, then so be it," Angelique said, amused but concerned at the same time. In a way, Wes' idea made sense to her. Angelique knew he was taking a deadly chance being the first to arrive at the gate, but somehow, someway, she felt he would survive.

Wes and Monsieur Chevalier changed shirts, as Angelique stood holding the reins of Wes' horse. Evan, having also climbed off his horse, stood gazing into a swampy area just off the path. Both he and Angelique had many questions on their minds but continued their silence while the other two chatted.

"So you think this will work, do you?" Monsieur Chevalier asked, making conversation.

Wes finished putting on the bloodstained shirt before replying. "Sir, I really don't know. But it will take the attention away from you three. My only wish is to get Katy back safe and sound. If I can't accomplish that, then I would rather haunt these swampy roads."

Monsieur Chevalier acknowledged his answer with a nod but mounted his horse in silence. Wes also got on his horse, ready to go. Reality set in as he stared down the path. He began to sense the dangers that he faced. Still, with his love for Katy, he believed his actions would conquer all.

"Wish me luck," Wes said, as his horse trotted toward the plantation.

"Godspeed, dear friend," Evan replied, feeling in his heart that he might never see Wes alive again.

While Wes slowly trotted away, Angelique walked up to Evan's horse. Evan, now back on his horse, extended his hand to help her up. As she grabbed his hand, Evan swiftly pulled Angelique onto the horse then tapped the horse's withers gently with the reins.

* * *

With the four slowly making their way east, the plantation was quiet, especially the house. Elisabeth tiptoed into the room where Fiona slept. She noticed Fiona was restless and mumbling in her sleep but could not understand what she was trying to say. Instead of waking her, Elisabeth felt it better to let Fiona sleep, so she left the room and closed the door behind her.

Elisabeth then made her way up the stairs to the room where Katy lay. As she slowly opened the door, she saw the same scene as that in Fiona's room. Katy was also tossing and turning, mumbling at times, but she continued to sleep. Elisabeth shut the door behind her then walked to the kitchen to see if she was needed there.

With both girls in a dream state, something else began to happen: Fiona's dreams became vivid. She dreamt of walking near the stables in the daylight as everyone was doing their afternoon chores. Fiona walked among them, but no one unnoticed. This confused her.

"Hello?" she said to a passerby, but there was no response.

"Please? Can anyone hear me?" she shouted, but still no response. No one saw her.

Was she dead? Was the tea meant for Katy actually poison? Fiona's eyes welled up with tears. She was frightened. Fiona knelt on the ground and wept. She was scared and alone, with no one to turn to.

Suddenly, a voice rang out from behind her. "No one can hear you," it said.

Fiona quickly turned her head to see who it was, but her anticipated hope for a return to normalcy was immediately banished: there, standing in front of her, was Alice. Pale and emotionless. She stared at Fiona.

"What has happened? Am I dead?" Fiona blurted out the questions, trying to make sense of her situation. "Help me!" she cried.

Alice stood in front of Fiona, betraying no emotion, then turned sideways, raised her arm and pointed to a tree. Fiona turned her head and, to her dismay, saw Katy sitting on a log under the tree in tears.

"What's wrong? Katy?" Fiona shouted, hoping to get her attention, but Katy just sobbed unaware of her presence.

"She can't hear you," Alice said, turning back to face Fiona.

"What's wrong? Please tell me," Fiona beseeched Alice.

"Time is short," Alice replied. "You must take her from this place, or she will perish. Behind the stables is a path leading to the cemetery. Beyond the cemetery, the path leads to the river. You will find allies there. Be swift and silent, or you will perish as well."

"But why? Who is trying to kill her?" Fiona asked, confused. "I believe her to be safe now. Isn't she?"

Alice, still impassive, turned and looked at the weeping Katy. "She is as safe from harm as I was," she said. Then she showed Fiona her wrists.

They had both been cut, injuries that surely would have caused her to bleed to death.

Fiona wiped the tears from her eyes. She knew Alice had died from a mysterious illness, like the maids before, but she had not noticed her wrists at the time.

"Who did this to you?" she asked, as a spark of anger began to grow inside her.

Alice turned to the house and pointed to the porch. Fiona looked and saw Lady Annabelle on the second story, looking out over the grounds. In Fiona's mind, this revelation came as a surprise, but in her deepest thoughts, it was not unexpected. She had never really trusted Lady Annabelle—or the others. Seeing her peers die one by one was too much of a coincidence.

"How do I get her out of the house?" Fiona asked. "She is lame; the house is heavily guarded, and I don't know where she is being held."

"Soon there will be a disturbance at the front gate," Alice replied. "When the Lady goes downstairs and onto the front porch, you will run up the stairs, find Katy and help her down to the room in which you awake. Climb out of the window and go to the stables. There will be a horse tied at the back, waiting. You must then go where I told you. Do not allow yourself to be seen or heard, or you will perish at the hands of the Lady Dragoness."

As soon as Alice finished speaking, Fiona awoke from her sleep. Disoriented and with her head aching, she quietly stood up from the bed and peeked out of the window. All seemed calm and peaceful outside, so she silently got back on the bed just in case anyone was to look in on her. Fiona was certain that it hadn't been a dream and that both she and Katy were in desperate trouble. She could only lie in wait until Lady Annabelle walked down the stairs.

While lying motionless on the bed, Fiona wondered how such a rescue could be pulled off. With her and the injured Katy severely outnumbered, only divine intervention would see them escape successfully. And who were the allies that Alice spoke of? In her heart, Fiona felt that they were not alone, and although their chance of escape was small, there was still a chance.

Katy tossed and turned, weeping in her sleep. The dream that Fiona had just endured had manifested to her as well. Katy sat on a log under a tree. She wept profusely, thinking of what the future held for her and possibly Wes and her friends.

"Katherine," a voice said near her, "the time for tears is over. You must face this with your head held high, for you will dictate the next path."

Katy looked up and saw Alice standing before her. Confused and frightened, she backed up against the tree.

"What's this? Why are you here?" Katy asked, slightly alarmed.

Alice stood in front of her, showing no emotion. "Why? Vengeance," she replied. "Awake. Those that cherish you are nearing. They are in danger. You—and only you—hold the key to the final end. Arise."

Katy felt weak and frail. She knew escape would be impossible just for the fact that her leg was injured and she couldn't walk. Not to mention that the house was surrounded with ranch hands on the lookout for her. The question still remained: how she would escape?

"How am I to walk, much less escape into the swamps again?" Katy asked.

Alice stood silent then extended her hand to Katy. "You will find a way, or you will become as I, one who walks the moors," she said, revealing her cut wrists. "Find the answers from within yourself. They will show you the path to freedom. You are not alone, even in this prison."

Alice pointed at Katy's hand. Katy slowly turned her hand over and noticed the black x on her palm.

"What is this?" she asked.

"It is a sign," Alice replied. "You have allies around you. Make haste your escape when the time arises. Fiona will be waiting at the bottom of the stairs. She will know the way out of the house."

Katy, still fearful of the situation, had no choice but to follow Alice's words. She was confused, and the showdown made little sense to her. So many innocent people along this journey were dead, but for what purpose?

"Why?" Katy asked in a soft voice. "Why me? Am I the cause of all this death? If so, then why me?"

"You have descended from much power. The one who came before you held tremendous power. The power is in your blood," said Alice, again showing her cut wrists. "It was in Catherine's blood as well; strong descendants from times past. Time has reached a crossroads. This will be the end, or this will only be the beginning of the next chapter of horrors. Go forth now, time awaits you."

As soon as Alice finished her speech, she disappeared. Katy awoke and raised her head from her pillow. She was back in her room with no one around. She tried stretching her leg, but the pain was excruciating. She knew she needed to somehow heal the leg, but that seemed impossible.

Scanning the room, Katy noticed a piece of rope hanging from the back of a chair. It gave her an idea. She continued looking around the room until her gaze fell on three wooden stakes lying under the dresser. They were what she was looking for. Katy dragged herself to the edge of the bed and managed to get her feet to the floor, holding onto the side of the bed for stability. She slowly made her way to the chair and picked up the rope, then knelt by the dresser to grab the stakes.

Katy sat on the floor and pulled her leg closer to her body. The pain was intense, but she knew she had no choice but to suffer through it. As she placed two of the stakes on opposite sides of her leg, Katy took the rope and wrapped it tightly around them, securing both her leg and the wood so that her knee would not bend. She then crawled back toward the bed, carrying the other stake in her hand.

Katy stood and tried to put pressure on the injured leg. It was not ideal: she could stand on it and walk with less pain, but what was good enough to get her out of the house, wasn't good enough to help her flee this place. Finally, she slipped back into bed and waited, hiding her leg and the wooden stake with a blanket. She knew time was short, but whatever happened, she would go down fighting.

CHAPTER 20

Etienne, William, Sophie, and Luke arrived at the edge of the Neches River where, luckily, the ferry was waiting. The travelers, together with their wagon and two horses, boarded the ferry, which took little time to make the crossing. Sophie seemed nervous and fidgety. She felt time was passing them by while Angelique was most likely near the plantation by now. As they prepared to move east, something in her felt out of kilter. She noticed that the blackbirds that had been singing all day had now stopped doing so. The denseness of the trees on this side of the river also gave her an eerie feeling, as did the parts of the swamp that reached up near the pathway.

"I don't like this!" Sophie exclaimed.

"I know, mama, but we'll make it through this somehow . . . some way," replied Etienne, edging the horse on faster and faster.

Etienne had become fidgety and irritable. He knew Angelique could stand her ground with most people but Annabelle, he felt, was pure evil, and death seemed to follow her. He could only imagine what horrors poor Katy was going through. This infuriated him to a point that he had never felt before. His normally happy-go-lucky persona had begun morphing into one of pure hatred. Certainly these feelings were not characteristic of him, but still, it was the way he felt.

"Sir, can I make a suggestion?" Luke asked Etienne.

"Sure, son; anything would help about now," Etienne replied solemnly.

"I've been hunting through this area many times," Luke stated. "I know there's a plantation about ten miles from here, and that's where I think we're going. But if we don't want to be noticed, then there is a path off to the side that runs between the plantation and the river. I think we could sneak in through there. I believe it's a shorter distance as well."

Etienne's head perked up, and he now gave Luke his full attention. "Are you sure?" he asked anxiously.

"I'm positive," Luke confirmed. "It's about half a mile up ahead off to the right."

"Can we get a wagon down there?"

"Yes, sir."

Etienne thought for a moment. It would be a blessing to be able to make up lost time. "Okay then," he announced, "let's go. We don't have much time."

"I believe I will stay this course," William said. Although he felt that Luke's shortcut was a good idea, he still felt that someone should stay on this path just in case someone returned.

"I guess that'll mean we got 'em surrounded then," Sophie said excitedly.

William laughed aloud. "Yes, dear lady, I believe we have."

With a light slap to the horse's side, William took off at full speed while Luke rode off the main path and found the shortcut. Etienne inspected the pathway then turned the wagon down the trail. As all four raced toward the plantation along different paths, Sophie felt certain that time was indeed running out. Her thoughts were focused on her friends, and her heart ached at the remote prospect of losing either one of them.

* * *

About ten miles east of her, Wes' thoughts were more focused on taking Katy back from her captors. Most of his life, he had been passive and silent, but the events of the past week and his newfound love had invigorated him. No more would he be the docile little ranch hand. Instead he felt confident and strong. Wes was aware of the dangers, but he doggedly pressed forward.

As his horse slowly turned the corner, Wes saw the entryway to the plantation ahead of him. He noticed three people standing at the gate talking, but they seemed unaware of his presence. Wes rode slowly forward, his head down. Seconds later, his horse gave a quick loud snort, which echoed through the trees.

Hearing the horse, Betty and the others turned to look up the pathway. Betty became uneasy when she saw the lone rider. Benjamin and Ezra, also uncertain of who was approaching them, drew their weapons and walked to the front of the gate. The slow sound of the horse's hooves clopping toward them made Ezra panicky.

"Who goes there?" Benjamin shouted, but the rider ignored his question and kept moving forward.

Benjamin pointed his weapon at the rider. "I said halt! Dang it."

Wes slowed the horse to a stop and looked up, tipping his hat at the three. Betty and Benjamin both now recognized the rider as Wes. Confusion filled their minds: surely Wes had died earlier in the week?

"Wesley?" Benjamin shouted, lowering his weapon.

Wes said nothing but removed his hat, revealing his face and a devilish smile. Benjamin immediately put away his weapon and motioned for Ezra to do the same, but Ezra was hesitant.

"Well, where the hell have you been?" Benjamin asked, walking up to Wes. "We heard you had an accident and died."

"Hardly," Wes chuckled.

Betty and Ezra looked at each other, trying to make sense of the situation. Ezra's revolver was still pointed at Wes.

Wes noticed their bewilderment. "Well? It is me. I don't think I'm a ghost."

Ezra lowered the revolver as Betty walked up to Wes.

"Hmmm . . . You look real enough. So, where you been?" Betty asked, inspecting Wes from head to toe. She noticed his bloodied shirt.

"Recovering," Wes replied. "It would seem that your new boss didn't take kindly to me."

"What happened?" Benjamin asked, glancing at Betty.

"Damn woman shot me," Wes said. "Ben was there. Didn't he say anything?"

"Hell, Ben don't give us any information," Benjamin answered. "I guess he's too highfalutin to mingle with the help."

Betty stood quietly, pondering Wes and trying to make sense of the situation. Her interest seemed to grow more and more with the knowledge that Lady Annabelle had tried to kill him. "So why did she shoot you?" Betty asked, her curiosity getting the better of her.

Wes looked at Betty, shaking his head. "I disagreed with her," he said. He stared into her eyes intently. "It would seem she's nothing but a nasty piece of work. If you don't play by her rules, then you're expendable."

No one commented for fear of being overheard by others. The three knew exactly what Wes was saying but were hesitant to speak out loud purely because they were afraid of Lady Annabelle and the power she had over them, especially Ezra.

"So why did you come back?" Ezra asked. "You know that if she did it to you once, she's bound to do it again."

"I want the girl," Wes stated simply, his gaze steady. "I'm not leaving here without her."

Betty saw the gravity in Wes' eyes. "You know she not gonna allow that," she said somberly.

"I know," Wes replied, "but all the same, I'm not leaving without her."

Betty turned back and glanced at Ezra, shaking her head in dismay. She knew that by taking this stance, Wes was on suicide mission and would cause certain death for others.

"You gonna get yourself killed, Wesley," said Benjamin. "It's not worth it."

"Oh, it's worth it alright," Wes responded quickly. "You know that girl don't deserve this. Now out of my way."

Wes picked up the horse's reins to move forward. "Oh, and one more thing," he added. "You might want to think about leaving yourself, 'cause this place is gonna be surrounded shortly."

Before Wes could finish speaking, a voice was heard shouting up ahead near the house. "My Lady! My Lady!" Sara screamed, dropping the bucket of water she had been carrying.

Sara had seen a rider at the front gate conversing with the other three as she had made her way back from the well. Upon further observation, she had noticed the rider looked eerily like the man who had died only days before. Stunned, she squinted both eyes to get a better look. When she noticed the bloodied shirt, Sara dropped the bucket and ran screaming onto the porch and into the house. "My Lady! It's a ghost!" Sara shrieked, running into the study where Annabelle sat dozing off.

Miss Sterling, hearing the commotion, stormed into the study to determine the source. "What's all this then?" she shouted.

"Pardon me," Sara replied, out of breath and with her head bowed, "but he has returned."

"Who?" asked Miss Sterling.

"The man who died a few days ago. His ghost is at the front gate all covered in blood."

Annabelle looked at Sara in disgust. Sara saw the displeasure in Annabelle's eyes and began to weep. "I am sorry, my Lady, but why does he haunt us? I am frightened!"

Annabelle rose swiftly from her chair. "Are you sure it is him, Sara?" she queried, glancing at Miss Sterling.

"I am positive, my Lady. It is he," Sara replied.

Annabelle's face grew dark. She grabbed her revolver from a nearby desk then walked out of the room without saying a word. In her mind, this could not be true.

Miss Sterling looked at Sara coldly. "Go look after Katherine. Make sure she stays in her room," she said, then followed Annabelle out of the room.

Shaking, Sara slowly left the study in tears.

The shouting had spurred the interest of all who heard it, especially Ben. He left the back porch and walked to the front of the house to see what was going on.

As Wes made his way slowly to the house, Ezra turned to Benjamin. "We need to get out of here now," he said. "That woman's wrong, and this ain't our fight."

Benjamin nodded his head in agreement. "Yep, but I got nowhere else to go."

"We need to go," Betty said abruptly, as she saw a small crowd taking shape in front of the house. "We can go through the woods, back to the stables."

Ezra looked at Benjamin. He knew that by leaving his post, he would surely be punished by Ben, even possibly killed. "I gotta do this," Ezra said uncertainly.

Benjamin looked at Ezra and sighed. "I know, just don't get caught. If he asks, I'll just tell him that we saw something in the woods, and you went out to investigate. Now go!"

While Betty and Ezra hurried into the woods, secretly making their way to the stables, Ben, Annabelle, and Miss Sterling had found their way to the front of the house just in time to see Wes stop his horse in front of the gathered crowd. Confused, Ben looked over at Annabelle, as did Miss Sterling. Annabelle, who was also slightly bewildered, clutched her revolver but was stopped from raising it by Miss Sterling. There were far too many people around, she thought, and she had no idea what the reaction would be.

"Afternoon, Ben, ladies," Wes greeted them with a smile, tipping his hat. He noticed the baffled stares he was getting from the three, and reveled in them. "Looks like you all have just seen a ghost." He laughed.

Meanwhile in the house, Fiona, hearing the commotion, got out of bed and tiptoed to the open window to see what was going on outside. Peering from behind the curtains, she saw no one but could hear that most of the hands and maids were in front of the porch, leaving the house empty. This is my time to make a move, she thought.

Fiona scampered to the door, opening it slightly to see if anyone was around. She saw nothing until she looked up the stairs and noticed Sara at the top, slowly entering a room. Her heart dropped as she quietly closed the door again. What am I to do now? she thought. I can't waste this opportunity.

Just then, a loud thud was heard on the ceiling of her room. Something had happened in the room above. Thinking of Katy's safety, Fiona raced out of the room and up the stairs. The door to Katy's room was partially open. Fiona peeked in the room and saw Sara lying on the floor, passed out, while Katy was trying to pick herself up off the floor. Fiona walked into the room. "Are you alright?" she asked, extending her hand to help Katy.

"Yes, just help me get her into bed," Katy replied briskly.

"What happened?" Fiona asked, looking at Sara.

"She must have run into a wall," Katy said nonchalantly, tossing a stake onto the bed.

Although filled with fear of the uncertainty that surrounded them, Fiona began to chuckle. Ever since the early days in England, she had not got along with Sara and indeed, hated her presence. Katy obviously shared her feelings.

"Come on then, help me before someone finds out," Katy ordered, trying to lift Sara by the arms.

"Hold on, let me do it," Fiona said, bending down to pick Sara up by the shoulders.

Finally, they managed to place Sara onto the bed and covered her with a blanket, showing only the top of her head.

"We need to go. Can you walk?" Fiona asked.

"I believe so. Not very well, but I think I can make it," Katy replied as she limped to the door.

Katy and Fiona made their way down the stairs and into the room Fiona had been sleeping in. Fiona closed the door, locked it and walked over to the window. She glanced outside quickly but didn't see anyone on that side of the house. From the chatter, it appeared that the hands were still out front and would not notice if they snuck out the window. So she opened the window wider and prepared to leave with Katy.

As they climbed through the window one at a time, Fiona and Katy heard the chatter of voices out front. Although Katy could not identify any specific individuals, she was certain she needed to leave—and fast. But her injury hampered her.

In the meantime, Annabelle gathered herself, smiled at Wes and asked, "And what brings you here, sir?"

"I want the girl," Wes said bluntly, his face betraying no emotion.

"And what girl would you be referring to?" Annabelle asked innocently.

"You know damn well what girl. The one you kidnapped."

"Hold on," Ben intervened. "You're insinuating that she kidnapped her? The girl's not well."

"I don't expect you to take my word for it," Wes raised his voice so all could hear. "Just march into that house and bring her out. She'll tell you herself. Anyway, you were there, Ben. Thanks for the help by the way."

Ben was silent, at a loss for words. He knew Wes was right, but he did not want to be on the losing end. Either way, he was stuck.

"She is very sickly and needs much attention," Miss Sterling said. "She is not, nor should she be, subjected to the sowing of your wild oats, so to speak."

"Ma'am, I'll have you know that she is my future wife, and I will treat her with the utmost care," Wes said confidently. "That is more than you can say. How many have died under your care?"

"Obviously one short," Annabelle retorted, referring to her failure at not finishing him off.

"Obviously," Wes reiterated, his voice dripping with irony.

As the discussion became more and more heated, another voice rang out from behind the crowd: the voice of Monsieur Chevalier. He, along with Angelique and Evan, had ridden in through the gates unopposed.

"I can attest to this," he said, stopping just short of Wes. "She murdered my daughter."

A ripple of silence flowed through the lively crowd—they were all looking at Annabelle, waiting for her response.

Annabelle stood silent. She was focused not on Monsieur Chevalier but on Angelique, who was sitting behind Evan on his horse. Her blood boiled at the sight of this gypsy woman, who had been a thorn in her side since the day they had met. Angelique, calm and composed, looked deeply into Annabelle's eyes, a faint smile on her lips.

Annabelle finally responded to the Monsieur, her eyes still on Angelique. "Where is the proof? You can make accusations, but they mean nothing without proof." She adjusted her gaze to look at him. "I would say that your daughter was dead to you, Monsieur, for a long time. Her troubled life only deteriorated as your antics and promiscuity piled on her already shattered world."

"Lies!"

"Are they now? And do you wish everyone here to believe that you have traveled a thousand miles to avenge the death of your daughter? Oh no, Monsieur Chevalier. You and I know the real reason for your journey: it has nothing to do with your daughter, and everything to do with your greed!"

Monsieur Chevalier became increasingly angry with Annabelle's rant and began to lose his composure. "Greed? You have the nerve to talk of greed when you yourself have taken something of mine!"

Annabelle began to grin openly, as a small feeling of satisfaction settled in. "And what is it that I have taken? What is it that you followed me halfway around the world for?"

"Yes, I would like to know, too," Evan added, seeing now the reason Angelique had warned him. "This is the first time I hear of this."

Monsieur Chevalier knew his temper had gotten the better of him. He felt his only hope was to be proactive and to come clean with Evan. "She took a shipment of gold en route to the Netherlands. It's worth millions."

"Pardon me for asking, Monsieur," Evan enquired. "I know you're a rich man, but may I ask how you acquired millions in gold?"

"The Ashanti wars," Annabelle intervened. "He had a deal with us. We were to confiscate a large amount of gold in the city of Kumasi along the Gold Coast of Africa and place it aboard his ship. He was to sail to Scotland and take his share to the Netherlands."

"Instead you had the Royal Navy raid my ship and take it all. They killed everyone onboard," Monsieur Chevalier replied furiously.

"Hold on." Evan was confused. "Let me get this straight. The Falsworth's are gold raiders?"

"No, we had confidants in the British military. We knew the Ashanti kingdom's fall was imminent," Annabelle answered. "We were just fortunate enough to beat the British forces to some of gold before they attacked and burned the city. As for his allegation of stealing, his ship never made it to Scotland. He tried to sail it straight to the Netherlands. Fortunately, we were tipped off by one of his employees and sent forth one of our many vessels."

Monsieur Chevalier stood by silently as Evan and Annabelle traded questions and answers.

At the same time, on the other side of the house, both Fiona and Katy had managed to escape out of the window. Katy limped—she was in obvious pain—and Fiona tried desperately to hold her up while they walked, but she struggled.

As Fiona and Katy approached the stables, the door suddenly opened, frightening them both. It was Betty. She looked at the two with nothing but compassion. Here before her stood two young girls on the verge of sixteen, in a strange land with the one injured. Betty could see nothing but helplessness in their eyes.

"Hurry up," Betty said, motioning for them to enter the stable.

They hurried into the stable, and Fiona closed the door behind them. Once inside, they saw Ezra saddling up a horse. As he turned around, he was surprised to see the young girls.

"What's going on?" he asked Betty.

Betty stared into his eyes. "I believe they need to escape more than us, Ezra."

Ezra looked at the girls and nodded his head. He knew they were in trouble and desperate. "I do believe you're right, Betty. Let's get them on this horse now."

"Bless you, sir" Katy and Fiona replied in unison.

Ezra first gently helped Katy onto the horse, then Fiona, as Betty opened the back door to the stable.

"Do you know how to ride," Ezra asked, as he led them out the door.

"Yes, sir," Katy replied, ". . . and thank you. I pray your good deed brings you a thousand blessings. Thank you both." Katy took the reins and trotted slowly out of sight into the forest.

Betty put her arm around Ezra, as they watched the girls ride away. "Yep, we gonna make that journey one day, but I guess it's not today." She laughed.

"I guess not." Ezra joined her laughter, as he also put his arm around her. "But I think we did good."

With the option of escaping to Louisiana out of the question, they now turned around and headed to the other door to go back to the house to see what was happening. Just then Ezra looked to his right, to a darkened part of the stable. He noticed a face smiling at him. Ezra jumped in fright, but Betty, seeing the same, quickly calmed him down.

It was the ghostly apparition that he had seen a few days earlier. She seemed different to him this time, but it was still something that he did not understand. The apparition stared and smiled at the pair until she finally disappeared into the darkness of the stables.

Betty grabbed Ezra's hand and clung tightly. "You know, I believe you just made a friend."

Ezra walked hurriedly out of the door. "Come on, let's get out of here."

Friend or foe, Ezra was not in the mood to deal with spirits. He figured he would leave that to Betty.

CHAPTER 21

Ezra and Betty walked up to the house. Seeing all of the staff listening intently to Lady Annabelle, Evan, and Monsieur Chevalier's exchange, they were convinced that their plans to leave would have been successful, but they had no regrets. There would be another opportunity to leave. Betty looked at Evan and noticed Angelique sitting behind him.

Angelique, listening and scanning the crowd, caught Betty staring at her. She gave her a quick smile then bowed her head in an act of acknowledgement. Betty did the same. She then walked back to her quarters while Ezra headed to the front gate. To Betty, the current disruption at the house didn't concern her, and she felt no desire to hear the rhetoric of those gathered, even though their voices could be heard in the distance.

"Say what you will," Monsieur Chevalier said, "but I have had no dealings with you. It is the elder Lady Falsworth whom I dealt with."

"Ah, but as Falsworths, we are one and the same," Annabelle responded snidely. "Your greed is your downfall, and you will not take advantage of either me or any others in my circle."

"Greed? Madame, you have no right to talk of greed!" Monsieur Chevalier shouted, becoming angrier with each passing moment. "I don't know who you are, or what you have done with the Baroness, but you will not get away with any of this."

All of a sudden a shot rang out, causing everyone to jolt. Wes had raised his revolver and fired into the air. The crowd went silent, along with both Annabelle and Monsieur Chevalier.

Now that I have y'alls' attention," Wes drawled, lowering his weapon, "I believe we've figured out that neither one of y'all's worth a damn. So now let's get back to what was intended in the first place. Where's the girl?"

Annabelle stared at Wes for a moment, her hand still on her revolver, when suddenly, from behind her, Sara appeared. She was holding the side of her head and crying profusely. Everyone turned to look at her.

"My Lady," Sara sobbed, "she hit me."

"Who hit you?" Miss Sterling asked.

"Katy. She is gone!" Sara bawled louder. "Forgive me, my Lady."

Annabelle glared at Sara bitterly. "How did this happen?"

"Sorry, my Lady, I don't know," Sara explained. "I went to check on her, and she hit me. Forgive me." Sara was becoming increasingly upset, her chest heaving with each word. The contemptuous look in Annabelle's eyes was far more painful than any blow from Katy. Sara had witnessed Annabelle's intolerance of failure, and she cringed at the possibility of Annabelle's wrath.

Wes and Angelique felt relieved to hear of Katy's escape, but they still needed to find her. Angelique whispered to Evan, "I need to leave here. Katy's out there somewhere. I need the horse."

Evan turned his head slightly to murmur his agreement before dismounting. Angelique moved forward and took the reins. She then quickly turned the horse and spurred it past everyone toward the woods. Wes followed close on her heels.

Annabelle instantaneously swept into action. "Someone! Prepare me a horse now!" she shouted. "This conversation is over!"

She stepped off the porch and headed for the stables. Ben immediately motioned for a couple of ranch hands to go ahead of her and organize some horses.

As Annabelle marched away from him, Monsieur Chevalier became irate: they had not finished their business. "Come back!" he yelled. "I am not through here. You will tell me where my gold is!" He raised his revolver and pointed it at Annabelle. "Halt! Or I will shoot!" he roared.

Annabelle stopped and turned to look at Monsieur Chevalier. "No, you won't," she said calmly.

Monsieur Chevalier sneered. "Do you mock me?"

"Yes, yes I do," she replied. "Now that you've stated your real reason for your journey here, do you really think anyone will give you the slightest bit of sympathy? I think not. And why would you shoot me when I am the only one that knows where the gold is buried?" Annabelle grinned at the Monsieur, who was becoming more frustrated by the second. "Well, here I am. Go ahead. Shoot me," she challenged him.

Monsieur Chevalier knew she was right. He knew that if he killed her, the gold would be lost forever. As he lowered his weapon Annabelle began to laugh out loud.

"So, we see your true self! All this talk of vengeance was just a ploy. Catherine knew you well, and so she shall again! The time for reckoning is here. Dear Catherine served her purpose. But then again, you knew this." Annabelle raised her revolver. She aimed it at Monsieur Chevalier, a wide smile on her face.

Monsieur Chevalier, seeing this, quickly took aim, but it was too late. Annabelle pulled the trigger of her revolver and shot him in the head, killing him instantly. Evan, watching this unfold, pulled out his pistol. Ben did the same in response, as did the few remaining ranch hands.

"It was self-defense!" Ben shouted. "You saw it!"

Evan knew he was outnumbered so immediately lowered his revolver. It would be pointless to die here for nothing.

As soon as Annabelle had pulled the trigger, she turned and strode toward the stables with Miss Sterling beside her. She didn't look back. Sara, now whimpering from the shock of what had just transpired, followed swiftly behind her, as did Hana. As the four moved toward the front of the stable, three ranch hands were hurriedly saddling up four horses.

"It is time to leave this place," said Miss Sterling, slightly irritated at having to deal with Katy's disappearance once again.

"We will leave when I see fit," Annabelle snapped back harshly. "In the meantime, gather the maids and wait for my return."

Annabelle grabbed the reins of a newly saddled horse and got on. After giving Miss Sterling a cold look, she turned the horse toward the path and rode into the woods. Both Sara and Hana stood staring at Miss Sterling as if looking for answers to what was happening.

"Gather your things and tell the rest to do the same," she said as she gazed into the woods. "Load them onto the carriage. We are leaving."

Sara and Hana were shocked, "B-b-but what of Lady Falsworth?" Sara stuttered. "Will she not be angry if we leave?"

"She will catch up. Now go!" Miss Sterling ordered, her irritation rising. She knew Annabelle wasn't thinking straight. Her obsession with Katy was clouding her normally cunning and precise way of thinking, which made Agatha feel that her survival might be in danger.

"We need the carriages ready," Agatha said to Ben, who was wondering whether or not to follow Annabelle. "We leave within the hour."

Ben hesitated at first but then instructed a couple of ranch hands to ready the carriages. He turned to Agatha, who was becoming frustrated by the incessant questions being asked by Hana and Sara.

"Silence!" she yelled. "Do what I told you. Now go."

The two maids walked quickly away from her toward the house. Ben also turned away and headed into the stables but was stopped by Evan and a slightly befuddled William, who had just arrived at the plantation and was unaware of what had led to the shooting. They had questions about what to do with Monsieur Chevalier's body and horse.

This left Agatha alone to ponder her next move. She knew she couldn't leave without Annabelle, but events had taken a deathly turn. For Katy on the other hand, they had come as a blessing.

Katy and Fiona rode down the path south of the plantation. Katy was not an expert rider by any means, so she rode slowly until they reached a fork in the path, near the cemetery. As the horse walked on, they heard a sound in the distance—the sound of a wagon speeding toward them. They were instantly afraid.

"Hurry," Fiona whispered anxiously, "Someone's coming."

Katy nervously nudged the side of the horse with her uninjured foot to make it speed up. She didn't know who was making their way down the path, but to be safe, she and Fiona needed to stay out of sight. The horse made its way down the southern path, away from the oncoming wagon and deeper into the murky landscape of the swampy river.

As Katy retreated farther and farther away from the plantation, Etienne, Sophie, and Luke moved closer and closer, finally arriving at the fork in the path.

"To the left," Luke said, pointing.

Etienne slowed the wagon and proceeded to turn left on the narrow path. Sophie leaned over the side of the wagon, making sure the wheel wasn't near the edge. The last thing either wanted was to be stuck in the swamp.

"You okay! Go!" Sophie shouted to Etienne.

Etienne continued turning the wagon north and then speeded the horses up. The three passed the cemetery with daylight swiftly fading amongst the towering trees.

"I don't like this," said Sophie, noticing the primitive markings on the gravestones.

"I know, but it's something we need to do," replied Etienne. He was apprehensive about the whole situation.

Sophie nodded in agreement, but her look of concern was noticed by Etienne. He reached his hand to her back, patting her lightly to offer his support. He knew Sophie was extremely upset, but there was nothing he could do under the circumstances.

Luke led the way up the path between the water oaks, cypress, and cedars. He felt that they were just a few miles from the plantation, if not less, and were making good time. Minutes passed before a sudden movement was detected up ahead.

"Riders," Luke said. Etienne could not see that far so took his word for it. Luke's young eyes definitely seemed to work better in the dusk.

"It's Gitane!" Luke exclaimed.

"This doesn't sound right," said Sophie. "How'd she get here?"

"We'll find out soon, momma," Etienne said quietly.

Further up the path, Angelique and Wes were riding at a furious pace. "I believe we have company," Angelique said, noticing Etienne's wagon.

Wes looked down the path, a bit confused about why Katy was not with them. Surely they had passed her? By all accounts, she would have had to travel this way. The five finally converged in the middle of the path. They had more questions than answers.

"Have you seen Katy?" Angelique asked Etienne breathlessly.

Both Etienne and Sophie shook their heads in confusion. "We haven't seen anybody," Etienne replied.

"She would have had to travel this way," Wes said, looking at the surrounding swamp. "It's the only way out."

"We didn't see anything," Sophie reiterated. "But what happened? Did she escape?"

"We believe so," Angelique said, "and I'm sure she made her way down this path."

"Where are the others?" Sophie asked.

"They are still at the plantation," Wes replied, "although it may be possible that some of them are somewhere behind us heading this way to look for her as well."

A mixture of confusion, uncertainty, and fear set in. The thought of Lady Falsworth and her hired guns on their trail didn't sit well with anyone, and they all knew they couldn't stay there. Etienne, knowing he couldn't move up the path, felt a bit unnerved. The path, although solid for travel, was extremely narrow and to turn the wagon southward without dropping it or the horses into the swamp was impossible.

"So, what are we gonna do?" asked Sophie, leaning over the wagon and looking into the murky water alongside the path.

Etienne thought for a moment. "We're just gonna have to take the horses off and turn the wagon ourselves I guess," he said, not very enthused. "It's either that or ride a few miles up ahead and hope for the best."

Angelique glanced at the horses then thought back to her journey through the path. "I believe it will be wide enough to turn the wagon about three miles up ahead," she said remembering a small treeless embankment along the way. "I'm sure you will be able to turn the horses safely, but it will be a tight fit."

Etienne nodded in agreement. "I think that's a good idea, Gitane."

"Just be careful. We don't know who is following us," Angelique warned.

"This path don't hold much of a place to hide for an ambush I reckon," Etienne said as he picked up his rifle, checked the scope and then handed it to Sophie. "I believe we'll be alright."

Sophie took the rifle, cocked it and, with a stoic look on her face, told him to ride on. The horses immediately started up the path. Luke followed them, making sure that everything was secure. Angelique knew in her heart that they would be fine. Her thoughts drew more and more to Katy, who was most likely out in the swamp, surrounded by danger. Luck had been with her the first time round, but it was not a good idea to tempt the cold hand of fate yet again.

"Let's go! We have no time to waste," Angelique said to Wes, popping the reins of the horse. The animal immediately sprang forward down the darkened path. The light of the day was dissipating by the second, which made travel in this swamp nearly impossible.

"If only I had a torch," Wes said as he rode alongside Angelique.

"Don't worry. Your eyes will become used to the darkness," Angelique replied. "Your horse is able to see; that's the most important thing."

"Yes, I've already experienced just how good a horse's eyesight is in this swamp," Wes grumbled, thinking back to his first night here when he chased Katy through the swamp. "My concern is not the dark, it's what's creeping around in it."

Angelique grinned. She sensed Wes' dislike for the area and all things slithery. "Tell me, did that torch help you last time?" she chuckled. "I have been around for a few years, sometimes the darkness can be your ally, trust me."

They rode into the ever-darkening swamp at a steady pace and finally reached the crossroads through which they had traveled earlier. They proceeded south, deeper into the swamp, but there was still no sign of Katy. Angelique, however, was confident that they would eventually find her. Wes, on the other hand, had put his trust in Angelique. In his heart, he felt they would find Katy, but it would be through the support and blessings of this gypsy woman whom he knew only vaguely.

As Angelique and Wes advanced down the path, Wes could not remove Annabelle from his mind. He knew she would also be searching for Katy and believed it to be entirely possible that she could be right behind them, hiding in the darkness like a demon waiting to strike. As his thoughts of Annabelle manifested, his arm began to throb in pain.

"Typical," he muttered to himself, but in his head, the pain was just a reminder of what and who he was dealing with. He would find Katy, and rest assured, no one would stand in his way.

With Angelique and Wes on Katy's trail, Etienne, Sophie, and Luke made their way up the path toward the plantation in search of the turnaround Angelique had told them about. Darkness had all but taken over what little light remained, which made Sophie a bit nervous.

"I can't see nothin'," she said, clutching the rifle tightly.

"Don't worry, your eyes will get used to it," Etienne said. "According to Gitane, the turnaround should be anytime now."

"I hope so. This dark is makin' me jittery," Sophie mumbled, staring ahead of them.

Luke, who was now riding in front of the wagon, looked forward. He could see the path expanding in front of him. The trees opened up to a small clearing of solid ground with the swamp to the left of the path. "I think this is it!" he exclaimed excitedly.

Etienne, his eyes adjusting to the increasing darkness, also saw the clearing. He drove the wagon onward, finally coming to a stop in the grassy highland, away from the murky swamp, and let out a sigh of relief. He felt very uneasy traveling in the swamp in the dark, not knowing who, if anyone, he would meet on the path. Still, he believed he needed to turn the wagon around in a hurry—for Katy.

As Etienne slowly turned the horses toward the south, Luke sat on horseback peering into the surrounding darkness. Sophie, feeling edgy, did the same. What had been left of the light of day was now dissolving into the pitch blackness of the swamp. This made the three even more jittery, and they wondered if traveling south was even possible. One wrong turn or riding too close to the edge could mean certain death.

"We need light," Luke said, shaking his head, thinking of the journey south.

"I have matches, but I don't see us making torches out of this moldy mess," Etienne said, speaking of the wood alongside the swamp.

Sophie looked into the back of the wagon and noticed two sacks and a crate. "What's in these things?" she asked. "Anything to burn?"

Etienne glanced into the back of the wagon. "I don't know. I think Thomas put them there. Probably just some hides."

Sophie laid her rifle down, climbed to the back and began sifting through the sacks. Etienne had been right, the sacks contained hides, mostly with a few cotton cloths near the top. After a hurried search through the sacks, Sophie turned to the small crate and noticed a few jars hidden amongst some dried seed sacks. After a thorough search through the sacks, Sophie returned her attention to the jars. A quick sniff of their contents made her cringe, as if smelling something foul. "Turpentine?" Sophie asked herself as she held the jar away from her nose and grimaced.

Etienne looked at her. "Are you sure?"

"Yes, I know the smell. I think we got something to burn."

Sophie put the jar down and pulled the cotton cloths out of the sacks. Luke got off his horse and picked a few sturdy branches from the ground, placing them near Sophie on the back of the wagon. Sophie quickly dipped the cloths into the turpentine, soaking them well, and wrapped the cloths around the sticks.

While Sophie assembled the torches, the horses started snorting and stamping their feet intermittently. They were clearly aware of something unusual, but no one was paying any attention. Their primary concern was light.

"Okay, here you go," Sophie said, as she handed a torch to each man.

Etienne pulled out some matches out of his pocket and proceeded to light his torch. The horses were still edgy.

"Whoa!" he said to the horses, pulling on the reins. "What's wrong with you? Settle down."

Luke's horse was spooked and restless. Luke was worried that maybe something was near them that they couldn't see. He became increasingly tense and asked Etienne for the matches.

Etienne was still fiddling with them. "Hold on. I'll get this lit," he said.

Just then, the snort of a horse was heard near the tree line a few yards away from them. As the three quickly whipped around in the direction of the sound, Etienne struck a match and touched it to Luke's torch.

"What was that?" Sophie asked, feeling around the wagon for her rifle. She was white-cold with fear.

Luke moved the torch forward in the direction of the tree line, backing up slowly to his horse at the same time. His rifle was in his saddlebag, and he was in desperate need of protection.

A click was heard from the same direction as the horse near the tree line, the sound of a gun being cocked. With light of the torches, all three could see clearly why their horses had been spooked: not thirty feet away was a horse, standing silently, with a rider on its back. The rider was pointing a Colt revolver at them.

"You, lad," the rider said in a gruff voice, "be very careful and hand me your rifle."

Luke saw that there was no chance of escape. He slowly lifted the rifle from the saddlebag, walked to the rider and handed it over. Through the flickering light of the torch, the three travelers watched on with their hands raised as the rider, a woman, grabbed the butt of the rifle from Luke and placed it in her saddlebag.

Sophie sat quietly. Etienne's rifle was just a few feet away, but she could not risk reaching for it without the woman seeing her. Etienne, still holding the torch, felt helpless. He had let someone sneak up on him. This had never happened to him before.

"You two, throw your torches down," Annabelle instructed Etienne and Sophie.

Both heeded her order then waited reluctantly for her next move.

"Well now," Annabelle said as she trotted the horse toward Luke. "This is your lucky day. I have no desire to kill you unless you provoke me. Take heed of this one and only warning." Annabelle continued pointing her revolver at the three. "You lad, hand me the torch, then kneel on the ground, nice and easy," she said, turning her attention to Etienne and Sophie. "As for you two, get off the wagon and kneel beside him."

Luke handed Annabelle the torch, then did as she had asked and knelt on the ground. Sophie and Etienne followed suit. Annabelle trotted her horse near the wagon. The other horses snorted nervously. Without dismounting, Annabelle reached to the back of the wagon where Sophie had made the torches. Seeing the jar of turpentine, she struck it with the torch. The jar shattered and the turpentine ran freely onto the wooded wagon but did not catch aflame.

Annabelle stared at the torch in her hand. Nervous whinnying from the three other horses filled the air. Etienne knelt in silence, his head lowered. He felt powerless to protect his wife.

"If you follow me, I will kill you," Annabelle said, extending the torch over the wagon. "Heed my warning!"

Annabelle touched the flames to the spilt turpentine. The liquid immediately lit up in flames. The horses hitched to the wagon were spooked and took off down the path into the darkness of the swamp. Luke's horse backed away from the fiery wagon but stayed close to Luke. Annabelle threw the torch at the horse, hitting its flanks. The horse instantly galloped off down the path.

"As I said, only death will be your fate if you follow me." Annabelle grinned, turned her horse and headed off down the path into the darkness.

Etienne, Sophie, and Luke got up from the ground, still in shock by what had just happened. They could see the flames from the wagon in the distance.

"We need to stop that wagon!" Sophie shouted as she started running down the path. "Them horses gonna burn up."

"Hold on, momma, it's not safe!" Etienne yelled, trying to stop her.

As Sophie ran down the path into the darkness, tears filled her eyes. She knew Angelique and Wes were in grave trouble—and Katy—but she was helpless to save her friends. "No! I can't let it end this way," Sophie sobbed as she dropped to her knees.

Luke ran up to her and put his hand on her shoulder. "You've always been there for me, madame," he said looking down the path. "I promise you, I will find your friends and whoever this woman is, she will pay for this." With that, Luke ran as fast as he could down the path after the horses.

Etienne, finally catching up to his wife, knelt next to her and put his arms around her. "Believe, momma. Believe," he said as he held her tight.

CHAPTER 22

The horse walked slowly along the narrow path leading to the river in the pitch blackness. Katy and Fiona, fearful of what lay around them, clung to each other. They both now felt that their escape may have been premature.

"What are we to do?" Fiona asked nervously, listening to the sounds in the darkness.

"I would hope to have seen the river by now," Katy replied. "It is near, I feel it."

"And what will we do when we reach the river?" Fiona asked, losing faith in Katy by the second.

"Relax," Katy replied, sensing Fiona's ambivalence. "There will be places to hide when we get to the river. We can hide until dawn and then find our way across to safety."

"Aren't you forgetting something?" Fiona was fretting. "If they set the dogs on us, we will be as good as dead."

Katy frowned. "They'll have to find us first. Anyway, we have a horse. We'll be fine."

"I pray that you're right."

A few minutes passed as the horse slowly made its way along the path. Fiona, still terrified that they were being followed, founded Katy's lack of riding ability unbearable. "Blimey. It'll be tomorrow evening before we even see the river at this pace," she said with no small amount of impatience.

"Okay, okay, but it's not every day that I find myself on a horse," Katy replied good-naturedly. "I also don't know what is ahead of us. There are many things here—dangerous, deadly things. I can't see in front of me."

"We need light." Fiona slapped her arm to kill a mosquito. "Bloody vicious creatures."

Katy listened to Fiona while staring into their pitch-black surroundings. Suddenly Katy noticed a tiny light flickering in the distance. She squinted her eyes to try to see more clearly but couldn't.

"Shhh . . .," Katy whispered. "Look, over there to the right."

Fiona silenced herself and peered out into the darkness. Her body trembled as she saw a small flickering of light hovering above the water and moving slowly toward them. "What is it?" Fiona asked, grabbing Katy's shoulder in fear.

"I don't know," Katy replied, her heart pounding.

The light drew nearer and nearer, pulsating through the air. They noticed another light behind the first, slowly floating toward them. Then another. And another . . . Until the murky swamp was filled with hundreds of tiny lights.

"Fairies?" Fiona asked as she watched the lights cover the area.

"No. Fireflies," Katy replied turning to Fiona and giving her an odd stare.

"Well, they could be." Fiona frowned, still uncertain.

"Whatever they are, they're here to help," Katy murmured. "By the gods, we're going to get out of here." With light cast over the area, Katy tugged on the reins of the horse, which made it speed up. Unfortunately, the trail ended only yards ahead. The fireflies seemed to hover around the path.

"What are we to do now?" Fiona asked, perplexed by the turn of events.

"We go back," Katy answered without hesitation. "There was another path leading away from the plantation. We'll retrace our steps and pray they haven't figured out where we are."

Fiona didn't like the idea of having to go back, but she knew there was no alternative. They could either take their chances on the path or wait in this godforsaken swamp and be eaten alive by whatever crawled out of it. "Okay, let's go then," she said with a sigh.

Katy turned the horse around and headed back north toward the plantation at a pace that was still too slow for Fiona.

"Hurry up!" Fiona exclaimed.

"I'm doing the best I can!" replied Katy, nearly in tears.

"Stop the horse," Fiona said and jumped off.

Katy pulled tightly on the reins, making the horse come to a complete halt. Fiona, who as a child, had had some experience riding horses, had decided to take over. As she pulled herself up, Katy let go of the reins and shuffled backward. Now in control, Fiona grabbed the reins and gave the horse a slight nudge with her foot. This immediately propelled the horse up the path.

Fireflies, by the thousands, continued to light the pathway, much to the girls' delight and wonder. A lit path meant a faster escape, especially with Fiona at the helm. The horse continued up the path, galloping faster, heading into uncertainty. Neither girl knew what would be waiting for them on the other side, but still they continued on, searching for a way out.

* * *

Further up the same path, Angelique and Wes were unknowingly riding slowly toward the girls. They however were in complete darkness. Fortunately, this didn't seem to faze the horses. Wes, however, still unnerved by his surroundings, was troubled but remained silent. He took some comfort in Angelique's confidence and determination to press on.

"We must be close," Angelique said, peering out over the blackened path.

"I sure hope so," replied Wes, trying to focus his eyes.

Minutes passed as they rode on through the darkness. Suddenly Angelique noticed a faint light up ahead. Could it be Katy, she wondered. Wes also seeing the light, grasped his revolver and raised it swiftly in front of him.

"Better to be safe than sorry," he said, his eyes trained on the light.

"Do not fire unless you know for sure who is in front of you," Angelique warned, aware that Wes was uneasy about being in the swamp.

"Yes, ma'am," he replied. "I'm just taking precautions."

The light drew nearer as they travelled down the path. Sparkling and lighting the way, the origin of the lights in front of them was soon revealed.

"Fireflies?" Wes called out in surprise.

"Yes, and by the gods they are welcome!" Angelique exclaimed. "You ask for light, and there you have it." She grinned at him.

The path became brighter with every second. The ghostly lights eased Wes' fear of the dark—and his nervous trigger finger—although an eeriness engulfed their surroundings; an eeriness that emphasized the uncertainty of their future. Suddenly, from up ahead, the sound of a trotting horse could be heard. It became louder and louder as it drew nearer until both Angelique and Wes could see a shadow heading toward them.

"Katy?" Wes thought aloud.

The shadow moved into view. Seeing Katy on the back of the horse, Angelique began to chuckle and Wes called out her name.

Katy looked up and saw both Angelique and Wes on horseback in the shadows in front of them. "Stop the horse!" she said to Fiona. "They're here to help us."

Fiona pulled the reins back, and the horse came to a halt in front of Angelique and Wes. Wes immediately got off his horse and ran to Katy. He held out his arms to her. Katy slipped off the horse, landing on one leg, and fell into Wes' arms.

"Blimey, is that a ghost?" Fiona gasped as she realized it was Wes.

"No, he's not a ghost. He's very much alive." Katy wept as she and Wes embraced. "I knew you would come, I knew it."

"She's not gonna harm you anymore," Wes replied, tears in his eyes, holding Katy as tightly as he could.

"She's evil!" Katy cried. "She's not of this world."

"Don't worry, we're here now and you're safe," Wes replied, still embracing her.

"But she will stop at nothing. I sense her watching us, even now." Katy rambled on and on.

The three could see Katy was stricken with a paralyzing fear of Annabelle. She wept uncontrollably, and mentally, she was in a shambles. Both Fiona and Angelique were still on their horses. Fiona knew Katy had been through immense stress in recent weeks and could only imagine how Annabelle had tormented her. Angelique and Fiona made eye contact, grinned and nodded politely.

"What kind of person would torture an innocent soul like this?" Wes asked, holding Katy in his arms as she sobbed uncontrollably.

"Not a person; a heretic," Fiona replied. "All of us maids were accumulated by the elder Baroness, but Lady Annabelle was forced upon us in a single night. I am still in the dark about what really happened."

"What do you mean you were accumulated?" asked Wes.

"All of us were and are homeless, orphans, runaways; children without hope," Fiona replied. "We found shelter in an old woman's home and were thankful for it. None of us realized the consequences since we hadn't a future that we could see. Now, after being sent halfway across the world into the wilderness to die in a moor, I am trying to grasp the reality of what is to come."

Angelique looked at Fiona's calm demeanor. "And what is to become of you?" she asked.

"I cannot answer this," Fiona responded matter-of-factly, "for only the gods know my fate, but sadly I know nothing of them. I truly am alone."

"You're never alone," Angelique said. "You've made it this far, haven't you?"

"Yes, by my own accord," Fiona raised her voice. "I have made it this far with the aid of no one and nothing. I await the same in my future." Fiona's pain was more heartfelt with each word spoken. Within her harsh speech flowed bitterness and contempt. Only a young lass of seventeen, Fiona felt her life was nothing more than that of an enslaved animal with no hope nor future.

"But you are free," Angelique said. "You have waited patiently for this night, and now it is upon you."

"Alas, I wish that were true, but I know she awaits me in the darkness. She awaits us all."

Angelique's horse nudged her horse next to Fiona's and extended her arm out to her shoulder. "I know well what you feel, the pain of abandonment and despair. To be abandoned and whisked away from everything you knew. To see the only one who loved you lie dying as a pauper with no help from either family or strangers. You lose faith in everyone and everything until you have no other alternative but to trust the only one who deems you worthy."

"Yourself," Fiona answered, glancing at Katy, who was now beginning to compose herself.

Angelique nodded and smiled at Fiona. "And she will never, ever abandon you."

"True, but she is frequently wrong," Fiona replied, cracking a smile.

The fireflies continued to swarm around the four but failed to light the path in front of them. As they all exchanged stories of what had happened to them over the past few days, both Angelique and Fiona noticed the horses becoming nervous.

"Shhh . . . It's all right . . . settle down," Fiona said lightly to her horse. She noticed Angelique staring out in the darkness as if looking for something.

"What's wrong?" Fiona asked her.

Before Angelique could answer, a shot rang out from the darkness.

"No!" Katy screamed as Angelique fell off the horse and onto the ground. Wes immediately jumped in front of Katy, reaching for his revolver. Unfortunately, he had left it on his horse, which was standing about twenty yards behind him.

Suddenly a horse appeared from the darkness; the rider's revolver pointing at Wes. Fiona's horse had started bucking violently, but she had managed to hold onto the reins and pull back tighter and tighter until the horse settled. Katy, seeing Angelique on the ground, rushed to her.

The horse stopped well in front of Angelique. "Do not move!" Annabelle's voice rang out. Her revolver was still aimed at Wes.

Fiona, filled with sheer rage, trotted her horse slowly toward Annabelle, while her one hand, hidden in skirts, reached for the long handled knife that Ezra had left in the horse's saddle. Her eyes were fixed on Annabelle.

"Get back!" Annabelle pointed the revolver at Fiona but kept a close eye on Wes as well.

Fiona continued to move slowly toward her. Annabelle could see in her hate-filled eyes that she was not going to be stopped. Wes again moved toward Katy. Though unarmed, his first instinct was to protect her.

"This is madness," Wes said standing in front of Katy and Angelique, who lay motionless on the ground.

Annabelle moved her revolver back and forth between Wes and Fiona. As Annabelle's eyes locked on Fiona, she could sense the strength of Fiona's hatred toward her.

"Before night falls upon this land tomorrow, I promise that you will see my face once again! By the gods, 'tis the last thing you will ever see!" said Fiona, the knife now raised as she charged the horse toward Annabelle.

Annabelle swung the revolver toward her and pulled the trigger. The bullet penetrated Fiona's side but could not stop the force of her attack. Fiona lurched forward and plunged the knife into Annabelle's side. Annabelle screamed in pain, falling off her horse into the damp mud and hitting her head on a rock. Fiona also fell from the momentum of the two horses coming together. She was bleeding profusely from the gunshot wound.

Wes saw the revolver lying next to Annabelle and ran to get it before she did. Dazed and confused from hitting her head, Annabelle felt someone rushing toward her. She opened her eyes and saw the revolver lying in front of her. Frantically she reached for the pistol, grabbing it while trying desperately to focus her vision.

Annabelle raised the revolver just in time to ward off Wes' charge. As she lay on the ground trying to get her sight back, Wes stood silently, like a wolf biding his time until his prey made a mistake. Unfortunately for Wes, Annabelle rarely made mistakes.

"Do not move!" Annabelle shouted. It was clear that she was in pain—blood was pumping from her wound.

Wes walked backward toward Katy, his eyes constantly monitoring Annabelle's shaky hand, which clasped the trigger uncertainly. Her eyes fluttered and a dark look dwelled on her face, as she attempted to rise from the ground.

Fiona also lay on the ground, blood flowing freely from her wound. Her body began to shake as the cold shadow of death hovered over her. Annabelle, finally gathering her wits about her, looked across at Fiona. She could see that her last seconds of life were near although her eyes seemed to follow Annabelle's every move.

Fiona slowly lifted her hand and pointed toward Annabelle, she tried desperately to speak. Stuttering and gasping for air, she could only blurt out a single word. One that Annabelle understood. "E-e-emlé . . . emlékszem!" Fiona gasped as her body became weak and the signs of her life faded.

She closed her eyes, uttering her last words, "Remember . . . me."

Hearing Fiona, Angelique's eyes opened. She was injured and confused, lying motionless; not knowing what evil surrounded her.

Annabelle, looking past Fiona's body, turned her attention to Wes and Katy. As she pointed the revolver in their direction, she felt intense pain on her opposite side. She looked down to her wound and saw her clothing was covered in blood. She knew she needed to get back to the plantation—quickly. As she grabbed the reins of her horse and slowly hoisted herself onto it, Wes grabbed Katy's hand and tried to pull her down the path as fast as he could. Katy with her leg feeling lame and hesitant to leave Angelique, trusted Wes and moved as swiftly as she was able.

Although in severe pain, Annabelle was now on her horse and thought it best not to pursue Wes and Katy but to rather head back to the plantation.

Seeing Annabelle ride away into the darkness, Wes and Katy stopped. Katy's thoughts were only on Angelique, so she hurriedly limped back to Angelique's side.

Katy knelt beside Angelique, noticing the movement of her arms and legs. The gunshot was to Angelique's arm, but apart from the shock and loss of blood, the wound did not seem to be fatal. Angelique lifted her head off the ground and attempted to focus her blurred vision.

"Where is she?" Angelique asked, feeling Katy's presence beside her.

"She is gone," Katy answered, her eyes filling with tears. "She killed Fiona."

Angelique, now slightly able to focus her eyes, looked over at Fiona's lifeless body. She tried lifting herself up, but the pain of the gunshot to her arm impeded her every movement.

"Hold still," Katy commanded. "I need to stop the bleeding."

Angelique lay her head back on the soft ground. With Katy's help, she turned on her back and faced skyward. Seeing Katy's tear-stained eyes, Angelique reached out and placed her hand on Katy's, holding it softly.

"Wesley, your belt," Katy instructed, wiping the tears from her eyes. "I need your belt."

Wes quickly removed his belt and handed it to Katy. While Katy tied a tourniquet around Angelique's arm, he hurriedly gathered the horses, checking to see that his revolver was still in place. Yet again, Wes felt on edge, but at least he now had some sort of protection.

Katy was able to stop Angelique's bleeding with the help of Wes' belt as well as a few strips of her gown. The three couldn't help but look at

Fiona, who lay bloodied and lifeless less than ten feet away from them.

Wes removed Ezra's blanket from the horse and laid it gently over her. "As I said, this is madness," he muttered, bending over Fiona and shaking his head.

"Complete and utter," Angelique agreed, rubbing the side of her head with her good hand.

"I can't help but feel that this was my entire fault," Katy said, staring at the blanket. "If I had stayed that night, she would still be alive."

"And you would be dead!" Angelique exclaimed. "You would all be dead eventually. Your escape was divinely influenced. You live for a reason. Do not be dismissive of that reality. She will be stopped. Unfortunately, more are bound to die before this happens."

As Wes looked out at the darkened path in front of them, he noticed lights in the distance. The lights flickered like oncoming flames. "What's this?" he gasped. "Torches approaching?"

Both Katy and Angelique could see them as well. They quickly helped each other to their feet and walked quickly over to the horses. Wes stood in front of them with his revolver raised. But the two on horseback riding toward them were Sophie and Etienne. Another horse followed. From her vantage point, Angelique could see that it was Luke and told Wes as such, thus settling his anxiety. They breathed a collective sigh of relief when they saw their friends.

The horses trotted up to the three. Angelique could see a look of shock on Etienne's face, an extreme departure from his usual joyous self.

"Gitane, you alright?" Etienne asked, noticing the blanket covering what seemed to be a body.

"Yes, but she is still out there," Angelique replied somberly. "Didn't you just pass her?"

"No, not now, but we did earlier unfortunately," he answered, shaking his head.

"Gitane! You're hurt," Sophie gasped, noticing Angelique's injured arm.

Sophie got off the horse and rushed to Angelique's side to inspect her wound.

"I'm alright." Angelique pulled her arm away. "Katy stopped the bleeding. We really need to move on."

Sophie eyed Angelique's arm, then turned to Katy, nodding her head in approval. "You did good, lass."

Katy stood silently with her head bowed.

"Where's the wagon?" Wes asked.

"Burned, and we nearly lost these here horses. Luckily they broke free from the wagon before the flames could get them."

Wes and Angelique glanced at each other and sighed.

"That is one damn evil lady," Etienne said, lowering his head.

"And now she is wounded," Wes confirmed. "I'm sure she will head back to the plantation for medical attention."

"Well, if you say she's heading down this path, the Peloat boys are guarding the crossroads, and she'll no doubt run into them," said Etienne bleakly.

"She passed both of you in the darkness, and you didn't see her," Angelique observed. "We will have to find her at the plantation."

Luke, sitting quietly on horseback and listening, nodded in agreement. "I saw it in her eyes: she's not human."

"Well, human or not, she's gonna pay for this," Wes said, as he began wrapping the blanket around Fiona's body. "As God is my witness, she's gonna pay."

After Wes finished wrapping Fiona's body properly, with the help of Luke and Etienne, he placed it on Katy's horse, as Katy had requested. The group then set off toward the crossroads and the grim uncertainty of what they would find there. They all now knew of whom, but not what, they were dealing with. The only sure outcome would be death—but of whose death, they were unsure.

CHAPTER 23

Evan and William sat on the porch of the main house of the plantation. After helping to bury Monsieur Chevalier and discussing in detail with Ben what had taken place earlier, they were both exhausted. Fortunately, Ben had agreed to let them stay there for the night and provided them with a meal. As he pondered their next step, Evan went through Monsieur Chevalier's belongings, hoping to find some clues about Lady Annabelle Falsworth.

"Interesting," Evan remarked, taking a few items out of a leather satchel, which had been on Monsieur Chevalier's horse.

"Something new?" William asked casually. He seemed uninterested as he stared out into the blackness of the forest.

Evan continued to remove papers from the satchel. He placed them on the small table in front of him. "It would seem that our dear friend was obsessed with the Lady," Evan said, squinting at each parcel by candlelight.

William turned his head and glanced at Evan. "He was obsessed with her gold or rather, his lack thereof," he grumbled, knowing full well that since their client now lay in the cemetery, there would be no hope of receiving any commission from this long journey. "So what are we to do now?" William asked.

"We plan our journey home," Evan replied, looking at William. "First though, I would like to chat with the others to find out a bit more information if possible."

"Others? More information? What on God's green earth do you need to solve?" William snapped. "Our client is dead. For us, the case is finished."

"Settle down, old friend," Evan replied, cracking a smile. "I just think it would be a good idea to find out a few more facts. We certainly can't go back to England without some sort of closure to this case. And you shouldn't forget John is awaiting our return. There is still an open case of multiple murders, and he will be expecting a full debriefing. The slightest clue might lead us to find out what happened to the elder Falsworth."

"I'm all for aiding Detective Stanley in his case, but I would jolly well like some sort of compensation," William growled.

"Well, there is still Monsieur's business. They will also want explanations," Evan replied. "Anyway, we can't leave just yet. I would like to talk to Angelique. She may be able to help us get out of this wretched place."

Evan continued to read the contents of the satchel, ignoring William's gripes and the noise coming from the stables as the ranch hands prepared the carriages for Miss Sterling and the maids' departure. Monsieur Chevalier's obsession was indeed with more than the gold," Evan said, as he pulled a small bag of gold coins from the satchel and tossed it to William.

Immediately William's face lit up, and a smile came to his lips. "Poor soul. I do believe he was tormented," he said, sifting through the coins.

"I do believe he was actually. There is a lot of Lady Falsworth's family history in these papers. I am certain he felt betrayed, especially after the elder Falsworth's disappearance."

"Does it really matter?" William mumbled softly, shaking his head.

"Obviously to him, it did," replied Evan. "Lady Annabelle was uncontrollable. With what we've learned here, he seemed to have had the upper hand with the elder."

"True . . . Till she ordered the confiscation of his ship and the extermination of its crew." William laughed, recalling Evan's recap of what had transpired before he had arrived.

"Point taken," Evan replied, as he continued sifting through the papers, trying to piece together the remnants of what Monsieur Chevalier had left behind. "I believe though, in his own mind, Monsieur Chevalier thought that he could control her, and therefore, when Lady Falsworth went missing, any power he had also disappeared, and this fueled his rage. The Monsieur's obsession enveloped all of his thoughts."

"Perhaps he even managed a bit of sorrow for poor Catherine then," William said with a touch of cynicism. The more William learned of his former employer, the more he felt Annabelle did the world a favor by bringing forward the time of his demise.

"In actual fact, yes, to a point, I believe he did," Evan replied. "His daughter's death must have initiated some sort of grieving process."

William shook his head in disgust, "You know, you're too positive you are. I believe he was nothing more than a snake in the grass. The more I learn, the more I believe he is where he belongs."

Evan nodded, then returned his focus to the contents of the leather bag. Suddenly a scream of pure terror pierced the air. It came from near the stables. Both William and Evan immediately jumped from their seats and ran to investigate.

"My Lady!" Sara was screaming at the top of her lungs.

Through the sparse torch light of the grounds, Evan could barely make out the shadowy figure of a horse with what looked to be a woman hunched over on its back. He and William watched three maids run hurriedly to the side of the horse and carefully lower her to the ground.

"Damn!" Ben exclaimed, as he ran franticly past them to see what had happened.

Evan and William followed close behind Ben, as they realized that the injured woman was Annabelle.

"My Lady, you're bleeding!" Hana shrieked.

"Get me Miss Sterling at once!" Annabelle said in a raspy voice, kneeling next to the horse.

"Lady Falsworth! Are you alright?" Ben asked, crouching down next to her. He saw that her dress was covered in blood.

"Yes . . . I am fine," Annabelle replied although she was obviously in pain. "Please, ready the carriages. We leave in an hour."

"The carriages are nearly ready," a calm voice said from behind the group that had clustered around Annabelle. It was Miss Sterling.

"Good, now help me inside," Annabelle commanded, her voice betraying the pain she felt.

Sara, Hana, and Helen surrounded Annabelle and lifted her to her feet. Annabelle's blood-stained dress and intense pain were apparent to all now, but she was silent about the pain and ignored the questions pertaining to what had happened. Her primary focus was just on reaching the house.

Annabelle, the maids, and Miss Sterling reached the porch and quickly went into the house while Ben headed to the stables to oversee final arrangements for the carriages. Evan and William walked to the side of the stable to chat. Evan's thoughts turned toward Angelique. He needed to find out what had happened to her, and the only way was to search down the path.

"I've got to find her," Evan said, as he peered into the stables. "Where's your horse?"

William, who was scanning the grounds, turned toward Evan. "Who?" he asked distractedly.

"Angelique, of course," Evan replied, trying to spot Ben amongst the ranch hands.

William looked confused. He knew Evan did not like to leave a case unsolved, but if they pursued this one further, there was a good chance that things would turn really nasty, and William wanted no part in that. "Leave it be," he said. "There's nothing good to come of your leaving in search of Angelique."

Evan turned to William with a look of disapproval. He raised his forefinger and pointed it in William's face. "We've come a long way. I believe we need to finish this, and I will—with or without you."

William shook his head. Although he did not agree with Evan, he wasn't going to let him trounce off into the forest alone, especially since he did not know what had actually happened there. "Okay, okay. Let's go before I change my mind," William said before turning and walking to the side of the house where his horse stood.

Evan followed him. "I knew I could count on you, old friend," Evan said, patting the uninspired William on the back.

William grumbled slightly, but at the end of the day, Evan was his best friend, and he would follow him anywhere. After hiding Monsieur Chevalier's satchel under the steps of the porch, they made their way quietly past the house, trying not to let Ben or anyone else see them leave. They silently moved toward the tree line where the horse was tied up. As they mounted the horse and turned to leave, they saw Betty staring at them from around the corner. Evan smiled at her and tipped his hat. Betty, her face showing no emotion, continued to watch them take a torch and ride off into the night.

After seeing them leave, Betty turned, made her way to the porch and went through the front door of the house. A few maids were dragging luggage through the doorway for their journey to East Texas.

"Be careful with that!" Hana scowled at Margaret and Rose.

Rose became irritated at Hana and snapped, "If you want to carry it yourself, then go right ahead. It would help if you would actually do some work and not just stand there and cackle."

Hana voiced her own irritation at Rose's remarks. The two had a history of not getting along, and these spats were common. "For your information, Miss Sterling has seen fit to put me in charge of her personal bags, and I will not have them thrown around or treated like saddlebags are handled by these heathen natives!" she exclaimed, turning her attention to Betty, who was eyeing the three from the foot of the stairs.

Without changing her expression, Betty turned away and trotted up the stairs. A confrontation on her part would not do a bit of good. She felt silence was the better option.

After a minute or two of brooding, Rose carried the luggage to the stables with Margaret while Hana returned to Lady Falsworth's room with clean towels and a bucket of fresh water.

"Hold still," Miss Sterling directed, trying to inspect Annabelle's wound.

"I'm fine; we must be on our way," Annabelle replied in obvious pain.

"My lady, here are the towels and water you requested," Hana said, holding the towels out to Miss Sterling.

"Thank you, Hana. Please put them on the bed," Miss Sterling replied, still inspecting the wound.

Hana did as requested, then looked on while Miss Sterling tended to Annabelle.

"You've lost a lot of blood," Miss Sterling commented. "I am surprised you're still alert."

"Do not underestimate me, dear friend," Annabelle replied with a notable grimace in her voice.

"Sara?" Miss Sterling shouted while delicately wiping the blood away from Annabelle's wound.

Almost immediately, footsteps were heard running up the stairs, and the door was pushed open, revealing Sara with a bottle of whiskey in hand. "Here, my lady," Sara said, placing the bottle in front of Miss Sterling.

"Excellent," Miss Sterling acknowledged, grabbing the bottle, removing the cork and handing it to Annabelle.

Annabelle clasped the bottle and took a huge swig, which seemed to give her some comfort but not much. After taking a few more gulps, she handed the bottle back to Miss Sterling, who poured the whiskey along the length of the open wound. Annabelle shrieked in pain. She was becoming weaker by the moment, but there was little that could be done.

"You've lost too much blood. You're turning pale," Miss Sterling sighed, as she continued to tend to the wound.

"I know," Annabelle replied in a weak and somber voice, "but we need to leave. Bandage it as best you can. We can't afford to stay here."

Miss Sterling reached for more towels, noticing Sara and Hana staring at them like soldiers waiting for their commands. Both sets of eyes looked troubled at the sight of Lady Falsworth in such distress.

"Sara, do be a dear and tell Brigit to come here, then check on the status of our carriages," she smiled at them. "Hana, please finish dressing the wound while I go make some tea."

"We don't have time," Annabelle grumbled, trying to stand.

"Do sit still, dear," Miss Sterling replied forcefully, though still smiling at both Sara and Hana.

Sara curtsied to Miss Sterling, then left the room, barreling swiftly down the stairs in search of Brigit while Hana tended to Lady Annabelle. Miss Sterling also left the room, but with a small pouch gripped tightly in her hand, and headed to the kitchen to prepare the tea.

Hana continued to care for Annabelle. Few words were spoken although

Annabelle's groans were frequent. Hana looked at Annabelle with a mixture of fear and sadness. She knew the blood loss was taking a toll on her, but there was little one could do.

A short time later, Hana heard the sound of someone clamoring up the stairs. The footsteps stopped outside the door.

"Hurry up!" Sara urged Brigit, who was slowly making her way up the stairway.

Even as Sara opened the door, most of her attention was still on Brigit, waving her hand as if motioning for her to come up the stairs.

"I'm coming, I'm coming," Brigit said. She had just made it halfway up the stairs. Brigit had still not recovered fully from her earlier illness, but she had improved to the point of being able to do her chores regularly, albeit more slowly than usual.

When Brigit finally appeared at the door, Sara whisked her into the room, "My Lady, here she is," Sara said, pushing Brigit near the bed.

Hana turned and looked at Sara. Sara could see Hana's eyes were glazed over and watery, as if she had been weeping. Since she was also distressed about Annabelle, Sara focused all her attention on Annabelle's wellbeing. She knelt down beside the bed, took a damp cloth from Hana and gently wiped Annabelle's forehead. Annabelle lay still, unresponsive to her touch and unable to even acknowledge any of them. She was sleeping.

A few moments later, Miss Sterling walked up the stairs holding a pot of tea. As she entered the room, she noticed all three girls huddled around Annabelle, visibly concerned.

"Ladies, please give her some air," Miss Sterling said as she placed the hot tea on the nightstand near the bed.

Hana, Sara, and Brigit all stood up and moved away from the bed to let Miss Sterling tend to Annabelle. As Miss Sterling looked at all three of their young innocent faces, she could see the fear and confusion racing frantically through each one's mind. She knew these three worshipped Annabelle unconditionally and for them to see her in this state was heart-wrenching.

"Sara? Are the carriages ready?" Miss Sterling asked in a slightly upbeat tone.

"Yes, my lady." Sara replied. "They are waiting for us."

"Excellent," Miss Sterling grinned. "Now I need you and Hana to go downstairs and gather the others. Load them onto the wagons and wait for us."

"But what of Lady Falsworth?" Sara asked, concerned. "Should she travel in this state?"

Miss Sterling took a moment before answering, "Fear not, dear Sara. Brigit and I will bring her back to the living. Your Lady shall once again be strong," she smiled.

Sara and Hana curtsied to Miss Sterling then walked out of the room and down the stairs toward the living area. They began to feel a glimmer of hope after hearing Miss Sterling's words; hope of the recovery of their mentor and, as Sara thought, the only one who had ever cared for them.

Meanwhile, still in the room, Brigit grasped the teapot and poured the contents into a cup, offering it to Miss Sterling.

"Oh no, dear," Miss Sterling smiled, "the tea is for you."

Brigit gave her an odd look. "For me?" she asked, confused.

"But, of course," Miss Sterling replied. "You have been sick, have you not?"

"Well, yes," Brigit replied, still not understanding the sudden interest in her health while Annabelle lay incapacitated. "But I am well, my lady.

Please do not waste precious time on me. Lady Falsworth is in dire need, and I would like to help in any way I can."

"Dear child, your Lady will be fine. Now drink," Miss Sterling said, gently touching the cup and nudging it toward Brigit's mouth.

Brigit stared at the cup for a moment, then put it to her lips. As she drank the tea, Miss Sterling looked at her, smiling with pleasure.

"There now," Miss Sterling said, "in a little while, you will feel neither pain, nor sickness."

"I do feel a little better," Brigit replied in between her sips of tea.

"Excellent," Miss Sterling said, turning to look at Annabelle. "You have no idea how much you are going to help your Lady."

With every sip Brigit became more relaxed and content. The aches and pains of her illness had dissipated. In fact, her mind was at ease and slowly drifting off to sleep. As Brigit's eyes became heavier and heavier, she lay next to Annabelle before finally drifting off.

Miss Sterling, hovering over both Brigit and Annabelle, took the cup from Brigit's hand and placed it on the nightstand. "Sleep well, dear child," she said, as she stared intensely at Brigit, "for tonight you are one with your Lady."

A short time passed as Sara and Hana rounded up the remaining maids and herded them into the carriages. They all sat and waited anxiously for Lady Annabelle and Miss Sterling to appear. Knowing the state of Lady Annabelle though, both Sara and Hana sensed the worst as time ticked away.

Ben, who was out roaming the grounds, thought well and hard about his future plans. To leave his employment on a whim could spell trouble down the road. The money was good but seeing Annabelle being helped off the horse drenched in blood did not set well with his psyche. Adding to his concern, Lady Annabelle and Miss Sterling's tardiness was definitely disturbing.

Finally, chatter from the front door broke the dull silence that had been weighing heavily on the early morning hours. Ben's head turned immediately to see who was leaving the house. As he walked across the field to the house, he could see Miss Sterling exiting the door in an almost gleeful manner. Behind her was Lady Annabelle, walking upright, with no visible trace of her injuries.

"Ma'am?" Ben crept up the steps with his hat in hand. "Are you alright? Can I get you anything?"

"Of course she is fine," Miss Sterling replied on Annabelle's behalf. "Are the carriages ready for travel?"

"Yes'm, they've been ready," Ben said, noticeably gawking at Annabelle.

"Good, we leave now," Miss Sterling said as she stepped off the porch and headed for the wagons with Annabelle close behind.

Ben's heart raced. All the grim thoughts he had had of Annabelle's demise now seemed to turn to the possibility of losing a good job. "Can I just speak with you for one moment, Ma'am?" Ben asked, almost pleading.

Annabelle walked silently, ignoring him until she reached the carriages. Seeing one of the ranch hands atop a horse, ready to lead them out of the plantation, she requested his horse for her. "I will be riding in front," Annabelle said addressing the hand. "You, sir, protect the second carriage in case of bandits."

The man agreed. He got off his horse, walked it to her and climbed on the second carriage. Annabelle, seemingly pain-free, took no time to mount the horse and ready herself for travel. Miss Sterling climbed aboard the first wagon with the maids.

Ben continued to ask Annabelle questions, but she completely ignored him as she rode to the front of the caravan. With everyone and everything on board and ready to leave, they were off. As Ben looked on in frustration, he turned away and threw his hat to the ground.

As Miss Sterling settled into the carriage, there was a constant chatter from the maids, especially Sara and Hana, who had now seen Annabelle.

"It's a miracle!" Sara blurted out excitedly.

"Your Lady is strong, dears," Miss Sterling replied jovially. "Good things come to the strong. Let not your weakest side show, and you shall also reign supreme."

For most of the travel time to the river, the maids remained joyous and happy. They were also excited that the trip to East Texas had finally begun. Hana was in such a good mood that she even attempted to joke with Rose, who sat quietly next to the window across from Miss Sterling. Of course, Rose would have no part in it. She just ignored Hana for the most part, yearning to change carriages.

As Rose looked sullenly out the window, thoughts of Brigit came to her. "My lady, where is Brigit?" she asked, still staring into the early morning darkness.

Miss Sterling turned her head to Rose and gave a quick grin, "Why I do believe she is in the other carriage. Why do you ask, child?"

"No reason really," Rose replied. "She usually rides in the front carriage with you, and I ride in the other is all."

"You're right," Hana agreed, "and that's the way it should be."

"Shut up, Hana, you tart!" Rose retorted angrily.

"Ladies! Both of you be quiet!" Miss Sterling ordered sharply. "This will be a long trip, and I do not want to hear another word out of either of you. Do I make myself clear?"

"Yes, my lady," Hana and Rose said in unison.

Silence now fell inside the carriage, as Rose turned back to the window. A feeling of dread was hanging about her this night, something she could not put her finger on. But unbeknownst to her, it would show its ugly face soon enough.

CHAPTER 24

Evan and William made their way down the pitch-dark path with only a single torch lighting their way. They were both uncertain about what they would find, if anything. Evan knew in his heart that Angelique was still alive, although the sight of a wounded Annabelle returning to the plantation made his outlook a bit grim. Nevertheless, he was determined to find Angelique even if it meant traveling through this darkened swamp all night.

A short time passed and William suddenly noticed a light up ahead. "Torches," he said, patting his side to make sure that his revolver was within easy reach.

As they got closer, Evan could make out multiple torches and a few young men with rifles. He felt certain that they were allies but couldn't be sure until he got a closer look.

"I know that one," William exclaimed when they were within shouting distance of the young men.

David discharged his rifle in the air. He had been eyeing Evan and William's progress for a while. "Halt," he shouted, "or the next one's gonna be in your gut!"

Evan immediately pulled the reins back and stopped the horse. "Don't shoot!" he yelled back. "It's Evan and William. We are trying to find Angelique and Wesley."

David lowered his rifle and motioned for Evan to continue riding up to the crossroads. Relieved, Evan and William continued until they were alongside a few of the Peloat boys. As they dismounted their horse, Evan spotted a light moving towards them from the path opposite that from which they had come.

"Possibly?" Evan said to himself.

William, who had also noticed the light, made out a few torches and riders heading their way. The riders moved closer and closer until finally they were in plain sight. The initial feeling of glee rapidly faded with the sight of what looked like a body wrapped in a blanket.

"Angelique?" Evan called out.

"Evan?" a voice responded. It sounded very much like Wes.

Evan watched anxiously as Wes slowly rode up with Katy alongside him. Next, Luke appeared holding a rifle close to his side, continuously looking at the blackened path. Finally, from out of the darkness, Angelique sluggishly made her way toward them. Evan could see she had been injured and seemed to be unaware of her surroundings, almost as if she were in a daze.

"Angelique?" Evan called out again. "Are you alright?"

Hearing Evan's voice seemed to awaken Angelique from her daze and confusion. "Evan?" Her voice was unsteady as she tried to focus her eyes.

"Yes, it's me," Evan replied, donning a big smile. "Are you alright?"

Angelique passed her hand over her face. "I'm breathing, so I feel that I am good," she said, trying to smile, but the pain was too great to ignore.

"Where is she?" Wes asked Evan and William, as he checked the bullets in his revolver. "I'm sure she's headed this way."

"Last we saw of her was at the plantation," William said, looking over at Evan, who had dismounted and was focusing all his attention on Angelique. "She was severely injured and appeared to have lost a lot of blood."

"That wouldn't matter," Katy said coldly. "She is indestructible, I fear.

It would seem that nothing can kill her."

Evan turned his head toward her. "Here now, no one is indestructible," he said. "She is due hers, and I believe it will be very soon if not already."

"Something just isn't right," Wes added. "It's as if she's not human."

"Of course she's human," Evan replied. "Ungodly and murderous, yes, but human all the same."

"Yeah? Then why can't anyone see her pass by them on this trail?" Wes asked in all seriousness. "You see how many people are here at this crossroads, but yet she passes unseen? Something's not right."

"I agree," Sophie added as she walked up to them, listening intently. "These young'uns could hear the flutter of a moth wing," she said referring to the Peloat boys, "yet they do not hear the Lady pass by. She's not from here."

Evan glanced at Angelique, who lowered her head as Sophie spoke. "And you? What do you think?" he asked her, reaching for her hand.

Angelique stared at the reins of her horse for a moment as if she did not want to answer. Her eyes appeared blank and lifeless to Evan as he waited for her reply. After a brief moment, Angelique raised her head and glanced at Katy, Wes, then finally Sophie. "More will die this day," she said, as she lightly tapped the horse's side with her feet. The horse began to move forward, away from the group. In the torchlight, all could now plainly see Angelique's eyes tearing up. Evan stared at her intensely, sensing the heavy burden that she seemed to place on herself.

"It ends today," Angelique said, turning to face them. She trotted her horse toward Etienne, who was talking with David and Luke.

Silence fell amongst them as they each pondered their own mortality. They all felt the cold chill of Angelique's words. Katy, in particular, grappled with these thoughts. She had feared that this day would arrive. Even worse, the feeling of guilt for Fiona's death lay heavily on her heart.

Angelique slowly dismounted the horse, the pain was immense, but luckily Katy had bandaged the wound well. "We need to leave," she said, walking up to Etienne.

Etienne nodded his head in agreement, then motioned for the others to follow. Evan, who was near Etienne, glanced around the path, noticing everyone who had joined in the search for Katy. He also noticed the inadequate number of horses to accommodate them all. "There are so many of us, yet many are on foot," he said, concerned.

"We use what we have," Etienne replied, "then adapt."

David walked up to Evan and tossed his rifle to him. Evan caught the rifle and lowered it to his side.

"You might need this," David said with a slight grin.

"Much obliged, good sir, but what about you?" Evan asked, tipping his hat.

"Don't worry, we will take the boat to the ferry in case they try to escape over the river," David said, sharing what he and Etienne had been contemplating. "Hopefully we will arrive before anyone else. Luke will go with you to show you the way back to the plantation. It is possible that they have left, but be careful anyway."

"I will. Thank you, and Godspeed," Evan replied, as he shook David's hand and turned to see Angelique and Sophie getting on Angelique's horse.

Evan watched as the torches, carried by the Peloat boys, disappeared into the darkness.

"Let's go, Evan," William called from across the path.

"I'm coming, I'm coming," Evan replied, hastily making his way to William. Evan tossed the rifle to William and then proceeded to hoist himself onto the horse.

Etienne, seeing that everyone was ready to go, set off down the path. They traveled onward through the darkness with Luke and Etienne leading the way.

The night turned to early morning and took its toll on a few of them, but they rode on and finally reached the outskirts of the plantation. Evan, through the light of the torches, began to notice the headstones of the cemetery, which he had failed to notice before.

"I believe we're nearly there," Luke said.

"Yes, I do remember this," Katy added with no expression or emotion, as she looked up the path.

Angelique looked ahead as if in deep thought. Sophie, sitting behind her, knew her well and felt it was better to let her be than to attempt to pry into her thoughts. She also felt that in time, Angelique would open up to her, as she usually did when her troubles eased.

A short time later, Evan glanced at his pocket watch. It was two fifteen in the morning. They had finally reached the plantation. All seemed quiet amongst the dimly lit structures and the main house. Wes scanned the area for life. He had learned the hard way on his inaugural trip to never let his guard down.

"Should we announce ourselves?" Evan asked jovially.

Wes raised his revolver and fired two shots in the air, hesitated for a moment, then fired another. Seconds later, they could hear voices from the ranch hands' quarters. Amongst the scurrying and confusion, a few eyes peeped out of the windows.

"Well, that should do it very nicely," Evan remarked, a faint smile on his lips.

"Ben!" Wes shouted.

"They not here," a voice rang out from near the stables.

They all turned toward the voice and saw a woman appear from out of the shadows. As she walked up to them, Katy noticed it was Betty.

"How long ago did they leave?" Angelique asked.

"Oh 'bout an hour or so," Betty replied. "She in a real hurry to get outta here."

"Were her injuries not too grave?" Evan asked, thinking back to what he had seen earlier.

"No, she walked upright to the stables and got up on that horse, sure enough," Betty said.

"Are you sure?" William asked in disbelief. "I saw her when she arrived, and there was enough blood on her to fill a body."

"Yeah, I saw her too," Betty responded, "but the fact is she left here better than she arrived."

"And how is that then?" William asked.

"I don't know," Betty replied, shaking her head. She couldn't really answer what she had seen since she didn't understand it.

"Did all the remaining maids leave with her?" Angelique asked, looking into her eyes.

"Don't know really," Betty answered, confused. "I'm sure they did."

"I believe it is in your best interests to check," Angelique said, in an almost commanding tone.

"What the hell's going on out here?" Someone was shouting from the front door of the house.

Wes looked over just in time to see Ben trip and fall onto the porch, breaking a bottle of whiskey in the process.

"Hiya, Ben!" Wes greeted him in an almost laughing tone.

Ben slowly picked himself up off the porch and stumbled down the steps. They could all see that he was intoxicated and in a vile mood.

"That's it," Wes edged Ben on, "you can make it."

"What the hell are you doin' back here?" Ben shouted, reaching for his revolver, but all he could feel was his trousers. No gun, no holster. "Dang it!"

Wes began to laugh at the sight of Ben so disoriented. This enraged Ben, who staggered up to the horses and noticed Betty standing there quietly. "Don't you have something to clean, woman!" he yelled at her.

Betty stared at Ben in silence. The rage was evident in her eyes yet she said nothing to him.

"Well?" Ben again scowled at Betty.

Betty smiled and walked toward the house, looking into his eyes as she passed him. Ben returned the smile before turning his attention to Wes.

"Where is she?" Wes asked Ben abruptly.

"I don't know." Ben sounded very irritable. "She probably going up north. Better off anyways," he rambled. "Damned English are just pompous asses."

Evan and William looked at each other, both amused by Ben's drunken assessment of the English.

"Well, he's right, you know," William whispered to Evan in jest.

Evan stayed silent and watched Ben while Wes, visibly amused, kept edging him on, almost as a payback for his earlier ridicule. Wes knew that Lady Annabelle was a sore spot for him, and he could not resist.

Angelique, hearing their petty arguments, became annoyed with all the unnecessary acrimony. "If she has left, then we must go," she said, eyeing Ben with a look of disgust.

Hearing Angelique, Ben became more belligerent. "Excuse me, woman, but I was talkin'," he said, slurring his words. "I suggest you be quiet, damn Gypsy whore."

Angelique immediately pushed the horse forward, knocking Ben down, and dismounted without a thought for her wounds. She revealed a knife, placing it under his chin and lightly jabbing his throat. "I am not in the mood for you this morning," Angelique scowled. "I suggest you tell us what you know, then silently crawl back into the swamp from which you came. Do you understand me?"

"Y-y-yes'm," Ben stuttered in fear.

Everyone could see Angelique's anger, as she continuously pushed the blade up against Ben's throat.

"Gitane! He's not worth it!" Sophie exclaimed. "Like you said, we need to go."

Angelique, hearing Sophie, pulled back the knife but continued to look Ben in the eyes. He pulled away and let out a sigh of relief, much to the enjoyment of Wes, who sat snickering on his horse.

Now with Ben in his place, Angelique, Etienne, and Evan discussed their next move.

"Well, she has over an hour ahead of us, and we are short a wagon and some horses," Etienne pondered aloud.

"The wagon and horses should not be a problem," Angelique replied, still glaring at Ben.

"N-n-nah . . . nah, go ahead and take a few horses," Ben intervened, stuttering over his words.

"Much obliged," Etienne said to Ben. "We could really use them. Also would like to know just where they goin'."

Ben had drastically changed his disposition. Being on the wrong end of Angelique's wrath seemed to have changed him for the good at a rapid pace. He now attempted to help them in their quest. "They left toward Beaumont, but the ferry doesn't run till early mornin', round four," Ben explained. "They will be sitting at the bank of the river for a while still."

"But you can wade horses through to the other side?" Evan queried.

"Yeah, but as heavy as the wagons are, you can't put them in the water. You'd never get them out," Ben replied.

"And what would stop them from wading across and bringing the ferry to the other side themselves?" Evan asked.

Evan's question was answered with a quick and simultaneous response from Ben and Luke, "Harold Brown."

"Who's he?" asked Evan.

"He's the ferryman and not a good sort of person," Luke replied.

"Oh yeah," Etienne added, "he's one ornery critter."

Both Evan and William looked a bit confused. They had passed on the ferry the day before and hadn't sensed any problems with the person in charge of the ferry across the Neches River. "He seemed cordial earlier," Evan ventured.

"Yeah, he's a nice guy till he starts drinking at nightfall," Luke replied. "After that he's just as bad-tempered as an alligator."

"Well, having seen firsthand what unfolded over the past week, I believe Angelique is right. We need to go. But what of Fiona?" Katy asked sadly.

Just then, a scream wailed from the house, across the grounds, for all to hear. Angelique rushed toward the house and onto the porch, followed closely behind by Evan, Etienne, and Sophie. As she entered the front door, Angelique saw Betty, in tears, running down the stairs.

"What is it?" Angelique asked, sadly knowing what Betty's response would be.

"The girl dead!" Betty screamed in horror, coming to a stop in front of Angelique. "There blood everywhere!"

Angelique could see the sheer terror in Betty's eyes as she reached out to her. "It's alright. Please stay here," she said, trying to comfort her, but to no avail.

"That woman has no soul! She gonna kill us all!" Betty shouted in fear.

Evan, gun drawn, ran up the stairs with Etienne close behind. He was certain Annabelle had left, but he did not want to take any chances. Now at the top of the stairs, both men could see inside the dimly lit room, which was illuminated by a lone candle.

"William! Bring me a lantern!" Evan shouted down the stairway.

William quickly found a lantern hanging on the wall near the foot of the stairs. He promptly lit it and prepared to make his way up to the room when Katy suddenly appeared and seized the lantern from him. She started up the stairs, limping noticeably, but she seemed determined to get to the top.

"No, lass!" William exclaimed, his arm reaching out to block her.

"No!" Katy shouted in anger. "I want to see!"

Katy slapped William's hand away and continued up the stairs, finally being contained at the door of the room by Etienne. Etienne grabbed the lantern from her hand and hastily passed it to Evan. Katy furiously tried to get past Etienne, but he would not let her.

"Let me in!" Katy shouted tearfully. "I need to see."

"No, young'un, it's not good," Etienne replied, pulling her into his arms to stop her from entering the room.

"Sweet mother of . . ." Evan blurted out, as the lantern revealed the true extent of the horror.

Etienne looked back at the ghastly scene and unintentionally let Katy slip into the room. Katy immediately fell to her knees at the grim sight of Brigit, who lay dead in a pool of blood on the bed.

"What is it?" William asked from the bottom of the stairs, where a crowd had begun to form, anxious to find out what had happened.

"You don't want to know!" Evan replied, as he inspected the body. "Horrendous."

Katy remained kneeling in front of the bed sobbing uncontrollably, as Etienne put his hand lightly on her shoulder in an attempt to comfort her. But alas, there was little he could do to console her.

The gruesome scene was upsetting to say the least. A young lass, who couldn't have been a day over sixteen, lay dead. Her throat and wrists cut, and her blood drained. Despite the horror, Evan felt he had to try and make sense of it all.

"How in the hell could someone do this?" Etienne asked, shaking his head in disbelief. "What would they get out of it?"

Evan continued to somberly look around for clues. "Someone or something?" he remarked with a certain coldness, obviously affected by what he was seeing.

It was about this time that Ben walked into the room. Seeing the departed girl, mutilated and soaked in blood, calmed his belligerence instantaneously and effectively sobered him up. "What the hell?" Ben was incredulous. His hands visibly shook at the hideous sight.

"Look!" Katy shouted. "Look well! For the Lady whom you serve has murdered another! This blood is on your hands. Take it in!"

Ben bowed his head as both the confusion and the reality of what had taken place since Lady Annabelle had arrived filled his head. He couldn't reply to Katy. He knew anything he said would only add to her misery.

"Let's go, young'un," Etienne said, as he gently tried to lift Katy's arm.

Katy reached for Etienne, sobbing profusely. As she rose to her feet, there was little comfort anyone could provide, but Etienne did his best. They made their way down the stairs as Angelique passed them on her way to the room. Upon entering, Angelique showed no emotion about the gruesome sight that confronted her. By now, William, who had also come up the stairs, went about the room, lighting more candles.

"Your thoughts?" Evan asked Angelique.

Angelique looked down at the body and then looked Evan in the eyes. "It ends today."

Evan could tell that Angelique was keeping something hidden from them. She appeared to know a lot more about Lady Annabelle than she was letting on. "Who is she? Or should I ask, what is she?" Evan asked, almost desperate for answers. "What are we dealing with, because if I'm to die today, then I would like to know something of my enemy."

Angelique stood silently for a moment, then placed her hand on the bedpost. "My grandmother used to tell me tales from the old country when I was very young," she said, remembering back. "Horrific tales of a woman who fancied the taste of blood. She tortured and murdered many a young lass. Some say the blood of a virgin kept her youthful and vibrant."

William turned toward Angelique, a smirk rested on his lips as he listened to her. "Vampires?" he asked in a disbelieving tone.

"Call them what you wish," Angelique replied, "but the family's reign was long, and the torment they meted out spread throughout the land."

"Superstition," William grumbled.

"Superstition maybe, but I do find all of this a bit odd. Don't you?" Evan asked.

"Point taken," said William, looking at the blood-soaked bed.

"It's in her blood; she will never stop," Angelique continued, as she moved around the bed and lightly touched her hand over Brigit's eyes to close them. "This is why it must end today."

Angelique knew that the conclusion would soon be thrust upon them but could not foresee the ultimate cost. In her heart, there was only one solution: Lady Annabelle had to be stopped, no matter the price.

CHAPTER 25

The living room exceeded its capacity, as the ranch hands and maids scrambled for information about what had happened. Death was no stranger to these people, but murder was only ever a concern if a poor soul ventured south to Sabine. To have it happen at the plantation was shocking.

Ezra and Benjamin stood near the foot of the stairs eagerly awaiting Ben. Both had spoken to Betty, and knowing that a horrific crime had taken place, felt compelled to do something.

"That's just not right," Ezra said. "What did that girl ever do to her?"

"It would seem we've been on the wrong side, Ezra," Benjamin said softly.

"Yeah, and we gonna make it right," Ezra replied.

"Maybe one day," replied Benjamin, noticing Fiona's body still lying on Katy's horse outside.

Just then, Angelique, Ben, and William walked solemnly down the stairs and into the living room where many were anxiously awaiting answers. Ben, silent since seeing the gruesome scene, pondered what to tell the ranch hands and maids of the plantation. He definitely wasn't a leader and felt sick to his stomach at the task he faced.

"Well?" Ezra asked Ben, a bit disturbed. "We going after her?"

Ben shook his head to indicate no.

Ezra's rage grew instantly, but he knew whatever words he spoke would fall on deaf ears. "Well, what are we gonna do?"

"Nothing," Ben replied. "If these folks need horses, a wagon, or any other supplies, then fine, but we're not gonna play sheriff."

"But they killed that girl!" Ezra exclaimed, angrily trying to understand Ben's thinking.

"She's one of their own," Ben replied. "Ain't nothin' to do with us. Let it be."

Ben's words cut right through Ezra and enraged him even more, but he knew not to push his opinion. He nodded in acknowledgement, then quietly walked toward Betty, Sophie, and Katy.

"Ma'am," he said to Katy, "I'm very sorry for you losing your friends. I will put them to rest with dignity."

Katy looked up at Ezra solemnly. "Thank you, kind sir. I am delighted to see that there are some who are as considerate as you. May Fiona, Brigit, and Alice see you as a man of great nobleness and integrity."

Ezra respectfully bowed his head to her, then left with Benjamin to tend to Fiona. Angelique paced back and forth, talking with Sophie. She knew Annabelle was attempting to leave the area, and they needed to get on their way.

"We have enough horses now. We need to go," Angelique said.

"I'll ready the wagon," said Etienne, acknowledging her.

"A wagon's too slow, especially if we are to cross the ferry," Angelique observed. "We need to keep with horses."

Etienne nodded, knowing she was right, but nevertheless, he wanted a wagon, even if it meant having a couple of people lag behind. "Okay, but we can have Sophie and Luke follow us with the wagon," he said, quietly thinking it would be safer for Sophie to be far behind them.

"Oh no!" Sophie chimed in. "You not gonna leave me behind. Whatever happens, I'm gonna be there."

Etienne did not argue with Sophie. He knew it would be a losing battle. "Okay, we'll get Luke to bring the wagon; he can meet up with David at the river."

Luke nodded in agreement, as he had been listening near the door.

"Okay, let us go," Angelique said, as she made her way out of the room.

Before she could leave, Betty grabbed her arm from behind. "Don't know what this means, but I believe you need to know this," Betty whispered. "The horse has again broken free. Someone awaits you; someone dear to your heart. The birds of Rhiannon shall guide you on your journey."

Angelique's eyes immediately teared up, but she continued out the door, giving Betty a faint smile. Katy, following Angelique, reached out for Betty's hand. "With all my heart, I am indebted to you," she said. "Thank you."

Betty stood in the doorway, a quiet smile on her face. "Missy, see with your soul and not with your eyes. The end is near, but it is bringing new beginnings. Through this, your future will be revealed."

Etienne, William, and Evan also left the house, meeting up with Wes on the porch. Sophie, who had hung back, finally made her way to the door where Betty took her hand. Betty's smile had faded, and her look of concern was evident.

"There is a choice for you. Know in your heart that you will make the right one," said Betty.

Betty's words disturbed Sophie greatly. She immediately pulled back her hand and walked out the door.

"This ends now. The future is in your hands!" Betty exclaimed, as Sophie hurriedly walked off the porch toward the awaiting horses.

As they all gathered in front of the main house, Katy stood near Wes and watched Ezra and Benjamin carefully remove Fiona's body from the horse, place it on a small cart and move it to the servant cemetery. Katy's eyes began to tear up as she thought back to her friendship with Fiona. Angelique, standing close, embraced Katy, trying to give what comfort she could.

"She never trusted anyone," Katy said over and over, as she looked at the body. "Maybe that is the trait of the gypsy."

"Gypsy?" Angelique asked curiously.

"Her parents came to England from Hungary when she was very young. They were accused of stealing and were brutally murdered by a few townspeople over a misplaced watch, leaving Fiona an orphan. She never opened up to anyone or trusted a soul. I feel that even I am fortunate to know the little of her history that I do."

"Well, she must have trusted you," Angelique replied.

"Yes, and she was murdered for it," Katy said, beginning to weep.

Angelique held Katy tightly, stroking her hair delicately with her fingers. "This is not your fault," she said. "None of this is your doing. Remember that, for your own health."

"It's as if I am cursed, as are those who come into contact with me," Katy sobbed. "Everyone who wanders too close to me faces the possibility of death and hardship. When will it end, I pray?"

"It ends today, dear Katy. For you will rise above this and live a good life with a good husband, who loves you dearly. I promise you, by the gods, these things will pass."

Angelique comforted Katy for a few moments more before they mounted their horses. Katy would ride with Wes and Angelique would ride on her own. With everyone ready for travel, the group set off toward the river in search of Lady Annabelle and her cohorts.

As they journeyed into the darkness of the early morning, Angelique rode up beside Wes and Katy. She eased the horse as close to them as she could, removed her necklace and placed it around Katy's neck. "See this charm and feel its protection through this time and always," Angelique said. "For as long as this necklace is worn, protection is certain. For the Goddess Cerridwen will watch over you."

Angelique steered her horse away from Wes and Katy. "'Tis time," she said, pushing the horse into a furious gallop, down the path and into the darkness, leaving her friends behind.

Evan and William followed Angelique as she took off down the path. Etienne, Wes, Katy, and Sophie sped up but stayed close to the wagon with Luke. With their torches lit as they rode on in silence, they thought of what was to come and how would this end. Angelique already knew what lay ahead and what sorrows awaited them near the river. Etienne could only hope that David and the Peloat boys would catch her first or at least slow her down.

* * *

David, commanding one boat, while his father commanded another, poled upriver in an attempt to reach the ferry ahead of Annabelle's entourage. Luckily for them, the wind had turned to the southeast, making it a little easier to move upriver. Their task was still a challenge however, and they were at least thirty minutes away. One could only hope that the ferryman would not cooperate with Annabelle, buying them some time.

* * *

As Annabelle reached the ferry, all was quiet. One of the hands shouted across the river to see if the ferryman was at his post, but his shouts were met with silence.

"It would seem that the ferryman is not here, or he is asleep, ma'am," one of her hands said.

"Two of you, cross the river and find out where he is," Annabelle commanded. "He shouldn't be too far off."

"Yes, ma'am," the hand replied, before riding into the river with another to find the ferryman.

Minutes later, on the other side of the river, the men got off their horses and called out for the ferryman, but there was still no answer. After a few more attempts, the men decided to guide the ferry themselves. While readying the vessel, a loud shout echoed down the river. Harold Brown had been asleep and seemed to be in one of his moods. He did not take kindly to people moving his ferry.

Annabelle watched through the darkness from across the river for a few moments, then turned to one of the hands. "Mr. Paine, your rifle." She held her hand out.

Mr. Paine hastily reached for his rifle and handed it to Annabelle. He watched as she placed it to her shoulder and aimed into the pitch blackness. Upon hearing more shouting from the other side, Annabelle discharged the weapon, hitting Harold Brown in the neck. He died instantly.

Silence fell on both sides of the river. They were all stunned by Lady Annabelle's marksmanship. Miss Sterling, who had leapt out of the carriage at the sound of the rifle being fired, strained to see across the river but saw only darkness.

"I congratulate you on a good shot, dear friend," said Miss Sterling, "although I will have to take your word for it that you indeed hit your target."

"Indeed," replied Annabelle, looking across the river. "I rarely miss, especially when the prey is as loud this one. Silence does have its virtues."

A short while later, the two men from across the river managed to move the ferry to the opposite side. Annabelle ordered the first carriage to board, followed by her horse and two more. She also instructed two maids, Rose and Hana, to stay behind to keep a close eye on the second carriage while the first group crossed. Hana didn't like the idea of sharing responsibility with Rose, but if her mentor requested it, then she would carry out her wishes.

Now full, the ferry left the river's edge and crossed to the Beaumont side of the river. Lady Annabelle kept watch through the darkness, like an owl stalking her prey, knowing her enemies were close.

Annabelle's hawkishness made the others very nervous, especially the men who had signed on for security. Starting from New Orleans, their journey had been cursed, to say the least, but some felt that the additional brutality was unbearable and pondered a way out. They were unwilling to make their feelings known publicly, especially now that they knew Lady Annabelle's full capabilities.

The ferry reached the other side of the river within a short space of time. The horses and carriage were swiftly offloaded, and the men prepared for the return journey to pick up the remaining horses and carriage.

"Ride forward!" Annabelle ordered the hands. "I will catch up when the other carriage has been brought over. Do not stop till you see me again."

The horses and carriage were hurried on their way up the path while Annabelle stayed behind, awaiting the other carriage. Suddenly a light appeared downriver. Annabelle could make out two boats coming toward them but was unable to see just how many people were aboard.

"Mr. Paine! Arm and ready!" Annabelle shouted across the river.

Mr. Paine, himself seeing the oncoming lights, reached for his rifle, but it wasn't there. He remembered that Lady Annabelle had used it and hadn't given it back.

"Halt!" David shouted from the boat. "Lay down your weapons!"

Annabelle quickly moved away from the side of the river into some brush to hide from the oncoming boats while the two hands on the other side of the river began randomly discharging their weapons at the boats. The Peloat boys returned fire, injuring both men and rendering them incapable of shooting back.

At the same time, Samuel, one of the Peloat boys, who had been let ashore before the boat had become visible to those on the riverbanks, ran up to the carriage, displaying his fifle, and disarmed those who had been left to protect what was left of the entourage. Seeing that all hope was lost, Mr. Paine raised his hands and surrendered.

Inside the carriage, Hana was stricken with fear. Lady Annabelle had placed her in charge, but she had been in no position to stop the events that had just unfolded. Hana did not want to be a prisoner or at the mercy of some nasty commoners.

"We need to escape," Hana said, trembling.

"Don't be daft!" Rose exclaimed, exasperated. "It would be foolish to go out there!"

"But if we stay, who knows what they will do to us," Hana retorted.

"There is no need to panic or go mad," said Rose angrily. "You'll get yourself killed, you will, and the rest of us as well."

But Hana, unable to sit quietly and wait for her fate, belted out of the carriage. "I can't stay here!" she shouted over her shoulder, as she ran to the edge of the river.

Meanwhile, the two boats, with three of the Peloat boys and their father aboard, were nearing the shore. David saw the frightened young girl running toward the river but took no action, as he could see that she was unarmed.

"My Lady!" Hana screamed. "Please, my Lady! Hear me!" Hana fell to her knees in tears at the edge of the water. "Do not leave me with these ruffians, my Lady! I beseech you!"

Hana knelt, sobbing, at the edge of the river. The Peloat boys took no notice of her. They were not out to harm the innocent. All the same, Hana was petrified and wailed endlessly. "My Lady! I am your true servant. Save me! I would rather die than for you to leave me!"

As Hana cried on the riverbank, Annabelle trotted her horse out of the brush and to the edge of the river. Through her sobbing, Hana heard the sound of the horse on the opposite side of the river. She became gleeful, as if all of her fear had suddenly been released. "My Lady, you have not abandoned me!"

Annabelle looked over at Hana coldly. She raised her rifle, placed it upon her shoulder and aimed at Hana. A second later, Annabelle shot Hana in the heart, killing her instantly. A scattering of rifles returned fire from across the river and the two boats, but no one could hit Annabelle. She immediately turned her horse and galloped away.

Rose, seeing what had taken place, climbed out of the carriage with her hands raised. The killing of the young girl had unnerved everyone, even the two Peloat boys on the shore, as they pointed their rifles at her apprehensively.

"Alas, we are unarmed, and no match for you," Rose said. "We surrender."

Seeing that the girl was telling the truth, the boys lowered their rifles and focused their attention on the men who were supposed to guard them. Rose lowered her hands and let out a sigh of relief. She walked up to Hana's body.

Hana lay on her back in a pool of blood with her eyes wide open. Her face had a look of shock, a sight Rose would not quickly forget.

"Madam, it wasn't us," David said, walking up to her after he had disembarked his boat.

"I know," Rose replied solemnly. "It was that wretched woman."

David was silent for a moment. "Yes, she has killed many, and she will pay for her crimes, but please do not fear us. We are not out to harm you in any way."

Rose managed to smile weakly. "I believe you, dear sir, and thank you for saving us from her."

David smiled at Rose. "You do not have to worry about her. We'll protect you," he said, tipping his hat to her.

"David!" It was his father, who needed help with the boat.

David again tipped his hat to Rose before turning toward the river to help his father. Rose retreated to the carriage to comfort the others.

Both sides of the river were now vigilant, as the Peloat boys waited for Etienne to arrive from the plantation. Less than thirty minutes had passed before a horse could be heard galloping toward them. With rifles ready, they waited patiently for whoever it was to ride forward.

"Hold your fire!" David shouted, seeing that the rider was Angelique.

Angelique pulled back the reins of the horse and slowly dismounted. "The two Englishmen should be arriving soon, and the others will follow." She walked near the carriage and noticed what looked like a body covered in a blanket. She shook her head in disgust.

"Sadly, we couldn't stop the woman from killing again," David said, as he watched Angelique scan the area.

"Where did she go?" Angelique asked.

"She escaped across the river," replied David. "The men say they managed to get a carriage and three horses across. They are headed for East Texas."

Angelique peered at the opposite bank. "Please tell Frenchy when he arrives. I need a fresh horse."

David pointed to one of the horses they had captured. As soon as he did, Angelique went over to it and got on. She rode into the river. "We have no time to waste. Bring the ferry to this side of the river. Luke will be bringing a wagon here."

As soon as Angelique crossed to the other side of the river, she rode determinedly up the path in search of Lady Annabelle. She knew that time was short, and even though she was a lone pursuer, Annabelle had to be stopped. No matter the cost.

Evan, William, and Etienne arrived at the ferry, just missing Angelique's departure. Wes, Katy, and Sophie were close behind, making the last turn toward the river.

As Etienne rode up to the carriage, he saw David standing near the door. "And Gitane?" he asked, quickly pulling back the reins of his horse.

"She's already crossed the river," replied David. "The English lady escaped with another carriage. There are two gunmen on the carriage and two on horseback." He paused for a moment then continued, "Watch out for that woman. She's a good shot in the dark. Killed this young girl from the other bank with a rifle." He pointed to Hana's covered body.

Etienne sighed as he turned to look at the body of yet another dead young girl. Evan dismounted his horse, walked up to the body and slowly removed the cover for him to see.

"Shot in the heart," he said sadly.

"We need to go," Etienne said. "Gitane is out there, and she's crazy enough to walk right up to that evil woman."

"Agreed," William replied.

As Wes, Katy, and Sophie rode up, Rose, noticing Katy on the back of Wes' horse, quickly got out of the carriage. Katy tapped Wes on the shoulder and softly asked him to ride to her. While scanning the area, Katy also noticed another covered body and could only assume it was another one of the maids.

Rose noticed Etienne looking at her and curtsied to him. "Pardon, dear sir."

"And yet another, I see." Katy nodded at the body as she and Wes reached Rose.

"'Tis Hana; one of the Lady's favorites," Rose said quietly.

"She now murders her own," Katy sighed. "And Brigit as well. I fear this will have no end."

"Rest assured, lassie," Etienne interrupted, "this will have an end. The killing will stop."

Katy looked over to Etienne. "I pray that you are right, Frenchy."

"I pray as well," Etienne affirmed.

"I believe we need to get these girls back to the plantation where they'll be safe," Sophie said. "They don't need to be out here in the swamp."

"I agree," Etienne replied. "David, take the carriage back to the plantation along with the injured and the young'uns. We'll head across the river to Beaumont. Luke will be here in a minute with the wagon."

David agreed, as two of his brothers finished moving the ferry to the other side. As if like clockwork, Luke turned the corner and immediately rode onto the ferry, ready to cross.

"Time to go!" Etienne said, turning his horse toward the river. "We will cross faster by wading through."

Etienne rode into the river, followed closely by Sophie and William.

Evan quickly mounted his horse and followed Wes and Katy. With the wagon on the ferry, the two Peloat boys began moving the ferry across the river. David, in organizing the trip back to the plantation, put the wounded men in the carriage beside the maids so that they could be tended to.

As he, his three brothers, and their father set off down the path with the carriage and horses, David's thoughts were focused on Etienne, and the trouble that lay ahead. He knew the danger that awaited them across the river, but believed that in the end, they would weather this storm.

CHAPTER 26

A few miles across the river, Annabelle has met up with the carriage and now rode alongside it. She wasn't nearly as confident as before. She had lost one carriage and all of her maids, except for Sara, the most loyal.

Sara, seeing Annabelle next to the carriage, stuck her head out of the window. "My Lady, where's Hana? And Brigit?" Sara enquired, seeing no trace of her friend or the other carriage.

Annabelle turned to Sara and without hesitation answered, "Dead; gunned down in cold blood by those ruffians. Unfortunately we are the only ones left."

Sara's eyes swelled with tears. Now all of her friends were gone. "But dear Lady, you have the power to bring them back to the living . . . Please, I beg of you!"

"The pain you feel inside?" Annabelle said. "The bitter, bitter emptiness that swells inside of you? Know that these people have caused this and that Katy has instigated our demise."

Annabelle rode away from the carriage and took the lead position, sending both hands to the rear of the carriage. Sara continued to weep loudly but was ignored by Annabelle.

Having heard Annabelle's conversation with Sara, the men atop the carriage became disillusioned. They had been hired along with eight other hands, but now they found themselves alone against what seemed to be overwhelming odds. It was only self-preservation that kept them moving forward along the path. To slip away from the Baroness on horseback was a luxury they did not have, unlike their counterparts who were riding behind the carriage.

The carriage continued north at a rapid pace. Although limited to a mere torch and lantern to light their way, the hands were able to maneuver the carriage sufficiently well. Miss Sterling, peering out into the darkness, was filled with conflicting thoughts. The horses were drawing the heavy carriage at a gallop, but she knew that they would not be able to keep this up and stood a great chance of collapsing from exhaustion if they continued at this pace.

"Mr. Kerrigan! Halt this carriage at once!" Miss Sterling commanded.

Mr. Kerrigan pulled the reins back tightly, slowing the horses to a trot before stopping in the middle of the path. Annabelle, hearing Miss Sterling's instruction, stopped and turned back toward the carriage.

"Do we have a problem, Miss Sterling?" Annabelle asked, visibly irritated.

"You know as well as I do that these horses will not last under this stress," Miss Sterling replied. "If we must defend ourselves, then so be it. But I do not want to walk to East Texas."

Annabelle knew she was right and acknowledged this. "Very well. Mr. Kerrigan, ride on at a steady pace, but be aware of your surroundings. We do not want to be ambushed."

As Annabelle turned her horse around, she noticed that the two men on horseback were missing. "What's this?" she questioned, immediately riding her horse to the back of the carriage. She stared angrily down the darkened path.

"What's wrong?" Miss Sterling asked, poking her head out of the window.

"It would seem we have deserters," Annabelle barked. She was furious. "Mr. Kerrigan, Mr. Carlisle, arm yourselves. Drive the carriage at a slow pace. If there is trouble, then do what you have to do. I shall be back."

Annabelle took off alone down the path in search of the two hands who had abandoned her. Mr. Kerrigan drove the carriage up the path at a moderate pace, understanding the need to conserve the horses' energy in case of trouble.

Miss Sterling also felt the need to arm herself. She took a box from under her seat and laid it on her lap. Sara, wiping away her remaining tears, looked on as Miss Sterling pulled out a revolver. It was at this point that Sara finally understood the danger they were in. Her hands trembled as she tried to calm herself and sit quietly in the seat across from Miss Sterling.

"Have you ever fired a weapon?" Miss Sterling asked, removing another, smaller pistol from the box.

"No, my lady, I haven't," Sara replied solemnly.

"Well, you are going to learn," Miss Sterling said, handing the small pistol to her.

Sara extended her shaking hand to take the pistol.

"Calm yourself, lass," Miss Sterling said, seeing her anxiety. "The gun is for your own protection. Keep it hidden under your gown. If, for any reason, you are forced to use it, then point and pull the trigger. It's simple really."

Sara took the pistol from Miss Sterling's hand and nervously placed it in a pocket in her gown. Miss Sterling placed her hand on Sara's knee. "Be strong, my child, your Lady needs you," she said, looking Sara in the eye. "We all have to be strong for her. Fear not, I promise you, she will avenge both of your friends' deaths and make those who do us harm pay for their meddling."

"Yes, my Lady, and I know that day will come soon," Sara whispered, wiping fresh tears from her cheeks.

"Good. We need you, dear Sara," Miss Sterling added. "You are our Lady's favorite, her one and only."

Seeing that Sara had regained some of her composure, Miss Sterling sat back in her seat and awaited Annabelle's return. Deep down, she knew that they were in grave trouble, but she also felt that, if they could make their way out of the area, they would stand a better chance of surviving. Sara, on the other hand, couldn't let her Lady down under any circumstances. Her renewed spirit would play an important part in the things that were to come.

* * *

The sun, which was rising slowly above the horizon, could not be seen due to the density of the trees surrounding the path. The two men rode swiftly, away from carriage that they were hired to protect. They had seen their chance and slipped away under cover of darkness. They were headed south toward Sabine, away from this desolate land and the even greater threat in the form of Lady Annabelle Falsworth.

As the men rode on, they could hear the sound of a galloping horse ahead of them. It rumbled louder and louder, closer and closer. Not knowing who was approaching, both men raised their weapons in anticipation of trouble. Suddenly, the sound stopped. Unnerved by the silence, they looked at one another in confusion, afraid to make a sound.

The men moved slowly forward, hoping to catch a glimpse of the horse and rider, but they saw nothing. Fearing an ambush, they dismounted and walked slowly down the path with their guns at the ready.

Minutes passed and still there was no sign of either a horse or a rider. Fear crept into their hearts as they pressed forward little by little. Suddenly they heard the sound of the horse neighing close by, followed by the clip-clop of hooves moving toward them.

"Who's there?" One man broke the silence; he was almost overcome with fear.

"Go ahead; show yourself!" the other man shouted. "We are armed!"

No one answered. There was just the sound of the horse's hooves echoing amongst the trees. Clip-clop, clip-clop, the sound became louder, till finally the men could make out the figure of the horse on the path ahead of them. White terror streaked through their hearts.

"Halt, or I'll shoot!" one man shouted, pointing his revolver down the path. But the horse just kept walking.

"Hold your fire!" the other man said. He could see that the horse was without a rider. "Dammit!" he exclaimed, sheepishly shaking his head. "Spooked by a damn horse."

The horse walked up to them and whinnied. Both men were embarrassed, like scared little children hiding in the dark.

"Well, at least it wasn't an ambush," the first man said as they both lowered their weapons.

"Hell, let's get moving, Jim. Daylight's coming, and we need to be far away from here by then," the other man replied, hoisting himself onto his horse.

Jim agreed and walked up to his horse, which was near the tree line. Just as he started to mount his horse, Jim suddenly felt a painful blow to the back of his head. He immediately fell to the ground in pain. The other man, upon hearing him fall, turned and saw a woman with a long-bladed knife bending over Jim, slicing his shirt and shoving the blade against his back and slowly pushing until he grimaced in pain.

"Drop your weapon!" Angelique shouted.

Jim lay flat on his stomach with his hands raised. He could feel the ice-cold steel of the knife press against his skin. Out of the corner of his eye, he saw a hand pick up his revolver, which had fallen next to him. The other man also raised his hands to indicate surrender. Neither was in the mood for confrontation.

"Hold on, lady. We don't want any trouble," said the man.

"Where is she?" Angelique asked angrily, putting more pressure on the knife on Jim's back.

"We don't know who you're talking about!" Jim shrieked in anticipation of the knife cutting him.

"Your lady, your Baroness, where is she?" Angelique asked again.

"Look, ma'am, we no longer work for that lady," the other man explained quickly, his eyes on Jim. "We just slipped away from her. All we want is to get out of here and leave this area."

"Where is she?" Angelique asked a third time, pushing the tip of the knife into Jim's back, penetrating the skin slightly and making him scream.

"Hold on!" the man replied. "She's not too far from here. They are headed to East Texas. She definitely seems like she's in a hurry to get out of this place."

"And how many surround her?"

"She only has the two drivers of her carriage, a maid, and her companion. This is all we know, I swear, that is all!"

Angelique raised Jim's revolver, removing the knife away from his back. She sensed that they were telling the truth, but still, she trusted no one.

"I would advise you to leave this area at once," Angelique said, as she stood up straight, holding the knife and the revolver in her hands. "Within five minutes, my friends will be here, and they will have no problem in gutting you. Do you understand?"

Jim and the other man agreed. The last thing they wanted was to be here. "Yes, ma'am," they chimed in unison.

Jim rose from the ground, clasped the reins of his horse and got on its back. "Thank you, ma'am," he said, tipping his hat to her. "I promise, you'll never see us again."

As Jim turned his horse, ready to head south to Sabine, a gun blasted. Angelique looked up just in time to see Jim falling backward off his horse. As he hit the ground, she noticed a gunshot wound in his stomach. Angelique quickly dashed into the trees. Another gunshot rang out, this time hitting the other man in the neck. He fell to the ground, dying instantly.

Angelique's heart raced. She knew the shooter could only have been Annabelle. Angelique was no match for Annabelle's expert marksmanship, so she hid silently behind a tree, contemplating her next move.

Annabelle's horse moved slowly down the path. It made almost no sound, so Angelique was not able to discern where it was. Angelique dared not stick her head out from behind the tree for fear of having it shot off.

"I smell you, gypsy whore," Annabelle said, taunting her. "I smell the blood oozing from your arm. There is no way your fingers are strong enough to pull the trigger. I should have finished you off while I had the chance."

Angelique looked down at her arm and noticed that her wound was bleeding again. The blow she had dealt to the man now made it almost impossible to use her hand. There was no way she could discharge the revolver quickly. Yet she would have to try all the same.

"I am here," Annabelle teased. "Out in the open for you to see; yet you hide like a frightened little girl all alone with no one to help you . . . Just as you felt when your Welshman lay dead from a fever you could not cure? Isn't that right, poshrati?"

Angelique's anger grew to boiling point, but she knew Annabelle was just trying to flush her out into the open.

"The great healer who could not even heal her one true love," Annabelle scoffed. "Your father was right to abandon his little poshrati. I'm sure he could not bear the sight of you. It is better to throw away rubbish than to let it sit and ferment, contaminating and rotting all that is good until there is nothing left but rubbish."

Angelique was raging inside, but still, she stayed silent.

"Come now, aren't you just a little bit eager to see me dead?" Annabelle sneered. "Well, you have your chance. Come out into the open and take your shot."

Annabelle eased down the path, eyeing the tree line closely. She knew Angelique was still there somewhere, and she had to find her before the others showed up.

Finally, as the morning sun rose, Annabelle caught a glimpse of what could possibly be Angelique's hair behind a tree. She lifted her rifle and took aim. "And so it ends here, poshrati," she said, trying to focus.

Suddenly the sound of muffled laughter was heard from the other side of the tree line. Annabelle whipped round to look but saw nothing. She then heard the laughter coming from behind her. Annabelle slotted the rifle into the holster on the saddle and simultaneously pulling out her revolver with the other hand. She turned to where the laughter was coming from but saw nothing.

Angelique, clutching her revolver, also heard the laughter. It sounded like a young girl running through the forest and laughing, but Angelique could not make out anything else.

Annabelle became annoyed. She could not see the source of the laughter, but whoever it was, they would pay with their life—right after she was finished with Angelique.

Annabelle turned back to the tree where she thought Angelique was hiding. She raised her revolver and prepared to fire when suddenly she felt a hand touch her leg. Startled, Annabelle spun around to see it was and fired the revolver in their direction. But no one was there.

Angelique, hearing the gun discharge, immediately ducked away, further into the forest, away from Annabelle.

Annabelle was furious. She twisted her body and fired all three remaining rounds into the forest at will but hit nothing. Again, an eerie, almost mocking, muffled laughter was heard in the trees.

"I will get you!" Annabelle shouted as she started to reload her revolver. As she was going this, she heard the sound of horses galloping toward her. With only three bullets in her revolver, Annabelle holstered the gun and pushed her horse to gallop in the opposite direction. As she glanced at the tree line, she saw the apparition of Alice, smiling—her dark eyes stared at Annabelle intently, as if looking through her, but Annabelle was unfazed. She just turned her head and continued on her path.

Watching from behind a tree some distance away, Angelique saw Annabelle ride off. Quickly, she ran toward her horse, which was standing in the brush. About this time, Etienne and the rest of the group rode up and found the dead men. Etienne instantly feared for Angelique's life but noticed her near the tree line.

"Gitane!" he called out, his gun raised, expecting trouble. "Where is she?"

"She's left!" Angelique replied, out of breath. "She's gone back up the path headed north. If we hurry, we will catch her."

Sophie looked at Angelique and noticed the fresh blood stain on her gown, "Hold on! You're bleeding again," she said, pointing toward Angelique's arm.

"It's nothing. Let's go," Angelique said as she attempted to mount her horse.

The group headed up the path with Etienne and Angelique leading the way. They could all sense that this traumatic episode in their lives was slowly drawing to a conclusion. Whether in a good or a bad way, they would end this today.

Etienne rode alongside Angelique. Although vigilant, he was deep thought. He had speculated about what awaited them further up the path but knew that, with Annabelle's trickery, anything could be there to greet them. "Don't know what's gonna be on the other end of this," he said, concerned.

"She has two men atop the carriage and a lady and a maid inside. She's killed the others," Angelique said. "She senses her world is coming to an end. She will be nothing but violently aggressive. We must keep our guard up."

"Absolutely," Etienne said. "We can't afford to let her get away this time.

"Please keep an eye on Katy," Angelique said, looking back at her and Wes riding behind them. "She mustn't be left alone."

"Agreed, but let us handle this from now on," Etienne replied, fearing that Angelique herself was at risk. "You are injured and to go out on your own again could mean certain death. We need you with us, Gitane."

Angelique was silent for a moment. "Don't worry this will end soon, and then you and Sophie can prepare for your new addition." She grinned.

"Yes, and what a good time that will be," Etienne smiled.

Angelique revealed a faint smile of acknowledgement, then moved ahead of Etienne, thus ending their conversation. Behind her, Evan, William, and Wes talked back and forth in preparation for yet another meeting with Annabelle, while Sophie and Luke rode close behind on the wagon. Etienne looked back at Sophie. He saw distress in her eyes.

"You all right, mama?" Etienne asked, as he turned his horse around and rode back toward the wagon.

"I don't know," Sophie replied, shaking her head. "This is just too much."

"I know, but this will be over soon," Etienne said, riding alongside the wagon and extending his hand toward her. "We'll make it, mama. I promise."

Sophie reached over and clasped Etienne's hand tightly. She wanted to believe him, yet still, fear of the unknown was flooded her thoughts. How she yearned for the quieter, calmer times, but she could only pray that they would once again return.

Betty's words haunted Sophie greatly. She repeated them over and over in her head, thinking about what the final outcome would bring. It frightened Sophie, replacing her usually sweet demeanor with one that was clouded with fear and apprehension.

CHAPTER 27

Light began to shine through the canopy of the tall trees that surrounded the path. Annabelle rode frantically to catch up with the carriage. She knew Angelique and the rest of her pursuers would be close behind her. Annabelle also knew that there was no way the carriage would be able to outrun them. She would have to deal with this when the time came.

Annabelle caught up with the carriage a short while later. Seeing her, Mr. Kerrigan slowed the carriage to a halt. Annabelle trotted up to it. "Mr. Kerrigan!" called Annabelle. "We are being pursued. I believe the time has come to see what these horses have in them."

Mr. Kerrigan acknowledged her and snapped the reins, engaging the horses in a full gallop. Hearing Annabelle's proclamation, Miss Sterling sighed and turned to Sara. "The time has come, child. Remember what I have told you," she said, turning her head toward the window.

"Yes, my lady. I shall," replied Sara, having seen the fear in Miss Sterling's eyes.

The horses raced up the path. Mr. Kerrigan, pushing both to their limits, knew well that they would not be able to last at this pace. Unfortunately, he had no choice.

Twenty minutes had passed, and Mr. Kerrigan could feel the horses tiring. Still, he pushed them to proceed up the path through the winding turns and increasingly dense forest. But no one could have foreseen the hazard at one of the turns. As the carriage turned the corner, one of its wheels hit a hole, causing the carriage to tilt and fall on its side.

Both men were thrown from the top of the carriage. Mr. Kerrigan rolled away from the falling carriage while his partner was crushed to death under its massive weight. Miss Sterling and Sara, who were passengers inside, were thrown violently against one of the doors.

Annabelle, fearing the worst, jumped off her horse and ran to the carriage. "Agatha!" she shouted, climbing up the side of the carriage. "Are you alright?"

Although she heard groans from Mr. Kerrigan where he lay a few feet away, there was no sound coming from inside the carriage. As Annabelle looked in the window, she noticed both Agatha and Sara lying listlessly at the bottom.

"Agatha! Hear me!" Annabelle shouted once again.

Finally, Annabelle noticed movement inside the carriage. Agatha, hazy from a blow to her head, attempted to stand. Sara, also dizzy and disoriented, did the same.

"Here, take my hand," said Annabelle, extending her hand through the open carriage door.

Agatha took hold of Annabelle's hand, pulled herself out of the carriage and slowly climbed down its side. Sara followed but seemed to have more trouble focusing. With both Agatha and the girl out of the carriage, Annabelle turned her attention to the horses that had pulled the carriage. Disregarding Mr. Kerrigan's woeful moans, she inspected the horses. One was fit for travel, but the other appeared to be hurt.

"At least this one will do," Annabelle said, as she began unhooking the horse from the carriage. "Will you be able to ride bareback?"

"But of course," Agatha answered. "It wasn't that long ago that I last did. Besides, what choice do I have?"

"Yes, but you are injured," Annabelle observed, removing the harness from the injured horse.

"Again, do I have a choice?" Agatha snapped at Annabelle.

"No, you don't, unless we leave dear Sara behind to hide in the woods," Annabelle answered.

"Please, my Lady, don't leave me here!" Sara pleaded.

"Do not worry, child. We are not leaving you behind," Agatha reassured her, looking at Annabelle in disgust.

"Good, now that that's settled, we need to hurry," Annabelle said.

Ten minutes passed, as Annabelle readied the horse for Agatha. Annabelle decided that Sara, who was not an experienced rider, would ride with her while Agatha would ride solo with the few remaining sacks of gold. Mr. Kerrigan's continuous moans made it hard to forget that he was still there, especially for Agatha.

"And this one?" Agatha asked, pointing to Mr. Kerrigan.

Annabelle, walked over to her horse, picked up her revolver and pointed it at Mr. Kerrigan. She pulled the trigger, shooting him in the back.

"Let's go," Annabelle said, walking away from Mr. Kerrigan's motionless body.

Agatha shook her head at Annabelle and then attempted to mount the horse. As she did this, a sudden rumbling was heard further down the path. Annabelle, who had already got on her horse and was helping Sara up, recognized the sound of galloping horses heading straight toward them. Sensing danger, both Agatha and Annabelle's horses began to whinny and buck violently, causing the women to fall to the ground.

Annabelle got up instantly and stepped away from Sara, who lay unconscious on the ground. She tried desperately to grab the reins, but the horses were frightened and ran away up the path. Without any other choice, she tried fleeing into the dense brush but was stopped by a single gunshot to her back. Agatha, still lying on the ground, opened her eyes just in time to see Etienne and Angelique's horses arrive. Knowing there was no escape for her at this time, she slowly closed her eyes and lay motionless on the ground.

With guns drawn, Etienne, William, and Evan dismounted their horses and secured the area. With his gun trained on Annabelle, Evan ran up to her to see if she was still alive. He examined Annabelle but could only find a faint heartbeat and little, if any, sign of breathing.

"She's alive but barely," Evan said, standing up, "I do believe that this one will harm no more, but who fired the shot?"

"I think I can answer that," William replied, standing over the body of Mr. Kerrigan, who still clasped a revolver in his hand. "It would seem our friend would have been wiser to finish him off before fleeing."

"Yep, I'm proof of that," Wes smiled, as he helped Katy dismount.

Katy was staring intensely at the bleeding Baroness. She could hardly believe that this dark saga of her life was finally drawing to a close. Katy walked slowly toward Annabelle, passing close to Angelique's horse. Suddenly the butt of a long-handled knife was thrust in front of her, near her neck.

"If you are to do this, then hide this under your gown," Angelique spoke softly, handing her the knife. "Just in case."

Startled, Katy looked up at Angelique and took the knife from her hand, hiding it in the sleeve of her gown. She walked slowly toward Annabelle, a swell of emotion engulfing her.

"You," Katy said in a raspy voice, "you are the cause of this. You've shed the blood of the innocent for the last time." As she spoke, her eyes filled with tears. "Hear me!" she said, falling to her knees beside Annabelle. "Hear my words! I am the reason for your downfall! Look at me!"

In a fit of rage, Katy pulled Annabelle's arm in an attempt to turn her lifeless body over. Upon turning her though, Katy found that Annabelle was far from dead. As Annabelle's head turned, her eyes bore fiendishly into Katy. Before Katy could move, Annabelle reached up, grasped her throat and began choking her violently. Katy tried desperately to free herself of Annabelle's grasp but failed. Still on the ground, Annabelle pulled Katy next to her body, shielding herself from anyone who might try to take a shot at her.

"Stay back!" Annabelle shouted, brandishing a small pistol that she had hidden in her coat.

"No!" Katy yelled, sobbing uncontrollably.

"Oh yes, dear Katy . . . dear sweet Katy," Annabelle said softly into her ear. "I hear you. Now hear me!" She jerked her hair harshly.

"You won't get away with this," Etienne said, aiming his revolver at Annabelle.

"That may be, but I will not be the only one dying here this day!" she shouted, pressing the pistol into Katy's neck.

Angelique walked in front of Etienne, pushing his revolver aside; her eyes fixed on Annabelle. She continued walking until she was within a few yards of them.

"Stop! That is far enough, gypsy whore!" Annabelle scowled.

Angelique stopped walking. "Your reign has ended. Set her free," she said, her voice calm and steady.

"The body may end, but I am eternal," Annabelle said assertively, feeling the continuous sting of the gunshot in her back.

"Nothing is eternal," Angelique answered, "but that of the gods."

"And I was here in the beginning, and I shall be here when this one's offspring breathe for the first time," Annabelle said, talking of Katy, "You can't get rid of me. I am eternal, unlike you—an unloved reject from a vagabond tribe. You are fodder and nothing less. How dare you address me!"

Angelique stood silently for a moment. "And you, of eternal greatness? Why do you need this loathsome child? You hide like a scared hare behind her? Stand and show your true self. You are a sniveling, worthless commoner. You are a Baroness of nothing."

"Your attempt to instigate and rescue this sweet dear child is amusing," Annabelle chuckled. She coughed, blood appearing at the side of her mouth. "No, I want you to see just how painful a death can be. I want you to feel helplessness again. Just as you felt when you let your one and only true love die."

Angelique was silent, showing no emotion while Annabelle was in obvious pain. Still though, she managed her usual devilish grin. "Yes . . . helpless and weak," Annabelle sneered, looking quite amused. "It's a shame really, unfortunate that he made a poor choice."

"Let her go," Angelique ordered, "and it's possible you will be spared."

Annabelle began to laugh. "Please do me no favors," she said, tightening her grip on Katy's shoulder. "For I am old and tired of these repetitive dealings with the likes of your kind."

"Old?" Angelique questioned. "Just how old? Twenty-four? Twenty-five? That is far from old. Everyone here sees that you are not old."

Annabelle paused before her response, trying to contemplate what Angelique was up to.

"What are you, and what did you do with Lady Falsworth? Did you murder her like the others?" Evan blurted out, unable to contain himself any longer. He walked up to stand near Angelique.

"Keep your distance, Englishman!" Annabelle shouted, pulling Katy's hair so that her head connected with the barrel of her pistol.

315

"Hold on," Evan said placidly, extending his hands to show he meant no harm. "Pardon, madam, but I have come a long way to find answers. With the death of Monsieur Chevalier, I am no longer obliged to see this case through. I simply would like to find out what happened to her. That is all."

"Maybe you will soon enough," Annabelle replied. "If you are truly an investigator, then the answer you seek may be in plain sight." She paused for a moment and coughed up more blood. "Who am I? I am the darkness you fear. I am the one who lives in the shadows. You shall never have peace; you will always fear me. I am eternal!"

"Please!" Katy sobbed. "Release me! I beg of you."

"Worry not, dear child," Annabelle said, holding the barrel of the pistol at the back of her skull, "it will all be over soon. Your life will transform . . ."

"Haven't you killed enough?" Evan was angry. "This is pointless!"

While all eyes focused on Annabelle, Sara, who had been unconscious, finally came to. Through her foggy eyes, she slowly became aware of what was taking place. Miss Sterling, on the other hand, remained on the ground with her eyes closed, pretending to be unconscious but listening to every word. The others seemed unaware that she had a pistol in one hand.

"My Lady, what's going on?" Sara asked, rubbing her eyes.

William, seeing Sara awake and sitting up, immediately pulled on her arm to move her to a place of safety. He thought she might be in danger, but he quickly found out that the exact opposite was true.

"No!" Sara shouted, as she pulled away from William. "What have you done with my Lady!"

Having escaped William's grasp, Sara ran to the carriage. She saw that Annabelle was surrounded.

316

"My Lady! What am I to do?" Sara shouted out in fear.

"Prepare, as you were told!" Annabelle replied.

Through all the shouting, a faint whisper could be heard near the trees across from them. The words were not clear but they got everyone's attention. As Wes moved to the tree line to investigate, the whisper turned to an echoing laughter. Still, no one had a clue from where or from whom the sound was coming.

Angelique moved her focus to Katy. Katy's sobbing began to cease, as she made eye contact with her.

"They have arrived," Angelique said to Annabelle, still showing no emotion.

Annabelle looked around, her anxiety apparent. "This is your doing!" she shouted, enraged at Angelique.

"No, this wasn't," Angelique responded, smiling slowly. "You've brought this upon yourself, and upon yourself it shall lie."

Annabelle, engulfed in rage, moved her pistol from behind Katy's head and pointed it directly at Angelique. As she pulled the trigger, her hand lifted up, as if someone had slapped it away. The pistol discharged harmlessly into the air. Annabelle looked up in time to see the ghostly figure of Fiona grasping her arm. Aghast by her presence, Annabelle froze. Fiona, unseen by anyone else, looked down at her, smiling.

"They await your presence," Fiona said, tightening her grip on Annabelle's arm.

With the pistol pointing away from her, Katy saw her chance to escape. She pulled the knife from her sleeve. A flood of angry emotion rushed through her, as Katy turned and plunged the knife into Annabelle's heart. Annabelle gasped, terror in her eyes.

"Heretic, die!" Katy screamed. "No more will you torture me!"

Annabelle, still gasping, lay slowly backward, onto the ground. More blood trickled out the side of her mouth, and her body shuddered violently. Seconds later, she was still. Annabelle was dead.

Sara, seeing her Lady lying dead in a pool of blood, screamed in horror. "No!" she yelled, retrieving the pistol from under her gown and aiming it at Katy. She was crying uncontrollably.

Etienne, seeing Sara raise her weapon, swung around and aimed his rifle at her. "No young'un! It ain't worth it," he said, hesitant to shoot a child.

Miss Sterling, forgotten by all, sat up with her pistol drawn. She knew that, with Annabelle dead, her life was as good as over. "I curse you bastards!" she screamed, aiming her pistol at Etienne.

Sophie, still sitting on the horse, had a full view of what was taking place. Sara had her weapon aimed at Katy, and Miss Sterling was aiming hers at Etienne. With no time to warn either, Sophie raised her rifle. She knew she couldn't afford to hesitate, but to her, the choice was simple. Her husband came first.

"Katy!" Sophie shouted, as she pulled the trigger. The rifle discharged, shooting Miss Sterling in the heart a fraction of a second before Agatha pulled the trigger.

Angelique, hearing Sophie's cry, turned and saw Sara, with hands shaking, attempting to pull the trigger of her pistol. With no other alternative, she stepped in front of Katy. Etienne had a clear shot and pulled the trigger, but the weapon jammed, rendering it useless. Sara discharged her weapon, hitting Angelique.

As Angelique fell to the ground, Evan discharged two shots into Sara, killing her instantly.

Katy, already distressed from killing Annabelle, bent down over Angelique. She was in shock. "No! You can't die!" Katy wailed, reaching for Angelique's hand. "You promised!"

Angelique reached for Katy's hand, her body shaking uncontrollably. "Never trust a gypsy. They lie," she replied, coughing up a little blood.

Angelique attempted to smile at Katy, but the pain was too immense. "I'm so cold," she said, as her body shook from the gravity of her wounds.

"Gitane!" Sophie exclaimed tearfully, as she dropped to Angelique's side, immediately trying to tend to her wound. "I'm so sorry, Gitane. There were two of them. I couldn't get them both."

Angelique reached out her trembling hand to touch Sophie's. "There's no need," she said, pulling Sophie's hand away from the wound.

"It's bad," Sophie replied, in tears.

"Don't worry about me," Angelique said, trying to grip both Sophie's and Katy's hands. "It's time. May the gods watch over and protect you both."

"There must be something we can do?" Katy sobbed, looking helplessly at Angelique.

"Yes, there is one thing," Angelique said. "Live your life and think of me; for I feel fortunate to have met you, Katy Morgan. If I had ever had a daughter, I would have prayed that she would be you."

Angelique began to cough up blood repeatedly. Sophie raised Angelique's head up, but her coughing still would not cease. Slowly, she began to lose consciousness. After a few minutes, Angelique took her last breath and died quietly between her two friends.

Silence now blanketed the area, except for the tearful sobbing of Katy and Sophie. Etienne walked toward the carriage, throwing his rifle in disgust amongst the trees. Wes moved quickly to Katy's side to give her support.

"There was nothing more you could have done," Evan said, following Etienne closely.

"Well, knowing that don't make it any easier, does it?" Etienne said bitterly.

"True," Evan answered somberly, as he put his hand on Etienne's shoulder to comfort him.

"Evan!" William called out. "I believe there is something here you need to see."

Evan turned his head and walked up to William, who was kneeling beside Annabelle's body. As he walked closer, he looked down at the bloodied corpse with a sense that something wasn't right.

"What's wrong?" Evan asked, staring oddly at William.

"Look at her," William replied, raising Annabelle's head off of the ground.

Evan looked down at Annabelle's bloodied face in shock. For lying before him on the ground, wasn't the body of Lady Annabelle Falsworth; it was that of an old woman.

"I don't know how this could be," William said, confused and shaking his head.

"You and me both," Evan acknowledged. "You and me both."

"Who is she? What is she?" William asked.

Evan stared at the body, then looked at William. "I believe we have found the elder. As to what this is, is a question that will haunt us for some time."

"But how?" William replied, still in a state of disbelief.

"I don't know," Evan replied somberly.

* * *

The carriage came to a halt in front of the plantation house. Behind it, David and Samuel followed on horseback. Ben, seeing the carriage return from his vantage point near the stables, quickly ran to see who had arrived.

"Mornin'," David addressed Ben as he dismounted his horse. "I believe this carriage may belong to this estate, as do these hired hands." He pointed to the few men who had surrendered earlier that morning.

"No, it belongs to an English Baroness who is no longer welcome here," Ben replied in an irritated manner.

"Well, be that as it may, it's yours now," David retorted. He got on his horse again and prepared to leave.

Suddenly a maid stepped out of the carriage. It was Rose.

"Pardon me, sir," she said to David. "We are much obliged to you for saving us, but may I ask another great favor."

"Yes, what is it?" David acknowledged with a smile.

"If you leave us here, the Lady may return, and alas, we will be in the same predicament that you found us. Do you know of anyone in this land who might be in need of our services? I beg of you."

David looked at Ben, who was observing the conversation with an annoyed expression on this face, then back at Rose. "Well, there are four of you, yes? I don't know, but I'm sure we can find you a place to rest for a few days. And I've no doubt one of the rich folk in Beaumont will be in need of your help."

Ben scowled. "Good, now that that's settled, take this dang thing and head it to Grigsby's Bluff."

David turned to Ben and nodded. "Okay, but the hands stay here. They're your responsibility."

"Fair enough, now go," Ben replied, not wanting anything of Lady Annabelle's at the plantation if for some reason she returned.

"Bless you, sir," Rose said, elated to finally be severing ties with the Baroness.

Rose climbed back into the carriage, and it started down the path, heading for Grigsby's Bluff and a new beginning for the four maids. A feeling of relief filled her soul as she stared out of the window into the dense forest. Although heading into a great unknown, she sensed that this path led to a brighter future for her and the other maids. Whatever lay beyond, she knew that she was now free.

CHAPTER 28

The following day, having trekked back to their home territory, everyone assembled near the river. True to her gypsy roots Angelique was put on a funeral pyre instead of being given a burial. This was by her own request, which she had made to Etienne years before in the event that anything ever happened to her.

Etienne stood in front of the pyre at a loss for words, a lighted torch in his hand. The usually strong man swelled with emotion as he looked at his friend lying on a pile of timber. Evan, seeing this, walked up to him slowly and gently took the torch from his hand.

"I only knew her for a short time," Evan said, "but her true passion and loyalty to those she loved was plain to see. By the gods, may you join them in peace."

Evan took the torch and lit the kindling, setting the wood ablaze. The pyre was quickly engulfed in flames.

After the ceremony everyone gathered at Etienne and Sophie's house. Ezra, Benjamin, and Betty joined them, along with the four remaining maids. Unsure of what the future held for them, Etienne took pity on the four young girls.

"You know mama, with the baby and all, you're gonna need some help," Etienne said. "Maybe these four young'uns can help out."

Sophie looked over at the girls sitting quietly on the porch. Their faces solemn, showing their fear and uncertainty as to what life had in store for them. Sophie could not say no and welcomed their help. She invited them into her home with open arms.

Katy stood silently near the edge of the garden, away from the group. She was clutching the necklace Angelique had given her and gazing into the forest. Her thoughts were filled with the events of her journey and its horrific end. Even as these images clouded her mind, she noticed something moving about the winter vegetables

"Cat?" Katy exclaimed, her arms extended.

Seconds later, a black shape raced from behind the leaves and leaped into her arms, purring wildly. Katy's sad eyes lifted slightly, as she hugged and petted the cat. "Well, I believe that now we are the same," she said, stroking the cat's head, "but we will make it."

Katy continued to look out into the surroundings, holding the cat, when some movement caught her eye near the tree line. Katy watched the area closely, her heart racing, until she saw what was rummaging through the trees. It was the buck that she and Angelique had seen days before. He seemed to be staring at her with a bit more than a passing interest.

Katy's heart warmed at the sight of the stag in all his magnificent glory. Behind him, she noticed a doe also peering curiously at her. In her thoughts, she could hear Angelique's words, "Behold, young lass. For even in this foreign land, the gods still watch over you."

"And may you be with them, dear friend," Katy said, smiling through her tears.

The stag and the doe remained watching Katy for a short time before they disappeared into the forest just as mysteriously as they had arrived.

Katy knew her life would be hard in this strange new world, but it would be nothing compared to what she had suffered these past years. Now, she had her freedom, thanks in part to a gypsy woman they called Gitane.

CHAPTER 29

Evan sat in his study and stared out the window, watching the snow fall gently upon the street. Midwinter's grip seemed to be holding tightly, with no sign of letting up. The chill of the season mirrored his thoughts. Two months before, he had been in a foreign land where many innocent people had died tragically at the hands of a lone Baroness. Now, after the long journey home, the time had come to put this episode of his life in the past.

Evan stood up and walked toward his desk. He could hear Helga, his German maid, preparing a pot of tea, as she did each day around this time. "Excellent," he muttered to himself. He had not noticed how much time had passed.

Evan walked to the kitchen, anticipating the tea and scones that had been part of his daily routine before his travels. As Evan entered the kitchen, the sweet smell of pastries filled the air. A nice change from the scones, he thought, but either one would have been sufficient.

"What a marvelous smell!" Evan proclaimed to Helga as he sat down at the table where the pastries were set. They looked delicious. "It's a good thing William isn't here, or he'd eat the lot."

No sooner were the words out of his mouth than the door opened. "Good afternoon!" William exclaimed as he walked into the kitchen, rubbing his hands in glee at the sight of the afternoon treats.

"You would show up at teatime," Evan said playfully as he lifted a pastry for a nibble.

"But of course! And I've brought a guest," William replied.

Detective Stanley, who had been working on the Falsworth case for the police five months prior, walked into the room. Again, this brought Evan back to reality. He thought back to his final days in Southeast Texas and his newfound friends. The day after Angelique's funeral, Wes and Katy had left for Nacogdoches. Wes had seen enough of Southeast Texas and all that slithered near the river. He felt that living in East Texas would certainly be a more appropriate and safe place in which to raise children. Katy, although saddened to move so far away from her new friends, Sophie and Frenchy, was happy to follow Wes anywhere.

Evan and William had also left that day but had headed for Sabine. Evan believed travel would be far safer if they sailed through the Gulf of Mexico than going back through Louisiana. So they had boarded a steamboat, which had carried them to New Orleans where a much larger ship had sailed them back to England. Seven weeks later, they had arrived in Portsmouth and made their way back to Newcastle.

As the three met in the kitchen, Evan knew William had been with the detective all day, explaining the events of the Baroness and Monsieur Chevalier's demise. He was eagerly awaiting news of any fresh evidence that the police may have uncovered.

"Good afternoon, John," Evan greeted, quickly trying to swallow the last half of a pastry.

"Afternoon," John replied jovially, seeing Evan stuffing his face.

"Miss Helga, I believe we will have our tea in the office, please—that is, if Evan doesn't consume it all beforehand," William said with a grin.

Evan backed away from the table and gave William an odd look before proceeding to the office. William and John followed Evan, snickering all the way. Helga, carrying a tray laden with pastries and tea, walked close behind them.

With the men now seated, Helga lay the tray on Evan's desk, removed the teacups and began pouring a cup of tea for each of them. "I do hope you enjoy this," Helga said as she finished pouring the tea.

"Oh, I am sure it will suffice," Evan replied, picking at another pastry.

Helga left the office and closed the door behind her, a smile on her face. All three men chatted for a few minutes while they consumed the pastries and tea. Their conversation then turned to the case at hand.

"Well, John, I am sure William has told you about Monsieur Chevalier and Lady Annabelle Falsworth," Evan said, lifting a cup of tea to his lips.

John nodded. "Yes, he told me about the deaths, but in your absence, we have been continuing our investigation."

"And what have you discovered?" Evan asked curiously.

"Yes, do tell!" William added eagerly. "I've been yapping to you all day but know little of what went on here while we were gone."

John took a sip of tea and then laid the cup down gently on the saucer. His face became serious, a far cry from what it had been just moments before. "Well, there were more bodies found on the premises," John said.

"I imagined so," replied Evan. "Not to be ghoulish, but she did have an appetite."

"Yes, she did," John agreed. "We unearthed 77 bodies in an area a few miles from the house."

Evan was shocked. "Seventy-seven bodies?"

"Yes, and it would seem that they were all young females," John replied calmly. "We really could not tell since many had been buried for a long time."

"Bloody hell! How long?" Evan asked.

"Possibly fifty, eighty, over a hundred years . . . I don't know," John said sincerely. He and his team of investigators were just as confused as Evan.

Evan was still aghast. "And who would acquire this many young girls without anyone noticing? I find it hard to grasp this. Is there a conclusion to your investigation?"

John shook his head, staring at the floor. He had been thinking about this for over half a year, but he had not been able to fathom how such a large number of young girls could have been murdered and yet missed by no one.

"We just don't know," John said. "Given that everyone is deceased, the case would be quite hard to prosecute, especially with all but one victim completely unidentifiable."

"And the ex-maid?" Evan asked. "Could she not have known more?"

Still looking downward, John shook his head. "No, that wouldn't be possible. A few days after your departure, we found her dead."

"What?" Evan gasped.

"A herder found her body in a field just south of town," John replied. "Her throat was cut, and she looked as if she had been badly beaten."

"For how long had she been dead before she was found?" William asked.

"Less than a day I would imagine," replied John after taking another sip of tea.

"Interesting." Evan was thinking aloud. "So she was killed two days after we left for Portsmouth."

"And four days after Lady Annabelle Falsworth departed," William added.

"There were no clues left at the scene, just blood," John said.

"A coincidence is not likely in my opinion," Evan observed.

"Could the killer have been one of Monsieur Chevalier's men?" William asked John.

"Possibly, but what would the motive have been? Anyway, all of his employees were rounded up, and his office and ships had been confiscated by soldiers. Monsieur Chevalier seemed to have had a tax problem as well."

"Well, I certainly wouldn't have put it past him," Evan said thoughtfully.

"Nor would I," William added. He turned to face John. "So would it be possible for us to have a look around the Falsworth Manor?"

"Sure, I do not see any reason why not," John replied. "Mind you, it would be best to announce yourself at the front door to the lady of the manor though. We really have no jurisdiction there now that Lady Falsworth is dead."

"Lady of the manor?" Evan asked "I thought the manor would be empty?"

"Oh, no. There are a few maids, stable boys, herders, and gardeners still employed there," John said.

"Who is paying them?" Evan wanted to know.

"The family, I would imagine," replied John.

"Family? What family?" Evan asked. He was confused.

"Lady Falsworth had a daughter living in Scotland. She has been cleared of any wrongdoing, so she freely commutes back and forth between Scotland and England."

"Are you sure?" Evan asked, knowing full well he himself had not been able to locate any documents.

"Yes, she is the last Falsworth," John replied, "and legally there is nothing pending against the estate. It would seem though that the

Chevalier estate was not so lucky. It has been gobbled up by debt and has disappeared."

"Into Queen Victoria's cupboard, no doubt," said William.

John grinned slightly in response to William's comment. "Possibly. I can tell you it certainly isn't in mine."

"Nor mine, friend." Evan smiled. "I believe we'll pop round for a visit in the morning. You never know; we might find something."

The conversation went on, as did the demolition of the heap of pastries. Evan managed to get a bit more information out of John that he felt could possibly help later, but nothing solid.

The following morning, Evan and William traveled to the Falsworth Manor with great hopes of putting yet another piece of the puzzle to rest.

Upon entering the gates of the manor, Evan's eyes took in his surroundings. Everything seemed normal to him. Nothing was out of place or unattended to. The shrubs and greenery were perfectly manicured, the cobblestone drive had been swept, and the windows were neatly washed and clean. Not really the look of abandonment that Evan had been anticipating.

In the distance, William noticed a few men and possibly a woman on horseback, riding toward the stables. He assumed they were hunters returning from an early morning fox hunt. Evan guessed the same but turned his attention to the house, especially the second story window. In the window, he saw a young woman staring back at him. She showed no emotion. Evan and William walked closer and closer to the house until they finally reached the steps leading up to the door.

"Utterly magnificent," William said, staring at the centuries-old building.

Evan had a different perspective. "Breathtaking, yes, but the bloodstained history of so many atrocities committed here dampens my view."

"Well, let's go then," William said, gesturing to Evan. "You first."

Evan climbed the steps and knocked on the huge wooden door. Seconds later, a young maid opened the door and greeted them with a friendly smile.

"Good morning, sirs," she said.

"And a very good morning to you as well," replied Evan, tipping his hat. Evan introduced himself and William then politely asked to see the lady of the manor. The maid acquiesced and led them inside, to the drawing room.

"Please make yourselves comfortable. I will return with my Lady shortly," she said before scurrying up the large staircase.

Evan and William were almost mesmerized by the antique furniture and décor in the room. Some of the pieces had to have been centuries old. The walls were adorned with beautiful landscapes, a painting of the manor, and a few portraits of different people whom Evan surmised to be relatives from time past. One painting in particular caught both their eyes. It was a huge painting of a young lady who was dressed exquisitely. She was standing near the same fireplace over which the painting was hung. Evan and William simultaneously turned and looked at each other. The young lady in the painting was the exact image of Annabelle.

Evan moved closer to inspect the painting more thoroughly. Below it, he found an engraved plaque which read "Annuska Běla Báthory Falsworth 1614."

"Annuska Běla?" William thought aloud.

"It's Hungarian," Evan whispered softly. "Annuska translates to Anne or Anna."

"Anna Běla," William replied, peering at the young lady's dark, piercing eyes. "Annabelle?"

A young woman entered the room, her eyes taking in Evan and William. She gave them a polite smile. "Good morning, gentlemen," she greeted. "My name is Victoria Sterling. I am the lady of the Falsworth Manor. How may I be of assistance to you?"

Evan turned and recognized her as being the woman he had seen in the window. Upon hearing her name, his mind back to the desolate land in which he'd so recently traveled, and he saw the minutes of his life after he'd fired two bullets into an obsessed young girl.

Katy stood up from her place beside Angelique's body, still weeping but now encircled by Wes' protective arms. Evan, checking amongst the dead, bent down near Agatha's body.

"Who is this?" Evan asked.

Katy, still being comforted by Wes, answered. "Her name was Miss Agatha Sterling. She was in charge of us. She was our keeper."

"And a very pleasant morning to you, Miss Sterling," Evan replied. "Thank you for seeing us."

Victoria looked at Evan and William, her face not betraying any emotion. She extended her hand to Evan and bowed her head slightly in a show of respect.

"We have come to impart sad news about the Baroness who lived here," William said somberly.

Victoria nodded, glancing up at the painting. "Sadly we already know of both her and my mother's tragic demise. It has left us all grief-stricken."

"My condolences, madam," Evan responded, "but if I may, there are a few questions I wish to ask about the Baroness."

"Certainly, sir. You are in luck. The Baroness' daughter is here from Scotland. I am sure she will be able to answer your questions."

As if on cue, a voice rang out. "Dorothy! I will have my drinks in the drawing room."

"Yes, my lady, at once," the maid was heard to reply quickly.

The first voice seemed familiar to Evan, as if he had heard it before. His eyes were drawn to the door, anxious to see who would enter.

"Ah, gentleman!" the voice said again, but this time the speaker had walked into the room for Evan and William to see.

William swiftly reached for his pistol but was immediately stopped by Evan's hand slapping his breast before he could open his coat.

"Forgive me if I startled you," the young woman said, grinning profusely, taking much pleasure in their uneasiness.

"No, madam, it is quite alright," Evan replied, holding back a thousand questions that were running rampant through his mind.

While the woman removed her riding hat, handed it to a maid and barked out specific instructions to another, Evan stood dumbfounded. He and William were looking at Annabelle, but he knew that was not possible since he had been the one who had burned the body, leaving only ashes and fragments of bones to bury. William, gazing into the woman's dark eyes, felt she must be Annabelle, but how, he could not explain.

"Well, gentleman, let me introduce myself," the woman said, extending her hand to William first. "My name is Anna, Baroness Anna Falsworth," she said, a wickedly bemused look on her face as she stared into William's eyes. "Would you care for some refreshments? Tea or whiskey perhaps?"

she offered cordially.

"Oh no, madam, but I do thank you for your kind offerings," Evan said, trying to appear as relaxed as he could.

"Well then, what brings you to Falsworth Manor?" Anna asked, grasping a glass of whiskey that a maid had given her.

"If truth be told, madam, we came to give you news of the Baroness' demise," Evan said, "but I can see that the sad news has already been given."

"You are correct, sir," Anna replied. "We were informed of the tragedy a month ago. Sad really, my mother was continuously obsessed, and in the end, her obsession was her downfall."

Lady Anna spoke with no anguish or even an ounce of sadness in her voice. She seemed upbeat, almost cheery and joyful. To Evan, Anna looked and sounded more and more like the Baroness he had last seen on a funeral pyre. The questions continued to stream forth in his mind. How did she know of the Baroness and Miss Sterling's deaths the month before? He and William had taken seven weeks to land in Portsmouth from New Orleans, and another three days to travel to Newcastle. To Evan, Lady Anna's knowledge of the news was logistically impossible, but knowing the events that had taken place, and seeing this woman, the exact likeness of Baroness Falsworth, standing in front of him, he felt anything was likely.

"And what of the two, madam?" William asked feeling the question should be asked.

"The two?" the Baroness asked in reply, a devilish smile on her lips. "Lady Sterling and my mother?"

"No, madam," William answered. "The elder Lady Falsworth and her granddaughter, who was your age."

Anna stared at William. She seemed almost amused by his question.

"Granddaughter? Do I look as if I am a mother to a woman in her twenties?"

"No, madam. You look the same as the woman in her twenties." William couldn't control himself. He felt angry.

Anna continued to smile at William, obviously she had enjoyed his passionate outburst. "Age can be deceptive, but in the end, we are all of the same blood."

The young Baroness finished her glass of whiskey in one swallow, then smiled at them. "Gentlemen, thank you for feeling obligated to inform me of my dear mother's passing, and I am sure Victoria shares my gratitude toward you, but alas, I need to bid you farewell."

"Well, madam, I will bid you a fond farewell until we meet again," Evan said, watching her walk toward the door.

The Baroness stopped at the door and turned to Evan. "And we will meet again, good sir," she said, before turning and walking out of the room.

Evan looked at William. The two were now alone in the drawing room, next to the painting. "I do believe we have just been put on alert."

William lifted a glass and filled it with whiskey, downing the contents with one swallow. "Hint taken. I will be there. As God as my witness, I will be there."

The End

www.ingramcontent.com/pod-product-compliance
Lightning Source LLC
Chambersburg PA
CBHW062018170626
46813CB00001B/204